DA

Cressida opened the door wider, to find Richard looking up into her brother's face with open admiration in his eyes. The room was stifling, in spite of the chill of the day outside. Both of its occupants were in linen shirts, and their golden hair gleamed dully in the light of the tallows. Their books lay forgotten on the floor between them. Then, as the draught from the stairway reached into the room, they turned and saw her.

The tallow lights flickered and brightened, and in their glow Richard smiled at his mother. She was never to forget the expression in his eyes. It was a faraway look, and the smile could have been meant as a greeting to a stranger. At that moment Cressida knew that her son had taken his first step on the path away from his childhood. With a painful stillness of recognition in her heart she knew that it was a path she followed at her peril.

Dark Tapestry

Anna James

ARROW BOOKS

Arrow Books Limited
62-65 Chandos Place, London WC2N 4NW
An imprint of Century Hutchinson Limited
London Melbourne Sydney Auckland
Johannesburg and agencies throughout the world

Book I, *The Rebel Heart*,
first published in Great Britain 1980
by Hamlyn Paperbacks
Dark Tapestry first published in Great Britain 1989
by Arrow Books

Printed and bound in Germany by
Elsnerdruck, Berlin

ISBN 0 09 940000 6

BOOK I

The Rebel Heart

1

It had been dark for three hours when Cressida opened the door of the hut and stood in the moonlight, drawing her heavy woollen cloak over the curve of fair skin above her small, high breasts. Her breath came quickly, and she trembled as she stepped into the intense cold of the January night. Behind her the single low-ceilinged room was in shadows. There was no light, and no sound. For a long moment she waited for some warning sign of life amongst the thin trees beyond the rough, frost-tinged grass at her feet. Then, as the utter stillness of the countryside reached out to her, she turned back into the hut and held out her hands.

The boy who ran towards her over the rush-strewn floor was a sturdy ten-year-old with the same high white forehead as her own, under a tousle of blond hair. His blue eyes did not leave his sister's face as she pulled the hood of his brown tunic up and over his head.

'It will not do for anyone who may see us in the villages nearby to remember that we are fair, Francis. Mother's death has not been enough for some of them. They know the Saxons and Danes never came to these parts with their golden locks – and there are those who would seize on any strangeness to prove that we are witches!'

'Mother was not a witch!' The boy's eyes filled with angry tears and he brushed them away impatiently. Looking down at the smudged cheeks, Cressida thought how young he was to have seen death. But in the last four months most of the children in the villages and forests of the south, living close to the great port of Southampton where the ships brought in their cargo of unseen dangers and death, had watched the victims of the plague in their struggle with fever and worse. At first she and her mother had somehow managed to keep Francis away from the sight of the village houses barred and sealed, the crimson cross smeared on each door, the words 'Lord Have Mercy' scrawled above the lintels by those who could write . . . and who were still alive. Then, as the carts had trundled heavily along the track above their home night after night, taking the dead to the common grave three miles away, the boy had begun to ask questions, and Margaret, his mother, had turned on him angrily, commanding him to go no further than their own small patch of garden until she told him otherwise.

Then the time had come when, though they lived on the village outskirts, they could not isolate themselves a day longer from the black, creeping nightmare that threatened to take all England in its grasp. Margaret was a wise woman, with great knowledge of herbs and healing. There were no doctors except at the manor house, where the wife of their landlord, Sir Robert, was already dead – and the physician was forbidden to minister to any but Sir Robert's own family and men. The village priest had died in the first week, catching the fever at the many confessions he was obliged to hear. The friar who should have comforted the dying in the next village had fled.

The knock on the door that was to take their mother from them for ever came late one night, soon after the feast of Christmas. Simon, the young peasant who had helped them work their strips of land in the open fields since their father had died in the French wars, had stood mutely in the light of the tallow that Margaret held high above her head.

'They call you Margaret the Good, in the village. Those who do not fear you. They are asking for you. My . . . my mother also. Will you come?'

In the days that followed, Margaret hardly saw her children. She bade them go to their beds early, before her return each night, and made them sleep under the window where the air was fresh and cold. All that winter, in defiance of the prevailing medical theory that the plague came on a flow of bad air, Margaret had kept the rough linen closure of their window open. She herself slept in the small outhouse against the main structure of the hut. She made her own latrine at a distance from the one her children used. And from the night that Simon came for her she would not touch them, nor let them touch her.

Cressida fastened the neck of the boy's tunic and smoothed the hood tightly on each side of his face. 'Mother was good, Francis. You are right. But that is why she was hated in the end. Those who knew she was not a witch sent for her on their deathbeds. She did what she could to save them, and – with no priest there – heard their last secrets when she could not. Now those who are left are afraid . . . afraid she told us what she knew.'

'But the confessional is sacred. Mother would never have broken her trust. I know she would not. It would mean she burns now – in Hell fire!' Francis stifled a sob, and Cressida knelt to him, holding him close. Although she whispered comfort to him, her heart beat fast at his words. They had always been taught such things. Everything in her spirit rebelled against a church that held the law of damnation over its flock; yet even as she rebelled she crossed herself fearfully. The habit was in-born, strangely comforting. Her voice, when she answered her brother, was brisk and firm.

'We know that cannot be. Why, Mother died because she nursed so many without a thought for herself.'

She had a sudden, vivid picture in her mind of their mother gasping for breath on the high bed of straw in the ramshackle wooden shed that had been her last home. In the five days it had taken her to die – longer than most of the plague's victims – she had screamed at them to keep their distance whenever they approached. She had crawled hourly, until she was too weak, to the spot where Cressida left a bowl of fresh water from the well; and on the fourth night, while Francis slept, she had called her to her and whispered her last request.

It had been almost dawn when Cressida began the grotesque, tormented task her mother set her. From the wooden chest where their most cherished possessions were kept she took a white cloth, and tied it round her own mouth. She forced the door of the outhouse back crazily on its hinges, and approached her mother's emaciated, gasping figure. Stooping, she lifted the nearest end of the ragged straw bed, and began to drag it towards the open.

As long as she lived, she would remember the moments that followed. She faced her mother as she pulled her, on her bed, the length of the path from their hut to the road above. Margaret's eyes never left her face, as if she willed her to do her last bidding. Her voice came in grating spasms, as her bed lurched to one side and Cressida reached out to save her from falling. 'Do not touch me!'

It was as if both mother and daughter were finding more than human strength. As they reached the track where the carts would pass that night, Margaret fell back, and wept. Cressida, her shoulders heaving, fell to her knees beside the dying woman, and forced herself not to vomit as the smell of plague plucked at her mask. Then both women were silent, until Margaret began to tell Cressida what Francis was to know.

'Tell him I died like those who needed me. Like Simon's mother. And the good priest who went before me. Tell him he will not see me again. And that I died peacefully, close to the sweet earth.' She closed her eyes, and her words became confused. 'When they come I will be ready for them. How easy it will be. So well prepared.' Cressida listened, in horror, aware now for the first time of what her mother intended.

'Mother, I will not leave you here to die like a beast in the open. I will not let you do this. I cannot.' She began to beat at the side of the bed.

Her mother's eyes flickered open briefly. 'But you have done it, child. It cannot be undone now. Unless you wish to return the way we came – and for your brother to watch us in the dawn?' Cressida bowed her head, helplessly aware of the strength of will that had always been Margaret's, ashamed of the exhaustion which left her no power to resist what she knew to be a cruel request. She seemed to be there for a long time, and as a thrush pierced the morning with a sharp cry for food she rose shakily to her feet. The only sign of life now in her mother's body was a soft, uneven rise and fall of her breasts as she slipped into unconsciousness for the last time.

The hands with which Cressida now clasped her brother's shoulders had seemed to her in the two weeks since then like those of a stranger. They had always been strong hands, used to helping her parents in their work, but she had taken care of them, proud of her slim fingers and neat wrists. They were more the hands of an aristocrat than a peasant. Now their smoothness was scarred, the nails torn by the ghastly burden they had dragged to the road, skin chapped by the constant washing which seemed never to shift the sickening smell of her mother's living corpse. For the hundredth time, she concealed them in the folds of her cloak, and told the boy that it was the hour for their flight.

'Are we to go to the house of Simon? Are you to marry him now that his mother is dead?' Francis looked anxiously up at his sister and Cressida tightened her rough hands in their hiding place. The man's name set her nerves on edge. She had much more important things on her mind.

'No,' she said levelly. 'It is true that he would wish it. And he has helped us in the years since Father went to the war in France. But it would mean seeking permission from Sir Robert, even paying a fee that we might be wed. I could not let Simon do that, and yet I know he would. And I – I can never marry a man who is content to be nothing more than a slave.'

'But we are all bondsmen, Cressida. And he is a good man. They say he loves you.'

Cressida frowned. She thought again of Simon's square frame, his broad shoulders, and innocent eyes, gleaming devotion for her. 'It's not my kind of love. Come!'

She looked once more round the place that had always been their home: the carved wooden chest in pride of place against the far wall gleamed in the darkness; the worn table and stools stood as they had stood since she was a child; the fire she had lit early that morning glowed lazily on the hearth. As she paused, the boy ran to a corner and picked up a roughly hewn model of a horse. At once, Cressida snatched it from him and threw it down. 'We take nothing, Francis, I tell you! Nothing. We have more things than toys to think of now.' When her brother turned to argue with her, she had gone.

A hundred yards from the house, the track forked into two wider paths. As they took the right hand fork the two dark figures crouched low, and began to run. There were no hedgerows, and the uneven banks of the open fields lent them scant cover from the moon. But Cressida had chosen her time with care. It was long past curfew, and there was little risk from inquisitive eyes. Even the roving horsemen sent out at intervals by Sir Robert to guard the ways to the manor house would not venture forth in such cold unless their master had some special task for them, and the ice that ridged the tracks was no footing even for his riders. The way to the next village and the house of Matilda, their mother's oldest friend, should stay unwatched till dawn. And by then Cressida planned to see her small brother sleeping in the warmth of Matilda's fire. They would have the hours of daylight in which to rest, and for the weeks to come the nights were long – for those who dared to travel.

It was as they reached a single oak tree set in the corner of a long strip of fallow land that Cressida began to think of her father. As a child she had waited there, watching his tall figure bent behind the clumsy one-wheeled plough.

He would strain at the turn at the far end of the field as the oxen shifted into the next deep furrow, then settle them into their path across the hard earth. In the summer she had brought food and drink to him and they had sat together under the oak tree in the heat of the day. When she was thirteen she had been tall enough to walk at his side and scatter seed with him, her long fair hair held back in a white coif from the teasing of the spring breeze. And then had come the summer three years ago, when they had left the field to find Sir Robert's horsemen waiting for them, under the same tree.

The wars in France had taken many men from the forest land in the south, but Cressida's parents had believed they were safe from such claims. Her father had great skill with the planning and phasing of crops and not only paid his dues in labour to Sir Robert, who owned all the land worked by the serfs away from their own strips of field, but was always sent for by Sir Robert's bailiff if a field went sour or a ewe was sick. Then, as the wars progressed and Edward the King made ever more ambitious forays into the French lands he believed were his by right, it became a matter of honour amongst his barons to rally all the men they could to the English flag – and the rewards came in the form of more power, more wealth, more land. Sir Robert was no exception to the general move by 1346 to raise the number of bondsmen taken from the fields and trained in haste for France. Cressida's father was seized a month before the opening of the triumphant campaign that led to Crécy.

Cressida would never forget the autumn day on which their father's close friend, Thomas, had come home to them with the news of his death. In spite of Edward's audacious strategy, few men had died. But Margaret's husband had gone down bravely, and with blessed speed, with a cut across the throat from a French dagger in a skirmish. They had been ambushed on reconnaissance and less than an hour later the English archery lines had let fly their magnificent defence. As Thomas dragged his friend back across the black mud left by the heavy storms of the night before, the small cannon grumbled uselessly around them, spreading more noise than destruction. Then from a distance, back in the shelter of the camp, he had watched the sun blaze down on the steaming surcoats of his comrades, and a flock of black crows had screamed into the sky above the French and English alike.

Now, suddenly, a crow squawked and flapped in the ditch that ran beside their path. Until this moment, Cressida had moved with her head down, watching for every stone and moonlit rift in their path. But at the thought of her father's death under the French sky three years ago she raised her face to the heavens, protesting to some power or providence she had yet to identify in her heart. At once she stumbled, and as her brother clutched fearfully at her cloak, each of them startled almost to the point of tears, Cressida began to talk, in low, fierce tones, to the boy who panted beside her in the dark.

'You say we are all in bondage, brother. And perhaps we are. In name at least. But we are not too humble for our father to die in the King's cause – why should we not *live* for such causes? For power, not serfdom. And gold, maybe. And land that is ours. I tell you, little brother, I swear on our mother's name, that I shall see you take your leave of this place . . . of this slavery.'

'But if we are caught . . . ' the boy whispered, not afraid, but seeking some answer in his sister's eyes. 'You know it means branding, Cressida. I have heard the boys in the village tell. And a fine that we could never pay.'

'You are too young to know of such matters. But we shall not be caught. That I promise you. Tonight, with Matilda's aid, I shall make our plans. And if we are wise, if we can stay on the road long enough . . . maybe you also know what that means?'

'A year and a day.' Francis looked at her steadily. 'If I can stay at liberty a year and a day it is the unwritten law that I become free.'

'Others have done it, Francis! Why not you and I? If

you do as I say, without question, I know it is possible.' She straightened herself, and stood at her full height. Her slim, tense figure had the aspect of more than her sixteen years. Other girls of her age had married, less ready to do so. Cressida had the bearing of a woman who would not easily be caught by a man, and yet everything about her promised that – once committed – she would love as fiercely as she would ask to be loved. But now it was as if she had no knowledge of such things. Her whole strength was concentrated on this dangerous bid for freedom. She started to walk again, and soon the walk became a run for them both.

'What if Sir Robert's men come after us?' They had reached one of the turnings that led to the manor house, and Francis, not pausing, had looked fearfully into the distance for some imagined pursuer. 'He has kept some fast horses in England, and they have caught other runaways – some after weeks on the road.'

'I have every reason to wish to outwit Sir Robert and his men.' Cressida spoke almost to herself. She could not tell her brother of the constant visits from Sir Robert since his wife had died. The dread of plague that made him keep his family and his physician within the walls of the manor house was apparently not so strong that it could keep him from his solitary ride, almost every day, to Cressida's home. He came at dusk, his mouth shielded against infection, his grey horse chafing and snorting as he held him in rein for half an hour or more, watching Cressida as she went about her evening tasks. She was feeding the hens one evening just after her mother's death when she looked up, aware that she was watched. He had never dismounted on these visits, nor did he speak, but this time it was Cressida who spoke, calling out to him that if he dreaded God's good air and the thought of death so deeply she wondered that he had found the courage to lead his men to France.

'I hear you are a wild fellow in battle, Sir Robert! But not man enough to have gone ahead in my father's place when he died for the King at Crécy!'

Then Sir Robert had smiled, letting the shield drop from his face. He was more than ever attracted by Cressida's show of spirit. He had guessed at this side of her nature the first time he had set eyes on her, when, as a very young girl, she had accompanied her father to his mill when the bondsmen brought their grain. He had wondered even then what the tall, blonde child, long-legged as a colt, would prove to be like if he could get her into his bed. The thought had sent a rush of blood darkly to his bearded face, and the moment's heavy promise and unanswered question had never left him. Now, years later, Cressida glared at him as he smiled. He had the dark looks of the Norman, with a low Breton forehead and brown eyes that were always narrowed in speculation. He was ambitious, cunning, and anxious to win the royal approbation. But in matters of love, it was rumoured, he did not seek in high places. Even when his wife was alive he would demand the *droit de seigneur* with any girl in their household whose looks caught his eye. And when he took a girl it was swiftly, without courtship, although in his own estimate he was fair to the offspring, if the girl became pregnant – taking the child into the manor house to be taught to serve at table or wait on the women of the family.

But Sir Robert's young sister Philippa, they said, would not allow the girls her brother had ruined to wait on her. More likely than not she would shelter them from him in her own room, or nurse them until the shock of his brutal ways had eased. Philippa herself had cause to defy her brother; since their father's death, when she was only twelve, he had been pressing for her betrothal to the Earl whose lands stretched for miles between their own territory and the next town. From the first mention of it, she had stubbornly refused. She threatened to go into a nunnery – taking her jewels with her – if Robert persisted. She knew that in his heart he was lonely, and would not like to lose her. But his choice of a marriage partner for her savoured only of his ambition and greed. The Earl, Ralph of Mansey, was powerful, rich, and at forty still unwed.

As she ran through the darkness, Cressida wondered what her life would have been had she given in to the unspoken demands of the horseman who in these last weeks had watched her night after night. Suppose she had weakened, and gone with him to the haven of his great house, with its warmth and men-at-arms to guard her? Would it have been any different for her than those who had preceded her in his bed? Would she have been wrapped in a liftime of luxury, or discarded like the rest? She smiled secretly to herself at the thought. Something told her that she was not a woman whom a man would so easily conquer, or discard. But, the dream persisted, would Francis have gone with her? At her side would he have become a member of a noble household, or even learnt to read? She ousted the fantasies firmly from her mind at this. She was not prepared to go to any man not of her choosing, whatever the price. When she loved a man, it would be in freedom. Somewhere in her dreams there waited an image quite different from that of this proud animal of a Norman. But the man was still a shadow, unformed.

'Nothing will happen to us if we travel fast: forget the bad dreams of branding and serfdom, Francis. I promise you that such things are not for us!' She drew ahead of him a pace or two on the rough track, and, lowering his head, the small boy gathered speed, his worn leather shoes pounding with the ring of iron against the frozen ground.

Soon the first scattered houses of the village where Matilda lived began to appear ahead, and they slowed down, glancing from left to right, anxiously, fearing to find a glow of light or a watching face in the narrow windows. It would be dangerous for their mother's friend if she were seen to be harbouring runaways. She lived alone now that her son Stephen was studying at Oxford, and her few humble belongings would soon be swallowed up in the great maw of confiscations that were the usual punishments for such an offence. But on most doors the rough red cross bade passers-by to keep their distance, and the dwellings scarred by this sign were all in darkness. For a moment Cressida thought she saw lights in the rare glass panes of a larger house at the start of the main village street, but it was a trick of reflection, played by the scudding clouds that now blurred the moon.

When they reached the large, single-storeyed house that was Matilda's home they huddled out of the view of the house on either side, under the lintel of the heavy door. Her finger on Francis's lips, Cressida listened for a full minute before she tapped at the wooden cross-bar, and waited in an agony of dread before she tapped again. Had Matilda also fled? Had she died of plague alone by her own hearth? If she was not there, all Cressida's immediate plans were doomed.

Suddenly there was a scraping sound, of wood on wood, as someone inside the house lifted the heavy latch that kept the door fast, and a narrow gap showed in the half-light as the door edged slowly open. But Matilda knew better than to show herself. Instead, she asked in a low voice who came to her at such an hour.

'The children of Margaret the Good. We believe you were her true friend. We need shelter, Matilda . . . for a few hours only. Then we plan to leave.'

The door swung further open as the brother and sister waited for the effect of Cressida's words, and the low voice bade them enter. Cressida turned to Francis, and almost pushed him into the house. Then, with a last swift look round at the sleeping, dying village, she slipped in after him and leant against the door, her heart thumping loudly, her eyes closed.

'Come.' Matilda led the boy at once to the glow of the hearth in the far corner of the large, single room in which she lived. He limped a little across the clean, rush-strewn floor, and the woman put a strong arm under his shoulders and half-lifted him on to the low settle in the nook beside the fire. 'We have a brave lad here, I see!' She turned to Cressida, who had not yet moved. She was a small, thin woman in her middle years, with quick but gentle movements. Bright, dark eyes in a weatherbeaten face spoke of long hours in the open air. Matilda had worked her own land for the ten years she had been a widow. She and Margaret had much in common.

As the hood of her cloak fell back from her fair hair, Cressida opened her eyes. She knew then that what she had done was right, the only possible path for her to take. The first thing she saw was her small brother, his face shining in the warmth of the fire and of Matilda's welcome. Their run through the night seemed to have left him completely untouched. For the first time since he had woken to a day without their mother he was the picture of a carefree child.

'Come.' Matilda fetched a small wooden stool from under the rough table in the centre of the room and placed it beside the settle where Francis lay.

Cressida moved as if in a dream across the room to where Matilda stood, and held out her hand. 'I cannot kiss you, though I believe we are free of the . . . the death that took our mother. There are no kisses in England now, they say.'

Matilda's smile was sad. 'Only the kiss of death, child.' She signed to Cressida to remove her cloak and sit closer to her brother. 'But I call you "child" as if your mother and I were still talking of our little ones, from habit I suppose – and I see now that you are no longer so! Cressida, you are a maiden with all the aspect of a woman. How Stephen would laugh now, if he could see you. With joy, of course! The little girl he played with . . .'

At the mention of Stephen's name, Cressida was surprised to feel her heart suddenly beat faster, as the shadow-image of her dreams flickered in her mind, and was gone. She remembered so much about Matilda's son:

their childhood games, she always teasing the solemn, dark-haired boy, and he always slow to give her his deep, secret smile. There were several years between them, but Cressida had always felt his equal. For some years, as children, they had stood brow to brow, the same height. Yet she blushed now, turning away from his mother's gaze, to learn that he still thought of her as a child. And blushed again at the discovery that she was curiously annoyed.

Matilda was busying herself with a jug of ale and a loaf of crisp, dark bread, apparently unconcerned at the effect her words had had on the girl. As she broke the bread into pieces she placed a slice of salted pork on each of the trenchers. Cressida watched the deft, gentle hands, and the neat, coifed head of her mother's friend.

'How is Stephen?' She tried to speak casually in spite of her racing thoughts. 'Is there news from Oxford? Has he been there since the death began?'

'So many questions. Here, take this good meat and ale. The pork was so good at Christmas. Little did we know there would be no merrymaking, when we salted it down.' She held the bowl of ale for Francis while he took his first hungry mouthfuls of bread and meat. 'Stephen was here at Michaelmas, before things got so bad. He was well.'

'And his work. Does that go well?'

'Aye. Well. But what do you know of that, Cressida?' She eyed her strangely for a brief moment. 'We heard again – word from a good man, a friar who was on his way to Exeter to sing mass at the great new Cathedral. They say the work there is almost done. The friar told us they were all as yet free of the plague. Stephen will try to ride this way once more in January – this very month – before their new trimester.'

'I did not dream when we played together as children that my playmate was a boy who would be a scholar, and read and write.' Cressida looked deeply into the embers of the fire. 'But then you are clever too, Matilda.'

'Clever enough to know that when his chance came to go to the friars he had to take it. They have their uses, whatever men say. The manor here can do with a scholar priest, and with the Lord Geoffrey's blessing we got Stephen away from the land. He belongs at Oxford, with his own kind. If it had been Sir Robert, now – '

Cressida put down her measure of ale, and brushed the traces of bread from her lips. 'That is one of the reasons why we are here. I know Sir Robert would never free my brother. His life will be nothing but slavery, scratching at our own poor land, and giving what profit he makes to the manor. Since Father died we have not worked the fields as well as we should. Even Simon . . . ' She faltered, and Matilda eyed her keenly.

'The man Simon could bring his own beasts to your land, and work for you well. If you would have him.'

'It's no good.' Cressida spoke quickly, shaking her bright head. 'The matter is left unspoken between us since I first told him I wanted something more – for us all. He is good, I know. And kind. But the thought of life here, perhaps for ever, with Sir Robert still our master . . . '

'Aye. Perhaps the trouble lies there?' She eyed the girl more closely.

Cressida did not reply. 'You are firm then, Cressida?' Matilda asked her quietly. 'This is the first step of your flight?'

Cressida nodded, and placed her hand on her brother's as he gave a slight cry in his sleep. She told Matilda then how she needed rest for them in the hours of daylight, and some disguise for when they took to the road. She did not know more than hearsay, but the tales of what might happen to young, inexperienced travellers on the highways of England were not pretty. Thieves, rogues, tinkers – these were the less desperate among the men they might meet. She thought it best in any case that Francis should darken his hair, and for herself she had planned to dress as a beggar, or even to pose as a poor mad girl thrown out of doors by her family. And they would need food, for the first few nights . . . until they had gone far enough from Sir Robert's domain to judge it safe to approach a strange hostelry. She had some coins, saved over the years by her mother, and she hoped that these would suffice when she had to buy victuals. Otherwise they carried nothing.

Matilda listened to the young girl carefully. 'I will do all I can,' she promised. 'But now you must rest.' Then, as Cressida began to speak again, she rose suddenly and signed to her to stay silent.

Her hand still on her brother's sleeping form, Cressida froze where she sat. She prayed that Francis would not wake just at that moment. Matilda's coifed head was poised to listen for something or someone in the small yard and shed that held her few hens in safety behind the house. At first Cressida thought she heard the pounce and predatory scuffling of a fox and its victims. But then Matilda herself would have been out of doors in a trice to the rescue of any creatures still unscathed. Then an unmistakable sound – the muffled whinny of a horse – reached them through the thin daub and wattle of the house walls, and round the side of the building came the swift, light step of a man.

Her caution thrown to the winds, Matilda ran to the door and raised the massive latch from its socket. Cressida watched in amazement as the older woman flung the door wide. Hastily, she stood back in the deep hearth, concealing herself and Francis as best as she could from any threatening presence in the street outside. But the man who stepped into the room, his dark tonsured head bent slightly under the low ceiling, dark grey eyes smiling down at Matilda as he took her in his arms, was known to her. As he turned to fasten the door again she stepped from her hiding place. Her breasts rose and fell imperceptibly under her plain gown as her heart beat suddenly faster. It seemed an eternity that they stood looking at each other in the firelight, and the man's eyes devoured her as Cressida spoke his name.

'Stephen.'

Stephen, son of Geoffrey the Wainwright and Matilda, peasant-boy turned scholar and novice-priest, had in his three years at Oxford grown into a zealous ascetic. His high forehead, fine brow, and the piercing eyes he now turned on Cressida – all told of a life of dedication. Yet there was nothing cold in his look, and the arm he still kept round his mother was protective, loving. As he held out his other arm to Cressida, he smiled gravely, and nodded. 'I always knew that you would be beautiful, little Cressida.' His voice was gentle, controlled, as if he had mastered the impulse of the first moment. There was something in his manner that disappointed Cressida then. Did he really see her as the little Cressida, still a child? She would have no man patronize her, of that she was certain, and she walked proudly towards him now, her slim body in its plain gown telling him with every step that she was no longer his childhood companion. She held her shoulders defiantly, and swung her hips with all the challenge of a grown woman. But his eyes were on her face. He saw a tilted chin, a wide, sensuous mouth quivering in its fight with tears, dark circles under brilliant blue eyes. 'You are in trouble, little Cressida. I am glad I came home tonight.' The voice was still that of a man who spoke to a child, and now Cressida could not be angry.

She gave a small, tremulous shake of her fair head: 'Do not call me little Cressida!' she said softly. Then the tears began to spill slowly down her face as she went into the shelter of Stephen's arms. For a moment she felt the strength of his whole body against hers. Then, as she pushed away from him briefly to gaze into his face, she remembered her torn nails and rough hands. She stepped back, holding them firmly behind her, shaking the tears fiercely from her cheeks. Then she told him, her head high: 'Yes. We will be glad of help, Francis and I. Our mother is dead. The village – and Sir Robert – are a danger to us now.'

'Sir Robert.' Stephen frowned, and Cressida wondered

if he was aware of the kind of interest Sir Robert might have in her. But he seemed to dismiss the matter. 'Your poor mother. So the plague has not shown mercy to you, then?' She nodded, and Stephen frowned. He pulled off his heavy student surcoat, and threw it to where he had dropped his wide velvet hat by the door. Matilda bustled to collect them, as if in the habit of a lifetime. Stephen, preoccupied, drew Cressida to the table. They sat together while Matilda brought more meat and ale, but neither of them wanted to eat. Stephen looked deeply into her eyes. She gazed back, suddenly aware that this man – whom she had known all her life – meant everything to her. Her face was burning beneath his gaze and in spite of her exhaustion she felt more intensely alive than ever before.

'What will you do, little Cressida?' Stephen asked her.

'I know what I *have* to do. I plan freedom for us both. For myself and my brother. Escape by tomorrow at nightfall. Sir Robert and his men will not guess we have stayed so close to home, and the roads for the first hours will be free of them, I am sure. They will be ahead of us, or have given up the chase. Then – it means we have to stay on the road for many months, more than a year perhaps. I plan to find work – but well-paid work, for work well done.' She spoke intensely, her low voice filled with such resolve that her weariness and tears were forgotten. Stephen looked at her with new interest. This was a young woman with beliefs and a will of her own.

Cressida went on to tell Stephen why she believed she should make a new life for herself and her brother. They could command high wages, as freemen – not slaves – now that the death had taken so many from the land. They could look forward to their own piece of land one day, and to money owing to no one but themselves. Then, she planned, Francis was to learn to read. It was his dearest wish. Maybe she too would learn, when there were books in their own, good English tongue. And she knew that one day there would be.

Stephen listened, nodding occasionally, waiting for her to exhaust her flow of words. Then he began to talk, and the two women listened for more than an hour while the boy whose future was in the balance slept peacefully on the settle by the fire.

During his rare, fleeting visits to his home in the three years now past Stephen had told no one in the village of his true task at Oxford. Now, listening to Cressida, he felt he could explain. There had been no one, before, who would understand. They might, on the contrary, have grown to fear him had they known. And when he returned for good, either as their teacher or a fully dedicated, ordained man of God, he did not want that. In the meantime he wished to avoid all suspicion.

'Suspicion of what?' Cressida broke in.

'Of heresy, Cressida. For in a fashion heresy has become my business.'

Her hands still concealed in the folds of her dress, Cressida was not tempted to cross herself at his words. She listened again, spellbound, as Stephen told them that at Oxford he had found young men who knew, as he did, that the church, far from ministering to the poor, deprived them of true religion. It ruled in fear, and in the Latin tongue, preaching some vague salvation from an all too well defined Eternal Hell. The rich bought their redemption. The situation gave the priests as much power as any ruler. There were prelates in the King's government, on every side. And this false power, Stephen believed, could only be challenged if the people could worship in their own tongue. They would know then they were as much God's beloved children as any rich or learned man. But church services in Latin, the rarity of any books save the painted manuscripts chained to the library walls, the inability of most men to read at all . . . all this must first be changed.

Cressida found herself strangely excited by his words. She had once seen a book, brought to their house by a wealthy noblewoman who respected her mother for her knowledge of healing. Together the women had studied the delicate paintings of plants and flowers, and the noblewoman had translated the Latin aloud. As she closed the book carefully, Cressida had sighed, and put out her hand to touch its rich covers. The visitor had laughed, and given her the book to hold. When she had gone, Cressida had asked her mother when she and Francis could learn to read, and at first Margaret had not answered.

When Cressida persisted, Margaret had said: 'When there are books in English, our true tongue. Not Latin for the priests, and not French for Sir Robert and his kind. But when that will be, my child, we cannot tell.'

As she listened to Stephen, Cressida remembered her mother's words. He too told them that it would take many years, but that there were now many good men, scholars and monks, who had already begun to translate the Bible into English. They worked in secret, in retreat. Discovery would almost certainly mean death. But in high places they had their secret well-wishers. There were noblemen who knew the time must come when the prelate-statesmen should be challenged. One day Stephen himself would have to go to London, maybe even to live for a time. The foundations of their movement must be laid so deep that once out in the open they would be strong enough to withstand allcomers.

'London!' Cressida breathed the name of the city softly, her eyes glowing. Forgetting her rough hands, she leant forward, cupping her chin, drinking in Stephen's words. When he saw the torn nails and raw cuts on her skin he gave an involuntary cry, and tried to take her hands in his. But she drew them away, shaking her head dumbly, unable to explain. Sensing her mood, he got up from the table, and went over to where Francis lay. He looked down at him for a long moment, and the boy began to wake.

'I have many friends on the road, Cressida. They would help you. I can give you names, places where you will be safe. But . . . ' Stephen turned to look at her, 'you will be safer if you travel alone.'

'No! I will not leave him! It is for him that I have dared even to think of escape!' Cressida darted to the corner by the fire where Francis was now rubbing the sleep from his eyes. She put an arm round his shoulder, and glared up at Stephen.

But he went on: 'The time will go quickly. You will see. Why – I can teach the boy to read. And remember – the plague goes ahead of you to London. It will wait for you at every turn. Do you not think that your brother will be best as a free man – in Oxford?' He paused. Then he reached out and touched a heavy strand of hair that had fallen across her breast.

'I would not leave it long before I came to you.' He glanced to where his mother sat, occupied with her own thoughts, in the shadows.

'But if I lose him now . . . ' Cressida said weakly, and as she spoke she knew that it was not only her brother she dared not leave. Suddenly Stephen had become part of her very being. If she let him help it would also make him an inescapable part of the new life she had planned.

'You are strong, Cressida. Whatever happens you will survive. But – I give you my word – you are not going to lose us. You will see.' Stephen drew her to him then with firm, gentle hands, and kissed her first on her high, white forehead. She kept very still, her eyes brilliant in the glow of the fire as they held his gaze.

'Your vows, Stephen. What of your vows as a man of God?' It was as if they were playing a slow, adult version of the games they had always played. A smile teased at the corner of her mouth, and she let it grow, as she tilted back her head.

Stephen bent to kiss her on the lips, then, and found her young mouth warm and open to his. 'You know I have not sworn my full vows, yet,' he whispered, and Cressida's answer was to kiss him back, swiftly and surely, before she disentangled herself from his arms.

It was Francis who broke the spell. Fully awake now, he leapt from the settle and ran to Stephen. 'Stephen! When did you get here? Have you brought your grey horse?'

Stephen laughed quietly, and swung the boy into the air. 'You are as heavy as ever, I see. You were always a very strong child, Francis. I remember you seizing the toys from your sister when she wanted to play alone.'

'I think I have given up toys, Stephen.' The boy looked down at him, suddenly serious, and slid to the ground. 'We travel light, Cressida and I. With nothing.' He allowed himself to be led to the table, where Matilda prepared a drink of warm honey and herbs, and drained his bowl at a gulp, his eyes not leaving Stephen's face. 'Where did you say I could learn to read? Was I dreaming?'

Stephen glanced across the table at Cressida. She sat very still, white-faced. Her golden throat and breasts were taut, and she seemed at first to be fighting the impulse to speak. Then, with an effort, she told Francis: 'No, you were not dreaming. You would learn to read and write at Oxford . . . if you went with Stephen tonight.'

'I ride in an hour.' The scholar smiled at Francis. 'Do you think the grey would carry the pair of us?'

Francis jumped from his stool and began to leap about the room in the firelight chanting a tune they had learnt as children: ' "Ride a grey horse to the shrine of Our Lady, ride a grey horse to the gates of Heaven." It would be like Heaven there, Cressida, would it not?'

It was the first time she had seen him in such spirits since the day she had told him their mother was dead. She knew then that she would have to let him go. The thought of the lone journey to London terrified her, but she must not let the others see it. Perhaps the road to freedom for her brother would be shorter if he went that night with Stephen. Perhaps it would be easier for her to find work if she travelled alone. And it was true that Sir Robert and his men would be looking for two of them if they decided to follow and drag them back to the village, to their life as serfs.

'Aye. You would be happy there, Francis. But – '

'We leave within the hour,' Stephen broke in, as if to avoid further discussion. 'The boy must assume some disguise, I think. And there are some clothes somewhere in my mother's store that I wore when I first went to study with the priest. They are right for a boy on his way to a great seat of learning.'

'I can dye my hair too, if you wish,' Francis said happily. Matilda stepped in then, removing him to a small annexe at the far end of the room where he could be washed and dressed for the journey.

'When would I see you both again?' Cressida tried to speak calmly, but her blue eyes were fixed anxiously on Stephen's face.

'If you can keep to the route I would suggest you will find that you can stay with true friends at least twice on your way to the city. Firstly, I have friends in Ashby who will welcome you. And at the second place, Grimthorne Abbey, we could meet. I would ride there overnight from Oxford, and bring the boy with me. In the spring. The weeks will go by so quickly, Cressida.'

He began to speak hurriedly, giving her directions, names, and landmarks by which she might keep to a safe path. That is, if anywhere were safe. When he asked her to repeat what he had told her, she went through his instructions without a fault, and he paused, gazing at her with admiration.

'You are quick to learn. As bright as your hair . . . ' He faltered, and looked away.

'It is of necessity, Stephen. I am resolved. If you think there is a life for – for me – in London, then it is the answer. Sir Robert will never guess that I should manage such a journey, or have such friends to see me on my way.'

*

'There are to be no farewells,' Stephen said later, as they stood ready to go, Francis in his neat student's tunic, the older man in his scholar's velvet hat and cloak. Francis's hair, now darkened by Matilda's labours, made Cressida feel that she took her leave of a stranger. She swallowed a little cry of thanks and sorrow as Matilda tucked a pack of food in the boy's tunic. Before the boy could respond, Stephen clasped his shoulder firmly. 'When you meet your sister again you will be able to read!'

She knew that Stephen meant it for the best, but there was something so unyielding about the way in which he was now prepared to take her brother from her that she wondered if he was not, perhaps, at heart as cold as his dark, lean good looks sometimes suggested.

The tight, brave smile on Cressida's face made him pause as he lifted the latch. 'You must sleep through the day now – before you take to the road.'

She nodded, unable to speak. She did not know how she would ever sleep again. The knowledge that her brother was riding north, away from her, that they had both left their village perhaps for ever, drummed in her brain.

It was as she raised a hand to call her brother to her for a last embrace that Stephen took three paces across the room to her, and kissed her again, full on the mouth. She went limp in his arms, astonished and deliriously happy for a second, then her body arched against his, and the kiss that followed, long and ardent as he sought her tongue and then broke almost angrily from her, was with her as she watched the daylight creep into the room some hours later, then closed her eyes in a determined effort to sleep. She would need all of her strength for the first night's walk, she told herself. By the next day she would aim to have left Sir Robert's domain.

But she woke once more before dawn, and as she again remembered Stephen's embrace, the fear of the unknown journey suddenly left her. She went into a light, easy sleep with the knowledge that there had been something reluctant, almost angry, in the way he had crossed the room to her, and later broken from her. She sensed that it was in her power to dispel whatever it was that held him back from her. In their kiss there had been no echo of their childhood games. And the long, menacing road ahead of them, the weeks and maybe months before she could seek his lips again, were not the fabric of children's dreams.

2

Before she had tried to sleep as day broke, Cressida had talked briefly with Matilda about a choice of disguise for the journey to come. The idea that she should pose as a poor mad creature rejected by her family had been discarded – such a figure would be a butt for mischief to all the rogues she might meet on the road, and if she sustained the role for any time it might come between her and the chance to work when such a chance came. Nor could she hope to pass for a pilgrim; a woman rarely went on a pilgrimage alone, and she had neither companion, horse, nor carriage. It was in any case no time of year for the pilgrimage to Gloucester or the journey to Canterbury, and her story would not be easily believed. Even the outriders from the monastic houses had to be in urgent need of supplies to take to the roads so early in the year.

In the end they had agreed that she should travel as a beggar girl, so that if she found herself still on the open road as daylight came she could take her rest whilst she appeared to ask the passers-by for alms. There were unwritten laws that guarded the unfortunates who had no means of living except as beggars, and if challenged she could frighten her inquisitors with pleading that both her parents had died of plague. Under her beggar-maid's clothing she would wear her own gown, ready for the day when she need no longer hide. And if the worst came to the worst and she was recognized as a runaway from Sir Robert's domain, then she could hope to bribe her way to safety with one of the coins she had saved. If this failed. . . it would mean surrender.

But she must not fail. Again and again as she combed her long hair back from her face in preparation for sleep she told herself that she must not fail. With each deft stroke she vowed that she would reach London in the end. So much awaited her there. It was true that she would be alone at first, but Francis would follow. And Stephen.

When at last she slept, she dreamed of Stephen. She knew him by the sombre, student's coat he wore, though he was at first turned from her, and by the pale circle of the tonsure, a token of Christ's crown of thorns, set on his young head. She thought as she watched his shadowy figure that though this showed him to be a novice man of God he did not belong to God alone, and had not as yet given himself entirely to the vows that would mean no return. She had called to him several times, very softly, in a strangely seductive voice that she did not recognize as her own. Then he had smiled, and vanished, and she woke to find herself smiling in the darkness, her young limbs stretched to their long, sinuous limits on the rough mattress that was her bed.

Cressida knew nothing of the formal, subtle interpretation of dreams believed by so many to shed meaning on the future, and on the true nature of the dreamer. But she knew by instinct that everything that had happened in the dream hinted of unnamed conflicts, unspoken desires – and in both conflict and desire it was she, not Stephen, who seemed to have been the victor.

Matilda stayed quietly in the house and garden during the course of the day as Cressida slept, but as evening came on she bustled at the fire with the preparation of a meal for them both. Then, as Cressida cleared the table, she disappeared into the annexe, to reappear within moments with a bundle of drab clothing under one arm and a small worsted bodice in her hand. 'You will need to hide more than your hair and your clean face, my girl. This bodice has pockets sewn into the seams. I fastened them strongly while you slept. This way you carry your money close to your heart. And if any man finds what you have stored away there, it will be too late; you will be as good as dead, and your money no use to you.'

Cressida shuddered, and begged her not to talk of such things. She knew Matilda meant well, but she herself was afraid that if she once started to consider all that could happen to her she would never start out on her journey.

'And food for your first day or two can be stored in your beggar-girl's skirt!' Matilda held aloft a wide, grey kirtle for Cressida's approval, and showed her a concealed panel under its ample folds. She handed it to her, and hurried to the window to draw the closure against the night. 'I do not believe we are watched, but now we have got so far with your plans we must take no risks. Curfew is soon. Then it will be safe for you to leave.'

Cressida thanked her warmly, and began to ease the clothes over her own neat gown. 'I have only one fear, Matilda – that my good shoes will give me away. And yet if I travel without them I shall not get far.' She looked down at her strong leather slippers and her slim legs in their warm woollen hose. Even as they had grown poorer, since her father's death, her mother had always made sure that she and Francis were well shod. Matilda looked thoughtfully at her own feet, measuring them against the smaller feet of the girl, then hurried once more into her seemingly endless store. She emerged triumphantly a moment later, and bade Cressida sit in the inglenook and hold out her feet.

Over the woollen hose and the good shoes, Matilda drew a pair of thick, bright red stockings she had worn once, years ago, at a great Fair. Then over the red stockings she slipped an ancient pair of her own shoes – wide, and shabby, but now a perfect fit. She knelt back on her heels as Cressida got to her feet, and shuffled at first clumsily and then with growing skill about the rushes. Then both women laughed delightedly.

'I will travel slowly, like this, Matilda! But warmly, and with every step I shall remember you – this house, your kindness . . . ' She sat at the table and looked about her as Matilda lit a tallow and placed it between them. The flames wavered at first in the airless room, and Matilda went to the door and opened it briefly. A shaft of light appeared from the street, and Matilda closed the door again swiftly. The tallow gleamed strongly now, and Cressida's hair shone in its light.

'Sir Robert's men have just passed,' Matilda whispered. 'They were riding out to the manor, as if going home for the night.'

'Then I am safe! Our plan is working!' Cressida got up, and walked about the room again restlessly. 'It means I must start, as soon as I can.'

'Not before we have darkened the fair line of hair that will show beneath your cloak,' Matilda reminded her. 'Come.'

Cressida had insisted that even if she risked recognition, or even if it seemed she were too well-clothed for a beggar girl, she would not take the road to London bereft of her cloak. It had belonged to her mother as a young girl, and it seemed to wrap her in the comfort of her mother's strength of spirit. It was a rare possession for a peasant woman, for even the merchants passed their rich cloaks down from one generation to another with cloth at the price it was. The weave was strong, and would see her through all weathers, perhaps for a lifetime.

They darkened the line of hair with the remainder of the soil with which they had smeared her face. There was no mirror in the house, but Matilda assured her she looked every inch a homeless, unwashed tinker of a woman – and Cressida believed her. She fastened the tie of her cloak at the throat, and stood motionless while Matilda checked every detail of her appearance for anything that would give her away. Nodding her small, coifed head as she stepped back, Matilda told her it was best if she left now, on the heels of Sir Robert's men.

'It is only two nights' walking, child, before you reach Stephen's friends.' Matilda spoke caressingly, sensing her fears.

'Yes, I know. If things go well I must find the house on the edge of the town of Ashby Cross. It is a holy clerk whom Stephen met in his first year at Oxford. He has a wife, and little ones. Stephen said their door is always open . . . ' She spoke as if to convince herself that all would be well. To hide misgivings in her face, she bent, pretending to push the store of food Matilda had given her more securely in its place in the wide skirts. The glimpse of red stocking this afforded her somehow gave her more heart, and as she straightened she hugged the older woman to her.

'Safe journey, Margaret's child,' Matilda whispered, and held the door for her. A moment later, she had gone.

Ten miles from Stephen's village the wide track would link with the main road to Ashby, and halfway to Ashby itself was the river that wound then beside the road until it reached the town. Cressida planned to rest, when the first daylight of her journey came, where the river could be crossed. Then, according to the number of people and conditions she found on the road, she would either walk on in the open or take to the river bank.

As she turned on to the main route she felt no tiredness, in spite of the fact that she had now walked for more than three hours. She blessed the knowledge of the stars that had made her choose this time, with its full moon, for her flight. The night was cold, but clear. Keeping close to the high banks that edged the common fields away from the village, she walked steadily, her gaze a yard or two ahead, watching for pitfalls in her rough path.

The point at which she would cross the river was spanned by the only stone bridge for many miles. Under it, the waters were always shallow, and the several arches that supported it were built deep into the river bed on raised, square platforms of moss-covered boulders. The platforms were usually clear of the tide, and Cressida – who had once crossed the bridge as a child on a cart her father had borrowed to move grain for Sir Robert – remembered thinking what a splendid game of hide and seek could be played down there in the swirling reeds. On the bridge itself there were spacious V-shaped bays, built in at intervals, where anyone on foot could take refuge when a cart or a horse plunged by. Cressida reached the bridge in the strange first light, when the countryside seemed more awake than at any other time of day. At first she thought the rhythmic pounding she could hear was the echo of her own footsteps, a trick of sound as she left the earth of the road for the stones. But the pounding grew louder, and suddenly she knew that what she heard was the beat of horses' hooves, no more than a mile away.

She stood completely still in the centre of the bridge for perhaps ten seconds. Then, with the speed of an animal racing for its life, she ran to the far end of the bridge and flung herself down the bank into the ice-cold river water beneath. As she touched bottom, the reeds and green slime caught at her skirts, and she stood gasping in their clutches. Then she walked heavily through the water, falling with each uncertain step, until she had gained the wide parapet under the last archway, the furthest point of the crossing from the approaching horsemen. Terrified that the sound of her movements in the water would attract their attention, she climbed slowly and painfully to the darkest spot she could find. Then, her long, wet skirts held back from the river, and her whole body shaking with the cold, she waited.

There were three horsemen in the party, Cressida guessed from the ring of hooves as they slowed to a trot in order to cross the bridge. From the jangle of bridles she knew they were riding heavily, maybe armed. She wished she could have seen their colours, and learnt whether they came from Sir Robert's band. But she was soon to know.

Having crossed the bridge and moved to a patch of meadow to one side of the road, the riders began to discuss the merits of going on. The man who seemed to be their leader was in favour of doing so. The other two were inclined to turn back. When the leader remonstrated with the remark that the girl was a strong wench, and the boy likely to stay the course if his sister bade him, Cressida knew for sure they were searching for her.

'Sir Robert will soon join us,' one of the others replied. 'He it is who wants the girl back. Let him decide how many horses we are going to weary in the chase.'

'Careful how you talk,' the leader warned him. 'There's the boy to think about. A good worker if he grows the way he was shaping when I saw him last. We're not on a wenching party, my lad.'

The third rider laughed cynically at this, and Cressida's anger seemed to calm her. She dared not move, but she settled more securely in her hiding place, and listened greedily for their next words. Sir Robert himself was out searching for them, which meant that he had called again at their house and found them gone. If he found her, she had no doubt what her fate would be. The fact that she had also deprived him of her brother's labours would make him doubly angry. But she made a vow to herself, as she crouched against the damp stones, that even if he caught her and threatened death she would never tell where Francis had gone.

As she made the vow, the sound of a fourth horseman, about a mile away, reached the others. Cressida heard it too, and as the search party turned and reassembled to greet Sir Robert she began to tremble violently again. Then the metallic beat of a horse ridden fast across the bridge made her clutch at her ears with her hands, and she became aware of the long, wet hair that had escaped from her hood and was clinging in strands of golden slime to her bodice. Stifling a moan of despair, she twisted and smoothed the hair back, and pulled the hood over her face. If the pursuers came down to the water's edge the slightest glimpse of a pale brow in the shadows would mean the end of her freedom.

As he drew close to his men, Sir Robert reined in his horse and gave an angry shout, demanding the reason for the halt. The leader muttered something which Cressida could not hear, and Sir Robert, whatever it was the man had said, was unappeased.

'I tell you that two mere children would not have got this far by night on foot. They must have had help. If you press on, you will come upon some carriage, or horsemen. They have been dragged to some other estate to work, for sure. And I want them back where they belong. They belong to me.'

Cressida thought grimly as she listened that Sir Robert had not deceived his men with his shouting. They knew what he was after, and maybe they too had daughters who had been subject to his rough wooing. But Sir Robert himself was deceived, if he believed that she and Francis would not have got so far on foot. She was glad that she travelled alone, now that she knew the search party believed she was with her brother and would be looking for two runaways, but for a moment she wished that she had him beside her. They would have listened together to the words that struck at the heart of the matter: Sir Robert believed they were his property, and pursued them as he would pursue a pair of hounds that had slipped their leash. With such a master as a threat to their freedom, they would have walked to the ends of the earth.

With a sigh of relief, Cressida next heard the small band of men ride away on the Ashby road, Sir Robert shouting that they would go five miles more before they turned for home. She settled down in her hiding place to wait. She dared not move, to dry herself, or seek warmer shelter, in case such a move coincided with the return of Sir Robert earlier than he planned. She knew enough of the man to guess that he was in an irascible, erratic mood, and could change his mind in a second and retrace his tracks to the bridge. With an effort, she controlled her shivering and chattering teeth, and tried to think. But she could come to only the one decision. She had to wait for the riders' return, and take the risk of discovery again, before she dare try to sleep.

It was less than an hour later that she was rewarded with the approaching hammer of hooves from the direction of the town. She had no way to verify that these were Sir Robert's horses, and if they rode straight on over the bridge she would never know for sure that they had given up the chase. But as the stone road above her rang again with the uneven trot that horsemen used as they crossed a spanning bridge she sensed the slower pace of the leader, and on the far side of the river the group of riders came once more to a halt. Then she held her breath, terrified, as Sir Robert, grumbling to himself, dismounted and strode back across the bridge, to come to a stand in one of the bays. She risked everything she had planned for as she leant precariously from her hiding place and glimpsed the heavy gauntlets gripping the parapet above her.

'The girl is clever,' Sir Robert growled. 'And a beauty. If she stays at large, it'll not be long before she is ruined.' He chuckled then, to himself. 'But I wager she'll put up a fight, by Mary. I'd like to see her struggle.' He must have picked a stone from the ground, for a moment later it came skimming across the green-brown waters in Cressida's sight. She watched the waters ripple back into place in the long winged path of the stone, as Sir Robert walked quickly away.

Moments later, as the riders disappeared into the distance and made for home, Cressida was out on the river bank, wringing her wet garments as dry as she could, and searching for what remained of her sodden food store in the folds of her kirtle. To her delight, the bread so well wrapped by Matilda was almost unharmed. But she would not touch the dampened meat. She had heard too often from her mother that however thirsty she might be she must never touch the waters of a river near a town. Returning to the low, stone archway at the water's edge that was her bedroom for the rest of the day, she closed her eyes and told herself that all she must think of was how to gather strength for the next night. The town could not be far. She calculated that she had gone more than half the way, by gaining the bridge that morning. As she slipped into an uneasy doze, a rat fell from the stone ceiling above her and sped from the bridge to the meadow above. She sensed its presence, but was too weary to be afraid.

That night, she made an early start on the road. It was barely dusk, and she knew that she risked discovery or attack if she passed any other travellers. But the incident at the bridge had spurred her on. She believed now that Sir Robert might tire of the chase, and if he thought some other landowner had her and Francis within his gates, he might change his strategy and start a search of the neighbouring castles. With this to cheer her, she trudged a good eight miles before she thought of resting. The walking eased her stiff, aching limbs after a time, and the fact that she had lost Matilda's slippers in the river meant that she now walked unhampered in her own good shoes. She had kept the red stockings, now inside her shoes, and rough-dried them by wrapping them in her cloak all that afternoon.

She took her first rest of the night in a ditch at the roadside on the edge of a small wood. She had nothing left of her food, and resigned herself to her growing hunger with the thought that Stephen's friends would take care of her less than twelve hours from now. She was rubbing her feet in an effort to warm them when she coughed slightly, and at the back of her throat tasted the unmistakable, acrid film of smoke from a wood fire. Slowly, she sat up until she could see over the edge of the ditch and into the thin wintry trees away from the road. In the moonlit clearing twenty yards from where she crouched, a man, his back to her, was sitting before a low fire. As she watched, he pierced something in the embers with a long slender branch, and held it to his mouth.

It was many months since Cressida had savoured a young chicken cooked on an open fire, and without concern for the risk she ran she climbed from the ditch and began to nose her way forward, stomach close to the ground, to where she could see and enjoy the source of the delicious aroma that was now wafting towards her under the trees. The carpet of wet leaves and bracken beneath her crackled as she moved, but she ignored it. As she came round to the side of the clearing she knew that she had been right: the man was eating delicately from the crisp browned carcase of a young wild hen.

In the light from the fire she also was able to see that there was a sturdy, low-built shelter of branches to one side of the clearing, and a travelling pack half-opened at the entrance to the shelter spilled an assortment of utensils on to the ground. This was a seasoned traveller, Cressida decided, and the odd homeliness of the scene she had come upon in the night somehow reassured her. She moved forward again on her stomach, wriggling through a patch of undergrowth until she was close enough to the man to study his face.

He knew then that he was being watched, and without stopping what he was doing, or changing his position by the fire, called in a soft voice: 'There is plenty for two to eat. If you are hungry, whoever you are, you may come closer. I do not fear you. That is if you do not fear me.'

If Cressida had known the figure she presented as she stood up amongst the trees and crept towards the clearing, she would have blushed crimson with shame. Her hair hung in strands from either side of her face, still mingled with dark slime from the river. Her mud-stained cloak was ripped down one side, and the red stockings twisted in her dusty shoes. She limped rather than walked, and her brilliant blue eyes gleamed with naked hunger. Her face, spattered with dried earth, was the face of an urchin. And yet, as she came into the range of light spread by the fire, the man who watched her was aware of her intense pride, and the beauty that matched it.

Three seconds later, she was sitting in the warmth, a leg of chicken in her hands, and a long strip of its flesh already between her teeth. The man was reminded of some fierce cat-creature, although he sensed in the girl some child-like need, to be nourished and cherished perhaps . . . or perhaps only to be spoilt? He said nothing until she paused in her feeding, then: 'My name is Dominic. I am known in the towns of this region. For my music. You do not seem to me to belong in this part of the country?'

Resenting the time that talking wasted while she still wanted to eat, Cressida took a second, and third, bite at the food, and shook her head. 'I do belong. But I – my family – we do not have the same looks as the Norman breed. It is an accident of birth, my mother said.'

'Where is your mother now?'

'Can you not guess? It has happened to one in every three. Have you not seen it in your travels?' She glanced at the shelter, and the goods spilled before it. 'Are you a tinker?'

Dominic threw back his head in a silent laugh. She had a glimpse of strong, white teeth and a firm brown throat. He was brown-haired, and looked at her again with soft brown eyes. She could not be sure that his look was harmless. She put down what remained of the chicken, and began to gather her cloak round her. As the man rose to his feet, she too rose, and backed to the other side of the fire. He seemed not to notice her move, and made for the shelter, where he started to gather his belongings into the bag. She watched him, warily. When she spoke, her voice trembled.

'Thank you, sir. For such generous hospitality. I would not find its equal in any mansion.'

'You would not find your way into any mansion at the moment, girl.' His tone was dry, and she looked down at her clothes, for the first time aware of her appearance since she had dived into the river ten miles back and twelve hours before.

'I am not a beggar girl, if that is what you think.' Her pride was regaining the upper hand, and her caution fled in the face of her embarrassment. 'I travel for a good purpose.'

'And so, I hope, do I.' Dominic walked back to the fire, and sat again in its glow. He motioned to her to do the same, and, slowly, she copied him. He gazed at her across the small clearing as she began hasty, feminine little movements to cleanse her face and put her hair in order. 'There is a mirror in my pack,' he told her, smiling. But she was at once suspicious.

'Mirrors are for noble ladies. They cost many pieces of gold.'

'They can cost nothing. Beauty deserves a sight of itself sometimes.'

'At what price? You do not state your price, tinker!' she objected, resorting to attack before he could make any move towards her that she might have cause to fear.

'I have told you. There is no charge. Perhaps – '

Cressida waited fearfully. 'Perhaps your story would be a fair price. Or I would accept one word, if you wish. Your name.'

'Cressida. My name is Cressida.' She sat very straight as she said it, and held out her hand. He studied the torn, reddened skin, but said nothing. Instead he went to the pack, and searched in its depths. When he turned back to her, he carried a small oval of burnished silver on a slim handle, and swivelled it, catching the firelight on the gleaming surface, as he walked over to where she waited.

The face that stared back at Cressida in the silver reflection was that of a wild, frightened child. But as she stared, her expression changed. She reached in the folds of her skirt for the roughly shaped comb she was never without, and, pushing her cloak back from her shoulders, held the mirror high in one hand while she began to transform her appearance. When she had finished, she stood, and asked Dominic, 'May I shelter here, for a short time only? I travel, usually, by night, and my time is short. An hour only, and I shall leave, I promise.'

'If you listen to me, while you rest, you may decide that we can leave together. I mean you no harm. But I wish I had by the throat the man who has brought you to this.' He was watching her with open admiration as he spoke.

As Cressida edged into the shelter he had made, Dominic moved away. From his belongings, he selected a small lute. Then he took his old place in the firelight, where she had first seen him, and began to sing.

It was not a melody she had heard before. It came perhaps from France, perhaps from the Kentish lands where the exiled French were to be found. As she listened, Cressida wondered how a powerful man like Sir Robert could so abuse the courtly game of love. The story was of a young man whose love had set him three tasks, and three years' exile in which to achieve them, before she would listen to his suit. When he came back to the garden where she had always met him, she had left word that she waited now in her bower within the house. There he found a rose, the symbol of perfect love. She had died the third year of waiting. But at least their love had been unspoiled.

'That would be a rare and lovely way to die.' Cressida spoke in the darkness.

'You should have no thoughts of death. Your whole life is before you. Is that not why you have fled?'

'How did you know? You are not what you seem – '

'Hush. You have the look of someone who runs towards the light. Towards freedom, if you like. And you must believe me – I am on your side. I can guess your story. There are many like you on the roads. But not so many who dare to walk alone, and at night. You must join me.'

'I dare not. I cannot – I have places, names of friends to go to. I am not as alone as you think.'

'It need not be all the way,' he insisted. 'I sing for my

living as I go from town to town, and my next fixed call is thirty miles beyond Ashby, for the Fair. Then – London.'

'London? I – I cannot promise. I have a brother, a young brother, with whom I must meet . . . ' She faltered. 'And in Ashby I am to call at the house of the holy clerk . . . ' She was almost too weary to talk, but she stopped sharply before she gave the name of Stephen's friend. How could she trust this man? He could sing prettily, it was true, and he was generous. But all that could mean he was out to win her confidence. He might be one of the enemies of Stephen's cause.

'I know the man,' said Dominic quietly, as if reading her thoughts. 'His name is Peter. And if you take me with you to his house, you will learn for certain that I am a friend.'

To walk in the centre of the road to Ashby in daylight, with a man ahead to protect her, was to Cressida the substance of a dream. She had slept long and deeply in the shelter Dominic had built, while he dozed and kept watch in turns by the fire. At dawn, she had found a stream at the far edge of the wood, and washed her face and hands in the fast running water. Then she had put her dress in order, bundling the old garments Matilda had given her together neatly, in case she should need them at a later stage of her journey. Now she marched with a light step, in her own shoes and hose, a yard or two behind the laden figure of her new guardian. She had offered to help with carrying his pack, but it was so well put together that he found it easier to manage it alone. As he walked, he sang – a ragged marching song in Flemish that sounded as if it were made for working men or soldiers. He had told her that they would be in Ashby, at the house of the clerk called Peter, by the middle of the day.

There were not many others on the usually crowded tracks, terrified as men were by the threat of plague. They had been on the road for perhaps an hour when a small band of horsemen appeared ahead of them, and Cressida ran for the side-bank, crying to Dominic to walk on without her. But he stopped, and came back for her, pulling her out of the ditch where she had fallen – in full view of the riders. As they came closer, she saw their colours, vivid blue and green surcoats and green bridles scalloped with silver. They were not Sir Robert's men – and they clearly came from a wealthier household than his. Cressida allowed herself to be dragged back to the road, while Dominic laughed and waved at the passing horsemen, making signs to show that he had a rebellious girl to deal with. The men laughed too, and rode on without slackening their pace. As they regained their own steady speed, Cressida asked Dominic sulkily why he had ceased his song. He told her that there was some music meant for the ears of honest men alone, and she walked in silence after that, pondering what he could mean.

With a short rest by the roadside three or four miles from the town, Cressida was ready for the last lap, and eager to meet Stephen's friends. They soon reached the crossroads where the way from the north-west traversed their own west-east route, and Cressida stopped for a moment to gaze into the distance to her left. This must be the road to Oxford, she thought – the road that Francis might take one day, to keep their rendezvous somewhere of Stephen's choosing. As she dwelt on the happiness the meeting would bring them all, two small black figures appeared on the horizon, riding south. Suddenly the younger rider, on a smaller horse, put on speed, and rode to where Dominic and Cressida stood, waving at them to stop.

'Say nothing of who you are or where we are going,' Dominic warned Cressida swiftly. 'It is I who will tell our story. These men are clerics, and they must have some devious reason for riding at this time.'

'Friends!' the young clerk called as he approached. He wore the severe clothing of a novice, and as he doffed his pleated velvet hat Cressida noticed the trim naked patch of his tonsure in his dark auburn hair. She took an instant dislike to his thin mouth and the sandy brows above steel grey eyes, and was glad to let Dominic speak for her. But Dominic said nothing until the second rider, an older man in the garb of a friar, joined them. At the sight of a heavy jewelled ring on the friar's hand, Dominic raised his own hat, and bowed.

'We would have your blessings, Father, for our journey,' he whined, in a voice Cressida hardly recognized. 'Will you not pray for this young girl and the souls of her dead parents when you reach the great Cathedral?'

The friar made a hasty, automatic sign of the cross in the vague direction of where Cressida stood. 'Both parents dead, child?' he frowned.

'Of the black plague, Father,' Dominic replied for her, and the friar reined his horse a yard or two back from them.

'How would you know that we ride for Chichester?' he demanded.

'Where else, my lord?' Dominic spoke lightly. 'They say there are great plans there for changes in the laws of England, and this road goes straight there if you do not turn for Ashby. You have the air of a man who would know how to make the laws.' He cringed in a fashion so foreign to him that Cressida had difficulty in not smiling, but she became serious at the friar's reply.

'What would a tinker know of such things? Where have you been to learn of changes?' He signalled to his clerk to rein in beside him and listen.

'The roads are great teachers, Father. The tales that travellers tell along its way are full of news and commentary. I could not help but learn.'

He did not add that he knew only too well that Chichester was a seat of secular rather than religious thinking, whose leaders' aims were to develop the power of churchmen as statesmen to such a pitch that even a popular king like Edward would be hard put to it to rule his own people. But for his own ends, Dominic wanted to be sure that he had judged the travellers aright. Their presence in the district was a bad sign, and there were those he would want to warn.

Cressida could not tell whether it was by accident or design that just at that moment a smoke-grimed, heavy kettle fell from Dominic's pack under the feet of the friar's horse, sending the animal rearing into the air, its nostrils dilated fiercely, and the friar rolling in his saddle, straining to regain control. The humble kitchen object came to rest on the track between them, and as if reassured by its mundane look, the friar wheeled and spurred his horse for the south. The clerk gave a last look down at Cressida and her companion, and something in the cold eyes left her inwardly afraid. As he rode after his master, she drew closer to Dominic.

'I know their kind,' he said. 'The sort of prelate who is always meddling in the halls of power. They must have some strong reasons for riding from Oxford at this time of year.'

'From Oxford? Why did you not tell me? I have told you my brother is there. They might have news.'

'No. It is too soon. They would have left before your brother reached the city, if what you have told me is true.'

'You know it is true!' Cressida blazed at him. 'Why should I lie?'

'Because you are not sure that you trust me,' he laughed, and with an arm round her shoulders he led her to the crossroads and the turn to Ashby.

All her life Cressida was to remember the night in the house of Stephen's friend Peter. It was a spacious, three-roomed house, in a patch of land sown with winter cabbage and thin stalks of maize. As they arrived, they were greeted by three tumbling children, whose little bodies were swathed in woollen cloth, their short legs wrapped in worsted leggings carrying them almost in spite of themselves as they ran across the frozen garden. Their mother came to the open door when she heard their cries, and called to them to stand quite still where they were, while the travellers were still at the gate. 'You are welcome, but I must first ask if you are free of the plague?'

Cressida called that it was some weeks now since she had contact, and all was well with her. Dominic answered, gravely, that he had walked for many months in the open air and had as yet met no victims of the terror. 'We would not threaten your little ones, Madam,' he called. 'We need shelter, but anywhere, outside, will do. And we need to talk with your husband. The girl – Cressida – is sent by – '

As a man appeared round the side of the house, Cressida hurried forward to speak for herself. In a low voice she asked if he were indeed the clerk named Peter, and when he nodded she explained that she had not told her companion everything: that she was from Stephen, the son of Geoffrey the Wainwright, and they had known each other since childhood. She was still too close to danger to seek shelter in the hostelries along the way, and Stephen had said she would find a haven here. Was it true?

Peter was a tall, heavily-built man wearing rough variations of a clerk's garments, and seemed to belong more to the fields than indoors with a quill pen. He looked down at Cressida with his keen, countryman's eyes, and then beyond her, to where Dominic stood. The shout of laughter he gave so frightened Cressida that she slipped as she turned to see the cause of his merriment – and came to her feet in time to watch Peter and Dominic embrace like old friends.

As Peter called his wife to meet the travellers, he explained that he had known Dominic for many years, and that they had met in dangerous times, in the Low Countries. 'And beware his songs, wife!' Peter went on. 'He will sing of a rose one minute, and the next you know he has you marching behind a drum and a rich man's sword at your throat!'

Cressida listened in amazement. She had guessed that there was more to Dominic than the man of soft music and quick wits, but this was a world of which she so far knew nothing. Peter and he were discussing what amounted to rebellion, organized revolt. No wonder he had taken a young peasant girl in flight under his wing.

As they assembled later for a simple evening meal, the twilight shed its melancholy on the figures seated round the table, and Peter did not laugh now as he talked. He warned Dominic that he believed he was a man born many years ahead of his time. That he came too soon to England. If he persisted, he would find that he stood alone. As he talked, Dominic shook his head.

'We shall see, my friend. We shall see. Look at this rebel I bring with me. Is she not true token of the times? And of good luck, with her strange golden hair and her fine spirit? I tell you, she will bring me good fortune, and allies. I intend to take her on with me . . . to London.'

'To London? Does her friend the scholar know of this? Stephen is a hot-headed man when he is roused. I know him well.' Peter looked keenly at Cressida, noticing the warmth of her cheeks as she heard Stephen's name.

Cressida spoke for herself, trying to make her voice sound casual as she mentioned Stephen. 'It is true I cannot make for London in haste. I am to meet with my young brother at the Abbey of Grimthorne, perhaps in the first days of spring. Stephen has given his word that he will bring him to me there. And they say there is sanctuary there for travellers, and those in flight.'

Both men nodded, as if they knew Grimthorne's reputation was safe. 'And you shall see your brother, Cressida. There is no great hurry for my journey. My next port of call is some sixty days from now, at the great Fair of Kent. There are men in Kent who await me, too. Until then I have business in the next village . . . and the next. It is I who will wait for you.' He sighed, and looked round the fast darkening room. The eldest child, seeing a good opportunity to ask him to sing, brought his lute from beside the hearth where he had left it.

Looking back at the scene, with the children and their

parents watching the singer, and her own heart aching with doubts as she strained to discern the meanings of his outlandish songs, Cressida knew it was the last time in her life that she had thought or felt as a child.

3

The village where Dominic hoped to stop next was a mile or two to the south of the road that led from Ashby to London. It was in the domain of an Earl whose tyranny was a legend, and yet in its own way – Peter warned Dominic – the life there was good. The mill was a large, efficient concern and the peasants received good service and fair returns for their grain. The priests were well paid and well fed, and in the care of their flock seemed more enthusiastic than most. The fact that the Earl was unmarried meant that the local merchant families behaved themselves, rather than lose any chance their daughters might have of winning them a share in his wealth. The life of the serfs was accordingly predictable, and happy enough.

It was said that the Earl remained a bachelor because the child of his choice some years before would not have him when she came to womanhood. The alliance was so important to him that he was prepared to wait. But time was running out, and the local candidates for his bed were kept on their pretty toes by the story.

The accounts of the apparently ideal state of life for the bondsmen thereabouts did not deter Dominic. He believed that a true rebellion would hold its own if its leaders were thoughtful rather than starving. In the Earl's domain he saw the potential that others less experienced in rebellion were blind to.

He walked into the village square early on a morning of winter sunshine, with Cressida a yard or two behind.

Together they made for the high preaching cross that dominated the scene. The cross was by custom a meeting place in most villages. There the holy friars would stand to give blessing, and the Pardoners' carriages would halt for the sale of indulgences to sinners. Dominic sat on a low granite step that ran round its base, and Cressida went to the other side of the square to wait for him.

He began with the song of the rose that she had heard in the wood the first night they met. The women came to the doors of their houses to listen. A young boy sat at Dominic's feet. A small group of menfolk gathered. quietly, Dominic began to talk. Cressida could not hear what was said, but it seemed to her that in spite of themselves the men stayed to listen, and to reply. There was no sign of trouble, and the group was preparing to disperse as the time came for the midday meal when a tight-knit band of riders appeared at the end of the street.

Cressida recognized the vivid blues and greens of their surcoats and shields at once. Then the colours, the silver trappings, metallic visors clamped down over flashing eyes, all blurred in a composite of noise and speed and fear as the riders thundered by. She had a split second in which to dive instinctively for cover with other women behind a group of gnarled oak trees across the square, before the riders reached the cross.

Dominic stood firm, too late to help a boy knocked unconscious to the ground. Two or three serfs were bludgeoned about the head, and fell heavily. Another staggered towards the women, blood streaming from his eyes. When Cressida looked back for Dominic, he had gone. The riders turned then, and the whip of a horse's hooves sent the young boy's body rolling again in the mud. As the horses passed on the route back to whoever had sent them, Cressida saw Dominic, slung across the last rider's saddle, arms and head swinging lifeless in the sun.

It was late afternoon when the street finally emptied. The women had dragged their men to safety. Some watched for the return of the riders, others waited for news in the doorways of their low, neat houses. The meaning of the raid was not yet clear. Then, as darkness fell and nothing happened, they moved back to their homes, and one by one the heavy latches fell into place at curfew.

Although the women had brought her food and drink, and tried to persuade her to take shelter with them, Cressida remained stubbornly out in the open. She knew that if Dominic escaped, if he was alive, he would come to her there. If not, she would either resume her journey, making for the Abbey where Francis might come in the spring, or retrace her steps for that night at least to Peter's house.

She did not have long to wait. She had settled as best she could against the tree, her cloak wrapped closely around her, when a single horseman appeared from the direction in which the raiders had disappeared. The horse cantered, without haste. At the cross, the rider stopped, and looked about him. Dismounting, he tethered the horse, and walked directly to Cressida. It was the auburn-haired clerk they had met at the crossroads two days before.

'I believe I knew we would meet again, demoiselle,' he began. 'Your story was too good to be true. The truth is also so much more interesting, is it not?' He spoke in an affected manner that made Cressida more angry than ever. The loss of Dominic had frightened her, but worse still it had ruined plans that seemed to be going well. And if she were frank with herself, to see a man of Dominic's quality thrown across a saddle as if dead had been more than she could bear.

'I do not know what your truth is, sir.' She tossed her hair back from her face as it escaped from her hood. 'We have been betrayed, that I know. And for nothing.'

'The man Dominic is known. His journeys are far from "nothing" in their intent. My master reported the meeting on our arrival at the prelates' palace in Chichester. I brought word back to Ralph of Mansey, as is fitting.'

Cressida gasped. The name was familiar to her, and yet she could not think why.

'The Earl awaits you,' the clerk told her, as if reading her thoughts. Then she knew why the name had struck horror in her heart. Ralph of Mansey was the man that Sir Robert's young sister had long refused. He and Sir Robert were conspirators in a bid for joint power in the south. The whole point of the marriage planned for Philippa was that her brother's sphere of influence would more than double with her wed to the man who owned the thousands of acres stretching along the boundaries of their own. Cressida felt that she was as good as dead, if the Earl discovered her true identity. Her only chance was to continue to act as Dominic's companion – and if she accompanied the clerk perhaps she would learn too if Dominic lived.

'Where does he wait?' She played the sullen wench that he would expect of her, reluctant now to arouse him to anger.

'In his castle. Where else?'

'And Dominic?'

The clerk's thin mouth twisted. 'Oh, yes. He awaits you patiently.'

Cressida concealed the shudder that went through her.

'We were on our way to the great spring Fair. There is no harm in music.' She played for time.

'Nor in kettles,' he reminded her. 'In their right place.' He prepared to mount his horse, and as he swung into the saddle told her: 'There is no way out for you until you have faced your betters. If you come without a fight, it would be in your favour.'

Hating the touch of his smooth gloves, Cressida allowed herself to be helped into the saddle in front of him. She wished, as they started off, that she had insisted on riding pillion. His hands were busy with the reins, but he pressed his thin elbows into her sides, and breathed too close to her neck. Irritated, she jerked the hood over her long hair. Her escort laughed, and the horse wheeled on to the road to the castle and broke into a gallop.

Their journey took less than a half-hour, through deserted countryside and along rough lanes. Towards the end, Cressida sensed that their path was steep. The horse slowed to a steady, climbing gait. The clerk did not speak.

Gradually, Cressida was able to make out a light ahead of them, further up the slope. It flickered and seemed to change from orange to scarlet in the night. As they approached it, she saw that it was a giant torch fixed in an iron socket on the stone archway that was the entrance to Ralph of Mansey's castle. Between them and the archway was a wooden bridge, and as they crossed it, still on horseback, Cressida looked down into the deep incline of a dry moat.

As if their approach were heralded, although the clerk was still silent, the door in the archway swung open before they reached it. They rode through into a spacious, square courtyard, and their horse's hooves rang on the cobbled yard. Three or four men-at-arms ran to take the horse, and as they dismounted a bailiff and an old serving woman came from another doorway at the far side. Cressida hesitated, trying to catch her breath after the ride. She pulled the hood of her cloak back on to her shoulders, and her long hair shone in the light of the torches that were hung on three sides of the yard. The old woman clucked her tongue, and tried to take the cloak from her. The bailiff stood to one side, as if waiting to attend her.

'See to her, man.' The clerk motioned them impatiently to take Cressida across to the entrance to the main keep. 'I have other work to do than fetch women from the village.' He studied Cressida briefly, as she stood defiantly before the old woman. Aware of his eyes, she glared back at him. 'Your anger will bring no good to you, demoiselle,' he smiled grimly. 'You have much to learn.' Then he turned to one of the men-at-arms, demanding a fresh horse for his journey south, and disappeared in what Cressida guessed must be the direction of the stables. It seemed then that she had no choice but to follow the old woman, and straightening her gown as best she could she transferred her attention to her hair. It was then that she remembered the gift Dominic had made her as she sat like a wild creature by his woodland fire. In the concealed pocket of her bodice, she reached for the small silver mirror.

The young woman who entered the main hall of the castle was a very different figure from the girl who had worked in the fields of her village home. In the few days since her escape, Cressida's golden skin had darkened, and her hair hung wildly in great pale strands on each side of her face. The long march had put a glow in her eyes, and the things she had seen and heard had set her shoulders back more proudly than ever. She took three steps into the hall ahead of the servants who attended her, and stood utterly still while she drank in the scene that waited her.

The hall ran for perhaps fifty feet, the length of the heart of the ground floor of the main keep. High on each side wall were the narrow windows that released the smoke from the great fire that burned on a central hearth. Rich tapestries hung beneath the windows, and the stones of the wall ahead were painted with pictures of birds and trees, and one scene that Cressida did not know to be a depiction of the Jerusalem beloved of the Crusader ancestors who built the castle long ago. Beneath this painting was a long narrow table, set on a dais. It was set with wooden platters and dull metal goblets – things Cressida had never seen before.

At first she thought that the hall was deserted, except for the dogs chained to the walls. She began to move forward, and the dogs growled. Then, from a recess to one side of the high table, the figure of a man appeared. She knew him at once. The broad build, and dark brow; the cunning eyes. She began to tremble as he approached her, but did not turn as he motioned to the servants to leave them alone. Somehow, she found the courage to speak then, and her voice was icy calm.

'Your authority reaches far, Sir Robert. I thought your men had lost me.'

'My men seek your brother. He is a strong child, and needed to replace the dead.' His eyes narrowed as he saw Cressida's breath come faster at the thought of her brother, now far away, she hoped, with Stephen.

'But as for you . . . ' his voice softened as his gaze stayed on her high, small breasts.

He does not even know my name, she thought. *He pursues me thus and he does not even know my name*.

'My name is Cressida, sir. Should you need to write in your records that I have slipped your bonds. Daughter of Margaret the Good, and of a man who died to make your reputation stronger with the King.' The words comforted her, reminded her of her childhood, secure with her parents. This man could do nothing to hurt her. Surely, if she read his gaze correctly, he was as vulnerable as she? Still he said nothing.

'They say Ralph of Mansey will never win your sister.' She spat out the words, waiting for them to take effect. The thought that this man's child of a sister, Philippa, could hold out so long against his commands gave her even more courage. If the stories were true, Ralph, the Earl, must be as unattractive to the young aristocrat he courted as Robert, standing before her now, was to Cressida herself. She eyed him distastefully, then let her eyes wander round the great hall. Impressed as she was by the height and length of it, by the warm tapestries that lined its walls, she contrived to look scornful. But as Sir Robert walked to within inches of where she stood, she faltered. She could feel his breath hot on her lips; they were almost within kissing distance, she thought, absurdly, and with the thought the memory of her last moments with Stephen flooded back. Her cheeks flushed deeply then, and her whole being ached for her childhood friend. She tried to speak again, suddenly disturbed by Sir Robert's long, amused silence. But she could only swallow painfully, her head held high as she held his gaze with hers. Neither of them flinched, and she felt suddenly that this man was even more dangerous than she had sensed before.

'But as for you . . . Cressida . . .' He chose to ignore the gibe at first. 'It is I who searched for you, myself. It took nothing but a little imagination. And as it happens, I had business in these parts. For you are wrong. Quite wrong about my small kin. My sister is here this night to honour her betrothal to the Earl. In fact, you are in time for the feast. It is fortunate for you that it has put me in good humour. For this night at least you will not be asked to pay the price for your escape. And your brother . . .' He assumed a careless tone that did not deceive her. 'When we have him too, then perhaps we shall sit in judgement on both cases.'

Cressida still said nothing. She was sure he did not know what had become of Francis, and if he tortured her to the point of death she would never tell him.

'I see you are as defiant as ever, demoiselle. But there are ways of breaking your spirit. Before the feast you must see some of the castle's secrets. And then my sister will receive you.' He looked disdainfully at Cressida's worn gown, but could not hide the admiration in his eyes. 'You cannot join the merrymaking until you are dressed fit to be at my side.'

'I am not here for that!' she blazed at him. 'You know that I came only because I was told my companion was here. I saw what Ralph of Mansey's men did to the innocent men in the village, and I will never sit at his table!'

Robert stood, his hands on his hips, laughing at her show of spirit. It reminded him of her attack on him in the twilight, when he had first come to watch her after her mother's death.

'But he is here. Did I not say?' He took the last step

between them that brought his face close to hers. His hands held her shoulders, briefly, and then slid with a practised touch to where her nipples showed delicately beneath the rough fabric of her dress. She froze. Instinctively, she knew that if she moved she was lost. The role in which the seigneur really wanted her at the castle was obvious, and if she roused him further she knew that he would take what he wanted even before the feast. His smile was dangerous now. His fingers pressed hard against her soft flesh.

'If Dominic is here, then I wish to see him,' she said in a low voice.

'Why, so you shall. Come.' Sir Robert dropped his hands from her, still smiling, and, with one arm lightly round her waist, led her to the curtains behind the dais. At once the dank air of closed rooms below ground rose into her nostrils. She covered them with her hand, but at her feet yawned a steep, stone incline, broken by rough steps, and she had to lean to the wall at one side for support as she made her way down. The slope turned and turned again, until she became giddy, and then suddenly they were in the annexe to a series of barred prison cells. A torch high on the annexe wall showed the slime of centuries on each stone. There were no windows this deep in the castle. But at once Cressida began to seek ways of escape. If Dominic were a prisoner here, she had all night in which to free him.

Sir Robert interpreted her quick glance correctly, and laughed. 'There is no need to seek a way out, little one. I am not keeping you down here. You came to see your friend. I have kept my word.'

The iron grille that ran from floor to ceiling between the annexe and the cells slid back heavily at Sir Robert's touch. Cressida was surprised that it was not locked. She stepped quickly through, and ran to the first cell, only to find it empty. The second cell was empty also, and she ran on, calling Dominic by name. In the fifth cell she discovered him.

She stood gripping the iron bars of what was no more than a cage. Her ashen face ran with sweat, and she vomited green bile within seconds of finding him. She could not think why they had caged him. She could only remember the strong throat, the wide mouth open singing or in silent laughter. For Dominic's head was now severed from his body, and the mouth, in rigid, closed agony, was a travesty of what it had been. The head had been fixed on the wall, in the clamp that should have held a lighted torch. The naked body lay slumped in the filthy straw beneath. Tunic and undergarments were flung beside it. With mounting horror, Cressida now saw what other, nameless act had been wrought on this man who had been her friend.

'When you learn French with me, demoiselle,' Sir Robert was saying, in a calm, matter-of-fact tone, 'you will understand the meaning of two words that are not spoken in this castle without intending death. They are: "*agent provocateur*". The Earl does not like his realm disrupted. His order of things is bettered nowhere. But that you will learn also, in time.'

Her head was spinning, and she screamed silently within as he half-lifted her the long nightmare spiral of the path back to the castle hall. She had no strength to resist the hated, demanding hands with which he held her. She had strength only to think of Dominic, and what he must have suffered.

As they brushed through the heavy tapestries that divided the stair from the hall, a flow of warm, smoke-laden air made Cressida violently sick again, and she staggered, trying to elude Sir Robert's grasp, until a slim girl ran to her side from the central fire.

'Do what you can to present our neighbour in the fashion we are used to for the feast tonight, sister,' Robert called. Then he motioned to a servant standing in an alcove to sweep the soiled rushes away from where Cressida had fallen. His sister, the Lady Philippa, helped Cressida to her feet.

She was younger, perhaps by three or four years, than Cressida, but she had the poised good looks of her breeding, and brought two more servants hurrying to Cressida's side with a brief lift of her hand. As they carried her, still half-fainting, through an arras on the other side of the dais, Cressida was aware of the sound of brother and sister quarrelling. The last thing she heard before she lost consciousness was the sweet, high voice of the girl who had helped her: 'Brother, this means that you and your noble Earl wait yet another year for my decision. We feast tonight, as you say . . . but we are not betrothed. I celebrate rather my freedom!'

When she woke again, Cressida found herself stretched under an embroidered coverlet on a high bed. At its foot the young girl who had brought her to the room sat alone. When Cressida stirred, she got up and moved swiftly to hold her hand and gazed anxiously into her eyes.

'You must not be afraid,' she whispered. 'I am sure no real harm will come to you tonight. And I promise you my brother will not dare to come for you here.' She helped Cressida raise herself on the scented pillows, and held a pomander of pungent, savoury aroma to her nostrils. Cressida inhaled, and then, remembering what she had seen in the cage deep in the earth beneath them, began to weep slow heavy tears.

'Hush,' Philippa soothed her. 'You must not weep for him. The day will come when you will grow accustomed to such things, and you must be brave. If you knew how many have died at the hands of Ralph of Mansey's men, and the world thinks him so fine a lord!'

'And yet he is patient with you, in your refusal to wed.' Cressida smiled weakly. 'I am from your village, Lady Philippa, and there is such talk of the dance you lead him.'

'Ay. And it is near its end. I'll not wed him after this day's work.'

Cressida looked with interest, in spite of her own heavy

heart, at the proud, lovely young face so close to her own. Philippa's complexion was dark, almost foreign, but had the bloom and glow of a dark English rose. Her long plaited hair was chestnut brown, and her slim waist and long legs showed in the folds of her velvet gown. 'I am still too young. Thirteen this summer. I would not have to wed if my father had not died. Now my brother sells me to the Earl as lightly as he would sell a slave – oh – ' She put a hand to her lips, afraid that she had hurt Cressida's feelings. Cressida sat up further in the bed, and her tears flowed less angrily.

'I am no slave, my lady. Not in my heart. There is no offence.'

'Thank you, Cressida. It is the way of things, I suppose. And I for one do not accept such ways. But – ' she frowned, biting her lip, 'I fear we cannot escape one form of bondage. The feast tonight. If we attend, it will perhaps assuage my brother's anger at your daring. And I promise you that it is all I ask of you. If I am to escape marriage this time I must play a subtle game, in spite of my brave words!'

Cressida nodded, and tried to stand. Philippa took her arm, and led her to an alcove built in the stone wall of the room. She explained that this was always her room on the many, fruitless journeys she and her brother made to the Earl's castle. She brought her own trustworthy serving woman with her, and travelled with several boxes of clothes with which her brother hoped she would keep Ralph of Mansey's interest in her alive. The alcove contained a wardrobe of these clothes, and there would surely be something for Cressida to wear. They were much the same height. She had heard that the King's lady Philippa, her namesake, was also tall, and one day she hoped to go to the Court at Kenilworth, or – much better – Windsor, and see her for herself. She chattered on, in an attempt to put Cressida at her ease, and as they stood in their plain linen shifts, golden and dark hair about their shoulders, sorting through the gowns that hung in the garde-robe, they were like any two girls of any station in life. Although her heart was heavy with anger and dread, Cressida tried for Philippa's sake to join in the business of choosing a gown for the night's feasting.

It was Philippa who decided in the end that Cressida should wear purple. It was the colour of royal pomp, and of mourning. The dark purple gown she kept for solemn occasions was the perfect choice. It hung almost straight beneath the breasts from a low, wide shoulder-line. It set off Cressida's firm shoulders and white skin to advantage, and the long, slit sleeves concealed her rough hands. The skirt flared at the hem, trailing behind her gracefully as she walked. She moved proudly about the room at Philippa's request, while the girl put her mind to which headdress she would wear.

Through the garde-robe there was a closet containing a high bath and a latrine, and the serving woman brought water to the bedroom at Philippa's request. When they were to bathe, she bade the woman leave them, and whispered to Cressida that there was something she must learn about the castle. While they waited for the scented water to cool a little, she showed Cressida that the latrine – a wide, shallow sink shaped in stone – was served by water running constantly down the wall behind it. Each room on this side of the keep had such a system, and at the far end an even wider sluice sent water constantly down behind the kitchen sinks. But the really interesting feature, to Philippa's mind, was the occasional iron foothold set as a ladder the height and depth of each latrine.

'The Romans were very particular in their household arrangements, and the Crusaders copied much of this castle in their style. The outside wall – did you see? They built to last. The place may be cold and frightening, but it is full of very useful things.' She looked meaningfully at Cressida, and pointed to beyond the garde-robe, miming the fact that they might be overheard. 'This ladder-system, for instance, so useful for repairing any fall of stone . . . do you know, it leads all the way down to a small service exit to the moat itself?' Her eyes gleamed as she put her finger to her lips, and Cressida tried to murmur a reply showing no more than polite interest. But she had understood Philippa's meaning at once.

An hour later the two girls walked proudly together along the corridor that led to the main hall. As they left Philippa's bedroom, Cressida had become aware of men-at-arms posted here and there close to their door – the green and blue livery to which she was now becoming accustomed a sharp reminder of the day's events. She lifted her head, the delicate wimple trimmed in grey and white poised like a helmet on her coiled, fair hair. The skirt of her robe swished behind her as she stepped through the arras into the light. The hall was already half-filled with men-at-arms, their women, and numerous servants and musicians. At the top table, Sir Robert sat staring into space, the goblet at his elbow apparently well filled by the boy who stood just behind the bench he shared with another man. This was Ralph, Earl of Mansey, Cressida guessed – from the way in which he stood hastily at Philippa's entrance and gave her a look that betokened a mixture of fury and lust.

To reach their places – Philippa between the two men, and Cressida at Robert's side – the girls had to traverse a set of shallow stone steps and then cross in front of the table where their host stood glaring down into the body of the hall. Their arrival had caused a stir amongst the others present, but their dignified, silent progress to their seats was met with a stunned silence. Cressida's beauty, new to them, was a rare, strange loveliness in those parts. They were not to know that the solemn maturity of her bearing had sprung, only a few hours before, from pain and grief. The purple of her gown hinted at a nobility no man there would have doubted or challenged. The delicate, fashionable painting of eyes, cheeks, and breasts served only to accentuate the natural glow beneath the colour.

But Cressida's impact was all the more startling in contrast to the figure that walked ahead of her. Philippa paused for a moment in front of the Earl, and bowed to him. Everyone in the hall held their breath. The exquisite girl-child whom they now all knew, from the gossip spread by the servants who had witnessed the scene with her brother earlier, to have refused their lord yet again in marriage, was dressed in the concealing, graceful black robes of a nun. The low coif hid all but a trace of her burnished hair. The wide sleeves showed slim hands lightly bearing a rosary. And – as a final taunt to her brother and would-be suitor – the hands and wrists were heavy with gold and jewels.

After her brief obeisance, Philippa walked to the end of the table, and took her place. The Earl sat slowly, anxious to maintain his dignity in the eyes of the assembly. Robert, waiting for Cressida, was white-faced with anger. Then, as Ralph of Mansey made an effort to pretend that nothing untoward had happened, clapping his hands for the meat and wine to be served, Philippa played her last card triumphantly. She held up both bejewelled hands in a delicate, sanctimonious fashion. The serving men paused.

'My lords,' Philippa said, her high voice carrying easily to the far end of the great room, 'I beg of you to hear grace from a novice before the feasting begins. My betrothal, thanks to your master, is royally celebrated here tonight, and I must give thanks. My betrothal, that is, to Christ . . .'

She lowered her head, and began to mutter in Latin. Somewhere at the end of the table further down the room, a friar joined in. Robert whispered fiercely to his sister that when he got her home she would learn what it was to mock him. The Earl, hearing this, raised an arm as if to thump the table and denounce both brother and sister, and then astounded them all by breaking into an agony of silent laughter, followed by a bellow that was at once an explosion of anger and a shout of amusement.

'By Mary! My patience has been well spent on this lady,' he roared at Sir Robert. 'A wench with spirit, and a gift of merriness to match! I vow, Robert, you have not lost our bargain yet! I'll wed her if it's the last thing I do!'

Across her brother, Philippa caught Cressida's eye, and smiled. Sir Robert, uneasy, yet for the moment mollified, made a show of drinking to the Earl's vow. He turned to Cressida, and began to study the pure, exquisite profile under the elegant headdress. Cressida did not turn to face him. Watching how the others at the table conducted themselves from beneath her lowered eyelids, she began to join in the feast as best she could. Then, as the girls had surmised while they dressed and bathed and chatted in the privacy of Philippa's room an hour before, the two men began to get heavily, irretrievably, drunk . . .

4

It was several nightmare hours before Cressida and the Lady Philippa were able to make their escape from the feast. By then even the servants were slumped against the walls; the dogs, surfeited with scraps and bones, no longer growled; and Sir Robert, making one last fumbling attempt to reach for Cressida's slim thigh beneath the oaken table, had lolled into snoring sleep by the side of the already comatose Earl. When a log slipped heavily into the dying embers of the fire in the centre of the hall and no one came forward to attend to it, Philippa gave Cressida a sign that it seemed safe for them to leave.

Edging to their feet, clambering over carls and dogs alike, the two girls began their perilous return to their room. More than once Cressida looked fearfully over her shoulder, sure that one of the sleeping guards would start into wakefulness and lurch across the straw towards her, calling on his masters that the birds were in flight. At one point she froze, unable to move, certain that her nerves had reached breaking point. Then Philippa, sensing that Cressida was no longer close behind her, returned for her, and led her gently through the heavy tapestry arras that concealed the entrance to the private apartments. Cressida responded by moving slowly, like a ghost, her hand to her pale forehead. The wine she had been forced to drink had been too much for her in the smoky enclosed air of the hall. The red-brown of the venison Robert had thrust under her nose had brought back vivid memories of the horror which lay beneath them in the dungeon. It was with the air of a sleepwalker that she at last followed Philippa into her room.

Less than ten minutes later, still fighting the delayed shock and grief at Dominic's death that now beset her, Cressida stood shivering, her white flesh gleaming in the torchlight as the purple gown slid to the floor. With a last, fleeting moment of regret, Cressida stepped from its circle, and reached for her own plain shift and gown which Philippa held out to her. Pulling them thankfully over her fair hair, she looked round, slowly gaining her nerve again, for her warm hose and leather shoes. Remembering that she had left them in the garde-robe when she bathed before the feast, she ran barefoot to retrieve them. Philippa watched her as she moved.

'You are very beautiful, Cressida,' she said at last, gravely. 'It is no wonder that my brother had made up his mind to have you. And this time he has been in a greater frenzy about it than I have ever seen. The sooner we get you out of this place the better.'

Cressida was touched by the earnest way in which the young girl who had befriended her spoke. She imagined this was not the first time, from what she had heard in the village, that Philippa had thwarted her brother in his intent to ravish one of his serfs.

'But what of you, Lady Philippa? What will you wear? Surely you do not dare to stay here after all that has happened now? Do you wish to escape with me?'

Philippa nodded grimly. 'Do not call me "my lady", Cressida. This night has brought me to the end of such things.' She busied herself then, struggling to conceal her emotion, by finding Cressida's long, green-black cloak. As she placed it about her shoulders, she patted it approvingly, noticing that her serving woman had cleaned and repaired it in their absence. 'After the games I have played with Ralph of Mansey my life would not be worth living if I remained. This was no place for me, even before – but now, if I could get to London and the Court, I am sure that the good Queen – my namesake – would put an end once and for all to this loveless match-making on my brother's part. She knows that marriage is a serious business – but from what I hear she knows also what love is. She has a great heart. And I do not believe she would have me matched with an old war-horse like the Earl.'

'London!' Cressida's eyes sparkled for the first time that night. It was as if at each turn of her flight the name of the city was put into her mind, reminding her that she was drawn to it, as a moth to the candle flame. 'But, Philippa, this could not be for many weeks. Did I tell you that now, with the death of the man Dominic, I have but one place to go? And there I must wait, for my brother. Had you stayed on here, and gone back to our manor with your own brother, I would not have burdened you with the truth of it all. It is a dangerous truth, and if I do not succeed in what I have planned only bad can come of it for anyone connected with me.'

'Is your brother a serf? Would he be free?' Philippa gazed into Cressida's eyes earnestly. 'You can trust me.'

Cressida nodded. 'He is young. Younger even than you, I think. And he is in hiding now. But he will be brought to me, in the first days of spring. And I am to await him at Grimthorne Abbey.'

'Then we shall await him there together!' Philippa gripped Cressida's arm fiercely. 'I know of the Abbey. It is a good place. The Order is Franciscan. They are men of peace.'

'Then my brother's name is apt,' Cressida whispered, her heart lightening for a moment. 'He is called Francis.'

Philippa smiled. 'The name pleases me. I would like to meet your brother Francis. And after all, I cannot travel far at this time of year. It would be easier for me to make for London by road a few weeks hence instead. Why do we not first go together to the Abbey? In this garment –' she glanced down at herself, and smoothed the dark folds of the nun's habit, which she still wore, 'I at least will be allowed through the gates, and you will be in good company! What do you say?'

Her determined little face told Cressida that she could not shake her off now, even if she wished. Her finely plucked, aristocratic brows arched slightly as she waited for Cressida's response. For a girl of such high birth, Cressida suddenly realized, the step they were about to take must be even more momentous, more insanely courageous, than for a serf. What bravery this young creature showed. How could she have hesitated to trust her? She stepped forward impulsively, and took Philippa swiftly into her arms. Their embrace, wordless as it was, sealed their bond. They exchanged in that moment the comfort and strength they needed if they were to survive that night. They did not know it, but it was the first moment of the long years in which their two lives were to be interwoven in a strange and complex pattern. A pattern in which they would not stand alone.

'It is this way,' Philippa whispered, as they stood back. She turned swiftly, pausing only to tie a leather jewel-bag fast in the folds of her dark robes. 'We may need to barter our way to safety,' she said with all the wisdom of an old crone, and Cressida was thankful that she too had the few coins she had saved with her mother, should they need to pay for shelter before they reached the Abbey.

Philippa led the way then through the garde-robe and past the heavy curtains that separated the bathing area from the latrines. Now they were without light, and they stood for a moment while their eyes grew accustomed to the dark. The only noise they could hear was the interminable drip of water against stone, softened here and there as it found contact with moss or slime on the great plunging walls. Somewhere far below them, as they began to see more clearly, they noted what could be the glimmer of a torch, its feeble flame coming and going in the moving air. It was probably, Cressida thought, a light kept there for some doorway – perhaps an entrance to the wide, unfilled moat she had noticed on her arrival at the castle. But none of this seemed important as she noticed the existence of footholds, in the shape of strong iron bars built into the stonework at intervals from a foot or so beneath where they stood. She tried to measure the distance between each of them, but the darkness was deceptive, and she could not be sure whether or not the gaps were too wide for herself and Philippa to clamber down. And what, she asked Philippa out loud, if it were too slippery? What if they were to fall?

Philippa put a finger to her lips, and whispered her reply. 'We'll not fall, Cressida. We'll each take one gap at a time, holding each other's hand. The one below guides the way. I've seen the carls do it when they clean such a place at my uncle's castle in Warwickshire. They were built for climbing after all. What else?'

The cool logic of the reply calmed Cressida at once. She had already witnessed how well Philippa knew what she was doing by her conduct at the feast. And surely she herself had not come this far to lose her courage now? She caught her skirts up in one hand, and with a quick, sure glance downwards stepped out into darkness. 'I shall go first,' she said, and as Philippa began to protest she placed a finger on her lips, refusing further delays now that she had regained her nerve.

Hands touching, guiding in the foetid, vertical gulley that was their path, the two girls moved as if by instinct. As their eyes and nostrils grew more accustomed to their surroundings, they gained more daring and with it more speed. They had perhaps sixty feet to go, for the lower floors of the castle were built into the moat, beneath the level of the main halls and kitchens. They were about half way when a groan from somewhere beneath her made Cressida tug sharply at her companion's skirt in warning, and both girls held their breath. They were immediately above a latrine that must have served the Earl's own chambers, and soon they were grotesquely aware of their good fortune that they were not beneath it. But they could think only of the inevitable outcome of discovery, and the price they would pay if the man who heaved his stomach's contents into the void, choking and cursing unmistakably in Ralph of Mansey's tones, became aware of their presence only yards from where he crouched. Shuddering at the bestial smell and sounds of the man, Cressida found a moment between fear and disgust to reflect that there were times when all men were equal. She looked up at her new friend then, as the noises beneath them receded into the muffled enclosure of what must be the Earl's garde-robe. And on Philippa's face she surprised a look of undisguised merriment.

Ten minutes later, the two dark figures stood in the cleft of the dry moat and examined the slope they must climb if they were to escape. They were grateful for the stars and the glimmering moon that lit the expanse of sky they could see above them. In the half light they were able to seek a route at an angle, decreasing the steepness they had to negotiate, though at the same time adding to the distance they had to cover and remain unobserved. But both girls were sure-footed, and the frost had not made treacherous the half-enclosed grass walls of the moat. In minutes they had reached the rough, narrow path that edged the moat itself and ran the whole circumference of the castle.

Glancing to both sides, they made sure there were no guards within sight, and then – knowing the grounds as she did – it was Philippa who led the way, swiftly and in silence, back down to the rough path by which Cressida had first approached the castle, pinned in the unpleasant grasp of the cleric who had betrayed Dominic. The memory leant wings now to her feet. She could not be rid of the nightmare too soon. As the path widened she began to run. Then, as they came to the shadow of a small, tangled copse of trees, she pushed the hood of her cloak back from her fair hair, took great gulps of the night air into her lungs, and sped on into the dangerous open of the crossroads. There she waited for Philippa, impatient, and for the first time since her flight with her brother strangely exhilarated and unafraid.

'We go on now, to the Abbey. The way lies there – ' She grasped Philippa's arm as the girl drew close again. 'I have the way clear now. We should be there by daylight if we take no rest.'

Philippa nodded, trying to catch her breath. She gasped: 'We need no rest, friend. We are both young, and if we do not stop by the way we are sure to make the distance if you think so.'

'There is one thing.' Cressida paused. 'The Earl's guard. Do you know when they patrol? At what hours of the night?'

'At dawn. And if they did ride out sooner, we would soon know. It is against the law in these parts to go abroad at night without torches, and Ralph is a great stalwart of the law,' Philippa said grimly. 'Besides, I do not think we will be missed. My serving woman is loyal. She was my nurse, and loves me too much to want me married to that monster. And my brother would not dare put *her* to the torture . . . she is too well respected in our manor and it would cause more trouble than it was worth to him. Come, Cressida, by the time the two beasts are on their feet again we'll be safe.'

In the chill grey of the dawn that followed, Cressida and her companion came to the gates of Grimthorne Abbey. Although they had trudged through the night for hours, sometimes running, sometimes stumbling and pausing all too briefly to regain their breath if they did so, the two girls now presented a neat and composed exterior. At their last hurried stop, they had used Cressida's mirror and the welcome half-light of the new day to put some order into their appearances. They both sensed that it was important to create a good impression if they were not to upset the good friars: a band of gentle, humble men of the utmost discipline. It would certainly have been a mistake to break in on their quiet world in the wild state which had been Cressida's for most of her journey so far, and both girls were glad they had dressed their hair and set hood and coif respectively at a modest angle when, in answer to their knocking at the high, wooden gates set in the Abbey wall, they were greeted almost at once – as the gates swung open – by the last thing they had expected, a tight-lipped, rosy-faced, disapproving old country woman.

Too surprised to speak straight away, Philippa, who had prepared a speech stating their business and asking for shelter, was forestalled by a rattle of words from the woman herself. 'The good brothers are at prayer. If it's food that you need, you must wait till they break their fast. An hour from now. You will wait at the gate. That's the place for all supplicants who arrive without warning. But if your errand is more urgent, then speak now! I'll not hold the gates much longer.'

They were aware of blue button-like eyes that were not as stern as the weathered face, of gnarled, work-worn hands holding back the gates, and of a general air of conspiracy that made the old dame seem like the keeper of a fort rather than of an Abbey.

'Lady,' Philippa began. She was at once interrupted by a snort of laughter from the old woman.

'My name is Agatha. Damoiselle Agatha. I serve the good brothers of St Francis, though thanks to them I also have my freedom from bondage. My own brother lived and died here. I am here on sufferance, as a woman, it is true. But I keep the gate well. I keep the world at its right distance.'

'That we can tell, Damoiselle Agatha. You are as lively a watch dog as one could wish. But pray, do not be so with myself and my companion.'

'We have introductions, Damoiselle,' Cressida chimed in eagerly, less afraid now of the first formidable image the crone had presented. 'To the Lord Abbot himself. From Oxford. We have a boon to ask, and we need shelter.'

The gates opened a fraction wider. Through them Cressida glimpsed a long, wide avenue leading to a great greystone building. An arch of wintry, leafless trees sheltered the avenue from the elements. In the distance, a lone figure of a monk clothed in a sombre brown robe bent in fierce concentration over a plant, tending its foliage as if his life depended on it. But Cressida had the impression that he also watched the newcomers at the gate. Briefly, she wondered why the man was not at prayer with his brothers. She was aware suddenly of Philippa nudging her as if to remind her of their purpose.

'If the Lord Abbot will grant us a few moments of his time,' Philippa was saying. 'My friend, Cressida daughter of Margaret the Good – from our village far south of here – has word for the Lord Abbot, as she has said.'

'You may wait within the walls, in my gate house, if that is so,' Agatha told them. 'And while we wait you can tell me more. Brother Oliver will take your message to the Abbot's clerk, no doubt.' She gestured to the figure of the monk who had now left his work and was walking towards them between the trees.

Moments later, the two girls found themselves sharing a warm hearth with two golden brown hens and a pile of drying herbs. And as Damoiselle Agatha set the table with mugs of ale and what seemed to be a succulent game pie from the savoury smell that wafted across to them, the monk who had now joined them stood glowering down at them in silence. Cressida's first thought as she returned his gaze was that he was very young, but that the expression on his face was as old as Time.

'Sir, we understand from the good Dame that you will take word for us to my Lord Abbot's clerk?' Philippa seemed to take the lead naturally, and if her disguise were to be accepted as genuine then it would be natural that she would be the one to address the monk. Not for the first time, Cressida was glad that she travelled with Sir Robert's young sister.

Brother Oliver nodded slowly. Cressida watched him, aware again of the intensity of the man. From the cut of his hair, which was thick and without a tonsure, she guessed that he was either a novice or a lay brother – one who worked for the Franciscans but was not a full member of the Order. But from his eyes, which glinted fanatically in the half-light of the room, she would have taken him for a dedicated man of God. They were almost black, flecked with hazel; strange, cat-like eyes she thought. His hands also were lean, nervously plucking at the belt on his robe. He was taller than average, and stooped a little, perhaps from his work in the garden. Something about him made her shiver slightly. She was glad when Philippa rose to her feet at a sign from Dame Agatha and they made their way to the table, amidst a fluttering of brown hens – Brother Oliver still all frowns.

Grumbling to herself at the shortage of labour, the menace of thieves at the gates, and the tear in her new apron, Agatha had in the meantime cut the game pie into generous slices, and now bade them eat. Having once decided to trust the two girls she had clearly made up her mind that they should be fed properly. At the sight of the meal, Philippa gave an involuntary cry of delight, and started at once to eat. Within a second, Brother Oliver had paced across the room to her side, and gripped her arm.

'I was right!' He almost hissed the words. 'Lady, whatever you are you are no Sister of the Church. You made no sign of the cross. Your hunger, your belly, comes first with you. If you were truly entitled to the robe you wear it would be second nature to you to bless your table thus . . . '

There was an uncomfortable silence, during which Philippa replaced the slice of food she had at her lips. Cressida did not know how to help her friend at that moment, and sat racking her brains for a way out of the trouble. If Dame Agatha chose to take the deception badly, it could mean that they would be thrown out of the Abbey grounds – within less than an hour of their arrival. There would be no time for leaving word for Stephen. It would be as if they had never passed that way.

But she had reckoned without Philippa's quick thinking. 'Damoiselle,' the girl was saying, as she got to her feet. She curtsied slightly to Agatha, who waited, lips curled and arms akimbo, for an explanation. 'I wear this habit as protection. Perhaps the only protection left to us poor women as we travel in these terrible days. I and my friend are bound for London. We flee from men who would misuse us. And a good Sister gave me this habit many months ago, when I was driven in despair to consider becoming one of her Order. But I was not worthy. It was not for me. And yet I retained my robes, I knew not why. Until I started on this journey. Now I travel thus to protect myself and my friend. I would not have deceived you much longer, please believe me. We were so afraid that we would not be received by the Abbot.'

'Two healthy creatures with their wits about them, why should I turn you away?' Agatha's blue eyes darted from one to the other of the girls, her arms still akimbo. 'Can you work? Can you sew?'

Cressida nodded eagerly, and Philippa said, 'I can sew, very well, Dame. It was a nun who taught me. And Cressida – '

Aware of Brother Oliver's eyes upon her, Cressida spoke evenly. 'I know how to cook, and – how to care for plants. I know the land. If we stay here, I can earn my keep.'

'If you are to stay, wench,' Oliver said coldly, 'we must

know your business. What is this nonsense of word for the Lord Abbot? How could you bring such word?'

'If you mean how can a peasant girl have anything to say to my Lord Abbot, then I will tell you, sir! My oldest friend, son of my mother's dearest friend, is a scholar at Oxford and has my brother in his care. My brother learns to read. He too will be a scholar. My father died in France to keep peace in this land for you and your brothers. My mother died, too – taking the role of priest in a village where no priest would stay!' She turned to Agatha, her voice gentle now. 'The scholar Stephen promised me that he would bring my brother here to me early this spring. He vowed to me that his friends here at Grimthorne would understand. Can we not get word to the Lord Abbot, as he bid me do? Is he too far above us to want word from the outside world? Would he really want my young brother to ride all this way for nothing?'

'Enough, girl.' Agatha spoke soothingly, then eyed Brother Oliver. 'She speaks with her heart. And the other one,' indicating Philippa, 'has no real harm in her. I'll swear it. What say you, Brother Oliver?'

The lay brother spoke reluctantly, as if he sensed he was outnumbered but wanted still to preserve a show of authority. 'All this will be passed to my Lord Abbot's clerk within the hour. I myself will investigate the truth of the existence of this – this scholar. If his name means anything to our good brothers, then no doubt the story is sound enough. And of course, if it is true, then the brothers would not turn these children away. But if there is a shade of untruth . . . ' He shrugged dryly, and made for the door. Then he eased the latch, and without taking his leave went out into the cold air.

Shivering in the draught that his departure had caused, Dame Agatha shook her head, tut-tutting at the sight of the food still unconsumed on the table, and encouraged the two girls to return to their meal.

'You'll stay here, in this house, with me. There's no sight nor sound of female creatures allowed up at the

Abbey, not even in the Cloisters, except when the cow wanders in from the field. But your friend, the man Stephen,' she looked quizzically at Cressida, 'I know this man. He must have been thinking of me when he bade you wait here for him. He is a humble man, is he not, like yourself? A clever man, and holy. But had I praised him before Brother Oliver, you'd never have been allowed to stay. A jealous brother, my dears. But he works with a will. And so shall you!'

In the days that followed no word came from the Abbot, but in answer to Cressida's and Philippa's doubts that all was well Agatha repeatedly assured them that were they not to be allowed to stay they would have been sent on their way the first night of their arrival. The Abbot was not a man to suffer deceit, and he had doubtless forgiven the Lady Philippa's masquerade had he been told of it. They could never be sure how far Brother Oliver would go in his lifetime's campaign against the fair sex.

'He likes spirituality, not spirit, in a woman. And when you go to work for him in the garden,' Agatha told Cressida as she sat one afternoon by the fire darting pungent cloves into an orange she was fashioning into a pomander, 'cover your golden hair.'

Cressida had known that if the weather improved while she still waited for her brother and for Stephen she would be expected to help in the work outside, but she had not carried this to its logical conclusion: that this would mean working with Brother Oliver. She was not at all sure, when she came to face the idea, that she liked it. It would have been pleasant to plant and weed and hoe again. A day or so before there had been an afternoon of warm sunshine, and she had sat against the stone wall in the seclusion of Agatha's own small garden within the Abbey grounds and closed her eyes, strangely comforted and at peace. The days were passing, their sanctuary was humble but pleasant, and she knew in her heart that Stephen would keep his word. But now, with a jolt, she had to face the fact that if she waited for him much longer, it would be with Brother Oliver's eyes constantly watching her, with the mixed expression of hatred and desire that she now saw in them. What she had mistaken on the first day of their meeting for religious zeal was in fact the look of a tormented man. She wondered if in his wisdom the Abbot – who seemed to keep silence on so many things – had some quiet, secret reason for keeping Brother Oliver from his final vows.

Cressida was in fact quite unaware of the ways in which her beauty had come to life in the days at peace at Grimthorne. The soothing nature of the simple, repetitive tasks she did for her keep restored in her a sense of order, and rested her exhausted young body. The roughness and scars on her hands healed rapidly as she worked with the herbs and unguents which Agatha prepared for the Abbey hospice. The good food rounded her face and brightened her look. But she kept her eyes lowered most of the time when Brother Oliver was near.

Fortunately, an unexpected change in the weather, ever capricious at this time of year, meant that her work in the Abbey grounds had to be delayed. It was heralded by a night of sharp frost, during which Cressida and Philippa slept huddled close together on the mattress Agatha had made for them. The next day they awoke to a landscape held in the grip of snow. The fields were already covered as daylight broke, and the snow still fell. The girls ran into the garden, their faces lifted to the kiss of the flakes, laughing delightedly. In the distance, the monks walked to early mass, like great brown birds on the move against a grey-white sky.

As she watched them, Cressida noticed one of the older monks slither on the path, and almost fall. She gasped involuntarily. And at once she thought of Stephen and Francis. If they had already started their journey to her, would they be safe? The snow might take a real grip on the country round Oxford, and they might be snow bound, or lost. But worse, what if with the change in the weather they decided not to travel? How many weeks might it be that she would have to wait? She went back into the house dejected at the thought, and spent the time before breakfast with her nose pressed against the one small window-pane of glass that the gate house boasted.

She was at the same window one afternoon a week later when a watery sun appeared in a yellow-grey sky, and as she watched the first crust of snow shifted slightly and began to melt. Before darkness fell, brown rivulets of earth had appeared amongst the white masses of the landscape, and early next morning the scrape of a spade against iron-hard ground told them that Brother Oliver was clearing the way between the trees from the Abbey to the gates. By mid-morning the sound was close to the gate house, and a loud knock on the wooden door broke into Cressida's daydreams. She had been thinking that now surely she would soon hear news from Oxford. *The snow is clearing*, she thought. *The new paths will bring Stephen and Francis to me. It is an omen.*

Ushering Brother Oliver into the room and closing the door sharply against the cold air outside, Agatha greeted him: 'I suppose, Brother Oliver, you are come to seek help in the garden now that the snow has begun to thaw? I knew you would not turn your nose up at my two good strong lasses here.'

Philippa, from her place on the far side of the hearth from Cressida, made a face. Not for the first time Cressida marvelled at her young friend's capacity for laughing, especially at men. She did not think it was a gift she possessed herself. As she waited for Brother Oliver's reply, watching his sad, hungry eyes, she found herself shivering.

'Agatha, you tempt me sorely to box your ears sometimes. Do you think I would have dug out the path all the way to your door if that were so? Why, the demoiselles could have dug their way to us, if they were so strong – and saved me the labour. But the path is for a special occasion. You can expect the Abbot's clerk within the hour. He will escort the girl Cressida. The Lord Abbot would speak with her.'

Cressida's hands tightened on the pomander she was making. Her heart began to beat painfully. If the Abbot himself wished to see her then the matter must be of the greatest importance. Had he decided he would not allow Dame Agatha to harbour them, and now that spring was on its way would bid them leave the Abbey? Was there bad news of Stephen, or of her brother? Worst of all, did Sir Robert's power stretch so far it could penetrate even the sanctuary she had found? She glanced fearfully across to where Philippa now sat very upright, her dark eyes alert. But her voice, when she spoke first, was casual, unafraid.

'Why, Cressida,' she smiled gently, 'we must prepare you for this meeting at once. It would not do for my Lord Abbot to find he has harboured a wanton in his midst. Your tunic is creased, look – and there is a spot of tallow on your shoe.' She rose from her seat, and came over to Cressida, pulling her to her feet and examining her gown more closely. 'Damoiselle,' she turned to Agatha, 'have we time to prepare our friend for this important meeting?'

'The Lord Abbot does not concern himself with the appearance of a wench,' said Oliver, sullenly. But he himself eyed Cressida's slim figure as he spoke. 'Wanton, wayward, it's all the same. The confessional screen hides the face of sin, though not its voice.'

Cressida's eyes widened, and Philippa turned to Brother Oliver, mild reproof in her voice: 'Surely my friend and I are too humble, women of the road that we are, to be allowed the honour of confessing to my Lord Abbot himself? It is a pity, truly, Brother Oliver, that you yourself are not entitled to hear us. For it seems you know the snares and pitfalls of such exchanges only too well!'

The lay brother took a step forward, his eyes blazing. 'What do you know of me? Of all such as me? Have I harmed you, that you speak to me thus?'

'Now, Brother,' Agatha broke in in her practical way, pushing him back to the door as she spoke. 'The girl meant no hurt. It's the long winter days getting at us all. The sooner she's out hoeing for you the better. You'll know then that we have two good creatures in our midst. Now – off with you, and tell my Lord Abbot's clerk we await him, at his leisure.'

When Oliver had gone, Agatha busied herself at once with Philippa, preparing Cressida for the encounter with the Abbot. But Cressida allowed them to fuss about her as if it were of no concern to her. The scene with Brother Oliver had made her uneasy. Philippa's teasing had, she felt, been ill-advised. There was perhaps no harm in the man, but whatever he was they could do with his friendship. With so little headway made on her flight away from Sir Robert she knew that it was a bad thing to make enemies. It was as if she were a swallow poised for that flight, the winter snow driving her to spread her wings before it was too late. She had waited for word from Stephen at first desperately in the past few weeks, and then with a numbed impatience tugging at her every thought. Beneath her surface activity, helping Agatha, sleeping at nights curled against Philippa for warmth, her whole being was straining every moment to return to her original purpose.

An hour later, she stood in the doorway of the Abbot's study, and for a moment her head swam. The Fran ciscans, it was true, were an Order that believed in the utmost simplicity. She had heard from her mother at times how well the priesthood lived, and what good, simple men some friars were in contrast . . . especially the Franciscans. And the Abbot of Grimthorne proved Margaret's words beyond measure. The room in which Cressida found herself was exactly the opposite of the rich and ornate scene she had expected as a background to the importance on the man who waited for her. Its vaulted ceiling was unadorned, its windows mere slits in the massive stones that formed its walls. The floor was also of stone, clean swept and bare. The only furniture was a long, low table, flanked by two benches, and at its head a plain high-backed chair, where the Abbot himself now sat. But the most impressive thing about the room was its air of total peace. The soft, dim light, filtering through to them from the winter's day outside; the small wood fire flickering in the hearth; and above all, the expression on the face of the man who waited for her.

As the clerk led her to the end of the table where the Abbot sat, and motioned to her that she was to kneel, Cressida could not take her eyes off the priest's face. Her own great blue eyes were held by his deep, mysterious gaze. She was aware, as the clerk slipped silently from the room, that no words had been spoken. As she rose to her feet, she brushed her long golden hair back from her shoulders, and stood, very straight, waiting. *This is the life that Stephen would lead if it were possible for him*, she was thinking. *Such isolation, and such simplicity. This man is totally alone. And yet his life is filled to the brim.* The power of the Abbot's presence was perhaps the strongest thing she had ever met with in her short life. It moved her, and at the same time troubled her. If this was what it was to be important, to be free, then it was not for her to question it. But something in her did protest, from the moment she had stepped into the room. For one strange moment she had the impression that she was in a play – one of the travelling mummers' plays that had come to her village once when she was a child – and that she was a character being led helplessly to the void of the tomb.

The Abbot began to speak, breaking into her reverie. 'My child, I hear good things of you and of your companion. The gate house has been blessed, these last weeks of the winter.' Cressida bowed her head, slightly, not knowing what to answer. There was so much more she wanted to hear. 'And your name has been sent to me from farther off. No – you have no need to be afraid. I know your story, or all that I need to know. You are safe at Grimthorne. But you will not be here for ever.'

'My Lord Abbot.' Cressida spoke in the knowledge that he waited to see if the thought of leaving Grimthorne troubled her. 'I have been happy here, in my own way. Yet my heart is always heavy. Until I have news of – of my young brother, and our friend –'

'It is a message from your scholar friend that has made me send for you, child.'

This time she could not wait. She started forward, her eyes shining. Whether or not it was appropriate to show the depth of her feelings in this quiet stronghold of celibacy she no longer cared. 'Stephen! Stephen has sent word? When will they come? Are they well? Will my brother ride with him?'

For the first time the Abbot allowed himself to smile. He held up a thin ageing hand in part blessing, part remonstration. 'Enough. I can see you trust the man Stephen . . . perhaps more. That is all I need to know – before the arrangements are made in detail.'

'Arrangements?' Cressida's spirits fell again. It sounded as if she were not to see Stephen and Francis after all. And yet, Stephen had sent word. Was it because he could not come himself? Or because he had no desire to see her?

'Child, you are full of fears. You carry your head high, it is true. But it is as if you approach the block. Life has been full of menace for you in these recent months. For all of us. But if you let that turn you into this proud, startled creature for ever, then you – and those around you – will be the losers.'

As Cressida strove to suppress her anxiety, the Abbot went on, 'The man Stephen rides from Oxford in three days' time. Whether or not he brings your brother with him, I know not. If he has arranged for his tuition as part of his duties at a choir school, which seems likely – it is the custom – then the boy will not be free to wander about the land as it pleases you. We will see. But as to the arrangements . . . I have spoken to Brother Oliver, and to our outrider. There is much to be gained, it seems, by a journey for the Abbey's representatives to London. There are supplies we need, letters to bring back. I have ordered our great cart to be prepared for the road. It goes empty to the city, for it will return filled with what we need here. There would therefore be a place in it for you, and for the young girl who travels with you . . . if it is London you make for.'

As the significance of what he said slowly dawned on her, Cressida could not believe her good fortune. She had anticipated days, even weeks on the muddy spring roads for herself and Philippa. She had always wanted to make her way to a big city, and now here was her chance to journey to the oldest and greatest in the land. And it was the Court, in London, for which Philippa aimed, to seek support from her royal namesake, King Edward's Queen.

'My Lord.' Cressida addressed the Abbot, her voice even and low-pitched now that she was in control of herself. 'It is more than we could have begged, or hoped for, were we ladies of rank, or Sisters of your own Order – ' her eyes filled with unshed tears.

The Abbot's smile returned, broader, more amused. 'But my child, I thought that is precisely what your little companion was? A Sister, a young bride of Christ. We know of her treasure of jewels with which she travels. We could not but believe our eyes, and she wears the garb of a novice. But – '

'Sir, I would not deceive you. It was our only chance of safety, of escape. If you knew how the Lady Philippa has suffered, how she has helped me at such risk to herself.' She knelt suddenly at his side, taking the soft hand in hers. It was against her ways, but as she imprinted her lips on the pale skin she wished only to express their need for mercy if they had offended. This man had arranged their way to London. He could surely not intend to judge and punish them? He had not the air of a hypocrite, like some churchmen she had seen, trundling through the towns of the south with their elaborate equipages, and pardons for sale.

The Abbot lifted her to her feet. 'Who am I to deny that such a guise as the Lady Philippa wears is the best protection of virtue, the only one perhaps in these times. And – she wears it with modesty. You have not gone unnoticed within our walls, my child.'

Wondering if it were Brother Oliver who watched and passed on reports concerning the two girls, Cressida asked then who it was who would travel with them to the city? And should Philippa continue in her disguise?

'There will be no need for masquerade. You travel as yourselves. Perhaps the young woman is, after all, entitled to enter the city as herself. We shall have the driver prepared, of course, with a story to protect the Abbey's good name.'

Cressida looked at him curiously.

'If challenged, he will declare that he carries two fine young ladies with their dowries, to be schooled in our sister convent on the city's borders. Yes, Brother Oliver knows what to say.'

At the mention of the lay brother's name Cressida gave a sharp hiss of surprise, which she was unable to check. The Abbot, who had risen from his chair as he spoke, seemed not to notice her reaction. But she was oddly afraid. She had thought that when they left for London they would be leaving behind the unwelcome looks, the suppressed anger, of the man who seemed to her half monk and half bad angel. But get to London they must, now that they had the chance. She stifled a further sigh, and began to thank the Abbot.

Ushering her from the room, he told her: 'Prepare yourself. And in three days your scholar friend will call on Damoiselle Agatha, no doubt. Then, if all is well, you ride for London.'

5

The news that they might soon be on their way to London, and would not have to walk, sent Philippa into a rapture of excited preparation to leave. With Dame Agatha, she packed small bundles of clothing and more precious belongings for herself and Cressida. She washed and dressed her hair, discarded her nun's habit, and roamed about the small gate house and its garden in a rough woollen gown the colour of flax, topped by a surcoat of good brown worsted begged from Agatha and fashioned on the first evening after Cressida's meeting with the Abbot.

But Cressida was not so light of heart. Restless, frightened of disappointment, she spent three days haunting the Abbey gates, listening for the sound of approaching horsemen. On the third day, she began to wonder if all was well with Stephen and Francis – and to ask herself what she would do if they did not come as the Abbot had forecast. The roads were dangerous; Stephen's own work was, she now realized, fraught with perils. Anything could have happened to delay them. The evening of the third day she spent at the window, her nose pressed against the pane, her eyes fixed gloomily on darkness, and a void.

'If they do not come tonight, Cressida,' Philippa said from the warmth of the hearth, 'then they will come tomorrow. Or the next day. You will see.'

'But what if the cart leaves for London before they come? You cannot miss such a chance of gaining an audience with the Queen. You will have to go with Brother Oliver and the outrider, but I – '

'I'll not go without you now. There are always travellers on the road to London now it is almost spring.

We'll let the cart go without us. It is the only thing to do.'

'But it would be just like Sir Robert to seek you in London next, and maybe go to the Queen himself and get his story in first! A fine tale it makes, of a runaway young sister and a great Earl she has insulted and refused. If you delay much longer in obtaining your audience with Queen Philippa it could go badly for you!' Cressida left the window, and crossed the room to her friend. In the new, simple gown she was wearing Philippa looked younger than ever – more like a peasant child than a maiden of the Norman blood. The two girls sat side by side then until Agatha reminded them sharply that no one would ride in that night and they'd best get their beauty sleep and be fresh to greet all comers tomorrow.

The next day was warm again, and Cressida, lack-lustre from a restless night, sat in the garden, leaning on the warm stones of the low wall that separated the gate house from the main Abbey grounds. After a while she nodded into sleep, and dreamed of fast horses riding through a landscape of ice. She awoke to find that the drumming of hooves was not in her dream, but a reality, and as they slowed down a shout at the gate told her that travellers had arrived.

At that moment Agatha herself appeared at the gate house door, rearranging her coif with plump hands. Hens scuttled to and fro in her path, and Philippa appeared framed in the doorway behind her, dropping a piece of needlework to the ground. But oblivious of them all, Cressida jumped to her feet and sped, hair flying, eyes shining, to the main gates. In the avenue Brother Oliver appeared, hurrying to admit the riders – but he was not fast enough for Cressida. Wrestling with the heavy latch, she dragged the gates apart. And as she found herself gazing up into Stephen's deep, grey eyes her brother hurled himself from a second horse – a young piebald – and leapt to her side. The impact of his embrace almost flung her to the ground, and her eyes left Stephen's to take in the tall, boisterous child her brother had become. They kissed, embraced again, and stood back to regard each other at more leisure. Cressida's heart swelled as she saw that Francis had grown almost an inch, wore a good scholar's surcoat and strong shoes, and looked in the best of health.

'I can read! Many words – some in Latin, some in our own English. I hardly know the meanings of the Latin, or any of the French they use. But I shall one day! And I can copy already, if I make a good quill!'

Cressida caught him up in her arms again, and smiled up over his shoulder into Stephen's face. She wondered for a moment why he did not dismount. He had doffed his velvet hat, and bowed to her from the saddle, from where he had watched her reunion with her brother. Now she noticed that he looked thinner, and strangely intense. There was less warmth, less expression, in the piercing gaze. And yet his eyes did not leave hers, and for a moment they both remembered their last kiss. Then, abruptly, Brother Oliver came forward and held Francis's horse, speaking in a low voice to Stephen.

The lay brother did not look in Cressida's direction as Stephen told her: 'I have urgent business with the Lord Abbot, and he bids me dine with him. I was delayed at Oxford. There are nothing but endless quarrels at the Colleges and I had to stay while yet another conflict was resolved. I cannot keep the Lord Abbot waiting longer. We will talk when I have seen him. Perhaps for an hour tonight – before I ride to Oxford.'

The words cut into Cressida like a knife. She began to speak, to object, suddenly desperately saddened by the thought that she was to see so little of this man she now knew she loved. But, with Brother Oliver's disapproving eye upon her, she stifled her protests.

'You have kept your promises, Stephen. You have brought my brother to me. But there is much to discuss. Even my thanks cannot be cut short. How can I ever thank you?'

'You are right, there is much to discuss,' Stephen

replied, unsmiling, and with a nod to Oliver to follow with Francis's piebald, he spurred his own grey and cantered on down the avenue under the trees.

Philippa, who had been standing at a discreet distance while brother and sister were reunited, came forward then, and curtsied, laughing, to Francis.

'You do not know me, sir?' she asked the boy, who regarded her with equal merriment, immediately taken with her brilliant colouring and vivacious little face. 'I was but five years old, and you maybe less, when my father came to your father's fields for Harvest. There was much merrymaking. It was before the men all went to war. We played at tag, only I remember you were too small to run from me, and fell in the stubble, and cried for your mother . . .'

At the mention of their mother, Francis and Cressida stood close, suddenly silent. Philippa came to them wordlessly, and put an arm through Cressida's. Together the three of them paced in the sunshine to the door of the gate house, where Agatha waited.

'These girls have been a long, hard road since last you saw your sister, master,' she told Francis, 'and we eat well in this house, to build their strength. You will join us? And there is much we would hear of your new life. Come.'

As he always seemed to be, Francis was at once welcomed by the women as if he needed spoiling and feeding, and as he took his place at the table and began to tell Cressida of his experiences at Oxford he had a willing audience in Agatha and Philippa as well. After the meal Philippa drew the boy aside, to the hearth, and plied him with memories of their lives back in the village – so different, and yet so full of shared places and people.

'Do you remember when you could not lift the sacks of grain in my father's courtyard, and I laughed? The next time, you succeeded!'

'I remember, but I did not know it was you, Lady Philippa, who laughed – and whom I would meet here with my sister, so far from home.'

Watching them talking non-stop, heads close together in the shadows, Cressida felt a wave of certain knowledge that what she had done for her brother had been the only thing possible. He had taken to his new life with ease. He talked with Philippa as if she were an equal – which now, in Cressida's eyes, she was. They were like any two children together, in any simple household. With a start, Cressida realized how young her companion seemed, as if she had reverted to her girlhood after all the hardships of the last weeks. For a brief interlude that evening, waiting for Stephen to come to her, Cressida was happy.

But the hours crept by, and Stephen did not come: and remembering the unfamiliar, steel-like gaze of the rider who had looked down at her at the gates that afternoon, she felt the same steel creep gradually into her heart.

At last she could stand it no longer. Agatha had retired for the night, to the curtained alcove where she had slept since she took them in. The children – for this was how Cressida now saw them – had fallen asleep where they sprawled by the fire. Making sure that the embers were safe, Cressida moved quietly about the room, searching for her strong shoes. Pulling them on swiftly, she went to the door, and from a heavy wooden peg carved in its frame she lifted her cloak. Seconds later, the cloak warm about her slim body, its hood closely wrapped to shield her face, Cressida let herself silently out of the gate house and made for the trees. Then, in the silvered light of a young moon, she began to walk steadily towards the dark mass of stone that was Grimthorne Abbey.

From her previous visit, to the Abbot's rooms, she remembered that at first on her right she would pass the cloistered infirmary. It was there that the monks practised their art of medicine, and nursed their sick. As she drew close to the graceful, low archways of the cloisters she thought she could detect a shadowy figure emerging from the infirmary itself. Thinking for a moment of inexpressible joy that it was Stephen, she ran in the direction of the building, only for the shadow to disappear. She drew her cloak closer about her, and retraced her steps to the main avenue. But as she walked on she was aware of a soft echo to her own footsteps, and when she turned to investigate the echo persisted, then stopped. But she could see no one.

Then, as she turned into the main portico of the Abbey buildings, she paused, suddenly afraid of what she had done. This was the very sanctum. Not even Agatha was allowed so far into the all-male territory that was bordered by these high doorways and flagged stone walls. And yet she must go on, she decided, until she could find Stephen and ask him whether or not he intended to come to the gate house that night. There was so much she wanted to tell him: of her stay at the man Peter's, and the children and their songs; of the terrible death of the *agent provocateur* in the dungeons of the Earl of Mansey's castle; and of her new friendship, with Philippa. She needed to ask him so much, too. Surely he would not leave her to go on to London with her brother without some word, some sign of the feeling between them? She knew for certain that he felt as she did, and that as they faced each other again at the Abbey gates he had remembered their last kiss. She stopped again, fearfully, in the darkness at the thought of that embrace in Matilda's house. Was it that which now stood between them? What had happened to Stephen since that spell-binding moment to make him keep his distance in this way? Her heart beating fast in a wave of angry despair at such a thought, Cressida leant briefly against a wide stone pillar, and at that moment decided she must turn back. She could not bear the thought of Stephen's anger, or of a rebuff.

As she left the shadows cast by the pillar, she sensed rather than felt a firm touch on her shoulder. She knew at once that a man stood behind her in the darkness, and that it was not Stephen. She stood quite still, the sound of her own heart hammering in her ears, the sinister, panting whisper of the man's breathing seeming to fill the air about her. As she spoke, she recognized the hissing, fanatical tones of Brother Oliver.

'How dare you come so far into the Abbey? Do you plot to tempt us all with your ways? Do you seek the man Stephen, to steal him from us? You will never do that.'

Cressida swept round then to face Oliver, and found herself in an even tighter grip, his strong hands hurting her arms where he held her above each elbow through her cloak. He was taller than Stephen, and his gaunt, slightly stooping frame concealed surprising strength. She wanted to run, but did not dare provoke him further by doing so.

'What is that to you? You know nothing of our friendship, of our mothers' friendship. There are other things – things a – a man of your nature would not readily understand.'

'What do you mean? My nature is that I do God's work. There is nothing else.'

'Isn't there?' Cressida spat the words out. The dark lines of the zealot's face drove her to sudden fury. They were a symbol of all that made her despair in Stephen – his elusiveness, his sudden coldness, his dedication to his secret work. Where she could not defy them in Stephen, she could now fight them in this man who had crept up on her in the night. Some devil must have possessed her at that second, for she stepped forward in her tormentor's grasp, the roughness of his robe only inches from her face, and her eyes blazed up into his as she tilted her chin in defiance.

To her horror, she at once sensed that the man who held her so tightly was excited by the move she had made. His hands slackened, only to hold her fast again. With a groan, he pulled her even closer to him, and as he did so she felt his manhood stir against her. She held her breath. If she cried out, in her mounting fear, it would bring the whole darkened building to life. And it was she who had been in the wrong, in coming to the inner sanctum in the first place. It would be the easieast thing in the world for Brother Oliver to persuade the monks that she had tempted him. And Stephen was under the same roof that night. What would he believe of her if she called for help?

Like a rabbit with a snake, she froze where she stood. The moment became a battle between Oliver's cat-like eyes and her own steady blue gaze. She made no sound. Again Oliver gave a low cry, and as he did so he broke the spell – pushing Cressida from him, and lowering his tormented face so that she could not see the expression in his eyes as he strove for self-control. Then, without a word, he turned on his heel and vanished into the Abbey buildings, leaving Cressida with slow, hot tears running down her cheeks as she remembered her longing for Stephen, and reminded herself that the man she had just brought almost to the brink of disaster was the man who would escort her to London.

Under the bustling supervision of Dame Agatha, the little household at the Abbey gates started the next day at the crack of dawn, and Cressida, who had managed to creep into her place beside Philippa the night before without waking her, woke from a heavy sleep to find her brother smiling down at her. 'It is not like you, sister, to lie abed! Did we keep you from your slumbers with our talk last night? There was so much to talk about.'

Cressida shook her head ruefully and got to her feet. She felt jaded, her limbs heavily reluctant to move. She was starkly aware of the fact that her sortie of the night before had ended without sight or sound of the man she had wanted to meet. It was certain that Stephen had intended to reject her, and had stayed at the Abbey in order to avoid an encounter. By daylight, of course, things would be easier for him. He could talk of nothing, of unimportant things in the presence of others. He was safely clear now of any discussion of their personal feelings. In the morning sunshine, her heart heavy with a sense of rejection, Cressida made her way round the gate house to the small yard where a butt of rain water glistened, fresh as ice since the melting snow had added to its depths. Leaning far over into the butt, she splashed her face and hair until her skin stung and her head cleared. She re-entered the gate house minutes later to find that Stephen was there, and having noticed Philippa feeding the hens with Francis beyond the garden wall Cressida knew that, with Agatha busy also in her vegetable patch, she and Stephen were alone.

Her first impulse was to run from him, out of the house, to the great Abbey gates, and through them on to the track that would take her far from him and the knowledge of what she had done the night before. Had Brother Oliver told him of her behaviour, she could never face Stephen again. A devil had got into her, and perhaps with good cause – she was not ashamed of her actions, so much as terrified of what they would do to her relationship with Stephen. As childhood friends they had shown affection, tumbled together in the fields, and more recently their embrace had meant much more. But even in its passion their last kiss had been innocent . . . on her side at least. She had not realized until now that she was capable of something much more violent, even more exciting. It was a side of her nature that she knew would discourage Stephen. His violence and strength seemed to be channelled entirely in his work. Now his face betrayed no emotion. He greeted her calmly enough, rising from the table where he had waited for her. She went to him, her hands outstretched.

'I wanted so much to tell you everything last night. Of your friends at Ashby, Stephen. They greeted me with all the love they feel for you. And of the part Philippa has played in my flight. And of the Lord Abbot's plans for our journey.' Her words trailed away. Stephen's gaze was friendly, but calm. Nothing more. She dropped her hands, and he began to speak.

'I am glad you are safe. And that you have transport to

London. It will save you many long days on the roads. Will there be place in the cart, do you think, for all three?'

'All three? Then I may take Francis with me this time? You would allow it?'

'Since you have company, yes. You will be a safe, brave enough little band with the Abbey outrider on horseback, and the man Oliver to drive you. I have spoken with him.'

Cressida's eyes widened in nervous anticipation. So Stephen had already met with Oliver! Then surely, from his quiet manner of speech, she could conclude that Brother Oliver had not disclosed that he and Cressida had met at the Abbey the night before.

'He is a devout Brother, though not fully sworn,' Stephen was saying. 'He knows of the street in the city where I believe you will find lodgings, and in time work. It is a friendly house, where I am known. An apothecary who will be glad of your help since you are the daughter of Margaret and know your simples. He is also a man who can read – and will see that young Francis progresses with his studies, at least as far as is possible outside the University.'

'The good Abbot was not certain Francis would be so soon at liberty to follow me. There was some mention of the choir school.' Cressida tried not to tremble as she spoke. Stephen still gave no sign that he wanted to embrace her.

'Such a life is not for Francis. He is quick to learn, and I have no doubt that he will find employment, maybe as a clerk, as soon as he is old enough. But I have studied this young brother of yours.' He turned a steady, serious gaze on Cressida. 'He is going to be an important young man, in a new world. He is a creature of action, and he has great capacity for joy. I do not see him, somehow, in the disciplined, unworldly role of a choirboy.'

'You have done so much for us already. How can I accept this too? The apothecary – '

'Master Valence. And he has a wife. And two little ones. You will like it there.'

'But how shall I pay our keep? It is all arranged so easily, so far away?' Cressida was suspicious that Stephen might be handing her some kind of charity. Everything seemed so simple. Things did not happen so easily in her experience, and the last thing she wanted in Stephen's present mood was to be dependent on him. After the agony of waiting in the recent days she knew she could not continue in this vague way with him, always waiting on his word, his coming, perhaps even his money.

'You will find in the city of London, Cressida, that it is quite usual for a young woman to work for such a man as Master Valence. Not only will your work in his apothecary's shop pay for your and your brother's food, but you will find you receive money too. It will be a good home for you, and in the crowded streets you and Francis will pass unnoticed. It is most important now, with still almost a year to go until you claim your freedom, that you go to earth. And the best place for that is a teeming city of strangers.'

Cressida's heart sank at the word. In all her dreams of life in London she had imagined herself at its hub, part of the splendid, colourful scene. And now she learnt that she was to become an anonymous, cowering creature . . . as much in bondage by reason of the need to hide herself and Francis as she had ever been whilst working her father's land. And yet – she sat at the table and cupped her head in her hands, thoughtfully. Then she raised her eyes to Stephen, and said in a small voice: 'I trust you, Stephen. I know from my journey so far that I cannot achieve great things on my own. I will work, and I will see that Francis continues his studies. But, if our life is to be so full, and so clandestine, are we to become total hermits? Shall we not see you again?'

Stephen crossed the room in a single stride. Before he had reached her, she had risen from where she sat and come towards him.

'Little Cressida.' He caught her up fiercely into his arms, as if in fear that he would lose her. He held her head close to his chest, and his voice muffled in her golden hair said: 'I am not yours this time as I was the last time we met, at my mother's house. There is danger in what I do now, and until my task is complete I have no right to give my strength to any other cause. One day, perhaps, the collegiate scribes, the men who help me in my task of writing the Bible for all of us in England to read, in our own tongue – maybe they will come out into the open and defy those who would cut them down. And believe me, little Cressida, the same enemies would have my blood. And the blood of those who are close to me. Until we have a real leader we work in total secrecy. There is such a man, but he is still so young that I cannot expect to call on him to lead my brothers. His name is Wyclif. One day, perhaps . . . Until then I will come and go at night, and work at night, and as for love . . .'

Cressida raised a tear-stained face to him. 'I try to understand. I know that in some ways we fight for the same things. And Francis is the living proof that such things will be. But Stephen, a woman cannot live without a fuller purpose – once she has met the man she is to love. I have learnt that in the weeks since I met you again, the night I sought shelter from Matilda. And I am not ashamed of it!'

Stephen caressed her hair gently, and as gently released her. 'You are still so young – '

'Others wed much younger. Or do not wed, it's all the same. I know of many who live together happily without churching. It avoids the marriage fee, and is not always frowned on by holy church. Why, the good father in your very own village had a hearth-mate.'

'Hush!' Stephen put a long, sensitive finger across her eager lips. Her eyes shone at him still, unashamed now that she had told him how she felt. 'Such titles are not for you, Cressida. When you become head of your own house, it will not be thus, with holy church not frowning. It will be an open happiness for all to see. I promise you, you would not settle for less.'

She drooped against him, clinging to his surcoat, sensing that he intended to leave her. 'Perhaps you are right.' She fingered a velvet button, and as it came away in her grasp, she laughed and held it up for him to see. 'It is an omen! A year from now, perhaps more, Stephen, you will bring me your coat, and ask me to mend it. And I shall do so.' She tucked the button into the concealed pocket of her bodice. 'You see, I'll not forget.'

He smiled down at her, easing her away from him. He could see that for all her jesting she was close to tears again. 'When I go,' he told her, 'you will at once prepare for your journey. You will be one night on the road. Prepare accordingly.'

Cressida quailed at the thought of so long in the company of Brother Oliver. She was glad that the outrider, who would buy the Abbey's provisions for the summer, would go with them. 'I have money,' she told Stephen eagerly. 'Still saved from the small store of my mother's.'

Stephen nodded approvingly. 'And you have a good small brother – not so small now – to protect you and the Lady Philippa. I am going now, little Cressida, to say goodbye to him – and to your new friend. And when I see you next, it will be because I have business in London. It is at Master Valence's house that I usually sleep. He is aware of the life I lead, and is on our side.'

'So you *do* come to the city, Stephen!' Cressida's eyes danced. 'How often? And for how long? And will you send word ahead?'

Watching her face light up, its golden beauty bathed in a glow he had rarely seen in any woman, Stephen could not resist her. He drew her to him again. Then, from the doorway, a shadow fell across the two figures as they stood in each other's arms. It was Brother Oliver.

In an even voice, the lay brother told them he had come to make the final arrangements with the travellers for the journey to London. There was no trace in his manner of the violent feelings Cressida had aroused in him only hours before. He was for all the world the humble, helpful servant of the scholar priest, as he bowed slightly to Stephen, and stood aside. Then, with a glance back to Cressida, Stephen told her: 'I leave you in good hands.'

In the garden, his voice mingled in farewell with the high-pitched voices of Cressida's brother and friend. Then the beat of the hooves which Cressida knew belonged to the grey. Then silence, except for the chirrup of birds in the sunshine, and the heavy sigh which Brother Oliver let sharply from his lungs, before he turned on his heel and left Cressida alone.

6

The trundling wooden cart that belonged to Grimthorne, with Brother Oliver in the driver's place, reins held tightly in his thin hands, eyes straight ahead under his cowl, was a familiar sight in the straggling villages between the Abbey and London. In the normal way it would have excited little notice, for Oliver was not one to have made friends on his journeys abroad for the Brothers. But their road now took them past whole streets where the only traffic for months had been the plague carts laden with dead. The survivors had begun to leave their houses, drawn by the rumour that Plague had left the land, and by the sweet spring air. They stood in small, silent groups as the great, high cart lurched by, its heavy leather awning flapping as it righted itself on its awkward passage through mud, over stones. There was no one now to be spared from the fields to clear the roads after winter.

Under the awning, further concealed by a mass of rose plants which Oliver was planning to trade for other goods in the city, Cressida and her two companions lay tightly bunched together. As the cart swayed and rolled, they all three swayed with it, grimly silent as they sensed they passed habitation, groaning loudly when they knew they were out on the straight road with no one to hear. With the Franciscans on their side, Cressida and her brother knew that no one from the Abbey would give them away in their flight from serfdom. There was such a strong, secret bond also, Cressida now realized, between Stephen and the Abbey that she never doubted that Oliver and the outrider who cantered beside them would fail to bring them to their destination. This was the last lap of their journey, and a prelude to their new life. If they gave themselves away now to any spies that might be out still after them, to bring them back to Sir Robert's manor, it would be their own fault. They suffered the tortured journey, their stomachs churning and their hearts beating fast, with a will. And beside them Philippa clenched her teeth, and clutched her small stomach, and lurched on the floor of the cart.

Philippa had decided, whilst planning this last stage of their flight, that she would leave Cressida and Francis south of the river, and make for the small, select Court at Shene. There she had a friend who, like herself, was the daughter of a Norman house and had been sent to Court to finish her education and serve the royal ladies. Through her she would get word to the Queen of her presence in London, and beg audience. In this way she could also be sure of being able to change from her rough worsted garments to something more suitable for the encounter. She could not plead her cause in old clothes, and it was doubtful whether the stewards would even let her past the door if she tried. The Court was the hub of fashion, and courtly manners were an entire way of life, not lightly to be flouted.

Brother Oliver had listened to her plan with tolerance, somewhat exaggerated by the fact that she had preceded her request with a gift to the Abbey of a jewelled necklace she carried with her. It was a handsome, precious offering, and would add greatly to the treasures at Grimthorne. Philippa had no trouble from then on in asking for their route to be planned so as to take her to Shene.

But that would be on the second day of their journey. Even if things went well and the fine weather held, they had to stop over at a hostelry somewhere on the way. It would be then, safely at a distance from the open country where Sir Robert's spies might still roam, that Cressida and Philippa would assume their roles of young ladies on their way to life in a convent, as the Abbot had suggested. And in his scholar's garb, Francis seemed a natural appendage to the little party.

As night approached on their first day, the outrider, a taciturn sallow-faced man with the well-fed air of a successful merchant, spurred his horse and rode on ahead. Hearing the stones fly up under the horse's hooves and the change in his speed, Francis whispered to his sister that the man must be seeking shelter for them all for the night.

'I trust we shall all be in the same room,' Cressida whispered back. 'We must keep watch for each other. Nothing must go wrong now.' She was thinking of what had happened at Ashby, and how fortunate they were to have come this far on their first day from Grimthorne without incident. For this at least she was grateful to Oliver – though she shivered still at the thought of what had passed between them. She had more than one reason for wanting to spend the night safely with her young companions.

From the sounds of a passing cart, a child's laughter, and the cry of its mother calling it into the house before dark, they knew less than an hour later that they had come to a village of some kind. And as the outrider rejoined them, calling into the back of the cart that they could prepare themselves to alight, they stretched their limbs thankfully and drew their cloaks about their faces. Cressida watched her brother pull on his scholar's hat proudly. His young face gleamed with excitement as the cart ground to a halt amidst the hurly-burly of what they guessed must be the yard of an inn.

As Brother Oliver came to help them descend from

their hiding place, he put his precious rose plants carefully to one side. Then, as Francis jumped down of his own accord, Oliver took Philippa's hands and supported her as she got down. By the time he turned back, his hands outstretched, to Cressida, she had already scrambled to the ground. He shrugged.

'Have no fear, girl,' he muttered to her, out of earshot of the others, as he made a semblance of once more shifting the roses neatly into place. 'There will be no further trouble between us. I share a lodging with the outrider tonight. You are to sleep with your companions. But,' he looked over his shoulder at her, 'do not think I have forgotten that I carry evil to London. Temptation. We are well rid of you at Grimthorne.'

Cressida's eyes blazed at his words. She tossed her blonde hair back over her shoulders where it had escaped from beneath her hood. 'It is a strange religion, Brother Oliver, that denies you beauty, and life itself. Even your roses have thorns. Is that why you allow yourself to love them, I wonder?'

She swept away from him and through the door of the inn, to where the others awaited her. She found it hard to forget the look of hatred in Oliver's eyes and was thankful when the outrider informed her that he had arranged for them all to sup in their own rooms. There would be no further need to traffic with the lay brother that night.

The parting with Philippa when they came to the village of Shene was swift, and without tears. The outrider called to Oliver as they approached the street that led to a side gate of the small palace Edward the King had built as an escape from the demanding Court life at Kenilworth and Westminster. The cart drew to a stop, and Philippa scrambled to her feet. She carried nothing but a small bundle of personal needs supplied by Dame Agatha, and – concealed in her bodice – the remainder of the jewels.

With her free hand, she grasped Cressida's shoulder.

'Wish me well, dear friend. I will come to find you at Master Valence's shop – I have the address by heart! – as soon as I have the Queen's protection.' She turned to Francis, her eyes smiling with mischief. 'And sir scholar! We will see who can read the longest words in Latin and French when next we meet!' Then, with a sudden brave downward twist of her lips as fear threatened, she hugged Cressida to her briefly, and reached for the hands the outrider offered her as she made ready to leave the cart for the last time.

As the whip sounded from the driver's seat and the horses pulled out into the main street again, Cressida had a glimpse of her friend standing at an open door in the palace wall. As she watched, Philippa stepped through the door, and it closed.

After Shene, their road led them for a while through open fields again. The spring day was alive with the sounds of birds, and the scent of the wild flowers in the hedgerows filled Cressida with nostalgia for her life before the long flight had begun. But the bustle of a street market made Francis sit up, and her sadness was temporarily forgotten as they clung to the side of the cart, their eyes glued to a peephole in the awning through which they could glimpse their first sight of the city. This must be only the outskirts, Francis whispered to his sister. He knew also that they would have to stay south of the river that led into the heart of London until they came to the one place where they could cross with a cart the size of Brother Oliver's pulled by two horses. It was the famous Bridge. And once over the river, they would surely be close to the city apothecary's shop where Master Valence would await them.

It was with mixed feelings of anticipation, fear, and instant delight in the teeming movement and sounds of the city into which they rode that Cressida emerged from her hiding place with her brother, unbeknown to Oliver and the outrider, who was some way ahead. Together the brother and sister edged their way to the open flaps at the back of the cart, and sat, feet dangling, clinging for dear life to the sides of the awning, as they came into London.

The first thing that assailed them was the acrid, decaying smell that rose from the ditch straddled by the cart wheels beneath their feet. Gazing down in horror to see what could cause such odours, Cressida at once averted her eyes. 'Keep your head up, Francis!' She gripped her brother under the chin with her free hand. 'Breathe only through your nose, not your mouth!' The amenities of the great city, she reflected, were strangely uncivilized in comparison with those of the good village life she had led under her mother's wisdom.

No sooner had she grown slightly accustomed to the stench of the road than she became aware that they were attracting a great deal of attention. Ragged children had joined them, running beside the cart, their hands flapping aggressively as they begged for food or alms. Fearfully, Cressida leaned as far as she dared round the side of the cart to see if Brother Oliver had detected that his charges were on display. But he was too occupied in avoiding the hazards of the crowded street. The distance between the high wooden houses was so narrow that anyone on foot had to jump back every few yards to escape the wheels of the traffic. And a plethora of small handcarts, men with packs on their backs trailing goods for sale, women with infants dragging at their skirts, hedged Brother Oliver's path.

The shops that they passed were unlike anything the children of Margaret had ever seen. In spite of her exhaustion and her nervousness, Cressida's eyes widened with pleasure. She glimpsed a counter laden with velvets in the dark interior of a clothier's. A basket of fresh fish, gleaming like pewter, some of them still thrashing their tails, made her catch her breath. A man clothed in velvet stood in the doorway of a tailor's shop, drawing long gloves on to slender hands as he made to leave, and the ruby and sapphire in the rim of his hat glinted in the afternoon sunshine. Cressida watched the jewels in fascination as the cart drew on gradually to London Bridge, until the glimmer of the man's hat was all she could clearly discern as the crowd faded into a blur, and the slowing of the cart wheels told her they approached the river and the city's heart.

Bidding Francis hide again in the darkness under the awning, in case they were about to arrive at the apothecary's and Brother Oliver would find them out in the open, Cressida herself stayed where she sat a moment longer. She gazed on the extraordinary sight of houses spanning water, the wide brown-green sluggish river that ran beneath them, and suddenly, rearing above her as they drove on to the bridge itself, she saw with terror the row of strong, slim pikes that flanked the approach . . . adorned with the staring, bloody heads of executed men.

As she looked, transfixed by horror, Cressida asked herself who these men were, and what had been their crimes. Under the matted hairlines and the clotted blood, she discerned young brows, old toothless mouths, fine complexions and the weathered skins of men who worked in the fields. With a stifled cry, she remembered Dominic, and her last sight of him. His death had been the beginning of a new awareness for Cressida, of the lengths to which evil and the lust for power could drive some men. But in the days since she had grown less disturbed by it, accepting his death gradually, remembering the good things about him. Now it returned to her with new force. She understood from the grinning, warning heads above her that she had not left the world which had killed Dominic behind. Trembling, she crawled back to sit beside Francis, hugging him to her, until at last the wheels braked and Brother Oliver's face appeared in the awning to tell them they had arrived.

With relief, she thought that this was the last time she would look into Oliver's face or have any dealing with him. Avoiding her eyes, he helped brother and sister down from the cart together, checked that their small bundles of clothing were complete, and busied himself once more making the rose plants safe. The outrider did not dismount, but watched them impatiently as they gathered themselves for the meeting with the apothecary. They were in a narrow street between the village of The Strand and the great church of St Paul's. At one end of the street a market was in full, noisy swing. At the other, they could see the line of a small jetty and the swirl of the river beyond.

The apothecary's shop was set under what seemed to be two high wooden houses. A curtained window prevented passers-by from seeing into the shop, but above the curtain there ran a painted sign, with all the emblems of the zodiac picked out in gold. Curiously, Cressida studied them. She had forgotten that there were men who practised medicine and the art of healing on a basis of the movement of the stars. Were the signs favourable, she wondered, for their meeting with Master Valence and his family?

She would not have been anxious had she been able to see the four people who clustered in the small shop waiting for her and her brother. Master Valence was a small, worried man wearing a strong white apron and a constant frown beneath a high forehead. His wife Alicia was apple-cheeked, with gentle hazel eyes. At her skirts clung two apple-cheeked replicas of herself – the tiny, brown-eyed, button-nosed Valence babies. And as the shop door swung open to reveal Cressida and Francis standing there, with Brother Oliver whisking the reins above the flanks of the two great horses as the cart drew away, the children ran to the street screaming with delight, to watch him go. Life at the apothecary's shop had finally begun.

It was an earnest, well-regulated little household, and from the start Francis studied well, and Cressida had plenty to do. For the first few days she was bewildered by the complexities of Master Valence's stock in trade, but his customers usually knew what they wanted, and if they did not Master Valence himself was quick to diagnose, to recommend, and to mix a remedy. While Cressida herself mixed unguents and potions under his supervision, a neat figure in the blue gown and white coif Dame Valence had provided on her first day in the shop, she also became gradually aware that the conversation between her employer and his customers was not always to do with their health. Sometimes their voices lowered, and she would catch a word or two that recalled the talk at Ashby, when Dominic was captured. Sometimes there would be no talk, but a paper or a package would change hands. Cressida was not surprised that this was the place Stephen had chosen for her to hide. There was no doubt that Master Valence was more than he seemed.

The house itself, which Cressida soon learnt was in a street called River Lane, was also a subject of some mystery. The fact that the shop ran the length of two houses, and that only the Valence family used the single door that led into the shop and the house, meant that there were numerous empty, unexplored rooms at the far end of the house upstairs. Often, as she lay unable to sleep in the room next to Francis's small bedroom, Cressida would imagine she would hear steps on the narrow stair that linked the two wings of the house. They would fade, in the direction of the empty quarters, only to return later that night or early the next day. The first time Cressida was allowed by Mistress Valence to go out (Francis was not allowed out at all), some two weeks after her arrival, it was to clean the sign above the shop window. Lingering over her task, she could not help noticing that there was in fact a second door that gave access from the street into the unused wing of the house. But it was out of use to callers, fastened with a heavy wooden cross-bar, such as she had seen used in houses afflicted by the Death.

It was some days later, on her first walk in the open air, now that they had become less afraid of pursuit and recapture, that Cressida realized how close they lived to the River Thames itself, and how easy it was for traffic to use the jetty at the end of River Lane – far easier, she was sure, than finding a way through the crowded streets she recalled from her first hours in London. It was in fact the great brown waters of the Thames, fast flowing in a summer tide, that brought her word at last from Stephen.

She was alone in the shop, putting in order a set of jars of which she had been learning the names of the contents by heart, when a waterman, in heavy leather jerkin and high boots, stepped through the door and asked for a remedy for a bruise he had received while retrieving an oar in the fast tide. The bruise did not seem too serious an injury to Cressida's increasingly practised eye, but she suggested a salve, which the waterman readily accepted. As she dressed the tender skin for him, his eyes did not leave her face. 'It is the Demoiselle Cressida, is it not? The friend of a friend at Oxford?' At once on her guard, Cressida continued her task, and nodded, without speaking.

'Word comes slowly by the river, but it's safer. We boatmen know each other; our families have worked the river for generations. Families you can trust.'

'I am sure that is true, sir,' Cressida told him politely, cleansing the surface grease from his skin and gently replacing his hand on the apothecary counter. He straightened, thanking her, and as he drew money from the purse strapped to his waist he glanced into the street from the half open door. It was deserted. Placing a coin on the counter, he began to speak in a low, quick voice.

'There is trouble. Your friend may have to leave Oxford soon if he is to continue his work. The work that means so much to the people – people like you and me no doubt, miss. If they leave, the scribes and the scholars, they'll do so by water, and by night. They'll need somewhere to work. You're to expect your friend soon, and he asks Master Valence to prepare a room for him.'

The blood rushed to Cressida's face. She tried to appear calm. 'But how can he be so sure that it is possible for Master Valence? How am I to ask such a boon? And who sent you?' So many questions hummed in Cressida's brain as she half-swooned at the thought of seeing Stephen again, that she sounded aggressive, mistrustful.

The waterman eyed her warily. 'If it were not for that golden hair I see peeping at the line of your coif I'd think I had the wrong lady. But the words were as plain as my boots – I was to speak with the golden-haired lady Cressida. There aren't many of that colouring, you know. The fashion's all for the dark beauties these days. And now I've seen you, miss, it's a fashion I think needs changing.'

Cressida could not resist the man's obvious honesty, and the admiration in his narrow, far-seeing eyes further comforted her. It was some weeks since any man had looked at her. She had kept herself to herself in the back room of the shop, and thought only of Stephen. Her evenings were spent with her brother, and it was from him that she had tried to begin to learn to read – a much-needed skill if she were to become of any real use to the apothecary's trade. Life had been an earnest, down-to-earth routine since they had watched Brother Oliver drive out of their lives, and now Cressida welcomed the rough masculinity of this man who brought her the news which promised to change everything. She smiled at him, to his intense pleasure. He began to back towards the shop door, unable to take his eyes from her.

'I thank you, sir. You have done so much for my friend this day. And for me. Am I not to know who sent you, and am I not to know your name?'

'My family works the run from here to the Bridge. We are known throughout the city. The name is Aske. John Aske. At your service.'

Cressida came round the counter and crossed to the doorway. As she held it open for John Aske to take his leave, she said: 'Master Aske, I'll not forget you. Perhaps one day, when I – when I am free to go as I please, I shall send for you, and you shall row me the length of the city and back.'

'The river will win you, miss. It'll win your heart when

you see it. Just come to the wharf, there at the foot of River Lane, when you're ready, and someone will get the word to me. As you know now, news travels surely on the Thames.'

When he had gone, Cressida stepped back into the shop and leaned breathlessly against the door, her heart beating so fast that she could hear it. So Stephen was to come to her! Whether he chose it or not, he needed to be in London, and he had asked for shelter where he knew she waited for him. If only she knew how he really imagined their future together might be, she could allow her own dreams to take shape. But at least she would be near him, soon, and he would not be able to elude her as he had at Grimthorne. That is, if whatever threatened him at Oxford did not strike at him before he was able to leave. Her heart sank as she realized she might once more have to face days upon days of waiting, perhaps indefinitely, if harm came to Stephen. But this time she would not bear it. She determined that if he had not arrived within the week, she would do as John Aske had told her, and go to the wharf and take to the river herself in search of him! Firmly, she locked the shop door as she saw what she must do, and raced up the narrow stairs that led to the Valence quarters to tell Mistress Valence what had happened. With a thrill of pleasure, she decided to ask if she could prepare the room for Stephen herself.

On a still, warm summer's night only five days later Cressida stood in the window of the long, low room she had made ready for Stephen and listened to the murmured voices of the Valence family in the quarters below. With the news of Stephen's imminent arrival, Mistress Valence had told her husband that they must now revive 'the other house', and after a quiet marital confrontation in the privacy of their own parlour, from which Mistress Valence emerged triumphant, Cressida was sent to fetch sweet herbs for a pillow from the shop, and Francis scampered down to the rear yard to collect straw for bedding. The thought of Stephen's living with them at River Lane had put the boy in a livelier frame of mind than ever. His enforced hiding and his studies (much as he liked them) had proved an ordeal of endurance for him. And though outwardly he bore them stoically he could secretly hardly wait for the day – now less than six months away – when he could mark his rough calendar with the end of his year at large, and the next day walk the streets a free man. In the meantime, Stephen's presence in the house would mean greater opportunity to study, and to talk. Apart from Master Valence, the household was far too predominantly female for Francis's liking.

Musing on her brother's obvious delight in anticipating the company of the man she herself loved so deeply, Cressida watched the flicker of torchlights as late passers-by made their way home beneath the window. It was against the law to walk abroad without light, she had learnt from Mistress Valence in one of her many informal lessons on how to survive in the great evil city that lay beyond River Lane. She was therefore curious to see, from the direction of the wharf, a lone figure make its way up towards the house in the shadows, no torch in his hand. At the thought of a petty criminal, or a smuggler perhaps, in River Lane, she drew back carefully from the window. She did not want to be asked to shelter a villain, or have her throat cut in the process. She had learnt enough from Mistress Valence of the outcome of such encounters.

Giving the man, whoever he might be, a few moments in which to pass, she returned to the window, and her study of the deep azure of the night sky. Stephen's temporary home was at the top of the unused wing, and between the high narrow houses there was a canyon of stars that drew Cressida to them each night as she visited the room, wondering if the next day, or the next, would be the day he would sit there with his books, his tonsured head bent earnestly over them, his eyes perhaps lifted every now and then to watch Cressida's face.

She shook herself at the thought, intent on driving her day dreams out of her mind. Idly, she looked down into the street again, and her heart missed a beat. The shadowy figure of the man was still there. And as her eyes grew accustomed to the darkness she knew that it was Stephen.

Leaning as far from the window as she dared, she waved to him in silent greeting. She was sure that he watched the house, and the white cuff at her wrist would perhaps catch his eye. She waved again, and in the shadows opposite the house the man raised a hand in reply. Then, searching the street to the left and right of the apothecary's, he crossed to the entrance, whilst Cressida raced from the far wing, through the linking passage, down the stairs to the late-night silence of the shop itself. She almost flung herself the last yard to the street door, wrenched at the heavy latch, and fell back as Stephen stepped inside.

The moment the door was closed again, Stephen signalled wordlessly to Cressida that she was not to speak. He took her hand then, and climbed with her to the upper rooms where the Valence family waited. They had heard Cressida's headlong flight downstairs, and guessed what had happened. In moments food was on the table, a tallow lamp lighted for Stephen's room. In answer to their enquiries about his colleagues, the scribes who worked with him, he told the Valences that they had sanctuary elsewhere – in a place where their papers could be safely stored. He would work with them there, daily. The place was to be kept secret. He could tell no one, even those close to him, where he would spend his days.

Cressida listened to every word with her whole being. Now she shared something real with Stephen. He too was a fugitive, from men who would stifle him. How strange it was that they had both ended in this narrow city street, under the same roof! Now she could surely get to know Stephen's plans for the future and prove to him how important a part she could play at his side if he would let her. As they exchanged glances across the table, Master and Mistress Valence clearly unaware of their interest in each other, Cressida searched for some sign of love in Stephen's eyes. When she found nothing but fatigue and a fanaticism that seemed not to be affected by his exhaustion, she told herself it was too soon. Stephen had spent countless days in fear of his arrest for his work on forbidden versions of the Bible. He was responsible for many others, who were also in danger. The plan to go underground, and to continue the work, must have taken all his strength. How could she expect him to think of their love, in his first moments of safety?

Later, the flow of words with which Stephen had told them everything began to slacken. She watched him in the dim light as his head bowed slowly to the table in sleep. Rising to her feet, she touched him gently on the shoulder. 'Stephen,' she murmured, careful not to startle him awake. Then as he stirred in his first sleep, she spoke his name again, and he woke, stumbling after her as she led him to his room. She held the tallow high above her head as he stood in the centre of the room, finding his bearings. He nodded approvingly. It had the simplicity of the Abbot's room at Grimthorne, and was warm. He took the light from Cressida and set it on the shining table she had found for him, thinking he would write here in this house.

'Thank you, little Cressida. I must sleep. I start early tomorrow – ' At her cry of protest, Stephen turned sharply from her. 'I will take no cries of women; nothing will stop me now from continuing my work. We have lost so much time. I have no choice, if I am to keep faith with my fellows, my fellow heretics if you like, but to work and work – until we have done.'

Cressida stiffened, and as always when she was challenged her small chin tilted proudly. 'I do not question that, Stephen. It is because of your work that my love for you has deepened into the lasting thing it is. It makes it possible for me to wait . . . for a while. Because I know I should be at your side.' She paused, searching for words. 'But you are right. Tomorrow, go to your work. Everyone in this house will care for you while you are here – I more than the others, perhaps.'

Stephen raised his hands helplessly, smiling now. 'You were always stubborn, little Cressida. We shall see. And for now – I must sleep.' He slumped on the low bed she had prepared for him, so heavily that Cressida started forward, alarmed, to help him. But a warning hand told her not to touch him. She stood looking down at him, her thoughts in turmoil. And by the time she had slipped out of the room and gently closed the door he was asleep.

'The life of a scholar,' Francis told the assembled Valence family some weeks later as they all sat round the great table in Mistress Valence's living-room, 'is a hard life, I can tell you. We may look soft, or well fed, or lazy, but the truth is we are lean, hungry fellows, with a lust for work. At least, that is what Stephen would have me be!'

Stephen led the laughter that followed. It was one of the rare days when he had stayed at home, a Sunday. Still in hiding from the eyes of those who would destroy his work, he did not even dare go to Sunday mass in St Paul's. Cressida herself, who did not feel the need to go to church these days, her faith neglected, half-forgotten in all that had happened to her, was glad of this. It meant that when he was absent, though she did not know where he worked, she knew that he was not abroad in the streets, perhaps with strangers, perhaps with women who might rival her for his affections. In the weeks since his arrival she had grown to accept his preoccupation with his secret work, and she knew that she must keep her distance if she wanted to win him in the end. She was merely biding her time. And as she learnt patience, her love for him still growing, her beauty became a much rarer, more subtle charm. She moved more slowly, and with more grace. She held her bright head modestly, always slightly bowed when Stephen was there. Now, as he laughed, she dared raise her eyes to his and smile. And her beauty at that moment, as she held his gaze steadily, made him falter.

Stephen also had changed since he came to London. He went quietly about his work, spoke to Francis as if he were father rather than friend, and seldom played with the Valence babies, as Cressida had thought he would. The carefree side of his nature seemed somehow totally eclipsed. He was also secretive, and hardly spoke even to Master Valence. Today was an exception. Would it be on such a day, Cressida wondered, that he would recall that he had once loved her, and would not pass her room without a sign that he remembered, as he went to his bed in the far wing, above where she slept?

One night, after a long evening in which Stephen had sat silently by the hearth, and Francis had sat with his books, Cressida had thought that her newly found patience would not prove lasting. She was astonished to find that with so much she had wanted now achieved, with her brother and her friends around her, she should be so much lonelier than when she had fled in terror from Sir Robert. If she had Philippa's company now, she thought, she would not be so desperate for some sign of affection from Stephen. She missed the laughter, the mischievousness, of Sir Robert's sister, and wondered where she was now, and when she would receive word from her. Surely the Queen had not refused her mercy? Cressida had heard since her arrival in the city that the Queen was renowned for her kindness. She had not only pleaded with her husband successfully for the lives of the traitor burghers of Calais, but even in the matter of a faulty stand that had collapsed during a jousting – a year or two before the Black Death had stopped such revelries, not far from River Lane itself – she had ruled that the guilty carpenters should not be punished.

It was almost Michaelmas, and the afternoons were drawing in, when Cressida decided that if she did not escape from the house for an hour or two, and breathe even the foul air of the streets, she would not vouch for her behaviour. She had spent the mornings of a whole week cleaning the house with Mistress Valence. She had minded the shop three afternoons running for Master Valence. She had earned the price of a new plough by her labours in a month, and had nowhere to spend it. And now, if the winter cold gripped the city as soon as the chill wind of the day seemed to threaten, she would never get out. If she waited till January, when she and Francis would at last be safe from the law, and from Sir Robert's claims on them, she knew she would pine into a sad, lackadaisical creature who would have no taste for her freedom when it came.

Mistress Valence was closeted in her small solar making a new gown, which she proposed to wear for Christmas. The children played at her feet, and Francis was engrossed in his studies. Master Valence and Stephen were both out, as usual. There were no customers in sight.

Once she knew what she was going to do, Cressida did not hesitate. She went to her room, found her old cloak, and wrapping it closely round her body went back down to the shop, let herself out, and dropped the latch into place as she did so. It was a trick she had learnt from Master Valence himself. No one could invade the shop once it was done. If a member of the household returned, they could call to the mistress for admittance.

Without glancing to left or right, Cressida walked away from the river to the far end of the street, where the city still went about its business. In the main street, she turned right. Ahead of her was Ludgate, and she felt suddenly exhilarated as she began to climb the slope to St Paul's. She had not walked so far for months, and found that she trembled with excitement as she increased her pace, jostling those around her as she herself was jostled, until she found herself part of a greater, slowly shifting crowd that seemed to have its centre close to the famous church. Cressida thought that she had never seen so many people all in one place. She wondered if it were safe, and if the plague had really left the city, then brushed the thought from her mind. There were wealthy, well-clothed people present, who surely would not be in the streets if they still feared the Black Death. Small stall-holders were selling autumn fruits and fresh fish along the side of Ludgate. She felt thirsty, but the crowd milled too thick for her to break from it and perhaps find an ale house where she could buy something to drink. Instead, she allowed herself to be carried the last stretch of the way to the great courtyard round the church itself.

As she edged through the people towards the front of the crowd, pushing away the grasping hand of a beggar, and ignoring the shifty but admiring glance of a young merchant, Cressida realised that this was no ordinary assembly. There was undoubtedly some attraction further ahead, if she could but reach it. It was possibly religious, for she had noticed people crossing themselves as they craned their necks to see – and in any case the church was known for producing great entertainment and spectacle, and she did not want to miss any novelty that might be offered.

At last she eased her way between an elderly friar who seemed to be praying as he watched, and a plump old woman whose eyes were almost popping out of her head at what she could see. As Cressida broke into the front line of the crowd between these two, she understood why. The scene was strange, the strangest she had ever witnessed. It struck fear into her heart, and as she continued to watch the fear became tinged with a sensation she could not recognize. The blood rose to her face, and her throat went dry. At the pit of her stomach an aching, hungry sensation took its grip. Her ears hummed with the rhythmic lash of whips, and the low, insistent cries of Latin prayers in a foreign intonation that came from the men who held the lashes.

In an open space before the great church of St Paul's there circled a stream of holy men in varying stages of exhaustion, pain, ecstasy and triumph. Each man held in his right hand a scourge. It was a heavy twist of rope, knotted at the free end, and the knot spiked with fine, sharp darts of some thin metal. The men moved in a wide circle. And with each step they raised the scourges, and brought them down on the shoulders, the buttocks, or the leg of the man in front. There was a great deal of blood. Their robes were torn. Their eyes were raised to the heavens. Cressida had a sudden sharp vision of Brother Oliver, and knew not why.

'Madam, please tell me,' she asked of the plump woman beside her, 'what is it? They speak with a foreign sound. For what do they pray?'

It was the friar who answered her. 'Pray with them, child. It is our last hope. Plague still rears its head in the land, and these holy men from the Low Countries are driving it out. Pray with them.'

Cressida looked at him in horror, and back to where the Flemish monks still circled with their grotesque gestures and entreaties rending the air. How could she have watched them even for a second, she cried silently to herself. It was a travesty of prayer to anyone who had seen the plague, as she had, close at hand. What did their ritual do to cleanse the land of disease? Never in a thousand years would she accept such madness. In disgust at herself as much as at the spectacle, she began to fight her way back through the crowd. The tears she had never shed for her mother began at last to flow. She wanted only to get back to her small room in River Lane, to find Francis and hug him to her until the tears were spent.

With a gasp, she found a way free in the crowd, and reached the side of the street. She was halfway down Ludgate, and stood in the doorway of a tavern while she thought how she might get home as fast as she could. Ahead of her, to the left, was a side turning that she believed might lead to the wharfs, and then perhaps she could make her way along the banks of the Thames itself to the far end of River Lane. She darted from the shelter the moment her mind was made up. Her country-woman's sense of direction was good, and she could be home in minutes if she ran. In the crowd behind her she thought she heard a cry. She was conscious of a struggle, and of a man breaking through the crowd. It was nothing to do with her, she thought, and turned thankfully out of the main street. She began to run towards the river. Her hood fell from her head, and her golden hair tumbled from its concealment. As she paused to cover her head again, a hand gripped her shoulder. Another hand clamped across her mouth. Unable to breathe, she twisted to see what thieves or rogues had her captive . . . and found herself looking into the eyes of Sir Robert, whilst two of his men bruised her arms and mouth with their hands.

7

As Sir Robert's men half-lifted, half-dragged her down the narrow, deserted street towards the river, the thought cut into Cressida's mind like a silent scream that she was going to be drowned. She bit, kicked at her captors, and arched her back again and again in a wild attempt to break from them. But they were too strong for her. Her mouth was gagged with a silken scarf by one of them the second time she tried to bite him. Sir Robert followed, laughing quietly, urging the men to move faster. It was growing dark. Her dragging feet struck the wooden planks of a rotting jetty. She felt splinters of rough wood tear at her shift as she was lowered for a moment to the ground. Then Sir Robert himself grasped her waist, and lifted her again. There was the soft plunge of oars in deep water. Then, mercifully, Cressida lost consciousness.

When she awoke, Cressida found herself stretched on a low, soft bed in what seemed to be a narrow room with wooden walls and ceilings. Her bruised mouth felt parched, her body ached. She blinked in the light of a flickering torch fixed in a clamp on a far wall, and turned her head. At her side, crouched on the floor, waiting for her to move, was Sir Robert. With a cry, she tried to sit up, but fell back, her head swimming. She was unable to understand why her body rocked, making her even more dizzy as she lay down again. She felt vaguely sick. It was some minutes before she had gathered her thoughts sufficiently to realize that she was in a boat, and that the boat was moving fast, rowed by perhaps several men. She could hear the rhythm of their oars above her. The boat rocked again. They were moving downstream, on a fast tide.

She swallowed nervously, trying to keep calm. If she let Sir Robert see that she was afraid it might trigger off more brutal behaviour on his part. And she must have quiet in which to think. She must play for time, she decided. The journey ahead had to end soon. A boat of this size – it was perhaps one of the private barges she had seen on the Thames from River Lane – could not go on out to sea. When Sir Robert reached his destination with her she would need all her wits about her to escape.

'You do not deceive me with your calm, pale face, girl,' Sir Robert broke in upon her plans. 'It is so easy to read your thoughts. Just as one knows what the rabbit is thinking in the snare. You are thinking that when we come to dry land you will escape me. But this time – you will not. If you do, I will follow again. And catch you again. And as you would doubtless also lead me to your brother, I would have a double catch. It would be well worth the chase. I am growing used to it.'

His voice was unusually low. As he spoke, Cressida watched his mouth, fascinated by the thin wet line of his lips in his beard, and the glimpse of gold-capped teeth. He leant closer to her where she lay, and she smelt wine on his breath. But he was far from drunk. He knew exactly what he was saying, and with a sinking heart she also knew that he was right. If she did escape, she would not dare to get word to her brother, to Stephen. Sir Robert was, as she now knew, too clever not to pick up her trail again. The only other way out of his grasp would be to run for it when they landed, if she could – and go to ground like a wild creature in the city. For the moment she had not the strength to consider such things. She turned her face to the wooden curve of the boat beside her. The wall was hung with the most exquisite tapestry, she noticed, and, half-dazed, she began to study the scene it depicted, of a boar hunt in winter. Close to her on the bed she also saw a discarded drinking horn, its leather edge trimmed with finely painted flowers in gold and white. She began to wonder if the barge belonged to Sir Robert himself, or whether he had purloined it from someone of high rank.

'There are no words left then, from my pretty rebel? Defeat at last, is it?' Sir Robert stood for a moment, stretching his limbs in the cramped space. 'Perhaps a taste of wine will ease your tongue.'

Cressida was indeed thirstier than she had ever been in her life. It was the result of shock, combined with the horror of the grotesque scene at St Paul's, she thought. Shuddering, she put the image of the spellbound crowds out of her mind. When Sir Robert held a goblet to her lips, she involuntarily took a long draught of the wine. It was very good, but she choked a little, pulling her head back from the goblet too soon. Wine spilt on to the blue bodice of her gown. She realized that someone had removed her cloak, and the surcoat she had worn beneath it. She remembered the splinters that had torn her shift, and looked down anxiously at her blue skirt, relieved to find it unharmed. Sir Robert's eyes followed her glance. He put out a hand glittering with heavy rings, and touched the blue skirt with extraordinary gentleness. The gesture mesmerized her, so unlike as it was to anything she had grown to expect of him. Her eyes shifted to his face, and he looked back at her with the glowering intensity she had seen in him the nights he had come to her house in the dark. She knew then that she had fled from him in vain. That there was no escape, as yet, from what he intended to do to her. Her senses swam.

'I – I am sick, Sir Robert. It is the wine, the river. It is too much for me.' Her obvious sincerity convinced Robert, and he took his hand away from her gown while he lifted her to her feet.

'The owner of this vessel,' he murmured to her, 'is a very wealthy and powerful man. He travels in the most noble fashion. Come, there is a privy – small, but well enough – beyond.' Then, to Cressida's astonishment, he led her swiftly, almost tenderly to the place. A curtain fell behind her, and she was able to vomit, and relieve herself. When she had finished, a pitcher of cold water beside the privy made it possible for her to moisten her face and wash her hands thankfully. She returned to where Robert waited, and sank back weakly on her bed, too exhausted to speak.

Robert looked down at her, his face impassive. He reached again for the wine, and this time she drank deeply as he held the goblet. She was becoming accustomed to the movement of the boat, and though her head swam she no longer felt sick. Robert studied her again as she lay back.

'I do not seek to tame you. I do not like my prey too meek.' His eyes narrowed. 'And if I failed, it is I who would be the fool. As I have so often failed with my brave little sister.'

At the mention of Philippa, Cressida's eyes flickered with interest. But she was too proud to ask after her friend of this man, and did not want to give away anything of her adventures with Philippa after their escape from the castle if it so happened that Philippa had kept her freedom and won her case with the Queen.

'Oh, she has beaten me, young Philippa. And I'm wiser for it.' Robert spoke grimly. 'She has a place at Court, and I have to keep my distance until our good Queen has decided whether her protégée shall wed Ralph of Mansey. Or Robin of Richmond. Or Cecil of Walmsley. They play a game with me, and they play it well. I have to admire it!'

'So she is safe. And she is well? Is she happy at Court?' Cressida was so delighted at the thought of Philippa's victory that she felt secure enough to speak of it. In answer to her sudden quite normal questioning, and the brighter look on her face, Robert threw back his head and laughed. Above them the splash of the oars in mid-stream told Cressida that they were not yet approaching land.

'The ability of the female to recover her strength never fails to astound me! Not a man in London would guess what you have been through this last hour, or these last months, if he could see you as you are now!' Robert bent over Cressida and his face came close. He shifted where he knelt, and raised himself on one elbow, leaning down even closer to look into the defiant blue eyes of the girl he had pursued for months.

With his free hand, Robert took a pleat of the soft blue gown between his fingers. With it, he pulled blue skirt, white shift, until the garments were at Cressida's waist and her long white limbs were bared. Still her eyes held his. She swallowed hard. She thought of her brother, and the need to protect him. She thought of Stephen, so remote from her now. The moan she gave was one of grief for him. Robert seemed excited by it, and his hand moved between her legs, tracing the soft curve of her inner thigh. She closed her eyes. She was strangely surprised by his gentleness but still not prepared for what followed. His fingers began to probe her warmth, and to play with the secret lips she herself had never touched or seen. She pulled back, but Robert followed, his fingers more insistent now, and began a strong rhythmic approach to her, until she cried out.

The kiss with which Robert silenced her second cry held her pinned to the cushions at her head. A black wave of despair mingled with strong desire she could not control banded her forehead in the dark moments that followed. She was aware of the light flickering beyond the man's shoulders. She sensed him untie his own clothing, and struggled once more to wrench away from under him as he mounted her. In a final effort to keep him at bay, she tightened her thighs about his thrusting legs. But it was too late. The hand that now reached for her breast stained her blue gown with her own blood. The piercing of her young body was complete within seconds, and Robert, his heavy body moving again and again within hers, began an assault on her in which there was no gentleness, no finesse, and which lasted almost the hour it took the men above them to reach their destination.

By the time the sound of feet on the deck above and a call from the shore told them that they had touched the river bank and were about to land, Cressida herself was moving in unceasing, rhythmic mockery of the act of love. Her eyes glazed, her breath coming in slow deep gulps, she watched the man who had been the lord of the manor where she was a serf lift himself from her, and minutes later, still in a daze, she followed him to the long, low manor house that waited for them, lights blazing in the courtyard, the dogs running, barking to greet them.

Sir Robert had leased the manor house from a great family which had bought new lands in France since the triumphs at Crécy and Poitiers, and would be away for some years. He had taken it to be close to his sister, whom if the truth were told he sorely missed, while she maintained her game with him under protection of the Court. It was convenient for Richmond, where a summer palace was kept by the royal family, and by boat he could be at Westminster within an hour. If Philippa was to marry, even if it was not to be the Earl of Mansey, Robert still wanted to keep control of the situation – if that were now possible. It was likely now that Philippa, fast becoming a beauty, would catch an even more powerful husband. It would not do for them to quarrel.

Meanwhile the manor house on the river had become a well-known rendezvous for the bachelor-knights in Robert's circle. A vast staff of servants whom he had inherited from the owners ran it for him, still in the lavish style to which their original masters had been accustomed. There were banquets every few days, hunting parties out to Windsor, and innumerable house guests, some of whom Robert hardly knew. He was spending too fast, and was out of his depth. Life in the country, however powerful he was in his own manor, had always been on an even keel, modest, even thrifty. He had worked the lands through his serfs, and wenched with the local girls, and run his home after his wife died in a rough and ready, soldier's way. But London had gone to his head. He wanted to cut a dashing figure, to hold his own with Philippa's new circle. That afternoon he had been on his way to an exclusive, clandestine cock fight in which he would have lost a small fortune, when he had been diverted by the crowds around St Paul's. The matter of Cressida and her runaway brother had never left him for long. One glimpse of the bright head in the crowd, and all else was forgotten.

As he brought Cressida into his personal suite of rooms at the manor house he noted that, for the first time since he had known her, her golden head was bowed. She moved like an automaton, taking the chair he placed for her by the fire that burnt brightly at one end of his solar. He left her for a while, and went through to his bedchamber. Returning in a loose, ruby robe thrown over his linen undergarments, he found her in exactly the same position as he had left her in. The silken shift he carried over one arm for her – left carelessly in his bedchamber by the woman who had last kept him company there – slipped unnoticed from her knees when he placed it before her. She continued to stare at the floor, and the knuckles that gripped the sides of her chair were white.

Pouring himself a goblet of wine from the graceful

flask laid ready on the table, Robert watched her warily. The unexpected turn of events had confused him, and he felt a strange mixture of exhilaration and regret. The picture of Cressida he had always kept in his mind was that of the country girl who was not afraid to defy him. Now he had her trapped, by her need to keep her brother from him still. And her defiance seemed to have melted in the hour before, as he made long, violent love to her with a brutal need to conquer he had not experienced for years. From the look on her face now, and the droop of her shoulders, it seemed that he had achieved his wish. But he knew now that this was not what he wanted of her after all. The girl who had lain with him in the barge as they sped down river, the woman who now sat before him, had the quality to become his equal. Studying her keen profile, her wild mane of goldspun hair, the delicate turn of her bare ankles, it dawned on him that here was a beauty he could present with pride at Court. With her at his side the scorn he knew so many at Westminster felt for him would turn to jealousy. It might even help his cause with his sister, whom he knew the girl befriended when they fled together from Mansey's castle. What he did not admit to himself was that he was so infatuated with Cressida after the single hour he had just passed with her that he would make out any case to keep her in his bed.

With a tact and gentleness that were unfamiliar to him, yet becoming more and more part of his dealings with the girl, he led her to the table, and raised a goblet of wine to her mouth. She sipped from it, automatically at first, and then greedily. Her ordeal had left her dazed and exhausted, and the wine warmed her stiff body. As she relaxed, she turned to examine the shift that now lay at her feet. She noticed that the floor here was covered with soft carpets in deep colours and complex designs. It was the first time she had ever seen such things underfoot. With a pang of sorrow, and growing anger, she remembered the rush-strewn floor at home . . . where the whole story of her relationship with Sir Robert had begun. For the first time, she raised her eyes to his.

'I need to wash, and I need to change my gown.' She did not use his title, or his name. She spoke coldly, as if she gave orders to a servant. If that was how she wanted to play it, Robert thought, he would not quarrel with her. Not for the time being, at least. He opened the door of his room, and called to a guard who stood a short distance down the corridor. Minutes later an old serving woman, her face a mask of disapproval, appeared, and led Cressida through to the bedchamber. Behind her walked two maidservants with the knowing looks and pert faces of girls Cressida had seen in the city streets. They carried pitchers of warm, scented water, in which Cressida was soon bathing her sore body.

When she had finished, and the servants had left, she stood in the curtained archway between the two rooms. As she washed her spirits had begun to revive. And she had begun to think. She was virtually a prisoner; she was too weary to try to escape that night; if she did get away, she had nowhere to go, for she would not lead Robert and his men to River Lane. There was also the fact that she dearly wanted to see Philippa again, in her new role at Court. If she stayed with Robert for just one day more, she could perhaps ask this as a boon. For he already owed her that. Her only regret was that her brother, and the man she loved, would think her lost. Mistress Valence always had too much to say about the evils of the city, and Cressida prayed that she would not frighten Francis with her tales. Stephen, of course, was so preoccupied with his devotion to his work that she would not be surprised if he hardly noticed her absence. She wondered, bitterly, what he would think if he knew that the girl he had kissed so ardently months ago in his mother's house had wantonly opened her thighs to a hated member of the very power-hungry set he was out to bring down. A Norman lord and land-owner, Robert was also a supporter of established régimes – when it suited him. And Cressida was fully aware that by the time Robert had finished with her on the river that evening she had been an active participant in his lust.

Now she suppressed the anger that the knowledge bred in her. She eyed Robert coldly, and when she spoke her voice was controlled, anonymous. 'If there is supper, I believe I could eat a little. I am weak, sir, after – after what has happened between us. I need food, and I need rest.'

Robert, completely taken in by her words and her aspect, almost bounded to her side, and led her to the table. He called more servants, and in no time an appetizing meal was laid before them. Cressida forced herself to regard the delicacies with simulated pleasure. She allowed Robert to help her to morsels of meat and fish in his own fingers. To her surprise, she found that she was indeed very hungry, and the food was the best she had ever tasted. But she gave no sign of her rapidly improving condition, and when she had eaten her fill she daintily refused more wine, and asked Robert if she might retire. His answer made her tremble. He took a great gulp of the heavy red wine with which they had finished the meal, and said: 'By all means. You will find a good soft bed in the chamber where you washed. It is my bed. And I shall join you there. I have things to do in my household first. In less than an hour I shall be with you. In the meantime – ' he took her hand, in a strong grip, and began to caress the palm – 'you are well guarded. There is a man every ten yards between you and the river. No one can get in – or out – without raising a hue and cry.'

As if to double the guard he had placed on her, Robert opened the door to the room and let in a giant black hound. As Robert himself left, and the door closed, the dog slunk to the hearth and circled until it found a place to sleep. Then it curled on the luxurious carpet, and lay with its eyes fixed on Cressida, as she walked slowly across the room and through the archway to Robert's bedchamber.

The room in which she lay and waited for Robert,

hoping against hope that he would be too weary or too drunken on his return to assault her again, was wrapped in the scent of musk and the ruby warmth of the velvet hangings that draped walls, windows and bed. The bed was a high wooden structure built against one wall, and was as wide as it was long. Climbing into it, Cressida flung aside the heavy furs that covered it, and slipped between sheets of silk. She began to realise how wealthy a household this was, and wondered if Robert found it too much of a contrast to the manor house at home. But soothed by the lavender pillows on which she lay she soon forgot such minor anxieties, and stretching her long limbs she inhaled deeply the perfume of her surroundings. For a moment she fell into a light sleep, and when she awoke she found herself curled close to the wall, her back to the room. She knew then that some sound had roused her, and she stiffened. With a sure, soft tread, not at all the gait of a man who has drunk too much, Robert was walking towards the bed.

A soft growl from the dog in the other room, and the deepening shadows around her as the tallows were extinguished and the outer door closed, told Cressida that she was alone in the dark with the man who had ravished her. As he climbed into the bed and settled heavily beside her, she lay motionless, her back still turned to him. To her relief he did not reach for her, but seemed to go almost immediately to sleep.

Terrified of waking him, she lay as if frozen for what seemed like an eternity. Then, lulled by the luxury of her surroundings, she heard the sound of music in the distance. A man's voice sang of love, and the lute player who accompanied him was a master. As she tried to sleep, Cressida remembered the songs Dominic had sung for her. Never would she forget that the man beside her in the darkness was capable of dealing torture and death as he had dealt it to the travelling minstrel she had known so briefly.

Thrusting the vivid picture of Dominic's corpse and its

terrible injuries from her mind, she turned abruptly on to her other side. As she did so, Robert also twisted in his sleep, so that as dawn came and light filtered into the room between the heavy curtains at the window, Cressida found herself tight in his embrace. She watched his cruel, foreign face in the half light. He was not a man who looked helpless in his sleep, she decided. She knew she had no choice but to go through with whatever the day might bring. Then, as Robert stirred and began to wake, she found herself forcefully thrown on to her other side, her back to him. She tried to scramble from him, but he had her pinned between himself and the wall. She scratched hopelessly at the velvet hangings, unable to find a hold on them from which she could fight back. He was too quick for her. His arms came round her waist, and from behind he took her nipples between his blunt fingers, finding them through the silk of her gown.

To her horror, Cressida felt them round and tighten at his touch. Grunting in a sleepy, animal fashion he released one hand and pulled her gown up from her limbs. Then gripping her above her slim, girl's hips, he entered her with a single long thrust between her small buttocks, and began the prolonged and cruelly violent attack on her that was his idea of love. With the first thrust, Cressida screamed. He whispered to her then that no one would come, scream as she might. They were used to such cries in this place. As he continued to move in her, she moaned a little, almost fainting. Then, in spite of herself, intoxicated by the silk and perfume that mingled with her limbs and her long hair, she gave herself up to the growing demands and increasing pace of his attack. When she screamed next, it was in angry, bewildered pleasure . . . and Robert drew back from her and rolled on to his pillows, sweating, and cursing her.

'I knew there would be such things between us,' he told her. 'But you are a miracle. I'll never be finished with you. Today I take you to the Court. And if any man looks at you as I do, then I'll cut his throat. But the women can envy you to their hearts' content. And I'll see that when you come before them all your robes will match your beauty.'

But Cressida had begun to weep bitterly, her face buried in her pillows. She had left the house in River Lane less than a day ago, she thought. All she had wanted was a taste of freedom, and a breath of air at the end of the long summer in the town. Well, her folly had cost her that freedom, and in the few hours since its loss she had changed irrevocably. She knew that all she had done had started as the only way to protect herself and her brother. But it had got out of hand, and as she rose to dress, in response to the serving women who now came to her laden with delicate undergarments, robes and tunics trimmed with fur, she herself did not know the woman who gazed back at her from the mirror held for her by a girl no older than herself.

The return to the city by water early that afternoon was very different from Cressida's journey with Sir Robert the night before. It was a fine warm day for late September, and she sat on deck, under a royal red awning trimmed with gold. Her hair was braided on each side of her face, its golden coils gleaming through the pale silver of the nets which held it in place. Her eyebrows had been lightly plucked, though she had not allowed the serving women who attended her to paint her face and breasts. Her skin had its own, natural glow, and her eyes blazed from a face that seemed to have grown thin and serious in the last few hours. The deep shadows beneath her eyes somehow enhanced her strange new beauty. The violet gown she had chosen was covered by a surcoat of bronze, slit at each side, embroidered with violet and gold thread.

As they moved slowly upstream, small craft bobbing in the water around them, the white sea birds wheeling above, Cressida had the sensation that she was coming to the city for the first time. All the buildings looked so much statelier from where she sat, lining the banks of the river as they did. For one terrible moment, she thought she could pick out what must be the wharf at the end of River Lane, and made to stand, a cry springing to her lips. But Robert, who had stayed close to her side all day, put a restraining hand on her arm.

Some minutes later, the oarsmen began to turn the boat, and Cressida saw that they were making for the south bank. As they approached a small landing-stage, two river boats, manned by watermen in heavy jerkins, neatly avoided them. Cressida looked down out of curiosity, and found herself looking into the narrowed eyes of John Aske, who had brought word to her of Stephen's arrival weeks before. There was no admiration in his eyes this time, and she had the impression that the man did not know her. But the way in which he looked at her, as if they were equals, in no way in awe of her or of Sir Robert, pleased her greatly. Almost imperceptibly, she inclined her head. Then John Aske smiled, and rowed off at speed. For an instant she wondered if he had after all recognized her, and had maybe guessed at her plight and gone for help. But it was too much to hope for.

The barge had called at the jetty, in order to take on two friends of Sir Robert before turning back down to Westminster. Cressida eyed them doubtfully as they took their seats under the awning. They were sophisticated, effete types, dressed with far too much attention to fashion and detail, she thought. They seemed strange company for Robert. There was talk of nothing but Court and Court politics as they proceeded, and when one of the men asked Robert with more than polite interest how his small sister fared, she noticed that he silenced him with a cautionary glance at Cressida herself. Could these be yet more conspirators, brought to spy on her friend? She must remember to warn her when they met, and set to examining the men in minute detail so that she could provide a thorough description of them to Philippa.

The thought of meeting her again made Cressida put

her immediate pain and regret to one side. She was in any case beginning to recover from the brutality of the early morning in Robert's bed, and she felt less tired than the night before. She was gathering strength for the chance to escape when it came – but only if she had somewhere to go. She hoped that the meeting with Philippa, which Robert had promised her, might lead to that. But she knew nothing else of Robert's plans for her once they arrived at Court.

Her entrance into the audience room at the royal palace at Westminster went at first almost unnoticed. Robert and his two friends were at her side, and the mêlée of clerks, petitioners, and guards who cluttered the main doors meant that they had to push their way through into the principal chamber. In spite of her troubles, Cressida was at once enraptured by the scene. The high vaulted roof was exquisitely carved with every kind of creature and flower, the walls were hung with tapestries as large and long as both houses in River Lane; down the centre of the chamber a wide carpet in deepest blue ran from the door to the two royal thrones. These were mounted on a dais, which was approached by steps carpeted in the same blue. The seats awaiting the royal entourage were placed at different levels. On each side of the room the courtiers waited, in groups or singly, and in a gallery which Cressida could not see a small orchestra broke into a graceful measured dance as the Queen Philippa appeared, accompanied only by her ladies-in-waiting, at the far end of the chamber. As they took their places, Cressida saw with a gasp of delight that among the ladies-in-waiting was Philippa.

It was then that the palace of Westminster became aware that it had a newcomer within its walls. Breaking from Sir Robert and his companions, Cressida began to run forward. Her golden head bobbed up and down in its silver helmet, and a murmur of surprise ran through the room: for the most part the women present were dark-haired, dark-eyed beauties, with heavy curves to their breasts and on their thighs. Here was a slim, long-legged creature darting like sunlight amongst them, with high small breasts and a pale beauty that made them all feel over-dressed and over-painted. She did not know it, but as she ran the length of the palace towards the throne on that September afternoon, Cressida created a new fashion in beauty that was to last half a century. And there was no Queen in Europe who would have stood for it, for the flagrant breach of etiquette by so young and exquisite a creature – except for Philippa of Hainault, whose heart was great and could forgive all things.

As Cressida drew close to the dais, her friend Philippa hastily whispered to the Queen. Then, apparently having obtained leave, she came down the steps to meet Cressida, and held out her hands. Eyes sparkling, the two girls hugged and kissed, while Sir Robert stood at a distance too astounded to take action – and not too anxious to be associated with such an outrageous incident. The other courtiers in the meantime had stood back, the women examining Cressida with undisguised antagonism, and the men with something rather more warm. Both men and women waited, however, for the Queen's reaction before deciding whether to smile or send for the guards that flanked the main doors.

Queen Philippa smiled. The assembly relaxed. All eyes on her, Cressida was led to the dais by her friend, and curtsied with such natural grace that the crowd began to think perhaps she did belong at Court after all. And Robert began to walk the length of the chamber to the throne, where he hovered for an introduction at Cressida's side: an introduction which was not forthcoming.

Looking up into the Queen's face, Cressida saw nothing but kindness and concern. Philippa, her friend, approached her namesake and whispered again.

'This is my dearest friend, Your Grace, and it seems she is in thrall to my brother, who has always pursued her against her will. Now he wishes to present her at Court as his paramour, even his betrothed – I never know with him. And she is therefore separated from her young brother, who has no one. Their father died for the King at Crécy, and their mother died nursing the victims of the Black Plague.'

Cressida stood quietly by while Philippa told her story. The Queen rose when it was finished, and the Court at once fell silent. Cressida waited still, until Philippa gestured that she should approach closer to the dais. She did so, and, kneeling, took the Queen's heavily ringed, plump white hand in hers. It was the hand of a sick woman, she thought, as she bent over it. The Queen raised her to her feet, and spoke so that all could hear.

'We know of our Lady Philippa's brother. He is a brave knight, and has much land. If he were to honour the lady Cressida with his hand in marriage, that would be a solemn matter and one which she should earnestly consider . . . at great length. But her duty is clearly for now with her brother. I know what it is to have lost dear ones in the plague. My own dearest girl. And my husband values the lives that have been laid down for him in France. This young girl who comes before us lost her father thus, and her mother died of plague. We will not see her maltreated. It is clear that her place is with her brother. And if it comes to our notice that brother and sister are molested by – ' she looked meaningfully at Sir Robert across the heads of Cressida and his sister – 'no matter what knight of what wealth or power, then there will be fines, punishment, and banishment from Court. Which would be a great sorrow to us all . . . '

Philippa and Cressida hugged each other at the words. They were both unable to take in the events since Cressida had arrived at the palace, and were almost speechless with the emotion of their reunion and the Queen's words. Cressida was the first to remember that she now owed so much to the Queen, and turned to curtsy deeply. She found that Queen Philippa had sent for a page who stood at the back of the dais, and was holding a small leather purse the page had taken from a tray he carried. As Cressida came to her feet, the Queen held out the purse. 'It is poor compensation for the loss of your father. You must use it well. It will provide a dowry for you, more than enough to please such knights as now keep you company. And now?' She turned to listen to a lady-in-waiting who stood at her side, and as Cressida stood back with Philippa, a supplicant with a boon to ask of the compassionate Queen came forward to the dais.

With Sir Robert's sister arm in arm with her, the royal purse clasped in her other hand, Cressida moved into the crowd of courtiers that flanked the thrones, and together the girls sought out Robert himself in the throng. He waited for them coldly furious, his jaws working like the gills of a fish beneath his rough beard. As Cressida drew near, he gazed into her eyes, and she knew that he was asking her if the night they had spent together made no difference. He pleaded silently, for in the presence of his sister he would show no sign of his desire to persuade Cressida to ignore the Queen's ruling against him.

Sensing his dilemma, and quite unable to take in the fact that she was free to go, Cressida tried to find the words to take her leave of him. 'Sir Robert, I would beg of you to let me go with your sister, and find garments more suitable for my return to my brother. I do not wish to cause you more anger, or more trouble here at Court. Your sister is my friend, and I would not have such scenes as this happen for her every day – '

Robert broke in on her speech. 'Your words are fine indeed for a runaway serf. No' – he raised a warning hand as she tried to speak again – 'have no fear, I'll not claim my rights with you. But your brother, now that's something different. It's a bad thing to lose a strong young serf like the boy. And Her Grace, or her councillors, would no doubt take the whole story very differently when they know that I am owed almost a year's labours. It's a matter for branding, and the purse you now carry might just cover the fines any court would grant to me if I had a proper hearing!'

Cressida held the purse tight. She thought fast. Then she spoke quietly in reply. 'Sir, when you say it is almost a year since my brother and I withdrew our labour from your manor, you speak a solemn truth. A year and day would mean that we had earned our freedom for ever from you. And that time is not far off. By the time you have proved your case, and defied the Queen, and brought her anger down upon yourself, it will be spring again, I should guess, and weeks before then – in the month of January – I shall celebrate the anniversary of the day I took my brother from his yoke, from under your heel! Twenty-four hours after that day dawns, there is nothing you can ever do to us again!' For a moment she thought she had silenced him. But she was wrong.

'So the last twenty-four hours, since you were abroad in the city,' Robert glanced uneasily at his sister as he spoke, afraid of rousing her suspicions that he had dealt as he had with Cressida in his bed, 'those hours mean nothing to you? Your reaction to the way of life I showed to you did not seem to me a bad one. In fact, lady, I would say you relished much of it.'

Cressida felt for the first time since she had lain with Robert in the barge the night before that she could hold up her head. 'I had no choice, sir. It is true I found much to enjoy these last hours. But they are over. Now, if you follow me, or, as Her Grace puts it, "molest" me or my brother, I will not hesitate to send for her guards. I defy you, Robert, to plead with a woman who wants none of you. And it is even weaker in a man to get what he wants by threats.'

Cressida was breathless with emotion as she finished speaking. Tears stung her blue eyes, but they were tears of relief, of happiness. The knowledge that Philippa stood at her side helped her defy Sir Robert, and as she rejected for all time the lure of luxury and the scented, passionate bed she had shared with him, she felt able to return to River

Lane with new heart. It was true that he was a man capable of pursuing her against the Queen's wishes, but she believed that time was on her side. It would soon be winter, and Christmastide. Less than six weeks into the new year she and her brother could walk freely in the streets.

Aware of her strength of purpose, and that she was probably right in her calculation that if he made trouble for her it would take him months to bring her to justice, by which time it would be too late, Robert stood at first in silence. He looked from one girl to the other, and bowing to Cressida he spoke to his sister. His tone was dry, sardonic. 'You may inform your friend, dear sister, that her cloak – which my serving woman had thought to discard – will be sent to you here, at Westminster . . . by special courier, of course.'

Philippa curtsied slightly to her brother, and made no comment. Like Cressida, she had learned that there were times when it was better not to answer, or to react. Then, with a brief, enigmatic glance at Cressida herself, Robert turned on his heel and made off through the glittering crowd. Conscious of the fact that all eyes were upon her, Cressida watched him go, her cheeks flushed in the knowledge that what might seem a small victory to these courtiers was to her a matter of life and death.

Cressida's one fear now was that with all that had happened to her in the previous twenty-four hours she would appear drastically changed to the household in River Lane on her return. More especially, to Stephen. The purse which the Queen had given her clutched in one hand, she took her friend's arm with the other. The small crowd that had gathered, its curiosity at fever pitch, parted as the girls walked to the far end of the hall behind the thrones. Cressida was aware that they stepped back to make way for herself and her companion as if they were people of importance. If her fair head in its sleek helmet could have been held higher, it could not have looked more proud – nor, though she did not know it, more arrestingly beautiful.

Together, once through the crowd, the two girls walked to the arras that concealed the entrance to the ladies' retiring-room where Cressida could no doubt, with Philippa's aid, select a plainer gown in which she could go home. But before they reached the arras, the eyes of the Court of Westminster still upon them, Philippa pinched her friend's arm, and whispered, with one of the gleeful smiles Cressida was to come to know so well: 'If only your brother Francis could see us now!'

8

It was in a dark velvet surcoat over a plain gown borrowed from the royal ladies-in-waiting garde-robe that Cressida left the palace at Westminster an hour later, and after a hurried kiss from the Lady Philippa she found herself lifted bodily on to the saddle of a sturdy black horse, in front of its rider. Her escort, on which Philippa had insisted, was a palace guard momentarily off-duty. He had at once agreed to take her to River Lane, finding it apparently impossible to refuse Philippa's dark eyes and soft beseeching lips. It was still daylight, and he held Cressida steadily in the saddle before him as they cantered up through Strand village, the river on their right and Ludgate and St Paul's ahead.

At the thought of returning so close to the scene of her capture by Sir Robert and his men, Cressida suppressed her inward conflict and sorrow at what had followed, and told herself firmly that whatever happened she would not let her brother fall victim to a similar accident. For all she knew, Sir Robert's men – and the guards from his newly acquired manor house on the river – were everywhere. And now that she had eluded him, it seemed, finally, with the Queen's edict to protect her, she had to allow for the fact that he was doubly bent on dragging Francis back into his employment – and no doubt the punishments would be all the harsher with Sir Robert himself smarting under his humiliation at Court.

Her way was clear now. With no more than four months and a day to keep her brother at large before he was free for ever, she would see to it that they took no risks. She would guard him with her life – and if he dared defy her orders to keep to the house, which she was still sure Sir Robert did not know about, she would not hesitate to make him a prisoner in his room until spring came!

With this resolution firmly implanted in her mind, she began to enjoy the last part of the ride home, looking about her with some interest from the novel viewpoint high above the crowded streets which riding on horseback gave her. It had turned intensely cold since she had left River Lane, and the people of London hurried about their business muffled in warm hoods and many-layered surcoats. Their faces pinched by the cold, and the anxiety the now receding Plague had brought, they seemed a saddened, humourless crowd. Cressida was aware that so far her impression of the city she had longed to reach had been of little but violence and suffering . . . except at the manor house where she had spent her night with Robert, and of course at Westminster itself.

Shuddering at a sudden return of the picture of comfort and luxury against which she had succumbed to Robert, Cressida turned to her escort and asked him to set her down. She wanted to walk the few remaining yards home, to clear her thoughts, and prepare herself. The palace guard remonstrated with her at first, reminding her that the young Lady Philippa had made him promise to see her safely back.

'There is no danger, now,' Cressida insisted. 'I am so nearly there – and perhaps for your own safety, sir, it would be better that you do not know where I live. That is, which house, at least. Then those who would harm me, and my family, cannot include you in their barbarous attacks.'

With a shrug, the man allowed her to convince him, and with his help she slipped lightly to the ground. The black horse was soon lost in the crowd as its rider made back the way they had come, and Cressida drew her dark surcoat close about her against the cold and walked on towards River Lane.

At the top of the Lane, the swirling waters of the Thames visible ahead of her now, and the narrow street waiting for her in the growing dusk, Cressida paused. Her mouth was dry with fear. She found that she was trembling. She knew then that her first meeting with Stephen after her ordeal, and the loss of her honour, was almost too much for her to face. If it had not been for the thought of her brother, and of the Valence family, who must be so anxious for her, she would have turned on her heel and hurried back the way she had come. But she had no such choice. Stephen might have had his misgivings over her disappearance, and would certainly be displeased if he knew the reality of what had happened to her. But she was sure he would have gone about his work as usual, whatever happened. And if her luck were in, she might be able to settle back into the house in his absence and recover her composure before she had to look into his eyes.

But she was wrong. As she stood in the low doorway of the apothecary's shop, silhouetted against the street, she was for a brief moment unnoticed by the group of people who huddled together in conference on the far side of the counter. In the centre of the group, his arm round her brother Francis, was Stephen. White-faced, his expression one of strain and shock, he was talking earnestly to the boy, who leaned on the counter, his face concealed in his hands. At their side, in quiet conference with Master and Mistress Valence, was the boatman John Aske. A sharp intake of her breath announced Cressida's presence to the little group, and as the Valence children ran to greet her she had only two thoughts running through her mind. Had John Aske recognized her as she rode to Westminster in Sir Robert's barge, and if so, had he told the others?

She was aware then of Stephen's haunted gaze upon her as her brother ran to her and flung himself into her arms. Then Stephen followed, slowly, and put his arms around them both.

While Stephen looked down into her face silently, as if seeking the truth of her disappearance, Mistress Valence asked her if she had fallen among the thieves she had warned her were on every corner of the city, and Francis asked her again and again why she had not sent word. Ignoring the questions, both silent and voiced, Cressida made it her business to catch John Aske's eye.

'Why, Master Aske,' she said lightly. 'It is Master Aske, the boatman, is it not?How is your hand? And were they asking you to dredge the waters for me? I hope not. For, as you can well see, I am safe and sound!'

In case the man had not realized it was she he had seen on the river, she did not want to complicate matters by seeming to ask what he knew, however indirectly. She had to content herself with a long look, and was both relieved and puzzled when he made no answering sign, but got up from where he sat and made as if to leave the shop. 'No, it hadn't come to that, my lady. Not yet. But you've saved us a hard task. And you've come home just in time to save much heartache here.' As he reached the outer door, he paused. Then, as if to the room at large, but Cressida could have sworn his manner meant that he intended the words for her ears especially, he added: 'All's well that ends well.'

'Oh, my dear!' Mistress Valence advanced on Cressida then, determined to have her to herself and learn the worst – whatever that might be. 'You are to come with me to my very own room, and to take wine. Some of Master Valence's best.' She looked to her husband as she spoke, and he nodded solemnly. 'Your adventures are to wait – shush, Master Francis! – until I am satisfied in my mind that you are truly safe and sound. Then – we are all to sup together. There has been no table laid today, and the small ones are to go to bed at once. Then we shall see what must be done to those who have kept you from us! Rogues and thieves, rogues and thieves . . . ' She led Cressida away, resisting Francis's cries of protest.

'A moment, Mistress Valence,' Cressida said, her hand on the woman's plump arm, pausing at the rear door to the shop. 'There is one thing I have to say to my brother before another second passes.'

Francis stood expectantly, his eyes round with curiosity. Now she was back in the fold all his anguish seemed to have disappeared swiftly, and Cressida wondered, not for the first time, at her brother's spirit and powers of resilience. It was not going to be easy to give him the orders she had prepared.

She put her hands on each of his shoulders as he stood before her. It was an effort to keep her voice from shaking, and to make what she had to say sound important and yet not frightening. 'Francis. You trust me?' The boy nodded. 'Then you will do as I say? You will not defy me, whatever I have to ask of you? It is important . . . to us all.'

Again Francis nodded, and Cressida spoke then to them all. 'I will tell you more later this night. But the truth is, to be brief, that I was foolish. I walked too far from home, and I brushed with Sir Robert and his men.'

Francis caught his breath, and Stephen took a step towards her. 'There is no reason to fear. He does not know where I am, nor who is with me. The Queen herself has forbade him to . . . to molest me. But – he threatens my brother, more evilly than before. He is determined to hunt him down. And I am as determined that he will fail!' She turned to Francis. 'Our only hope is for you to stay in this house this winter, if Master and Mistress Valence will agree, and on, past Christmastide, into the new year. Until your year and a day has gone by. Do you understand me, brother?'

'We spoke of it when we first fled,' Francis reminded her. 'I know what is at stake, Cressida. But now so much more matters, too. It is you who must trust me! If I were captured and taken back to the manor, to work the land, all I have learnt now would be wasted . . . '

'And you care? You would not lightly throw it away?' Cressida looked proudly at Stephen, and he smiled back at her. 'We owe so much to all our friends here, brother. I would not like them to think we would put our freedom at risk again.'

Francis turned to Stephen, a mock frown on his face. 'If I am to be confined so long, Stephen, there's one thing certain – I'll be a great scholar by the end of winter. You'll have to work hard to keep up with my studies!'

'It is no laughing matter, Francis,' Cressida told him, sharply. Stephen raised a warning hand, as if to show her he did not mind the boy's jest. But she ignored it. 'Whether you work or not, you stay in this house. And if you cannot accept that – then you stay in your room, and I will guard the door! We have not come this far for Sir Robert to win you back . . . '

'Cressida, the boy understands. As we all do. You are both safe here. You are overwrought from your ordeal – ' Stephen crossed the shop to her, but she did not wait for him to reach her side. She began to climb the narrow stairs to the quarters above, and her brother and Stephen watched her go.

'It was no ordeal, friend,' she called over her shoulder, as she gathered her long skirts about her, forcing her voice to remain calm. 'I found I had friends at Court, and I am safe, after all.' The words trailed into silence as she followed Mistress Valence to her room.

Stephen put a hand on Francis's shoulder, and gave it a reassuring grip. 'You spoke well. And now – supper, and sleep. Your sister will tell us, in her own time.'

*

It was not until the house in River Lane was quiet and in darkness, and Cressida stood alone in her room, that she remembered the purse she had received from Queen Philippa. As she undressed, it fell from the deep pocket in her undertunic where she had concealed it. She retrieved it from the floor, and poured its contents on to her bed. As silver and gold coins tumbled haphazardly out on to the woollen coverlet, she gasped. There was more money there than she would have seen in a lifetime, had she stayed in Sir Robert's manor and worked the land. She ran the coins through her hands several times, aware that she hardly knew the value of some of them. A sense of menace gripped her as she wondered what the reaction of the others would be if they knew she had so much wealth at her disposal. Then she remembered the Queen's words . . . that the purse might serve as a dowry. How ironical it was that the man she wanted to marry cared nothing for such things. It was Ralph of Mansey and Sir Robert himself, men hungry for power, who expected their womenfolk to bring the goods of this world as well as themselves to their beds. Whereas Stephen . . . his secret work, and his dedication, seemed to suffice him. If she had not surprised the anguished look on his face when she returned to River Lane she might have continued to believe that these days he had no thought for her.

Deciding to hide the money in her room, and tell no one until real need of it arose, she began to gather the coins back into the purse. As she did so the door swung slowly open, and, startled out of her reverie, she looked up to find Stephen standing there, his eyes fixed in amazement on the gold and silver that glittered in the soft light of the single tallow by her bed. He closed the door firmly behind him, and walked towards her. She stood up, about to ask him what business he had in her room at this hour, but he spoke first, indicating the purse and its contents:

'Am I not to know the truth of your escapade? And will

you not tell me how you won such reward?'

'That is my affair, Stephen. I am surprised that you ask me. What right have you? And since when have you cared?' Her heart beat slowly, steadily. Her first surprise as he entered her room had subsided. She watched him now as he began to pace about, and her eyes held his as he turned and walked towards her. She knew that a moment of truth had come for them, and that somehow from this visit to her room much more would be resolved than the matter of the Queen's purse.

'I am a stranger to you these days, Stephen. We live in the same house, but we are further apart than we have ever been . . . we were closer as children. Since the night at your mother's house, the night I fled with my brother, I have not known a moment's peace about you.'

Stephen looked down at her, his deep grey eyes darker than ever with anguish in his white face. 'My right is plain. It is that I love you, Cressida. That you are my beloved. But until such time as we know what we are to make of our lives – when all danger is past, for you and your brother and for me and those with whom I work – I can only watch over you. From a distance. Maybe much farther off, if my work demands it. But watch over you I shall, whether you ask it or not.'

He had scarcely finished speaking when Cressida went to him. He held her gently at first, and she nestled her head in his shoulder, like a lost child that had been found, and scolded, and embraced. For the first time in all the months since their first kiss there was no tension between them, no suppressed desire. His embrace was all tenderness, and her response in his arms was the innocent fluttering of an injured bird. She was amazed to find that the thought of Sir Robert's violent attacks on her meant nothing now that she was in Stephen's arms. Her body felt as fresh and new to love as it had on the night she had faced Stephen in his mother's house. But the memory of what Robert and she had been to each other, their short-lived, animal passion – in which she herself had in the end participated – made her shudder, and all at once the trembling became uncontrollable. The reaction to her nightmare, which she had staved off in the warmth of her welcome home, had begun. She began to shake violently, and her teeth chattered. Stephen, his lips on her forehead, whispered to her that she was fevered, and must rest. He led her to her bed, and drew back the coverlet. She could not resist as he lowered her gently, and placed her under it. Then, as she lay still trembling he studied her face in the glimmer of the tallow, and took her hand.

Her lips quivered, and she controlled them angrily, determined not to cry. 'Stephen, my love,' was all she could say, as another attack of shivering swept over her. He sat beside her, gripping her hand strongly now.

'You must tell me, Cressida. You are more troubled than I thought. You know, do you not, that you must tell me everything that has happened to you?' She twisted her head from side to side at his words, and the coins scattered from the coverlet to the floor, unnoticed. Then she began to weep, and Stephen, his eyes never leaving her face, let her weep. Once he touched her hair, lifting a rebel strand and letting it fall back into place. The gesture brought a torrent of wilder tears from Cressida, and it was a long time before she was able to speak.

'Have I woken the house? I was so sure I would not cry.'

'It is good to weep, sometimes, little Cressida. And you have a gift for silent tears!' He smiled.

If it had not been for his smile, Cressida might have kept to what her instinct had all along told her would be best, and told Stephen no more than he already knew. But she found herself searching for words, plunging headlong into the story of what had really happened between her and Sir Robert, from the moment his men had snatched her to the morning he had her bedecked for his swaggering arrival at Westminster. She spoke in a low voice, without emotion. She gave only the facts, but once put into words their cold ugliness, the plain hard truths of hideous implication, were all that emerged. What she herself had really undergone and really felt was submerged still. In any case, she knew that those feelings were the only thing she would never – could never – let Stephen know.

When she came to the scene at Court, Stephen raised a hand as if to silence her. Until then he had listened without moving, without comment. He had kept his head bowed, and avoided her eyes. Now he looked straight at her, and it was a regard that pierced her like a knife. But his voice, as he spoke, was dry, frighteningly controlled.

'The rest I know. Are you not safely here, to prove it? And, though this I did not know, have you not become a wealthy woman since you stepped out for your afternoon walk in the great city?'

Neither of them glanced at the coins that now scattered the floor. Cressida waited for Stephen to continue, but he seemed to have no more to say.

'And the rest of my story? Do you have no more to say to me?' Cressida's voice was low with fear of hurting him further rather than with shame. She did feel ashamed, but of something that had after all been outside her control. She had tried as she told the whole story to explain to Stephen how she had been trapped, and once trapped how she dared not put her brother at risk. As soon as her chance of escape had come, she had seized it, and her friend Philippa could have told him how willingly she had fled for home. But his cold manner, and the low, bitter tones in which he began to speak to her, showed that she had failed to convince him.

With his back to her, he rose from the bed. As he walked to the door, he said, 'No, there is no more for me to say. Except that I do not and cannot accept your story. Until the day I die I can never tolerate what has passed between you and Sir Robert. The very man from whom you first fled, and who has it in his power to make your brother's life a misery for the rest of his days! There is no excuse. There can be no forgiveness.' At the door he paused, and turned to look at her. His face was dark with cold anger. Watching him, Cressida could have wished he had less control, and that he had dealt with his pain more violently. She could have coped with that. It might even have broken the tension that had been mounting between them ever since she had stopped weeping. With the realization that he was about to leave her with nothing resolved between them, her head spun. She sat up, and tried to climb from her bed. But her legs were weak, and she was aware that Stephen was speaking to her again.

'It is utterly abhorrent to me . . . You must see that. What I felt for you – what I feel for you – was precious, unstained. All that is lost. If I dwelt on what has passed between you and this man I would go insane.'

He raised the latch, and at once Cressida flew out of bed and across the room. With one move, she stood between him and the door. He stood back, watching her carefully, almost as if he were afraid she would attack him. She looked a half-wild creature as she stood there, her shift falling from her shoulders, her hair in a cloud of gold about her head. But at that moment there was no desire between them, and Cressida almost spat at him as she whispered, fearful that they would now indeed wake the household:

'So – you would leave me with such cruel words? Is that what you really feel for me? Why, it is no more than your own self-pity – that Sir Robert has had from me what you yourself wanted. What hypocrites men are! You condemn me for something outside my control, and yet it is what you would once have had me do. You pretend you are affronted, disgusted – but I have known you at times disgusted by your own lust for me. Yes – do not deny it – there have been times when you wanted none of me, when you wished your full vows had been taken and there could be nothing between us!'

Stephen stood in silence before her onslaught, and in his tall dark figure she saw a momentary glimpse of Brother Oliver. All her anger against the lay brother's hypocrisy and frustration, and his attempt to come between her and Stephen, now welled up in her. 'And what do you know of the world and its ways? How can you tell what forces were brought to bear on me? You spend all your days in your secret, dry as dust closet at your work – with your dry as dust clerks and monks and friars. In my few short months out in the world, Stephen, I have learnt that they too are men – as you are, and as Robert showed himself to be!'

The growing disgust on Stephen's face angered her more than ever, and with the mention of Robert's name her own anger – at all that had happened to create this rift between her and the man she loved – drove her to violence. It was as if it was the only way open to her to communicate with Stephen, and to rid herself of her pain.

There was no more than a yard between herself and Stephen. She flew at him, her hands reaching wildly for his face, her expression that of a wildcat facing its enemy. But Stephen stood his ground, and was too quick for her. Before she could touch him, he had her wrists in his grasp. She had a sensation of extraordinary, unexpected strength. He held her just out of reach, and she knew that her impulse to kick now that her arms were held was absurd. They stood as if locked in position, like some strange and ancient carving. The little room seemed filled with the angry gasps with which Cressida drew breath. Stephen himself breathed calmly, but his eyes did not leave her face.

For the space of a minute, Cressida held her ground. Then she relaxed, and when she spoke it was without anger. Stephen still held her wrists, and kept her at a distance. But at that moment she longed to go into his arms.

'You called me your beloved. Can such things change so easily?'

'You had not told me the truth then,' Stephen answered relentlessly.

Cressida raised her head. 'I knew I should have continued to keep my secret. I knew it would destroy us if you knew.' Her voice was dull, lifeless now. She intoned her words as if she had no hope left, nothing more to lose. 'You have not wanted me near you for months. The life I had thought possible for us here is not what you wanted, I see that now. You are using what has happened to me as an excuse, to bring our love to nothing.'

Stephen dropped her hands suddenly, the first sign of anger since she had sprung at him. 'I see I do not have to go to Oxford to find a master – or should I say mistress – of logic.' His voice frightened her with its coldness now. 'It is you, Cressida, who twist things to your own purpose. And nothing I can say now will divert you from that purpose. A house. Wealth. Marriage. These things are too much, too soon – when only a few weeks ago all you wanted was the freedom of God's air.'

'You are wrong! I have not lost sight of that need for freedom – for my brother, if not for myself.'

'Let me finish. You say I do not have time for you. Well, now I wish for time – to talk with you. But it will be the last time. It is true I have been an ascetic, a celibate. A man of God who might have taken his full vows. The fact that I came to London, to this house, did not mean all that had changed. I came because I was in danger – my work was in danger. I have known for some weeks now that I must settle in London, and that if that were the case the subject of marriage between us had to be settled one way or the other. It would have been a problem which together we would have overcome. Since my arrival I have had no time for anything but work, it is true. We have to press on with our translations as far as we can before we are stopped. It could happen any day. We are in constant touch with the man Wyclif, who is still in Oxford. One day he will lead us, out in the open. But it is too soon. All these things have meant that I had no chance, no inclination even, to discuss the future with you.

'But – little Cressida – ' he half-groaned her name, and

the tears came to her eyes again. 'It is not that I have been unaware of you. If anything my feelings for you have grown deeper. I am a celibate, it is true, but I know what it is to love, for I have loved you. My place was here because of my work, but I stayed willingly because of you. At Christmastide I had planned to talk with you, of the future. Now your – your escapade has made all that impossible. Oh, Cressida, there was even this whole empty house we might have made our own.' His last words were torn from him, almost against his will, and his voice was rent with a grief he had so far concealed from her. She stood back, her arms held out to him. But he ignored the appeal in her eyes. In moments he had opened and closed the door silently, and had gone.

The dawn light breaking over the city hours later found Cressida at the river's edge. Heedless of any threat from the dark streets, she had crept out of the house when Stephen had left her, and taken refuge under the cold stars. Instinctively, she had made for the swirling water of the Thames. She had no thought of self-destruction, but sought comfort in the constant movement of the great river through the city she had so longed to see. She had walked for an hour, meeting no one. A flickering watchman's torch in the distance had sent her scuttling down the bank into the foul-smelling mud as the tide ebbed. There she had crouched, in the shelter of a crumbling wooden jetty, until day broke.

In the course of the night she had decided what she must do. She knew that Stephen loved her. She accepted that what had passed between her and Sir Robert had for ever destroyed her innocence. And the life Stephen himself led meant that nothing was sure.

But there were other things to live for. Her brother's future, in which Stephen himself must still have a role to play; her friendship with the Lady Philippa, who no doubt would spend many months to come in the sanctuary of the Court. And such circles were no longer forbidden to Cressida. The Queen's own edict was her protection, and she was – by reason of the gold and silver she had left scattered on her bedroom floor when Stephen had gone – in her own right a wealthy woman. Well, she would make that wealth work for her. She would see that Francis wanted for nothing while he studied. She would rent the empty house in River Lane from Master Valence, for a sum that no doubt he could not refuse. She would transform it into a setting that was right for her brother and would make a home for him and herself that would for ever erase the boy's memories of the past. The fact that Stephen would be in the same house was almost irrelevant. But not quite.

If Stephen stayed in River Lane, as he had admitted he needed to, he would watch her grow more beautiful. There was much that money could do. And she would show him how well she could run a home. She would entice him with things other than the beauty that she had begun to realize was hers as she stood in the Court of Westminster, all eyes upon her. Her heart beat faster, and a slight flush came to her pale, tear-stained cheeks as she remembered also what she had learnt so recently in Robert's arms. There were indeed many ways of bringing Stephen back to her. Even his despair at what had happened to her when he learnt the truth was proof that he was a man.

Stumbling to her feet, her legs aching in the cold of the morning air after her long vigil, Cressida made her way home. She let herself in, and went straight to her room. Somewhere in the living quarters Mistress Valence called to the children, and the household came slowly to life as Cressida knelt, gathering the gold and silver coins into her skirt. When she had retrieved them all, she returned them to the purse the Queen had given her. Then, from a corner of the heavy armoire that was the main piece of furniture in her room, she took a worn leather box. In it she placed the purse, but before she returned the box to its hiding place she took from it the only other treasure it contained, and held it to the grey light at her low window. It was the button she had stolen from Stephen's scholar's tunic, and it seemed to her now that she had teased him about it an eternity ago. With a sigh, she replaced it in its hiding place. And returning the box to the armoire, she went in search of water, to wash all trace of the night's grieving from her face.

9

As the icy fingers of the winter that followed began to sculpt the usual quagmire of the city's streets into a frosted semblance of order, and the plague receded in the sparkling, cleansing air, Master Valence found that his previously hectic days in the apothecary's shop began to ease, and he was more able to manage without Cressida than he had anticipated. He had willingly given her the lease of the empty rooms for which she asked on the day after the disastrous scene between herself and Stephen, although the section of the wing of the house where Stephen himself slept was, as the apothecary expressed it, 'reserved'. He also granted her the sole use of the second front door, next to the shop's entrance, that gave on to River Lane, and as he handed her the heavy key, rusted and gnarled with age and disuse, he wished her joy in her task of running a home for herself and her brother.

Some weeks later, a brilliantly sunny December morning found Cressida as usual at her new duties very early, and she was startled by the sound of a knock on the door in the street below. She paused and listened. She had no wish to answer, and her breath came faster as she wondered nervously who the caller could be. But within moments the knocking was resumed, and sounded imperiously through the half-empty house. Reluctant to leave Master Valence to see who her visitor was, Cressida had no choice but to make sure that the door to Francis's room, where he was already engrossed in his studies so that he might take full advantage of the short-lived light of day, was firmly closed, and to hurry downstairs.

Standing in the narrow street, one fur-trimmed wrist poised delicately as she held her skirts from the ground, was Philippa. Over her other arm was neatly folded Cressida's beloved cloak.

Philippa's dark eyes shone mischievously. Her cheeks glowed with a most uncourtly, healthy radiance in the cold. She dipped a curtsy to her friend. 'Master Apothecary informs me that you now possess your own front door, my lady! May I humbly request permission to be the first this morning to cross the threshold?'

'Philippa!' Cressida gasped, torn between joy at seeing her, and fear that they were watched, perhaps from the houses on the other side of the street. 'Quickly, quickly, come in. Are you alone? Did you come here all the way from Westminster on foot?'

The two girls embraced warmly in the small hallway at the foot of the stairs. 'Cressida, you are not to worry. Of course I came alone. And I made sure I was not followed. I used a side door to leave the palace, and was out before the men-at-arms had even changed the morning watch. I am quite aware that Robert only kept his word to bring your cloak to me in the hope that he could have his men spy on me when I came to return it. But they are a weary lot at Richmond these winter days, and their easy life there leaves them far too bleary-eyed in the mornings to be up in time to catch me when I decide to go abroad!'

'I should have known you were too clever for – for Robert.' Cressida embraced Philippa again as she placed the cloak in her hands. She made herself repeat the name of the man who had so recently wrecked her life, and who still threatened her brother, and stiffened inwardly as she realized it was the first time she had said it aloud since the night she had returned to River Lane from his bed.

Philippa regarded her affectionately as she clasped the

cloak to her, as if seeking comfort from its well-remembered roughness and the folds of the warm wool. 'They say old clothes are best. I swear you will wear that cloak until it crumbles into dust! But you're not in old clothes now, I see.'

She examined Cressida's outfit admiringly. As she ran downstairs, Cressida had hastily unpinned the plain apron she used as she worked, and under it she wore a deep blue woollen tunic over a skirt of paler blue embroidered with small golden flowers and delicate leaves, also in gold. Low on her hips was slung a silken belt, and beneath the hem of her skirt there was a glimpse of small feet clad in soft blue leather house shoes.

'And you have excellent taste!'

'The city is a good place in which to learn what is good as well as what is fashionable,' Cressida told her. 'The merchants' wives want value for money, and I find that the river brings all I could wish for, right into the heart of the district.'

'You are right,' Philippa sighed. 'And by the time the merchants themselves bring their goods down to Westminster they cost double what I daresay you pay. The city really has got the Court by the throat in all things, you know.' As they chatted, Cressida led Philippa up the dark oaken staircase, and they stood briefly in the passage above, their eyes growing accustomed to the dim light that came from the open door of the main living-room.

'Now,' Cressida announced, 'you are the first to see our new home. Where shall we start?'

'Why, with your brother, of course! He is here with you, is he not? How I miss his high spirits, and how often I have wondered if he has been able to continue with his studies!' Philippa's eyes shone as she mentioned Francis, and, more than somewhat surprised at the girl's interest after such a lapse of time, Cressida said nothing. Placing a finger on her lips, she made for the closed door at the far end of the passage, and slowly opened it. Philippa waited silently in the frame of the doorway while Cressida stepped into her brother's room. At first the young, blond head bent over the manuscript on a small table beneath the window did not move. Then Philippa, unable to contain herself another second, suddenly laughed. And Francis, turning sharply as he realized it was not Cressida's voice, gave a cry of recognition, and almost knocked over his chair as he bounded across the room to greet the new arrival.

Watching them together, Cressida realized that in the few weeks since he had been confined to the house Francis had grown even taller. He was now the same height as Philippa, and as she studied the young fair head close to the girl's burnished crown of hair, revealed as the hood of her cloak fell back to her shoulders, Cressida realized also that these two people, both so close to her, and so important, were fast leaving their childhood behind. With a pang, she remembered that she had forgotten her brother's birthday in the traumatic days of the late summer, and that he was now in his thirteenth year – less than two years younger, in fact, than Sir Robert's sister. She forced herself back to the reality of the moment, and tried to take in what Francis and Philippa had to say to each other. To her amazement, Philippa was speaking in the clipped, elegant French used at Court – and to her even greater astonishment, Francis answered in a few quite fluent phrases. But aware of Cressida's scrutiny, he broke off abruptly, exclaiming: 'But you must not encourage us, sister! We have not come so far to talk with the tongues of our conquerors. By the time you yourself have a place at Court, no doubt Stephen will have seen to it that they talk English there.'

Cressida's fair face grew dark at the thought of Stephen. But her pride in Francis and his display of newly acquired knowledge made her smile. 'You are right, little brother. But I do not seek a place at Westminster. I have come to love the city, and I have my own small palace here within it. Now – you must work. Philippa, you must let me be your guide through the Court of River Lane!'

Francis turned obediently enough back to his desk, and Philippa watched him sympathetically. She glanced round the room as he took his seat under the window. It was furnished very plainly, with a narrow bed over which was slung a heavy fur coverlet, and the table and stool where Francis worked. Cressida seemed to guess her thoughts.

'There are no trimmings – and no lights. At night we sit together in the living-room, at the back of the house. I have to be sure that there is no sign that this room is inhabited, and if ever the house were searched the intruders would be hard put to it to detect who lives in it.'

Philippa turned to Francis. 'It will not be long before Christmastide, Francis. Not much more of this strange secret life for you before you can count the days before you walk out of this house and into London – a free man! How we shall celebrate.' She laughed, her spirits as always irrepressible however solemn the moment. 'How angry my brother will be!'

Cressida gave a warning glance towards where Francis sat, his attention still drawn from his work as Philippa spoke. 'We must be patient still, Philippa. Francis understands. If we set our hearts on such celebrations, we will become careless. We are not yet through our ordeal.'

Francis nodded, and Philippa listened earnestly as he told her: 'Nor would it be fair to the others, if we grew careless. There must be no word of my existence here. No betrayal of theirs.'

'The others?' Philippa asked, surprised. She looked from brother to sister. Cressida blushed with vexation, but it was too late.

'We can trust her, Cressida, I'm sure of it.' Francis pushed his work away impatiently, and crossed the room again to where the girls stood. 'Did you think I knew nothing of those others who also hide here? And who work with Stephen here, by night?'

Cressida bit her lip. She had not intended that Stephen's name should be introduced into the conversation. It was a name she whispered only to herself these days, in the privacy of her room when her day's work was over. 'Francis, you forget yourself.' She tried to speak lightly. 'Do you think that your secrets will earn you a respite from your studies? Our visitor is no excuse for a holiday.' She suppressed a sigh of relief as the boy smiled, and nodded goodbye to Philippa, walking back to the table with a philosophical shrug of his slim young shoulders. The sight of his vulnerable boy's head bent once more over his book in the poor light tugged briefly at her heart, but she gave an approving smile, and gestured to Philippa to follow her. As they left the room, Cressida softly closing the door behind her, they did not see that Francis had once more raised his head from his studies and was gazing thoughtfully out into the grey winter's day through the window.

The corridor which linked all of the rooms that now were rented by Cressida was carpeted with a long, soft rug, which Philippa paused to admire. Cressida explained that she had first seen it in the city streets, slung over the shoulder of a swarthy carpet seller who offered his wares from a stall in the market at Cheapside. She had at once admired its dark, subtle colouring and the intricate formality of its design, and with the Queen's purse tucked securely inside her surcoat, where she always carried it, she had been able to embark on a thoroughly enjoyable session of bargaining. Eyes narrowed as he described the priceless item, hands weaving the air as if he himself had woven it into being, the dealer had enjoyed the occasion as much as she had herself, and had been so impressed with her skill as a buyer that he had suddenly capitulated and thrust the beautiful, silken carpet into her arms just as she thought she was on the verge of defeat.

On the wall of the passage hung a tapestry of a hunting scene which, Cressida told Philippa, had stopped her in her tracks when she had noticed it under the awning of a merchant's shop in Ludgate. The close tangle of the trees in a winter landscape, the dark figures of the huntsmen, the furrows of the fields they had crossed on their run into the kill, all spoke to her of home. She had carried it back to River Lane blissfully unaware that she had paid for it a sum that in the old days would have kept the entire family for many of the winters it portrayed. And though she considered when she hung it that evening on the wall of her new home that a year before she had never dreamed such things would be hers, she did not care in her heart what she had paid for this reminder of the depths of the English countryside where she had been born. But she had no need to explain to Philippa: the girl stood quietly studying the tapestry for some minutes before she asked:

'Tell me, Cressida. Do you think you will ever settle here? Become a citizen of London?'

Cressida stood beside her, her eyes also on the dark trees in the embroidered forest. 'My place is with the people I belong to, and who belong to me. It matters not where we are. Others have made the great change, from forests to the city streets. And they have done well. Master Valence tells me that our own Lord Mayor of London walked a hundred miles or more, as a boy, to become an apprentice, and is now the richest man in the city – '

Philippa interrupted: 'But I do not mean riches, or fame, Cressida, when I talk of citizenship. If I were free to choose, I would settle for a good solid daily round, of work, a house to run, friends to call in at the end of the day, children whom I would want to see grow up like little flowers in the forest of the city.'

'If flowers do grow in that murrain of a forest outside this house I'll think about the rest of the idea, but as for you – you are too young to plan. Come, have you all the morning to spend with us? Can you sit with me at our table?' Cressida took her arm.

The great sturdy oaken table which Cressida had ordered from a local carpenter for the living-room was her pride and joy. It was flanked by a high-backed settle in whose seat she kept her ever-increasing collection of fine linen. She had bought it because it had reminded her of a settle she had seen on her night in the castle of Ralph of Mansey, the night on which she and Philippa had fled to the Franciscans. But in the agony of her discovery of what had happened to Dominic, the *agent provocateur*, she had been unaware of her impressive surroundings except as an added spur to her anger and distress. It was many weeks before she realized she had bought the piece of furniture almost out of revenge, as an avowel that she too could purchase such things as the devils who had killed Dominic lived with every day of their lives. Somewhere in her heart there lurked perhaps the need to avenge the rebel spirit who had befriended her in her first hours of flight.

Unaware of all that passed through Cressida's mind as she sat opposite her at the great table, Philippa brought the conversation back to the subject of her own future.

'I am not too young, though you may think it, to plan my life.' She cupped her chin wistfully in her slim hands. 'My brother thought not. And Sir Ralph agrees with him still.'

'You may meet a nobler lord than Ralph of Mansey if you stay much longer at Court. There are princes there, after all.'

Philippa laughed her mischievous child's laugh. 'After Ralph I do not think I could ever seriously consider the nobility. I shall always doubt their reasons for wanting me. My brother's land, or my jewels, or the need for an heir to their own little domains – there are so many reasons such men ask for my hand. I would, for my part, find a man who loved me. Who loved me for myself!'

Cressida found herself unable to answer. This young

girl who had become her friend, who had suffered so much less than she, knew more of truth than Cressida herself. Her words echoed in Cressida's head – a man who loved me.

'Of course,' Philippa rattled on, oblivious of Cressida's distracted air. 'Her Grace is gracious enough to pretend to my brother that she awaits a suitable offer for my hand – and I do not think she will hurry me. No' – she looked about her – 'I would like to do as you have, Cressida. You have done well. The house is warm and safe. You have spent your money wisely.'

'It is not all spent.' Cressida spoke almost to herself. 'There is one more room to furnish properly. My own room.'

'And I daresay you will spend on the Christmastide festivities!' Philippa's eyes sparkled at the thought. 'Your brother is fortunate, Cressida. And I believe he loves you well. He will be a fine man one day and you will be repaid a hundredfold for your courage in seeking his freedom. You'll see. Now, let me tell you the latest scandal at Westminster, of a knight who has broken his word to his lady and still wears her favour, though she forbids it!'

The romantic tale which Philippa went on to narrate echoed much of the poetry from the French which Cressida had recently come to know through Francis, who read aloud to her and translated into English in the long evenings they spent together. When her guest had gone, Cressida smiled grimly to herself at the thought of how the decorative scandals of Court life contrasted with her own relationship with the man she loved. Life with Stephen had become a routine of silence, of lowered eyes, and of hands that did not touch. Since the night he had come to her room and she had all but attacked him he had made sure they were never left alone together. If he came to the living-room in the evenings, it was with the excuse on his lips that he wished merely to check on his pupil's progress. Refusing her offers of refreshment, he would sit stiffly at Francis's side on the high settle, his tonsured head bowed earnestly over a manuscript he had brought for the boy to read.

The sight of his strong, slim hands holding the parchment, his dark curls, and the finely-shaped beard outlining his jaw, all roused in Cressida as she watched him covertly a mood of bitter resentment – of herself, of Stephen and his hardened heart, and above all of the part Sir Robert had played in their destruction. But she stifled the feeling as best she could, and held her peace. From the wreckage of their love, she told herself on such nights, she had already salvaged the scene before her: a room that was her own domain, her brother safely within it, and Stephen, his tutor, still at his side.

The pain and anger of their last encounter was a chasm that neither of them was able, in fact, to cross. Their mutual pride, their natural disgust at what Robert had done to Cressida, and her own anger at Stephen's refusal to forgive, all contributed to the impasse to which they had come. And Cressida was woman enough to sense that even if they made some false gesture of reconciliation, the unforgivable things she had said – and the bigoted attitude Stephen had assumed – would not simply fade with the passing of time. It would take more than a few months, or even years, before the insults ceased to come smarting back at them, whatever she did to salve them. For the moment, she had to learn to live with them as with a roomful of shadows, and she also had to face what truth there had been in the torrent of words that had at last burst between her and Stephen on the night of her return from Sir Robert.

But as she watched the man who sat with her brother, she hoped in her heart that she had already taken the first, subtle steps towards winning him back, however long it might take. In her very silence as he sat with them she voiced her need of him, and her soft glance expressed her patience. Whatever the apparent reasons for his presence, she did not discourage them by a look or a word. Their only hope of reconciliation was in the fact that he still came. And she did not know it, but the new poise she had acquired with such knowledge, the added beauty of the sorrow in her face, had not escaped the notice of her brother's tutor.

The evenings when Stephen did not appear, however, became more frequent – and they coincided with greatly increased activity in the nocturnal life in the further wing of the house reserved for him and his callers. Muffled footsteps on the stair, shadows in the street outside as men came and went without lights, whispered voices in rooms that were empty by day, told Cressida that the men with whom Stephen worked in secret were becoming more numerous than ever. She was glad that the diversion of Christmas, which she was determined to make as enjoyable as possible for Francis in his enforced imprisonment, gave her something else to think about.

As Advent approached its climax and the city streets filled with stalls and lurching carts and countrymen selling everything from good cured pork to the Smithfield butchers to wizened apples to the housewives who passed by, the household in River Lane became frantic with its own preparations. Although they lived separately, Cressida and Mistress Valence shared the kitchen in an amicable fashion, and for the festivities they joined forces and shared the costs. While a stout capon strutted the yard behind the shop waiting for the voice of doom, and a brace of Valence babies tumbled at her feet, Cressida found herself happily chopping and mixing and baking, a tough canvas apron round her plainest skirt, her hands warmly pink with the first real work she felt she had done for months. Recipes from her childhood at her mother's side came back to her. The kitchen swirled with smoke, and the air swam with the aroma of herbs and sauces and preserves.

It was there, two days before Christmas Eve, as daylight crept into the room, that Stephen came upon Cressida unexpectedly, and they found themselves without warning completely alone. Cressida had come down to start her last batch of baking early, and there was no one else about in the Valence family's quarters. The cat and her kittens mewed from their niche by the stove as Stephen came in. Cressida, sensing his eyes upon her, continued with her work. Her heart beat painfully fast. Determined not to be the first to break their long silence, she waited for him to speak.

She was not disappointed. His voice was low, and slightly hesitant, but he spoke civilly to her. 'Is Mistress Valence not about? I am too early, no doubt. And usually – '

Cressida was unable to let him stumble on alone without some word from her. Her presence in the kitchen had obviously surprised him, and his usually stern face betrayed his embarrassment. 'Mistress Valence has perhaps left nothing ready for your breakfast, Stephen, because we – she was under the impression that you were away from home. We did not see you last night, nor hear your return.'

'It is true. I have only just returned. There is a crisis. . . ' His voice trailed away, and he turned as if to leave the kitchen with no more said between them. But Cressida sensed that in this moment was her chance to re-establish contact between them. She wiped her hands on her apron, and drew a stool from the hearth to the scrubbed white table on which she worked. 'Then you must eat. I will prepare something. Come.' She did not look him in the face as she spoke, but she felt his eyes upon her.

She turned to raise the heavy lid of the food chest where she knew Mistress Valence kept her bread, and was relieved that Stephen took the opportunity to cross the room and sit at the table as she had asked. They were silent again as she cut the slices of bread and covered each with a layer of cold meat. Placing them before Stephen, she went in search of ale in the stone larder by the door that led from the kitchen into the yard. The cat mewed happily, stretching itself, and followed her. She opened the door to let it out, and a flurry of snow blew into the room, making her give a small cry of surprise. Stephen raised his head at the sound, and as she turned back to him they found themselves looking deep into each other's eyes.

Stephen smiled ruefully. 'A wife – or mother – would ask where I had been, little Cressida. But you are neither.'

'I am not your keeper, Stephen. I know that what you do is secret.' She looked round for some task with which she could continue, rather than have to decide whether he would fall silent again if she were to sit with him. To her relief, he seemed to need to talk, and went on as she resumed the mixing she had left on his arrival.

'My colleagues from Oxford have gathered here, by night, in the city. They are scattered at many secret addresses.'

'And some of them are here, are they not, Stephen?'

He nodded. 'We are discredited, and in danger. The penalty for heresy is still death. And rather than bring down the wrath of the establishment on our innocent friends at Oxford we have decided to break all links with the University – at least for the present. Our plan is to work here in London, where we can go unnoticed. We are to continue with our translation of the Bible into the people's tongue – but we intend to write many things. Original work, sermons, tracts. Then, when the crisis has died down, and we are least expected to return to the attack, we shall come into the open again, in more force. We believe that we shall be missed, but we know we need to be stronger. We are going to use this time of hiding to work. Then, with our task much closer to completion, our case properly stated, we believe the people – many more than now – will find the courage to flock to our side.'

Cressida trembled as he spoke. She forced herself to conceal her delight that he was talking to her again, and of the things she knew to be closest to his heart. 'The plan sounds worthy. You will have to leave Oxford, though.

And I know the life there has meant so much to you.'

Stephen stood. He seemed to have guessed the rest of her thoughts. 'More than that, Cressida. If I do not return to Oxford, then this house becomes my only home. It means that I shall live here as the guest of Master Valence and his good wife for much longer than I had originally planned. And it means that, whatever has gone before, you and I must live here, in the same house, in peace. Do you think that possible?' His voice was terse now, and his tone discouraged her from speaking in any detail of the rift between them.

'We are not made to quarrel with each other, Stephen,' she said in a gentle voice. She did not detect the slight smile that crept to Stephen's lips at her words. For all he had suffered since the disaster of her escapade at Sir Robert's hands he had not forgotten the image of the firebrand of a girl he had found in his mother's house almost a year ago. If any woman was made to quarrel, it was this fair-haired creature, her apron askew, her face flushed with the warmth of the kitchen, who stood before him.

'But I will not ask of you the embarrassment of sharing the Christmastide celebrations with me,' he replied. 'You are right – we will not quarrel. But if I ride fast, and can find a good horse to carry me, I should get to my mother in two or three days, and return here for Epiphany. The roads are neglected since the Death, and I think that is the first snow we saw just now, but I should get through without mishap if I start soon.'

At the thought of the road he would take, and of the last time she was in her mother's house, Cressida felt the tears start to her eyes. Fiercely, she blinked them back. She nodded. 'Yes, you should be with Matilda at this time. You will give her my love, and wish her well? You will tell her that we are safe, Francis and I? It is thanks to her that we survived – and to you, Stephen.'

The way in which she controlled her emotion brought a look of admiration into Stephen's eyes. Cressida was unaware of the shining beauty of her face and her golden hair in the light from the fire in the hearth. Her slim body in the rough apron tightly wrapped round her plain gown had the strong, supple look of the peasant girl she had once been. 'I will tell her. But that is all I shall say. You understand?'

Again Cressida nodded, but her lips quivered. She knew her capture by Sir Robert and what had followed could never be made acceptable to Stephen, but she guessed that in her wisdom his mother would have understood. She knew more of the threat to women in serfdom than her son. She had seen that life could offer even worse than the things that had happened to Cressida. But Stephen seemed to want to deny her the chance of his mother's understanding, and the knowledge cut into her heart like a knife.

'Tell her that the children of Margaret are well,' she told him, and her voice was calm.

'I must go. There is no time to wake Francis, but tell him nothing of what I have told you. He is to know only that I have gone home for the sacred festival – it is the right thing to do.' Stephen turned towards the door that led to the hallway of the Valences' house. Bitterly, Cressida reflected that he did indeed always know what was right – but he had no farewell for her. In the doorway he paused. 'And tell him that a month from now we can go to the scribe's house together, and he can spend some of his well-earned money on parchments – a freeman.'

'His money?' Cressida, astonished by this first sign that her brother had money in his possession, echoed the words almost stupidly. The significance of the fact had still to dawn on her. If Francis had money and had not told her, he must have some reason for concealment. And if he had money and was spending it, then where and how did he do so? 'I did not know he had money!'

'We scholars have to live, you know. The Church pays very well to some, and modestly to others – but it does pay. And Francis has already earnt his keep at Oxford; so the fact that I do not have to maintain him now means that he receives payment instead.'

'But Stephen, how could you? Do you not realize the temptation it must be to him, to be a prisoner when he has the means to go out into the city? And why was I not told?' Her voice rose as she became increasingly incensed at what she now saw to be a deliberate attempt to deceive her. At once Stephen's eyes turned cold.

'He is not the child you think. And we did not intend to deceive you. But as you yourself remarked – you are not our keeper. You must realize the boy will soon have a life of his own. For all I know he plans to surprise you with his savings. Can you not try, for once in your short life, to see that you are not in charge of our destinies? That we do have wishes of our own?'

'And as you yourself remarked – we are to try to live in peace! Does that mean we have to do as *you* say, and nothing more?' Cressida's eyes blazed, but her anger was wasted. Her words floated on the warm air of the room as the door to the street outside opened and closed again, and Stephen left her. In exasperation, she reached for a large wooden bowl in which she had left a half-finished dough mix to stand, and seizing it in both pink hands she lifted it out on to the table and began to knead it mercilessly.

An hour later, as the household in River Lane began to come to life, she remembered that she had not climbed to her own rooms to waken her brother. Her anger with Stephen abated by her frenzied activity in the kitchen, she hung her apron in the corner, and climbed the stairs. The passage was silent, and calm. The tapestry glowed darkly in the shadows. Softly, Cressida opened the door of Francis's room. And one glance at his deserted desk, the narrow, unruffled bed, told her that he had gone.

Shivering in the grey light of the early morning as he walked quickly along the river bank not five minutes from where his sister stood and gazed helplessly at his empty room, Francis looked from left to right every yard of the rough path, making sure he was unobserved. Although there were signs of activity on the city wharves that lay ahead, he could see no other lone walkers like himself. The snow had kept everyone indoors, he decided, and pulling the inadequate collar of his scholar's tunic closer to his neck, he hurried on. If he reached the markets before the crowds began to form for their day's shopping, he might make his purchases at leisure. The money he had received since he left Oxford jingled happily in the purse concealed at his waist. He was certain there was enough in it to buy the presents he wanted to give Cressida, and the Valence children – and perhaps Philippa. At the thought of his new friend, her mischievous ways, and the life she must lead at Court, he paused and looked back again to see if the great palace of Westminster itself were visible from where he stood. But the fall of snow clouded the air, and the horizon of the town that sprawled on the banks upriver was a blur.

Once he had reached the wharves just south of St Paul's, Francis calculated from all he had heard of Cressida's shopping expeditions, he must leave the river and walk north to the markets. There were more people about now, and he became anxious that he should not be challenged. His fair hair had already attracted notice. A well-dressed, elderly stranger was eyeing him with more than polite curiosity. He put up his hand to hide his face, and turned quickly away, so that he did not see the man smile and shrug. But the look had been one that had been directed at him more than once by some of his older colleagues at Oxford, and as he remembered this he blushed, but thought all the same that if that were the only interest he was likely to arouse then he was sure to reach River Lane in safety. There were worse things to be feared than well-dressed effeminates on their way home – and in the days of his early childhood in the country, when he knew nothing of such things, he had braved a wild pig in a covert or leapt into a racing stream after a fish with no thought of danger. But that was before his father and mother had gone, and at the thought of those days he squared his thin shoulders and marched boldly up to the next stall, on which a plump woman, her face hardly visible beneath the layers of hoods and coifs with which she fended off the cold air, was hanging out a display of baubles. She glared at Francis from beneath her headdress when he stood examining a tray of purses, and, momentarily reminded of the wild pig in the covert, he began to bargain with her in his high boyish voice.

It took him no more than five minutes to select a blue purse for Cressida, and a red for Philippa, but in those five minutes his voice had aroused the notice of a tall leather-clad figure who had been examining the wares at the adjacent stall. As he paid for the gifts and looked round for a merchant who might have sugar plums for the Valence children he found himself gazing into the piercing blue eyes of John Aske, the waterman. A heavy hand on his shoulder, clamped immovably on his tunic, told him at the same time that there was no sense in trying to run.

'I tell you, boy – Francis is it, I think – that this is the end of your shopping for today.' The blue eyes twinkled, but the face was aloof and unbending.

'But – '

'Your sister would permit no "buts". Have you learnt no lesson from her? Do you not realize this city waits for the likes of you? It's not only Sir Robert – oh yes, I know it all,' John Aske brushed Francis's attempt to interrupt him aside, 'it's the rogues who would find it very helpful to sell a young runaway back to his master, or to the highest bidder. And before any of those rogues catch up with us, we're for the river, and the apothecary's shop.'

There was no remonstrating with John Aske, and the waterman's huge strides back down towards the wharves made Francis gasp for breath as he ran at his side. Within ten minutes of their meeting, they were stepping into a light vessel, and at John's bidding Francis almost fell into concealment under a pile of skins which served as rough shelter if rain fell when the waterman was in midstream. Almost stifled by the stench of the uncured hides, his heart racing, Francis crouched obediently in the boat, listening to the heavy swish of the paddle in the broken rhythm which the watermen used. As they moved at speed back upstream to where they could beach at the foot of River Lane, John Aske began to talk.

He told Francis that he was a brave rebel lad, and good material. There were men who could use him, when the time came. Friends of his. The men of Kent, in the orchard lands beyond London to the east. One day, maybe not until Francis was a grown man, or had young rebel children of his own, the men of Kent would lead the people against their feudal lords. They would break the power of the Church, of the hypocrites who grew fat by its laws, and they would call on the King to lead them. But until that day, Francis should take care to stay alive, to stick to his books, and to obey his betters.

Shivering with the damp and the cold, still breathless from his adventure, the boy clutched the gifts he had bought for his sister and for Philippa close to him. He listened avidly to John Aske's sermon. How strange it was that wherever he and his sister went they came upon people who thought as she did. It seemed that rebellion was everywhere – but still no more than a secret wish in the hearts of the poor. As the boat grounded heavily against shingle and mud, John Aske's voice made him stay exactly where he was, and on no account to move. Sir Robert's men were standing guard at the corner of the street above them on the river bank. Now he would learn at last what it meant to be a rebel.

'If you move,' John Aske growled softly, and it sounded as if he spoke between closed teeth so that he would not appear to be talking to anyone, 'if you move,' he repeated, 'I can promise you that in two days' hard riding from now you will be back scratching the cold earth of your father's land, a whip at your shoulders, and the brand of a runaway on your brow. I am going to leave the boat here, and warn them at the house – if I can. Your Sir Robert's men will conclude if I leave the boat that I am alone. Or so I hope. But of course I cannot promise. While you wait – and it may be many long moments before I return – you will have plenty of time to remember my words.'

The receding sound of the waterman's boots as he climbed to the bank, the murmur of gruff voices in an accent he knew came from his own village, the lapping of the water against the side of the boat were all that Francis had for company in the hour that followed. He dared not move, and his limbs slowly became frozen into the crouched angles at which he lay. He breathed with increasing difficulty. The pulse at his temple throbbed as he strained to hear what his enemies were saying. But he could catch none of it, and at last, after what seemed an eternity, the countrymen's voices faded, their arms clanking rhythmically as they marched heavily away. Moments later he heard the sound of horses moving off, then silence.

'Now it is,' he told himself, clenching his teeth to stop the chattering that the fevered moment had induced, 'that whatever I do *I must not move*.'

And to pass the time that followed before John Aske came for him again, he went over in his mind all that he had learnt from the waterman of the men of Kent, pausing only once or twice to remember with regret that he had gone to all the trouble of risking his freedom in the streets of the city, and had seen nothing of note – nor brought home sugar plums for the children of River Lane.

10

The flood of relief which swept over Cressida when she knew that Francis was safe did nothing to assuage the anger she vented on him when he returned. Fear for his life, terror that all she had done so far to work for his freedom could have been wasted, had churned her emotions into a whirlpool by the time the boy staggered into the house with John Aske's arm about his shoulder. Glaring coldly from one to the other, she told Francis to go to his room and wait for her there. And he would have no food for the rest of that day, she added as an afterthought as she watched him clamber painfully up the narrow stairs to their quarters. Head down as if to fend off her wrath, the boy muttered something she did not at first catch. She asked him, sharply, to repeat his words in a voice that became a scholar – one they could hear in the church, if that is they ever went to church again.

'I asked, sister, if you would wish to see the Christmas gift I went to buy for you. And the same for your friend, Lady Philippa.' He turned and looked down at her. 'It is your favourite colour.'

His frank eyes, and the audacious tilt to his chin as he spoke, defied her to scold him further. With a small choking cry Cressida rushed to where he stood, and held out her arms as she ran. Moments later, brother and sister sat on the stairs together, both in tears, like two children who have survived a family squall and are forgiven. Cressida clutched the purse in one hand, and ruffled her brother's hair with the other.

'You have the stench of the river about you.'

'It is the stink of the raw hides under which I hid. We must be thankful John Aske had them in his boat.'

'There is much we have to thank the waterman for,'

Cressida said, thoughtfully.

'He thinks as we do, Cressida. I believe him to be a friend of Stephen, too.'

'No doubt,' his sister said quickly. 'But you are not to speak of these things. Now – you have done enough harm for one day to the peace of the household. Off with you to your room – '

The boy sighed. 'There is one thing I would ask of you.' Cressida eyed him quizzically. 'I would like to tell Stephen of this myself. I would not have him hear a report of me, as if I had been a runaway pupil. And he would have been so angered had I been caught by Sir Robert's men.'

Cressida caught her breath. Did Francis know anything of Stephen's real reasons for hating Sir Robert? 'There is no need for the incident to be mentioned between us, Francis.' She was glad now that Stephen was on his way to his mother's house. She had no wish for the subject of Sir Robert to be mentioned again. 'Even if he should have told me you were receiving money for your studies, I would rather not anger him with this story.'

'Oh, I shall tell him. But I shall choose my moment. Ishall tell him all I heard from John Aske too. It will be more a tale of adventure when I come to describe it. And I shall tell him how I was sent to bed without victuals, by my unfeeling sister!'

Unable to sustain her anger, Cressida pulled his hair and sent him scampering to his room, his mischievous laugh echoing through the house.

She turned then, to thank John Aske for all he had done. 'We are much in your debt,' she murmured. Still she did not know how much this kindly, mysterious man knew of her own recent adventures at Sir Robert's hands.

'There are no debts between us common people,' he replied. His accent, that of the man born in the great city, harsher than the soft country voices with which Cressida had been surrounded all her life, was still unfamiliar to her ears. She found it hard to decide whether it masked his good heart on purpose, or whether his words sprang from fierce belief, and hidden violence. 'And if there were, one day they will all be forgotten. You'll see.'

Still pondering his words as she returned to her work in the kitchen, she reflected that she would do well also to have forgotten the matter by the time Stephen returned. It would not do to give range to the anger she still felt at the deceit he had used on her with regard to her brother's money. Yet, at the thought of what he had done with that money, she could not resist an impulse to smile.

It was Stephen himself who introduced the subject, some nights later. He had returned from spending the festival quietly with Matilda, and had moved all his belongings from Oxford into the rooms beyond Cressida's own. It was the first evening he had spent in the house for some time. He sat at Francis's side at the big table in the living-room. Between them lay a manuscript, which Francis deciphered slowly, instructed by Stephen. As the boy's voice ran monotonously on, Stephen looked across the room to where Cressida sat.

In the light of the tallow candles her pale beauty had a golden calm to it that made him swallow to hide the sudden emotion that engulfed him. Aware of his gaze, Cressida did not look up from her embroidery. It was a new piece of linen she tackled, and she pretended to study a line of stitches as if seeking a fault. But her hands trembled.

'Your brother's escapade in the city must have caused you much alarm.'

'He has told you, then.' Cressida attempted to keep her tone casual. She looked up at him. 'I was afraid, it is true,' she went on. 'And at first very, very angry.' She decided against reminding Stephen that it was to all intents and purposes his fault that Francis even had the means to go to the markets in search of gifts. She smiled softly. 'But when I saw him standing there on his return I cared only that he was home again. You know how it is?'

Francis tugged at Stephen's sleeve, as if to bring him back to his proper task for the evening. But his gaze held Cressida's eyes.

'Yes,' he said softly. 'I know well how that feels.' They both knew that he spoke of the night Cressida had escaped Sir Robert for the second time and returned to River Lane. The night when everything between them had been changed.

'Those men of Sir Robert's were everywhere.' Francis laughed. 'The waterman taught me a lesson I'll not forget. I smelt like a pig, and I thought I'd never walk again!'

But Stephen was not listening. At the mention of Robert's name his body visibly tautened, and his face darkened. Cressida flushed, and lowered her eyes. The effect on them both of reviving the memory of the man who had taken her honour was as dramatic as if it had only just taken place. Anger flared between them, but it was sorrow that deepened Stephen's grey eyes and made Cressida lower her own gaze. She picked up her embroidery. Stephen turned to Francis, and selected a newly cut quill from the table. He toyed with it, his eyes narrow. Cressida let her frame of linen fall back into her lap, and stared blankly into the embers of the fire at her feet. She wondered how long she could bear their enforced intimacy if it were to be spiked with moments like this. For a second she felt more surely trapped than she had ever felt as a bonded serf. Would she have to leave London again once she was free to travel? Stephen himself could not risk leaving River Lane; his ordeal of secrecy and captivity had only just begun. Hers, and her brother's, was almost over.

'A penny for your thoughts, Cressida!'

She started. It was Francis who spoke. She looked up to find him glancing anxiously from Stephen to her and back again, in spite of his light tone. He was old enough, Cressida reminded herself, to know that a quarrel was in the air. Maybe something much deeper than a quarrel. It was as if war threatened between her and the man she still loved. But she loved Francis, too. She would not put him at risk now. He needed a good atmosphere if he were to continue to progress with his studies. She straightened her shoulders, and avoided Stephen's eyes. 'That's an easy question to answer,' she said banteringly. 'I was thinking that it is time for sleep. If you are to be up at first light for your reading, then it is time for bed.'

Stephen stood quickly, pushing his heavy chair abruptly away from the table. 'Then I must leave you. Forgive me.' His voice was low, and Cressida had the impression that he feared to be alone with her. Alone, that is, except for the sudden and insidious storm that had begun to rage silently between them.

'There is much I have to do,' Stephen continued. 'There are many people I must see now that I am back.'

Cressida shrugged. Suddenly she wished only that he would make his way from the room at once, without speaking again. If it were always going to be like this, then she could not trust herself to maintain the calm exterior at which she had worked so hard since his return. She wanted to scream at him to leave her if he could not bear her company and the thought of what had happened between her and Sir Robert. And at the same time her heart ached for him, and she wondered if she could see in her eyes that she still loved him.

But he had turned away, and was at the door before she could reply. With one hand on the handle, he spoke to Francis. The boy paused in gathering his papers together.

'Francis. You have done well.' Stephen's voice trembled slightly, then came under control. He stood in the shadows across the room from Cressida, a lean, still youthful figure in his dark scholar's clothes. She had a vivid, momentary sensation of being held close to him – and yet, she told herself, the chasm between them had never been wider.

'Should you need me, I am not far off.' He was still speaking to her brother. 'My home is here now, in this house. Did your sister tell you?'

Francis nodded. 'I do not know how you were able to leave Oxford. It was your whole life. I saw that in my short time there with you, Stephen.'

Cressida heard her brother with astonishment. For such a young boy he spoke as an equal to his tutor. She had almost forgotten that they were all childhood friends, and with the knowledge that Stephen had indeed found it possible to leave his life's work and come here to London and survive, her heart lifted.

'I can make my home wherever it is that I must work. In the coming months there is work for me, in your city. I cannot tell you more.' He took a step back into the room, and placed a hand on Francis's shoulder. 'You know enough to understand that what I do is subject to the strictest laws of secrecy – if our cause is to flourish when our time comes.'

'My city?' Francis had seized on the phrase, and sounded puzzled.

Cressida rose from where she sat, and went to his side. 'Stephen is right, brother. In less than one month you and I have it in our choice to become citizens of London. We belong here now. What do you say to that?' But as she spoke she looked at Stephen, and it was his reply she was seeking.

'I say Amen,' Francis said.

Above his bright hair, Cressida and Stephen looked into each other's eyes. The storm had passed as swiftly as it had come. Cressida's whole being ached for the slim, proud man who stood at her brother's side. The anger and jealousy that formed such a rift between them was, after all, no more than an aspect of love. With a surge of recognition of what she must do, she shook her long fair hair back from her shoulders, and held out her hand.

'Good night, Stephen. Keep safe, as you go about your work. Now I must go to my room – for I too have much to achieve.'

She reached the door before either of the others could

move. She squared her young shoulders almost arrogantly, and her skirts moved gracefully about her long limbs as she walked quickly out of the room, leaving Stephen with the same ache in his heart and his body that held her in its grip.

For a girl who had begun life in a one-roomed village dwelling, and spent her days in the fields, Cressida showed a startling degree of sophistication in the task she now set herself, and Mistress Valence watched her go about it with increasing admiration, slightly mingled with apprehension. Each time Cressida came in from her hurried shopping excursions into the city streets, always at first light or just before dusk, when she could escape notice more easily, she carried some parcel or trinket, or had news of some craftsman who would call at the house next day with his wares. She had determined to pass the final weeks of isolation for her brother and herself in the decoration of the last room in their new home, her own bedroom. Oblivious of the fact that until a year before she had shared a mattress of straw with her mother in the corner of their low-roofed house, she now planned for a high wooden bed, a chest at its feet, a settle for one wall, and a great new armoire for another.

The carpenter who came to the house to build the new armoire had been recommended by Master Valence himself, so there was no need for Cressida to exercise too much caution in her dealings with him – though she took care to conceal her brother's presence, and to make sure that the approach to Stephen's wing of the house was concealed by a heavy arras. But the little carpenter, who was reputed to have come all the way from Holland and practised somewhat in the shadow of the frowns of the guildsmen who plied the same trade in the city of their birth, was a dedicated worker, and hardly knew what went on about him as he sawed and cut and tenoned the stout oak his apprentice brought in for him. It was more than a week before he had prepared the cupboard and settle, and Mistress Valence gasped as Cressida paid him the twenty shillings due to him on account. But there was more to follow: in the carpenter's wake came the carver, and the rasping and banging of the previous week gave way to the quiet chipping and scraping of the wood-carving tools as the furniture took on its final luxurious appearance. But no sooner had the wood carver left than the carpenter returned, a cart at his heels in the street. On the cart were the long oaken planks that were to make Cressida's bed.

Cressida's bedroom was a long, low room overlooking the street from a single small window. It had no hearth, and for warmth she had covered the floor with rugs and heavy furs. The bed itself was built into one corner of the room, which formed a natural alcove between the beamed arch of the two inner walls and ceiling. It was high and almost square, with a carved head to it and a deep mattress of straw tailored to fit exactly into its solid oaken flanks. A bolster of straw covered in white linen served as a pillow, and stretched right across the bed. The coverings consisted of a length of blue velvet, and a white fur coverlet. The velvet was edged with gold embroidery, and the fur had the softness of the ermine worn only by royalty. A small bedside table was also covered in the blue and gold fabric, and on the opposite wall was a tapestry depicting a summer scene, a pilgrimage of riders, dressed in brilliant colours in progress under a pale blue sky.

When the room was finished, Cressida stood alone by the low window, her back to the light, and examined the whole effect with a critical yet glowing eye. It was a room of simple beauty, and of extreme intimacy. It had cost her most of the remainder of the contents of the royal purse she had received from Queen Philippa, and she was like a proud delighted child as she stood there gravely. She had shown the room to no one else, and the sense of secrecy, of the first real privacy she had ever enjoyed, sent a glow through her whole being. But for a moment she frowned, then went swiftly to the armoire, and from its depths produced two objects. One was the small burnished mirror the man Dominic had given her when she first met him in the forest clearing in her flight. The other was the box that contained her memento of Stephen, the velvet button from the scholar's uniform.

Placing the box on the table beside the bed, Cressida went to the window with the mirror. In the grey winter's light from River Lane she turned the silver circle to and fro until she had a clear reflection of her own face. She studied it solemnly, detached from any judgement of her own beauty. She knew from the effect she had on Sir Robert, and the way in which the Court at Westminster had reacted, that she must be less than plain. What she did not know was that in the months in London the pinched look on her face – a look of sorrow, of apprehension – had given way to a smooth roundness, a look of confidence and maturity. The eyes that had been quick to flash in anger were softened. But their blue had deepened, and the whites gleamed with a healthy, startling pallor. The blonde hair, now drawn neatly into the white coif she wore about the house, shone as if in response to the circlet of pearls that was seeded in the coif itself. The mouth was as full and sensual as it had always been, but as Cressida placed the mirror on the table and turned again to examine her room it had the pleasurable hint of a smile at its corner – a slow, secretive smile that had nothing in it of the child she had been.

Still smiling, she sat on the white bed coverlet, and ran her hands through the smooth, soft fur. With a delighted leap of her heart, she realized that the memories of what she had been to Sir Robert in his bed at the Richmond manor – briefly recalled by the touch of the fur – now hurt her and shamed her less. She had thought she would never wipe the remembrance from her mind, and she had been aware for some time after the night at Richmond of her own participation in the events. But they now seemed to belong to another world. Her body had forgotten its bruises, and her heart was quieter at the thought.

She reflected that she had heard her mother once tell a woman friend that one forgot the pain of childbed as the months went by. Could it be the same of violation, and a night spent in the closed, silken world she had shared with a man who was wrong for her in every way? She prayed then, suddenly, with the fervour she had sometimes prayed with as a girl, that this new sense of well-being, of new birth even, would not leave her.

Then she climbed further on to the bed, and took the box from the table into her hands. Opening it, she retrieved its solitary contents. (The royal purse had long since taken up a new place under her surcoat, before it had grown empty.) Placing the box back on the table, she held the small velvet button in her long fingers, then raised it briefly to her lips . . . before she tucked it gently under the white linen pillow. Then she lay back and closed her eyes in the first sweet sleep she had enjoyed since the night she slept by the hearth in Stephen's own house, while he rode with her brother into the darkness towards Oxford.

When she woke again, the light had gone from her window, and downstairs she could hear the laughter of the Valence children, and Francis laughing with them.

Hurrying to bring him back to their rooms upstairs for an evening that was almost the last he need spend in isolation, her small feet sped down the narrow steps to the Valence family's quarters, but paused on the last stair as she heard the unmistakable, familiar sounds of Stephen's return home. There was no escape from him, she told herself. She stood at the foot of the stairs, and he had to pass. He was shaking rain from his cloak, and seemed not to have noticed her. He turned, and in the half light she could not be sure of the mood his expressive face would announce. His voice was soft when he spoke to her. At first, he said only her name. She did not know how to reply. It seemed foolish to speak of the weather, and yet that was the way strangers would greet each other in such circumstances. Fortunately, he sensed her hesitation, and spoke for her.

'It is a wild night. They say on the river that the rain comes from the south-west.'

'That means it will stay. It will blow itself out in the city, and maybe take days about its work,' Cressida said lightly.

'So you remember your countrywoman's wisdom, little Cressida?'

His words made her blush furiously, and for a moment she could not speak. It was weeks since he had called her that, and now – in contrast to the anger it had always wrought in her – she found that it delighted her beyond expression.

'The rain and wind have come from where we were born,' she said at last.

'And as you tell me, they are come to stay. Will they blow on their way after these next few days?'

'No, I think rather they will storm themselves out of their wildness, and settle into being small city breezes, racing round street corners and lifting rose petals in the town's gardens.' Cressida spoke as if her words were the words of a song she had heard. Her heart sang as she stood, still on the lowest step, and she had a vivid memory of Dominic's voice and the songs he had sung for her. His ghost seemed to stand there with her, and she could have sworn she heard his voice, urging her to happiness. She was aware that his spirit had taken over from the painful haunting Sir Robert had exercised. She was suddenly, unaccountably, wildly happy.

Stephen studied her, his dark eyes giving nothing away. 'I am glad you are in poetic mood. Your brother is not the only one to have a way with words in the family, I see. And I need to listen. My work has been demanding today. The problems increase, rather than diminish. We had meetings with those in high places . . . and I cannot be sure that we truly have their support. I seem to be playing some complicated game, in which I have no control.'

'You will always have control, Stephen. You would not have got so far at Oxford if the tasks were beyond you. And see how you have succeeded with my brother – '

'Francis? Where is he?' Stephen's voice lightened.

'I was about to fetch him. He has strayed again – but not far.'

'Let him be. It is not long now.'

'That is when we must be most on our guard,' Cressida said firmly, and took a step towards the kitchen, calling Francis's name.

The spell between them broken, Stephen put his cloak over his arm, and began to climb the stairs. 'I shall join you both later,' he called, almost casually, over his shoulder. 'I have made a momentous decision this day, and I need to be with my childhood friends.'

Cressida hardly had time to react to what he had said before he had disappeared out of sight at the head of the stairs. She paused before calling Francis again, hoping that Stephen would realize she wanted to speak and come back to hear her. But she could sense that he climbed further into the far wing of the great old house, to his own rooms, and she turned, bewildered, to bring Francis to her. Her heart beat fiercely now. She could have no idea of what a man like Stephen, usually so taciturn, could mean by what he had said. But the fact that he had even hinted to her of matters of importance, matters which he wanted perhaps to discuss, after these months of silence, was enough to make her pulse race. If she had thought about it, she would have found that she also had been lonely for her childhood friends – or for one of them at least.

Less than an hour later, Francis sat at the table as usual, his manuscript books close to a bright candle, and Stephen sat at his side. Cressida was in her usual place, but she had not brought her embroidery into the light of the tallow by her seat. Instead she sat thoughtfully, watching Stephen and her brother openly, hoping that Stephen would speak. She had not long to wait. Stephen seemed unable to settle to work, and Francis asked him if he did not have greater things on his mind than teaching Latin verbs to a scholar who would one day teach in the speech of the people?

'There is no greater matter, Francis,' Stephen answered gravely. 'You are within your rights to correct me for straying. But in a way it is just because of such issues that I am uneasy.'

'Stephen, you talked of a momentous decision earlier? What happened today?' Cressida was unable to contain her own questions once she saw that Stephen was indeed ready to talk.

He left his seat at the table then, and walked to the hearth. The soft embers lit the aquiline features of his face as he began to speak. Cressida thought he had never looked more handsome, or more serious.

'I told you there were meetings today, with powerful men. A prince of the royal blood was there. Two members of Privy Council.'

'Such men were present when heretics met?' Francis gasped. Cressida frowned him into silence, but Stephen raised a forgiving hand.

'It is true that I and my co-workers are heretics, by some creeds. But we are not alone. And there are leaders of men who know it can be a wise strategy to be ahead of the times – as we are now. If they sympathize with a cause that others think is already lost, but which one day they sense will gain in strength and conviction, then they can hope to remain in power when such a time comes. They have nothing to lose – so long as they act in secret at this stage.'

'But that is false, Stephen,' Cressida said. 'And dangerous.'

'The danger is to us, the true heretics. The new thinkers. We do not want to trust such men, and yet we grasp at straws through them. We need money from them, to finance our work. We cannot starve, or let our brothers starve. And if we are found out, we need protectors in high places.'

'But how could they protect you?'

'By still playing false,' Stephen said. 'If they are not known to sympathize with us, they can always plead from a place of strength with the other side – suggesting that it would be unwise to execute a heretic well-loved of the people, or reading omens into the signs given by the heavens advising clemency. There are many ways to sway a court – if you sup with the judges the night before.'

'Then what do you fear?' Cressida asked him. He turned from the fire, and she was momentarily shocked at the lines of exhaustion in his face as he looked at her.

'I fear that such men take us scholars for unworldly clowns: that our cause is diminished by such attitudes. I fear that we should deal with hypocrites, even those who side with us for their own lasting reasons. Such things rub off on those who share them. And I want our work to be rooted more strongly. There are others who work with me who disagree. They are ready to confide our secrets to such men. I – I am not.'

'Then what would you do in its place? You cannot surely quarrel with your scholar friends. You have all endured so much. And now you are torn from Oxford, you must needs stay close.'

'You are right, little Cressida. And this is what has played on my mind these last few days. If I bring the matter to a head, I risk my friendship, and should I lose the argument I may even find myself parted from the work for which I live.'

Francis watched Stephen silently as he spoke, his young face alive with passionate involvement. Cressida was astonished at the expression on her brother's face, catching it by chance as she looked away from Stephen briefly.

'Then what will you do?' she asked. It was as if she asked them both, and it was Francis who answered eagerly.

'Why, join them, of course! Break into their ranks, the ranks of those who use the cause for their own ends – and sort out the true believers, if there are any!'

Stephen nodded slowly. 'The boy is clever. He has gone right to the heart of things. And that is what I have to do. I have determined to make a show of siding with these great ones, and to live cheek by jowl with them, in pursuit of the truth. I have been forced to London, away from my ivory tower at Oxford. Everything tells me I must use that.'

Cressida looked doubtful. 'But will you ever learn truth from such men? Everyone at Westminster seems to me to be caught up in petty bids for power, short-lived, long-term, whatever suits the moment. And will even the sincere ones amongst them trust their innermost beliefs to a heretic priest?'

'But who says it would be a priest in their midst, Cressida?' Stephen's face was white now, and he spoke so softly that she had to lean forward to be sure she heard what followed.

'This is my torment. I have decided that my only hope of working for our cause now is to discard my role as cleric, even as scholar. I am to mix with the world, it seems, for the least worldly reasons. I intend to make it known publicly that I will never take my full vows. That I can be trusted by priest and prince, but that I shall owe my allegiance neither to the church nor to the King. But those who would use us will never know the truth. That I shall work solely for the day when the humblest of men stand equal with priest and prince . . . in God's eyes it is already so, I know it.'

'Then how will such things be achieved, if not by a priest?' Francis asked. Cressida, suddenly aware of the significance of Stephen's words for herself, was unable to speak.

Stephen seemed completely unaware of the effect his words had on her. He began to pace up and down the room, and told Francis: 'They will be achieved by making our cause respectable in the halls of power, as a school of thought, a new way of seeing and thinking of the ordinary men and women. I intend to be the one to make this happen – to get what we all believe accepted – ' he laughed strangely ' – fashionable, if you like. By the time our Bible is ready, the men and women for whom it was written will not have to read it in secret. And if I am to achieve such things, then I will not let them be built on the shifting sand of false support. I have decided to come into the open . . . but as a layman . . . here in London.'

He stopped pacing, and waited for one of them to speak. At first taken aback by the way in which he had seen fit to confide in her, Cressida had realized as she watched him speak that he was in some ways as unsure as the weakest of men. He was brilliant, a born scholar, but still a very young man. There were three years between them, and she felt at this moment as if she had lived longer, seen more of life than he. It was the first time she had ever felt stronger than the man she loved. And she gloried in the knowledge that he was seeking an answer from her, seeking her approval and support, even though he had evidently made up his mind.

But between her answer and the words she wanted to express it stood the knowledge, too, that this decision meant only one thing to her as a woman. She struggled with her thoughts, trying to produce a clear, sympathetic reply to Stephen's news. But drumming through her brain, refusing to be stifled, was the cry that if Stephen came out into the open and renounced his work as scholar and novice priest – then he would be free to marry.

As if he could read her thoughts, Stephen sat at the table again, his head in his hands. 'It is in some ways the end of all I have worked for so far – and it bites deep into my being to do this. But I know it will have effect. I know it is the right thing to do.'

Cressida rose from her place by the fire and went to

him. She did not touch him, but stood close to him, looking down at him, longing to touch the dark hair that curled softly at the nape of his neck. Francis watched them both. The room was silent for a long moment.

It was Cressida who spoke first. Her voice was calm, and still she did not reach out to make contact with this man who she now knew needed her, at least in this moment of decision and crisis. 'I have seen enough of the ways of Court, of the barons, to know you are right. In their way many of them are bumbling, over-eager, power-hungry men. They are far from subtle. I think that if you were to befriend them, in their own world, you would soon sort out the true from the false. Then you could build on it. I know you are right, Stephen. And I know it will not be easy for you, to take such a step.'

He raised his head. Still he looked straight before him, not wanting perhaps to see the expression in Cressida's eyes. Perhaps he too had thought ahead, to the inevitable moment when he would realize that a new way of life would bring with it the right to marry. But there was nothing in his demeanour at that moment to show he had thought of such things. Instead, he gave a deep sigh. And the sigh was echoed by the boy who sat at the table with him. At the small, weary sound, Stephen stood up, smiling.

'But I have exhausted you both. Francis – it is your bedtime. We have done so little work, it is not worth resuming our studies for tonight. And the longer days of spring will soon make our task so much easier – at least for our eyes, if not for our brains!'

'We are not too weary to listen, Stephen. Stay. Tell us what you will do. How will this thing be done?' Cressida put her hand on his arm, for the first time since he had started to speak. To her delight, he did not move away. She looked up into his face. It was an exhausted face, and yet the eyes, deeper and greyer than ever, were calm now. He smiled down at her.

'We start by sleeping. I think I will sleep now. And then

I must see Mistress Valence early in the morning.' He glanced down at his neat, worn scholar's tunic. 'If I am to breach the halls of power, then I must look the part. And my wardrobe is in sad disrepair.'

Cressida followed his glance. She caught her breath. Her hand went out involuntarily, and was drawn quickly back again.

She smiled shakily, and brushed her hair back into place from where it had escaped from her coif. The gesture was a purely nervous one. Stephen smiled down at her. He seemed to be teasing her wordlessly, challenging her to say the words they both knew must come next.

'You have lost a velvet button from your tunic,' Cressida said. She was not smiling now.

'Why yes, I remember the occasion. I remember it well.'

As he watched her recover her composure, again tucking a strand of gold into place under the white coif, Stephen's heart contracted in sudden recognition of her beauty. She was no longer a child to be teased, nor a rebellious, desirable woman to be regarded with suspicion. There had been feelings between them that he could not pretend had faded on his part. It was these deep, fathomless emotions and desires that had made his anger at the loss of her honour to a man like Sir Robert such agony to him. But perhaps the time had come for him to re-examine his feelings towards her. With no obvious effort on either side, the chasm between them since the night of their anger had imperceptibly narrowed. Now he had asked for her approval, sought her comfort. And though she had given him all the strength and support he could have asked, she stood before him like a slender, flaxen willow. He fought a sudden, mad impulse then to bend to her and gather her into his arms. But even as he conquered it, Cressida, her cheeks flaming, had gone to her brother, and with an arm about his shoulders led him to the door.

She turned. Her small breasts rose and fell swiftly

beneath her plain gown. She shivered slightly in the current of air that came from the corridor as Francis opened the door. She could not bear to see Stephen in such open conflict in his relations with her. She was totally aware of what raged in his heart, and his body. And she was as determined not to be the one to make the first, pleading move towards a reconciliation.

'We start by sleeping. The words are yours, Stephen.' Her eyes blazed at him across the room, and with Francis already out of the door and on the way to his own bedroom Stephen made as if to speak again. He took a step towards her. But before he could reach her, her trailing skirt had disappeared through the doorway, and he was left alone in a darkening room.

11

But Cressida did not sleep that night. Her long naked limbs stretched beneath the soft white coverlet of her new bed, she lay stiffly, listening for the sound of the keepers of the watch in the street below as the hours passed. The knowledge that Stephen was to renounce all plans for taking his full vows, even for following the true scholastic life, had driven sleep from her. Her mind darted from thoughts of what this could mean for the future, to anxiety for what it might mean for those people and places who made up the picture of the past. Stephen had been a natural, brilliant boy scholar, selected by the lord of the manor for his studies at Oxford. It had been understood that he would return to the manor one day, to his parents' village, and use his learning for its good. His commitment had been clear; it was the custom. As scholar or priest, Stephen would have spent his life in the service of the small community. And though such an arrangement could perhaps be shelved in the months of disorganization that followed on the heels of the plague, it could not be altogether discarded. Cressida knew too well that the feudal lords had a way of claiming their dues in the end.

She knew, also, that it was in her power to leave Stephen free to pursue his new path without the embarrassment of her presence in the house in River Lane. In a day or two she would be at liberty to walk into the streets of the city without fear, her brother at her side. Free to move on, out of Stephen's life. And in a way, she realized, such a move would also free her from the humiliation of waiting, and of wondering whether Stephen would ever come to her with love, of his own accord – for she had secretly vowed to herself that from now on, whatever happened it would not be she who would seek him out.

As the night dragged on, she became haunted by other thoughts – of the last sight she had had of Dominic, who had died almost a year ago; of her own mother's death, the anniversary of which had just passed. How much had happened since then, and yet how little. How the months had sped by, and yet – for Cressida and Stephen – how things had stood frozen in despair.

And those who had seen her on her flight to the city – the drunken Earl of Mansey; young Philippa; Dame Agatha with her round, smiling face; and the gaunt figure of Brother Oliver walking the snow-covered paths of the Abbey at Grimthorne – they too were frozen images that now seemed to stand about her bed, silently asking the one question, over and over again: had her long journey led her to nothing after all? At last, twisting and turning in an effort to get to sleep, she threw back the fur covers in spite of the coldness of the night. When the dawn watch passed, crying that all was well, she slipped from the bed and crossed the room to the window. The watchman was right – the city was at peace under a dark sky from which the stars had not yet fled. Shivering, she returned to the warmth of her furs, and snuggled under them again with a sigh as she waited for the day.

Then, as she tried once more to sleep, it was Stephen's face that came to her, and she knew that she would not leave him unless he told her plainly that he no longer loved her. Love's fair face had eluded them long enough, and Cressida chose to give herself one last chance to reach out and touch it before she gave up all hope of happiness. But still it would have to be Stephen who made the first move.

Three days more passed in an agony of waiting. Philippa called at the house on the third morning, to remind her friends that within twenty-four hours they would no longer be her brother's serfs. Francis told her that he too had counted the days, and was determined to celebrate the anniversary of his flight with his sister quietly. It was a serious moment in his life – a turning point.

The bright-faced boy Philippa had encountered on her previous visits was growing fast, and into a thoughtful, strong character, she thought. She was glad that he trusted her with his true feelings. She herself was a radiant figure, the bloom of womanhood on her cheeks and in the curve of her slim body. There were girls at Westminster who were married at her age, and looked and behaved like children. She confided to Cressida, when Francis had left them alone in her room, that one girl had recently been brought to bed of a child and that both had died. She herself would never let a man bring her to that – before it was time. And in less serious vein, she described to Cressida her latest strategy – with the Queen's help – in avoiding marriage at all.

Her young friend's mood was in such contrast to her own, and her opposition to enforced marriage so unlike Cressida's plight, that Cressida fell silent.

'Cressida, you are not listening! And I have news that will make you wish you were!'

'What news is that?' Cressida smiled. 'You are a human chronicle, I sometimes think, with the tales you bring.'

'It is not a tale. It is an event. A personage. Someone you – someone we both know is at Court.' She eyed her friend, waiting for her to beg to be told.

'Not your brother again,' Cressida said dryly. 'I try to forget him, Philippa. Pray do not open the wound.'

Philippa sat impulsively beside her on the white fur of the bed, and took her arm. 'I know, I know. And he knows he is defeated, you must believe me. He departed for home more than two days since. I think in his drunkenness – which is perpetual these days – he believed you had at last gained your freedom. I did not disillusion him, for I too have counted the days! And I would not have come to River Lane simply to tell you that. No – now think! What other personage do we both know? Young, and handsome – and extremely clever. I saw him but once, and I did not forget his face. Those grey eyes.' She laughed teasingly, but Cressida shook her hand from her sleeve and stood up, looking down at her eagerly.

'It is the scholar Stephen.' She did not have to ask. It was she who stated what Philippa was trying to tell her. That Stephen had achieved the first move in his new strategy, and presented himself at Westminster. Her mind was in a fever at the thought. How had he manoeuvred such a step so soon, and under what pretext? She tried to keep her voice steady. 'Is he to preach at Court, in the chapel? Is he to become tutor to an Earl?'

Philippa shook her head, still teasing, her eyes shining with the knowledge she had to impart.

'Have you not heard of the new plans for the great Abbey at Westminster – for the building of the nave? There will be such monuments to God and the Angels. It will take a lifetime. It is to be a masterpiece. And advisers are needed, for it is to be perfection – '

'Advisers?' Cressida spoke breathlessly. If Stephen had contrived an appointment on such a project he would be in the company of the highest in the land.

'And this young and handsome stranger, known to us both,' Philippa concluded, 'is to be in charge of all transcriptions, of all records. By order of King Edward himself.'

'Oh, Philippa, he will excel, I know he will. It is the answer to all of his problems. I – ' She stopped, for fear of giving away even to the young girl at her side the true nature of Stephen's ambition. 'I will see little of him. Will he live at Court? Does he stay there now?'

She had not seen Stephen for the last three days, but had thought he came back to the house late at night, and was avoiding her. Now her heart beat faster, painfully, at the thought that he might already have left for good.

'I imagine he will have the choice,' Philippa replied. 'This house is not far, after all.'

'Yes, that is true. And it could be that with such a building in hand it would be useful to have a base close to the city . . . the guilds will have much to say in the matter.' She spoke wistfully, as if trying to convince herself. Sensing her innermost feelings, Philippa rose to go.

'You are right, friend. But then you have learned so much since we first met. You and your brother have travelled far in more senses than one.' Impulsively, she embraced Cressida. 'I will think of you both all day tomorrow. I shall never forget you.' She turned then, and made her way down to the main door. Cressida followed, and let her out, opening the door as usual only a fraction of its full width, and glancing into the street b fore she closed it again, leaning wearily against it, her eyes unaccountably filled with tears, as she told herself that in less than two days she would never have to take such care again.

On the morning of the day which saw their release from serfdom for ever, Cressida woke early and went straight to her brother. It was still dark. The street outside glimmered as the last watch turned into River Lane, torches held high, and called that all was well.

It was a year and a day since they had left their home by

night, the moonlight glimmering on the snow as the torchlight now flickered between the tall, narrow houses of the city street. As the watchman's cry reached into Francis's room he slipped from his bed and ran to the window. Involuntarily, Cressida put out a hand to restrain him as he parted the dark linen curtain she had kept fastened there for his protection from prying eyes. But he brushed past her, and when he had opened the curtain he pressed his face to the window pane and stared eagerly out at the night sky.

When he turned back into the room their eyes met. Francis's face glowed with excitement, but he walked slowly now as he crossed to where his sister stood. Cressida found herself at first unable to speak. Her elation at the knowledge that she had outwitted Sir Robert, and gained her brother's freedom for life, was mingled with an inexplicable desire to cry. Her heart ached for the very fields in which they would no longer have to toil; the memory of her mother's death, which had started the whole train of events, which had brought them to this room, stabbed at her heart. Just as she had held her arms out to her brother on the night of their escape, she held them wide for him now, and as he came into her embrace they each found that the other wept. It was a long moment before the words came.

And then they tumbled out, mixed with laughter, blurred with tears, as brother and sister hugged each other again, and Francis began to dance about the room as if he had suddenly remembered that he was free.

'Hush! You will wake the household!' Cressida whispered as he jumped on to his low bed and began to bounce up and down on it in delight. When he paused, it was only to shout with laughter, and to catch his breath, before he whirled across again to where Cressida stood, and kissed her.

Then for a moment he fell silent. His face became serious, and the solemn young eyes that stared into Cressida's were full of questions.

'What is it, brother? Is there something of which you are afraid?'

'No,' Francis said. 'But I have a profound problem. The philosophers at Oxford would find it an absorbing matter.'

'Then tell me. We can have no problems today.'

Francis paused before he spoke. 'It is – that today, the day of our freedom, has dawned, and I find myself perplexed because I do not know what I would do with it! I thought that I would run into the streets, shouting. That I would take a boat to the sea itself, or ask you to prepare a feast for our friends, but – '

Cressida waited for him to continue.

'But I find that I have work to do! That I have promised to prepare a translation for Stephen's return, and that I *want* to do it!'

Cressida smiled slowly. She understood so well the sense of anticlimax, of sorrow even, that could creep up upon them if they made too much of the day that was a turning point. She understood also that Francis was trying to tell her their daily routine was in itself a freedom. That the ultimate freedom now that he could walk the streets without fear of abduction was to choose to stay in the house.

'Tell me Francis,' she said. 'Would it please you if we made today like the other days? And spent it quietly here?'

'Yes, that is what I meant. My real freedom came perhaps a long time ago – the night I rode to Oxford, or the day I was trapped in John Aske's boat and learned my lesson, and you did not scold me!' He began to gather his clothes from the settle at the foot of his bed. 'I am free now to choose – and I choose a day like any other day!'

Cressida went to the door. 'Then I too shall celebrate by passing the day as if it were an ordinary day. Except that I have prepared a game pie, and Mistress Valence has saved a flagon of mead for us to drink as honeyed as that served at Court itself, and – '

'Then I agree to eat and drink a little more than usual, and maybe you will allow me to stay up later and read to you?' Francis asked.

Cressida nodded. Their decision to pass the day quietly had somehow eased her sadness at the memory of their flight. She told herself firmly that there was no one now to wait – or watch – for them in Sir Robert's village, and that their life there belonged to a past era. Swiftly, she stepped into the corridor, and closed the door of her brother's room behind her. Then, fastening her long golden hair into a coil at the nape of her neck as she walked, she made her way to the kitchen.

That night Francis tried in vain to keep his eyes open as he sat with Cressida until long after their usual bedtime. The book he had begun to read aloud to her, a romance from the French which he translated as he went, slipped from his hands. He rested his head on the great oak table, and slept. Cressida watched him in the light of the tallow lamps, and smiled. He had spent the day as planned, in working with an obsessive concentration, and by dinner time was so exhausted that the mead they drank had sent his senses swimming. She feared that if he slept too deeply now he would not easily waken to get to his bed, and when he stirred she called his name softly.

He raised his head, and rubbed his eyes. Then he swayed to his feet, and gathering the parchments into his arms, turned to the door. 'It has been a perfect day,' he told her. 'And if I do not go to my bed now I will sleep here where I stand.' He yawned, and suddenly gave a low, delighted laugh.

'What is it?' Cressida asked.

'I was thinking,' he said, 'how the Lady Philippa will rejoice that we have escaped her brother for good.'

'And that we still have her for a friend,' Cressida reminded him.

'How could I forget? She is so different from the upstart barons who would rule us with iron. With her, true friendship is possible, I think.' And he blushed slightly as he spoke, leaving Cressida gazing thoughtfully into the fire long after he had left the room.

When she looked up again, there was a tall figure standing in the doorway. She found herself gazing into deep grey eyes – eyes which held no hostility, no wariness, for the first time for many weeks.

'Stephen. You are back. We did not expect you . . . '

'I had to return. Tonight of all nights. Surely you know that?'

'Because of your new appointment?'

'Did your friend at Court tell you that?'

She looked up at him sharply. He raised an expressive hand, as if to beg her not to attack him. 'I had to be with you on this day which ends with your brother asleep in a free man's bed, and the curtains wide for all the world to see that you no longer need to hide.'

Her face glowed. 'I am glad, Stephen. But we have spent the day quietly, as if it had always been so. It was what Francis wanted, when it came to it, and I thought him right.'

'He no longer thinks like a child, that I know. There will be work for him at Court, with me.' Stephen smiled down at Cressida.

She smiled back. 'My "friend at Court" has told me of your new appointment – I cannot pretend otherwise. But – you must tell me yourself, Stephen. I want to know everything. We must drink wine to your future.' Cressida turned to the table, where a flagon of mead stood half filled. Two goblets she had bought shone in the light of the fire beside it. As Stephen watched her, she filled each of them with the dark, golden wine. Then, taking one goblet in her two hands, she stood and offered it to Stephen. For a moment he did not move. Then he came swiftly across the room to her, took the goblet from her, and raised it to her lips, before he reached for the other vessel on thc table. Then they drank together, still looking into each other's eyes.

'My future is here. There are no obstacles now, little

Cressida.' He took the goblet from her again, and set both drinks on the table.

Cressida lowered her eyes. She could not believe that this moment had come, and she trembled at the thought of its passing. 'No obstacles to what, Stephen? Have I put obstacles in your way?'

'It is you I need to keep my way. To remind me every day of my new treacherous existence, what I came from, and the nature of my purpose.'

'I would be proud to be of use to your cause. But I am not a clerk, I cannot read or write – though I will learn, soon.' Cressida looked up at him, frowning a question. 'If that is what you want.'

'I want much more than that, little Cressida. I know I forsook my vows as part of this new game I play. You knew that. But what you did not see was my innermost relief when I did so. It was *I* who built obstacles between us, or let them grow.' With a gesture now so familiar, he reached out to take a strand of her hair between his long fingers. She wore no coif, and the golden chain she wore at her throat mingled with her long, golden hair as Stephen began to caress her.

For a long time they stood close in the centre of the room, Stephen's arms holding Cressida's young body so tightly that she thought he would never let her go. Sometimes he spoke to her, his voice low, his breath warm against her throat, telling her of his regret for the long, wasted months of waiting. She stopped his mouth with her kisses, and again they were silent. She wanted no regrets, and no recriminations. She felt that now Stephen had wiped out all his past anger and disgust by coming to her as he did, and that they faced each other as equals.

The fire died slowly as they stood in its light and warmth, and suddenly Cressida quivered in Stephen's arms. 'It is late. Are we to part now?'

He placed a finger on her lips, and shook his head. Then he led her to the door, his arms still about her. 'We have finished with doubts and hesitation. And of all the nights since I found you in my mother's house this is the one I would choose, from the whole year past, to stay with you.'

'I hoped so often that you would come to me – yet I too wanted our love to be fulfilled when I was really free, and not before.'

'You are also free to deny me. It rests with you still, little Cressida.'

They stood in the doorway, and in the shadows Cressida saw on his face such open, adoring love that she flew back into his arms, clutching him to her, every movement an echo of their first embrace a year ago.

'You are wrong, Stephen, my dearest love. I have no choice. And if I had – why should I deny you? I would only deny us both.'

This time their embrace was fiercely assertive. Cressida knew there was no going back, and she kissed Stephen with open lips. With a low cry, he drew back from her, to hold her head in his lean hands and look into her eyes with a fathomless, questioning look.

'We must seal our troth. I would not have you think I had used you. It – it is not my way with women.'

'Hush.' Cressida's eyes shone. She sensed that Stephen was perhaps an innocent in love, and the knowledge excited her. It might even be that she was his first woman, as she knew she was his first real love. 'You are not to tell me of such things. There is no need. All that matters is the future. You have taught me that yourself, this very night.'

All Cressida wanted now was to be alone with Stephen in the beauty of the intimate sanctuary she had created – almost subconsciously – for the consummation of their love. Taking his hand in hers, she led him out of the room, and together they walked silently along the corridor to her own door.

In the hours that followed Stephen did not seem to be aware of the surroundings she had so lovingly designed. And Cressida herself soon forgot where she was, once she had proudly shown him the furnishings and the blue and white-furred bed. On the blue velvet coverlet and the gold embroidered flowers she regained the fresh innocence that was hers before Sir Robert captured her, lost it again in Stephen's searching, demanding love-making, and as the first light came into the sky slept in his arms as if they were both children again.

It was Cressida who woke first. She lay quite still, her slim frame close to Stephen's hard young body, from her small high breasts to her feet. In the growing light, she studied his face. The fine brows were tensed, and the mouth set in a strong line. It was the face of a man at peace, but not at rest.

At the memory of Stephen's touch, and of all that had passed between them in the darkness, she blushed deeply. Her bruised mouth broke into a smile, and she stretched her limbs as if to savour her new being. The movement woke Stephen, and he opened his eyes. At once his arms were round her again, and he lifted her towards him, murmuring her name. She could not have refused him had she wished. Then for a moment he drew sharply back, frowning down at her. For a terrifying second she thought she had angered him but she saw that a smile lurked at the corners of his mouth. He shifted his weight, and moved one arm from beneath her head. Then he burst out laughing, and she whispered to him to make no more noise. The house would soon wake for the day, and they would be discovered. But in his hand was the small velvet button she had taken from him months ago, and with a delighted smile, caution thrown to the winds, Cressida began to wrestle with him for possession of the secret token of her love for him – until she lost, and the button fell to the floor, and Stephen pulled her down to him and entered her and began to love her as if he would never stop.

As she lay beside him drowsily afterwards, the sound of life in the house below reminding her that she must start the day in spite of their wakeful night, Stephen said: 'I have sealed our troth in my heart. When you wish, we can exchange vows before others. You will tell me when you wish it?'

'I thought to marry a scholar, and I find myself the hearthmate of a great administrator, the King's own. It is a strange feeling.' Cressida sat up, and looked down at him solemnly. 'Yes, I believe we shall marry, Stephen. One day. Perhaps when – '

He pulled her to him, refusing to listen to conditions and reservations, but she insisted. 'I was going to say perhaps when I find myself with child. Then it would be my deepest desire, to marry the father of my son. I know of no sweeter thing than a family, close-bound, protecting.'

'You have done your best to create what was lost for your brother. You have earned your happiness,' he replied.

Cressida caught her breath. She was about to make the sign of the cross at her forehead and breast, but remembered she had put away such things.

'Do not tempt providence, Stephen. I am happy, it is true, here with you. But all I have seen since my flight has taught me that one does not *earn* happiness. Or even expect it. The important thing is to live!'

12

'If I do not learn to read and write before the child is born,' Cressida announced to the royal ladies-in-waiting in general, and to Philippa in particular, 'it will be too late. My brother and Stephen will have no eyes for me when the infant rules the household, and I shall have no tutors and no time.' She bit through a length of thread with her small, white teeth and made a knot in it, bending her fair coifed head awkwardly as she started a new seam in a tiny, half-fashioned robe which rested on her large stomach.

Philippa looked up at her from her own embroidery, her eyes squinting in the pale autumn sunshine that filtered into the women's solar through the narrow palace window. 'If you do not *wed* before the child is born, then it will be too late for anything! The world and its wife knows 'tis a love child you carry!'

Cressida smiled. Philippa's sense of mischief had not changed as she grew older, and she meant no harm. 'Yes, it is a child of love. There is no disgrace in that. But all these months Stephen has had so much on his mind and now, just as my time is near, the French architects are here in London to advise on the next stage for the Abbey. There are so many reports to be written, for the master masons, and the bishops – and for the King himself.'

The ladies-in-waiting nodded. The building of the great new nave at Westminster had brought many strangers to Court, and they were all deprived of their husbands' attentions, though one or two in their ranks had acquired new admirers and new lovers in their beds.

'I hardly see Stephen as it is.' Cressida acknowledged their sympathy. 'And when I do it is a hurried meeting. I do not choose to appear to hurry to church as well!'

'But your nights are not hurried, Cressida. They say the lights are extinguished early in your windows across the river,' an old retainer, whom Cressida knew to be a favourite of Queen Philippa's, murmured, not pausing to raise her eyes from her work. The others laughed softly, and Cressida joined in. The woman who spoke had thick, dark hair that was just beginning to turn grey, and to the tolerant amusement of her companions she had begun to use a solution of camomile wrung from the herb's white flowers to bleach the grey streaks to the pale gold that was fast becoming fashionable since Cressida had become a familiar figure at the Plantagenet Court.

Cressida had taken the imitation as a compliment, and she knew no hurt was meant now. In any case she was used to the banter and gossip of these long hours spent at the palace amongst the women who served the Queen. Good-natured teasing helped to pass the time, which often hung heavy on their hands as they waited for one or other of their band to be summoned to the royal presence. And Cressida preferred their company, now she was so far gone with child, to that of her two bustling, well-meaning servants, Beatrice and her young husband Henry, who helped her in the running of her new home.

Claire House, the great town dwelling Stephen had taken in the third, lucrative year of his appointment to the King's entourage, was a beautiful, rambling manor house on the south bank of the river Thames. But it seemed to Cressida that its rooms echoed as she walked about them alone. It would be different when the child was born, and her days would be filled with so much more than waiting for Stephen. She was also happy in the companionship of Queen Philippa's ladies, who were kind to her, and less suspicious of her now that her proudly misshapen body presented less of a temptation to their menfolk. They knew the story of how she first had come to London, and she intrigued them. They had not yet forgotten Robert and his swaggering ways, and were secretly glad to have seen a man they suspected of being a rapist meet his match. Philippa was also still in their midst and it was accepted that she had become a confirmed spinster rather than prolong her feud with her brother and the Earl of Mansey. Both men had kept their distance since Robert's downfall at Court, and with the new Statute of Labourers to deal with they had long since returned to their adjoining estates, to lick their wounds, and restore their fortunes after the great plague – with a less easily bludgeoned work force, greatly diminished in number. Philippa hardly mentioned them now, but she had once, in the early days after Cressida and Francis became free of their bondage, told Cressida how glad she was that Francis had not been dragged back to their home to face the harsh life the boys he had played with as a child still endured.

Cressida herself was now an accepted visitor at the palace of Westminster. She came with Stephen each day by river, from their private jetty at Claire House. It would have been too arduous in her present condition for her to retrace her steps from the house to London Bridge and then traverse the Strand, approaching the palace by road. And she enjoyed the daily voyage on the dark green swell of the water, through the heart of the city of her adoption. The countless smaller vessels crowded round their own barge, the great sailing ships from France, even the clutter of foul-smelling litter on the mud banks made a hazardous, enthralling business of their passage each morning into the world where Stephen now worked.

Francis also accompanied them when he was needed by Stephen in the Abbey offices to help with the copying of records and reports. His studies were well advanced, and he now spoke French, and could write in Latin. The fact that he also wrote in the new dancing tongue that England herself had evolved from the French and the strong, living Saxon language that was his inheritance was not lost on Cressida – but they did not speak of it. It was all part of the secret aspect of the work she also knew Francis undertook for Stephen, on the nights he did not come home. The nights when John Aske the waterman, one of their first friends in London, called for him after darkness and rowed him swiftly away across the wide reach of the Thames, on their way into the rebel garden that was Kent. In spite of her apprehension, Cressida said nothing of what she knew. By her own flight with Francis years before she had condoned these rebels, and since the night she and Stephen had consummated their love she had wanted nothing but his happiness. This happiness, she accepted, depended as much on the success of the clandestine heretic movement of which he was an acknowledged leader as on their continuing love.

But once together in the seclusion of their home, that love still blossomed for them. Claire House had been allotted to them by King Edward himself as Stephen's work had become increasingly important to progress on Edward's beloved Abbey. The churchmen who had first ratified Stephen's appointment, close on his decision to leave Oxford as it was, had watched him with interest. If they knew of his committal to other, forbidden causes, they chose to feign ignorance. They were men used to balancing power without coming to grief, and it did nothing but good to the ecclesiastical image at Court to have at the royal right hand a brilliant administrator and scholar like Stephen. Claire House was simply further evidence of a fact that they hugged to themselves with approval: Stephen had arrived.

From the start the luxury that befitted their new situation had also delighted Cressida. She had been briefly saddened by the need to leave River Lane and the Valence family, but her first glimpse of Claire House won her round. It was a long, low building set in its own garden, and the lawns led to the river's edge. Its two-storeyed timber frame and white walls were freckled with honeysuckle, and a trailing creeper gave the house a mellow aspect. Built only a decade before, the house had more front windows than Cressida had ever seen in a domestic building, and as she leaned out of a downstairs window on the first morning Stephen had brought her to it the scent of the honeysuckle wafted into the empty room on a breeze from the river. She breathed deeply, gazing out across the garden to the city growing into being on the other side of the wide, swirling waters of the Thames. It was a moment to be remembered, and sensing that Stephen had come to stand close to her shoulder she chose it to tell him she believed she was with child.

She had hardly completed her sentence before she found herself caught up in his arms, and in his violent embrace her hair fell from its fastening and the scent of the honeysuckle mingled with Stephen's kisses in its golden strands. Tears of happiness started to her eyes at the unexpected force of Stephen's emotion. She closed them, wanting the moment to last. It had never occurred to her that a man who had once been on the brink of a celibate life could take such joy in her news. Yet, with the great issues of the day demanding every ounce of purpose he could muster, he still felt deeply about an unborn child. His delight took her completely by surprise, and she could not speak. But he spoke for her.

'Now perhaps you will agree that happiness exists – and that you have found it,' he whispered to her.

As they left the house and crossed the lawns to the jetty, Cressida noticed with interest a stretch of land on the opposite bank that had not been developed. Calculating that it must stand almost exactly half-way between Westminster and the city of London, the two rivals for power and influence throughout England, she thought what a perfect site it would make for a building of importance.

'A good place for one of the young princes to build,' she pointed out to Stephen, as he settled her in the small barge they had hired to bring them from River Lane. He was glad to see that the sad implications of what might be their last journey from and to her first London home in River Lane had escaped her, and that she had taken so quickly to Claire House.

'So now you have plans to run the royal family as well as your own?' he teased. He laid his hand gently for a moment on her waist under her breasts, as if to remind her of the new life that waited there, and as she settled in her place in the prow of the boat, the breeze lifting her hair from her shoulders, she felt a glow of serenity steal softly through her whole being.

Now as she sat, some months later, with the ladies-in-waiting, she felt the same gentle rush of happiness suffuse her whole body. She paused in her needlework, and shifted in a search for a more comfortable position on the narrow window seat which was her accepted place. It would not be long now, she told herself, before she would have to watch Stephen take the barge to Westminster without her. She sensed that their child would be born very soon. In the palace garden beneath the solar, she heard a child laugh. She looked down into the dark reds of the late roses which Queen Philippa loved, and saw a young boy at play. A young tutor, dressed in a fashionable short tunic and long silken stockings, sat at a distance, apparently dreaming of some courtly ideal love. The thin reed of a pipe played mournfully somewhere further off in the gardens, its plaintive note a perfect reflection of the scene.

Cressida recognized the small boy as the young prince, John of Gaunt, whom the Queen had borne far away from home, during the earlier French campaign. She shivered at the thought of the ordeals to which a royal mother was submitted, trailing after her sire in battle, bearing his sons with a chorus of judges and bishops and privy councillors gazing under the coverlets as the heirs to the throne struggled into a war-torn world. Such things were not for her. With a sudden longing for the large, airy room where she and Stephen shared a bed, she leaned her forehead on the cooling window pane.

The boy, sensing that he was watched, looked up to where she sat. She was aware of piercingly honest and intelligent eyes, and a determined chin. Not a prince to have as an enemy, Cressida thought briefly. There was something in the boy's regard, too, that recalled a look she had more than once seen on her brother's face. It was the look of solitude.

In spite of the current truce with France, the boy John did not see much of his elder brother, Edward – the 'Black Prince' – and there was an age gap of ten or so years between the two princes, emphasized by the death of Joanna, their sister, from plague when she was only fifteen. Cressida still remembered the look of compassion on the Queen's face when she learnt from Philippa how Cressida's mother had died. With a sigh, she turned from the window. She had begun to accept her parents' death now that she herself was to become a mother. If she became morbid, it would do no good for the child in her womb.

As she stood, she was aware of a dull ache low in her spine. She stretched, and rubbed her back as best she could round her wide girth. The robe she had been making fell unnoticed to the floor. Moments later the pain returned, and this time it did not leave her.

Crossing the room to where Philippa sat, Cressida tried to weave her way through the groups of women as if nothing were wrong. But once at Philippa's side she whispered to her urgently, asking her to send word to Stephen, wherever he might be. As fast as she could.

'And on your way, dearest Philippa,' she whispered, 'would you find a page who can hasten to our mooring and see that the barge is made ready? I want to be at Claire House as soon as they can take me there. I must get home.'

Philippa wasted no words on comfort. She nodded briefly, and ran out of the room. Cressida followed, her head high. But in the doorway a single stab of pain stopped her in her tracks. She leant in the doorway, panting, waiting for another attack, and at once the other women realized what was happening. Two of them ran to her, and each took an arm as Cressida started to walk the length of the palace corridor to the main courtyard. By the time they had reached it, Philippa awaited them there, a page at her side. The barge was ready. But Stephen could not be found.

'Then I will go home alone. Now. There can be no delay,' Cressida said.

'And I go with you,' Philippa enjoined. 'You cannot go alone.'

'No. You must find Stephen for me. Or at least get word to him. He is at the Abbey, I am sure, or if he is not then word left there will reach him. He can hire a boat, and come to me.'

'Oh, Cressida, why will you not stay here, at Court? The ladies will look to you. They are skilled; look how they minister to our dear Queen each time! There is everything you could possibly need here.'

'No.' Cressida walked on towards the river. Her voice was quietly determined. She had not realized until this moment how deeply she felt about this birth of her first child. And Stephen's. The baby was to be born in freedom, under their own roof. 'I must reach Claire House. I must. It is our home. And – ' She paused, her face straining under the onslaught of a new spasm of pain, and tried to smile – 'I will not be delivered in midstream, Philippa – of that you can be sure!'

Impulsively, Philippa hugged her as she stood where the barge waited. 'Can you be sure that all is prepared at the house? Did you know you were so near your time?'

Cressida took the hand of a boatman who came to help her embark. She turned and looked down into Philippa's face from the barge. 'I find it hard to remember, but I have servants now, and Beatrice is good. She is young, but she is a country girl – like her mistress! And Henry, her husband, will be there, and it is he who will go for the goodwife I have asked to attend me. Now, Philippa, if you love me – go for Stephen. If he does not get word of this he will never forgive me.'

Philippa sighed. 'Perhaps you are right. And I can see that you will not be refused. But dear Cressida, take care.'

'I am certain of one thing,' Cressida smiled. 'Bearing my child is a simpler affair than escaping from castles at night! Think of it, Philippa. If it were not for that night, and the winter at Grimthorne, we would not be standing here with Stephen's child hurrying into the world.'

Philippa stepped back. 'I wish you well then, dearest friend. And – I think that I envy you more than a little.' Then, as the boatman called to the oarsmen to pull away, Philippa ran back towards the palace, and took the path that would lead her to the Abbey buildings.

For the first minutes of the journey to Claire House Cressida sat stiffly under the canopy in the body of the barge, staring ahead, as if silently willing the men to row faster. Then in midstream a long breeze suddenly caught at the barge, and she reached thankfully for her ancient cloak, which she kept under the canopy for just such an emergency. But as she bent down for it a wild spasm of pain, stronger than the previous attacks, gripped her whole body. Before she could prevent it, she had given a sharp cry. Hearing it, the boatman who stood at her side half-lifted her from where she sat and wrapped her in the cloak. For the rest of the journey he held her fast. But as they came to Claire House she asked him, quietly, to let her try to stand. She knew it was better for the child if she could walk the last yards to her childbed. And with strained, white face and taut lips, her mother's cloak about her shoulders, she crossed the grass to the house, the cries of sea birds above her head under scudding clouds. By the time she reached the main door and Beatrice ran to meet her, it had begun to rain. Lifting her face for a moment to its sweet coolness, Cressida went into the house.

While her husband Henry ran for the goodwife, Beatrice accompanied her mistress to the great bedroom on the first floor that looked out over the river. But Cressida had no eyes now for the world outside. She loosened her clothing, and sank thankfully on to the wide bed, allowing her first real cry to escape, before she bit her lips.

'Is my brother in the house? I do not want him to hear me. He is too young. It is not his concern.'

Beatrice hurried over to the bed, a linen robe for Cressida in her hands. 'We are alone, demoiselle. The man John Aske came for your brother this morning. They will not be back until tomorrow. They left word.'

Vaguely Cressida took in the name, trying to remember where she had heard it before. Her head was swimming. She was briefly thankful that Francis was not in the house, and suppressed a fear that he was on yet another of his clandestine journeys into Kent. But Beatrice eased her back, removing the heavy coverlets from under her, smoothing her hair back from her high forehead. Then she busied herself at the chest at the foot of the bed, taking several long pieces of white linen from it, and a number of smaller dressings. 'We should have sent for the wise men, too,' she muttered as she worked. 'I need to know that the signs are right. It's more than a body can do, without aid. And I would that we had a good surgeon standing by.'

'How can you talk such nonsense,' Cressida groaned. 'We both come from the great forests of the south, not from some gilded palace. We have seen other creatures in the byre. We both know that this thing will take its course, whether the wise men or the surgeons stand by. As will the life of the child I bear. Now come, hold my hand. I have the strangest urge to scream now that I know the house is empty.'

Moments later, with a long strangled cry, Cressida arched on the bed, while Beatrice gripped her hand. Sweat beaded on her forehead and again Beatrice wiped it away. Breathing heavily, Cressida sank back. 'Grip my hand. I must stay conscious.'

Beatrice did as she was asked, and silently prayed that the sounds she could hear in the house below meant the arrival of Henry with the goodwife. 'Help is at hand, all will be well,' she told her mistress as bravely as she could. She only hoped that her words were true. But Cressida seemed to have gone into a world of her own, and had not heard the steps now mounting the stairs. She brushed Beatrice's hand from her almost angrily, and began to mutter to herself. Then she dragged herself on to her side, and twisted deftly, in spite of her cumbersome shape, into a kneeling position in the middle of the bed.

She was squatting in this position, breathing and exhaling with quick, shallow little gasps, when Henry opened the door to the bedroom and stood gaping at her. Behind him the plump, coifed figure of the goodwife bustled to enter and pass him. With a screech, Beatrice ran to them, and pushed Henry out of the room. Then both Beatrice and goodwife turned in amazement as a cry of laughter came from the bed. Cressida was between spasms again, and breathing steadily. Her voice shook, and she laughed again, the laughter edged with determination. 'I am glad indeed that we are not a household in the grip of Roman modesty.'

The goodwife sailed across the room to her then like one of the small ships on the river below them. She gazed in astonishment as her patient, as if it were an everyday experience, conducted what seemed to be the last stages of childbirth entirely on her own. But as she reached the bedside and put a hand out to steady the wild, primitive creature who knelt before her, she watched her slowly sink her golden head on to her knees, and then roll back wearily on the covers.

'My husband must know. The child's father, Stephen,' Cressida moaned. 'He would want to be here with me. It is his place. He has no patience with convention. He would be with me, I know it.' She began to toss her head from side to side, and watching her Beatrice was suddenly reminded of the awkward, primeval thrusting of married love as she knew it with her husband. How like these last moments before birth were to the dark moments of impregnation – and yet how laced and bruised with pain. Only a woman could know how love and agony mingled if she loved a man, but in the greatest moment of all, when she bore his child, then the pain became evident to others. Her head swam as she thought of it, and the floor of the bedroom tilted towards her. Sharply, the goodwife called her to attention. She was to fetch water, and plenty of it.

In the moments that followed, Cressida's bravura, and the instinct she had used as she waited for help to control the earlier stages of birth, deserted her. Her body was racked with blinding, demanding waves of pain. She was aware of a voice crying out, and of an answer. She did not know both voices were her own, and that she called for Stephen. Then, in a lull from the pain, she looked about the room, and finding he was not there she began to weep, hot slow tears running down her cheeks, whilst the goodwife took her young body into a firm, guiding hold, and began to give her commands for the last stage of her labour.

She was fully conscious, and gave a cry of triumph as she felt herself at last caught up strongly, irrevocably in the moment of birth. Her body spun in a vacuum of no pain, and with the impulse of the eye of a hurricane the child seemed to leap from her and slither down her thighs. A silence followed, and the goodwife moved quickly somewhere at the foot of the bed. Cressida sank back as if into a whirlpool in which she would now willingly drown – if it were not for the fact that she waited for her child's first cry. When it came, it was a thin, scratched wailing call to her. She became acutely aware again of everything about her as the baby was thrust at her breast by strong, experienced hands. A quick, rhythmic tugging at her nipple began almost at once, and she raised her head to look down at the child. Beatrice leaned over them both, smiling in blurred close-up.

'It is a boy child, Demoiselle Cressida,' she announced as grandly as if she had herself given birth.

'Yes,' Cressida whispered to the baby himself. 'It is Richard.'

For the rest of the day Cressida lay in the great bed half-asleep, always listening for the sound of an arrival at the jetty. The baby beside her, firmly wrapped in its robes and outer tunic, slept and fed and slept. The goodwife had long since gone, leaving the bedroom door half-open so that Beatrice, busy now in the kitchens, could hear if Cressida called.

It was late when the flicker of torches out on the water and the drifting voices of the boatmen announced Stephen's return home. Cressida, moving carefully so that the child was not disturbed, sat up against her pillows, straining to catch some glimpse through the darkened window of his arrival. But the barge he had hired to bring him back was already moored, and before she could sink back Stephen stood in the doorway.

Cressida looked up to see him drop his cloak and velvet hat with the familiar, impetuous gesture she had grown to know and love. Then in three strides he was across the room and at her side, embracing her and the child in a single tender grasp. First he looked into Cressida's eyes, as if seeking assurance that all was well with her. She knew then that he had been detained against his will, that if he could have reached her side for Richard's birth he would have done so. She had no wish to ask him what had happened, nor to complain. As they gazed down together at the miniature bundle on the bed between them her cup of happiness was full.

'He has your eyes. Blue eyes. And his father's nose.'

'His nose is round, not Roman. But he has your eyes – they are grey. Or they will be. All good Saxon infants have blue eyes for the first weeks, but they change.'

'But there is one thing wrong,' Stephen said thoughtfully. He studied the baby again, frowning slightly. Warily, Cressida put the baby on the bed and held her breath. Surely there was nothing that could spoil this moment? Was there something abut the infant that the goodwife or Beatrice had not dared to tell her? She had heard of imperfections concealed from the mother lest childbed fever should be induced. But if there were anything wrong with Richard, she would demand to know the truth.

Stephen moved away from the bed, and stood looking out at the night sky. Cressida froze. There was something he could not say while he still looked into her eyes.

'Not with the boy. He is unblemished.' Stephen's voice was low and hesitant. 'But rather with his parents. Cressida – ' He turned and walked back to the foot of the bed, and smiled at her. 'When the Frenchmen have left for home, and my work gives us time, and you have left your bed – then we go to the church.'

Her heart leapt with joy, not at the thought that some legal and religious bond would thus be set upon their union, but because it was Stephen who had, without prompting from her, expressed the need to seal their happiness in mutual commitment. Their life at Court had done nothing to lessen her view that marriage was not always desirable between man and woman. It was true that she wanted Stephen, her childhood sweetheart and now the father of her child, to be bound to her for life – but only of his own volition. Marriage for the Plantagenets was so often a worldly-wise contract between two houses, a dynastic move, a bid for heirs and territorial expansion. But for the child of Margaret the Good, now that it was within her grasp, it was a simple underlining of a love that already bound her innermost being to another's.

'If that is your desire, Stephen, then it is mine. But – ' She held out a hand, and he came round to the side of the bed and clasped it between his own long fingers.

'But?' He seemed momentarily annoyed that she had not shown greater pleasure.

'It is not only your work, and the constant visitors, that takes your time. There is your secret task. I know you must spend more time on it when you can. This winter will be soon upon us, and the days will be short. I would rather . . . ' She was interrupted when Stephen abruptly returned to the window, so that she could not see his face.

'It is not a matter for teasing,' he said over his shoulder. With a sigh, which she quickly suppressed, Cressida wondered if the way would ever be smooth with this brilliant, temperamental man.

'You were saying that you would rather what?' Stephen continued, his voice laden with suspicion.

With another effort at cheerfulness, Cressida called him to her. Reluctantly, he came to her side. She patted the bed, and waited for him to sit close to her before she spoke again.

'I was about to say, Stephen, that – given the choice – I

would rather go to church with you, and be wed, in the month of May. It is the perfect month for marriages; I have always felt so. Do you not agree?'

13

Cressida's first outing from Claire House after the birth of Richard coincided with an Advent service to be held in a completed section of the Abbey. In thanksgiving for the continued success of the progress on the new nave, the King, Edward, had announced that he would himself attend. And Cressida, who on her previous visits to the palace had only glimpsed the King in the distance, a dignified figure always surrounded by councillors and servants, prepared herself for the occasion with mounting excitement.

Although her origins, and her anger at the continuing plight of the serfs, were never quite forgotten – and her brother's involvement with their cause would not have let her ignore them had she wanted – Cressida had, out of love for Stephen, thrown herself into their new life with a will. Even if he dissembled his taste for authority, and walked with princes only in anticipation of what lay ahead, Cressida herself found the ways of the Court of endless fascination. The day-to-day ceremonies, the petty jealousies and protocol on which they thrived, the endless jostling to take the fancy of the members of the royal family, all seemed to her a kind of complex game, to be observed at a distance – and to be joined only when she was required to do so as Stephen's consort.

The Advent service was just such an occasion, and when Stephen had asked her anxiously if she were able so soon after Richard's arrival to be at his side in the Abbey for the first great public event in honour of the work he had undertaken, she sat very straight in her favourite seat, by the downstairs window looking out over the river, and reminded him that if their son had been born at home and they had never seen their fine house or London, or the Abbey where Stephen now worked, she would have returned to her daily duties within hours of the birth.

Stephen had smiled at her response, and walked swiftly across the room to her side. She had looked up at him, new-found confidence in his love lending a glow to her whole face. The birth of their child had brought her closer than she had ever dreamed she could be to this man whose aspirations demanded so much of him in the world outside. But during the few hours he spent at Claire House, she knew that Stephen cherished her. And the way in which he had planned their wedding, agreeing that it should be in the spring, had finally convinced her that he had willingly committed himself to her, now that his new role no longer forbade him to marry.

It did not trouble her that they were still unwed as they walked together in the solemn procession that wound its way from the palace to the Abbey on the cold December morning of Advent Sunday. They were not the only couple at Court, she observed wryly to herself as she looked around her before the procession had started, who were not linked formally in wedlock.

But all such thoughts evaporated completely as she and Stephen walked side by side into the Abbey itself. The great nave, half completed now, stretched before them like a wide street paved with stone. On each side the numerous pillars of the same stone reared like giant trees into the dimness of the vaulted ceilings above. There was a deserted air about the buildings, which at first Cressida could not understand. And then she saw that the walls beyond the pillars were lined with the masons and carpenters and their apprentices, their hats doffed and their aprons with their deep pockets still tied around their midriffs, as they awaited the arrival of their patrons. The sounds of their work were temporarily silenced. Here and there, piles of unhewn stone and sections of half finished screens told that their work had been only suspended for the occasion – Cressida knew from Stephen that these men would maybe spend their whole lives in this one, dedicated task.

She glimpsed young faces gleaming with anticipation at the King's approach, and old faces pinched with cold and engraved with dust. The Abbey was a draughty, wind-swept place at the best of times, and Stephen had often come back to Claire House chilled to the bone. But in mid-winter, and for a slow-moving procession, it was an ordeal. She was glad that her new tunic, slit at the sides, was lined with ermine, and that her fashionable new sleeves came low upon her slim wrists.

Then, without warning, the whole scene changed. From a side aisle the royal party approached. At the same time, a choir of young boys began softly to chant an Advent hymn – Angelus ad Virginem – in the high, plaintive voices that could swell to the rafters and move the listeners to tears. There were tears in Cressida's eyes as she heard the sweet treble harmonies. The fact that she could only just understand that the words were the story of the Angel's annunciation to the Virgin Mary did not seem to matter. For a moment she felt a traitor to Stephen's ideas, and even to herself. She had never believed that the Church should have power over its children, power at least to rule through fear of Hell – and the behaviour of the priest who had fled from the plague and led to her own mother's death was something she was not likely to forget – but the exquisite beauty of the music, and Stephen's presence beside her under the soaring roofs of the Abbey, moved her to heights of something akin to adoration. For the first time she knew a little of the spirituality experienced by those who were truly religious – men like the Abbot at Grimthorne perhaps, and even the fanatic, tormented Oliver whose memory had not left her over the years.

Her attention was drawn next to the entrance of King

Edward and Philippa his Queen. The King was a handsome, elegant figure, with light brown hair and a neat beard of a slightly darker shade of brown. He wore ornate robes of white and a fur-edged short cloak. Philippa wore an overtunic of 'royal' silk, dark blue shot with gold, and on her left arm gleamed the blue and gold emblem of the Garter. They were too far from where Stephen and Cressida stood for her to see the Queen's face. But as if it were yesterday she remembered the first time she had been presented. Or rather, the time she had run the length of the great hall at the palace to greet her friend, and found herself telling her story to this kindly woman who ruled England and half of France with Edward Plantagenet.

As the thanksgiving service ended, the procession of courtiers and Abbey officials parted for the King and his consort to make their way out. As Edward and Philippa drew near to where Stephen and Cressida stood, the King stopped.

'We have much for which to give praise this day,' he told Stephen. Around them the courtiers exchanged glances, of mixed admiration and jealousy, Cressida noticed. She wondered what they would do if Stephen's true mission were known to them. It would be like most of them to cut his throat in the name of loyalty, and this sign of the King's approval could only create enemies for Stephen in the long run. But the moment of apprehension passed as the Queen herself bowed her head in Cressida's direction.

'I know your face, child,' she said.

Cressida curtsied deeply. 'Your Grace once saved my life. I am the friend of your lady-in-waiting, Philippa, whose brother's lands were my home.'

'Ah, yes. Of course.' The Queen frowned. 'Little Philippa is not with us today. Some question of a visit from her brother, who would not wait. The roads are bad, and they had much to discuss before he left.'

Cressida felt the blood drain from her face at the

Queen's words. Robert at Court! She looked swiftly about her, to make sure that he and his sister had not after all been able to attend the service. Then she glanced fearfully to where Stephen stood, talking still with Edward. She was relieved to see that they were engrossed in their discussion, and it was unlikely that he had heard the reference to Sir Robert. They had long since put their quarrel behind them, she knew, but then they had not had cause to revive it. And the thought of meeting the man who had once so ravished her and threatened Stephen's love for her, now made her blood run cold.

At that moment, the King himself approached her, and Stephen stood at a distance, his face expressionless. Had he heard what the Queen had said? But the King began to wish Cressida well for her wedding day, and teased her with the fact that the father of her son had wanted the day to be sooner.

'Yet to be married in the early summer is the height of joy,' he said, a brilliant smile playing on his sensitive face. 'And the royal purse shall see that the day is blessed in more down-to-earth fashion. Your husband-to-be has earned our approval this day. And your own presence adds a golden light to our solemn house of worship.'

Cressida curtsied as the King moved away towards the great west doors, and it was Stephen's hand that raised her, moments later, to her feet. Her heart beat faster at the stern look in his eyes. She did not know whether the scene and the King's compliments had angered him, or whether he waited to open old wounds and challenge her about Sir Robert's presence in London. But with a sigh of relief, she felt the pressure of his hand on hers that told her his serious expression only concealed a wave of passion. The love that suddenly flowed between them at the touch of his hand reminded her that he had not come to her bed since the birth of their son, and that she had begun to want him with as much longing as she had ever known for his lean, handsome body and the murmured words of love and desire he used in the long nights they had spent in each other's arms since they had come to Claire House.

Outside the Abbey the air was crisp, and a pale sun made the day seem warmer than it was. They made their way down to the river, where their barge waited to take them home. From the way in which Stephen held her arm as she stepped ashore, she knew he wished they were alone.

But across the short, wintry grass a figure ran to greet them. She laughed with delight as she saw it was Francis.

'So you do need your home sometimes, brother?' she teased.

He panted in the cold air as he stopped for breath. She had not seen him for some days, and each time they met now she became increasingly aware that Francis was approaching manhood. His frame had thickened, and the golden curls of his head were echoed by a fine gold down on his upper lip. But as ever, he was evasive about where he had spent the days before.

'I have come home to study, Cressida. For the rest of the winter, I think. And to be at my sister's wedding, of course!'

He walked back to the house with them on Stephen's other side, the two men in companionable silence, and Cressida hastened her step as she saw Beatrice standing in the main doorway with Richard in her arms.

'Beatrice,' she called, a strange note of authority in her voice which made both her brother and Stephen glance in her direction with some surprise. 'I have told you the child is not to be brought into the cold air. It is a most treacherous time.'

As Beatrice, her round face reddened with puzzlement, tried to stammer that she had only wanted the baby to greet his mother on her return, Cressida tried to cover her own regret by walking ahead of them to the stairs, with Richard in her arms. The others exchanged glances. They perhaps attributed her outburst to some reaction to child-bed, or to the strain of her first outing. They were not to know that the knowledge that Robert was in London had returned with force as she saw Stephen's child in its nurse's arms.

Every instinct she had told her that she must guard herself and her child against this danger from the past. She now had so much to lose. With a muttered excuse that she was tired, she hurried upstairs and carried Richard to his cradle, sitting at its side for almost an hour before she rejoined the others, her hand gripping its wooden rail possessively, as if she would never let it go.

Richard, dark hair curling on a high rounded forehead from beneath his linen cap, slept on, unaware of his mother's vigil.

The next day, Francis had agreed to go to Westminster with Stephen and see the progress made on the Abbey before he settled down in earnest to the studies he had planned for the winter. Stephen himself wished to make a last survey of work in hand before he rode to his own village. He planned to spend Christmas this year at Claire House, pretending it was nothing to do with the presence there of his newborn son, and he had therefore to make the journey to see his mother before the snows.

Regretting the way in which she had shouted at Beatrice the day before, Cressida showed the girl how she wished the baby to be wrapped in its robes and shawl if it were to be taken out of doors, and then decided, as a beam of bright sunlight crept through the nursery window, to take Richard into the garden now that he was properly dressed for the open air.

'You shall take him another time, Beatrice,' she said, more kindly, 'I promise. But I have little to do, and the air will do me good.'

With Richard in her arms, she took the path that led away from the river, and bordered the grounds of Claire House on the Richmond side. There was a small gate in the fence which their friends used if they came from the palace at Shene, and Cressida, noticing that it stood half open, walked to close it. She supposed that Francis had been on some whirlwind visit to Philippa at Court and had not bothered to shut it on his return.

She was walking back in the direction from which she had come, avoiding the small heaps of golden autumn leaves that now clung together damply on the paths, when she knew, with a tingling of fear that ran the whole length of her spine, that she was being watched.

It was a familiar sensation, and it came from the past. From the nights when she had crept into the garden of her mother's small house and tended their few hens. And Sir Robert, masked against the plague, had waited and watched, knowing that he would some day have her at his mercy.

She did not have to turn to know who it was. A black horse rode towards the fence that surrounded Claire House, appearing so quickly out of the trees beyond that she feared for a moment that it would not halt, but would come hurtling towards her, jumping the barrier, and ride her down. She stood as if transfixed, Richard clutched in her arms as if someone already tried to snatch him from her. Her blue eyes blazed in anger and fear as she watched Robert rein in his stallion only inches from the fence.

'What do you want of me?' Her words rang on the cold air, and her breath came in white clouds. She managed to conceal her inward trembling, but beneath her long gown she knew that her limbs shook almost uncontrollably.

She wanted also to look round to make sure that they were not observed. She could trust Beatrice and Henry, she knew that. They were unlikely to come closer when they saw the tell-tale blue and green of the horse's livery. Both had come from Cressida's own village district, and were not to gain by any encounter with the seigneur at this late date. But if Stephen himself were to return from the Abbey, or even Francis, and find this man at their gates, she sensed that all hell would break loose.

Still not speaking, Robert turned his horse again, and rode along the fence, closer to where she stood. She held her breath. Her face remained devoid of anything but cold anger.

Only yards from her, he spoke. 'I want nothing but to look on you, as I once did. And to confirm my memories of what there was between us. My anger against you died long ago, but not against your brother and his kind. You will warn him? His sympathies are known, and the war between his rebels and us who must work the land with their reluctant labour is not resolved yet.'

'I do not know what you mean. My brother is a boy still. He has won his freedom, and the Queen has already ordered you to keep your distance. I have only to call the river guard to see that her orders are enforced.'

Robert smiled. She had forgotten how unpleasant it made his face. The swarthy features and the dark beard revived other memories at the same time, of a musk-ridden bed and rough handling in silken surroundings.

'That is how I remember you,' he said. 'And how I wish to carry your memory home with me. It is the last time. My sister will never return, I know that now. And I have been to see her to make certain things clear. There are those who wait for me, and are glad of my company, at home, you see.'

She tilted her chin proudly. 'That is nothing to me, sir.'

At the use of the respectful title, Robert threw back his head and laughed aloud, making her glance fearfully around them to see if they were watched.

'You did not call me such things in my bed, Cressida.'

'So you remember my name,' she said. 'That must be quite unusual.'

He nodded, serious once more. 'Oh, yes. I remember. Everything. But – I have heard of your new role in life, and I wish you well. Does that surprise you?'

She did not respond. The softer tone in his voice made her suspect a trap of some kind. She lowered her eyes.

'I can see that it does. And I see also that there is nothing more to be said between us. I did not come to snatch your child from you, Cressida. Will you not slacken your hold on the poor brat?'

The term of abuse, as if Richard were some peasant child in his thrall, was all that was needed to fire Cressida into action. It was the one thing Robert could have done to bring her to life, and he had done so unconsciously, just a moment before he would have turned and ridden out of her life for ever.

Before he could do so, she began to run at him. She made for the fence like a wild creature, Richard still clutched to her, and when she had reached it she stood almost spitting hatred, glaring up at the stallion and its rider.

'Get away from my land!' she hurled at him. 'This is my land, and this is my son! What passed between you and me, Robert, was a mere token of slavery. And I have put all such things away for ever!'

She paused for breath, her breasts heaving under her tunic, and with her free hand tried to replace a long strand of golden hair that had slipped from the warm coif that held it in place.

The black horse snorted violently at the movement, and began to paw at the ground. Cressida eyed it fearfully. It could do more harm to her and the child than its rider, if it leapt the fence. She swallowed, and went silent. Robert looked down at her, the old admiration in his eyes.

'I am glad you have not changed, girl,' he told her. 'But be warned. I too have kept my old ways, and my old power.'

Then, as Cressida stood rooted to the spot and watched the horse and rider disappearing into the trees, a cry came from the house. She turned to see Francis racing towards her.

Brother and sister faced each other as the sound of hooves receded into the distance.

'Cressida,' Francis said. 'I must know what that man is to you.'

Cressida thought quickly before she replied. If Francis

had identified the livery, then it was Sir Robert he meant by 'that man'. But his question was sure to be prompted by his political activities, not by any suspicion of what might have passed between her and their seigneur as man and woman.

'I had heard he was at Court, Francis,' she said lightly. 'For some last discussion with his sister Philippa. It seems there are many new things happening at home. Sir Robert has other interests now, you can be sure of that. But – I would beg of you not to practise your rebellion on his doorstep, as it is not so many years since we fled for ever. I do not think I could bear it if everything were revived again.'

They walked back to the house side by side. The baby slept through. 'But that does not answer my question,' Francis persisted. 'Why was he here, of all places? What do you think Stephen would say?'

Cressida stopped dead. She looked into her brother's eyes. 'If you say one word of this to Stephen,' she said, 'to my future husband, and the scholar to whom you owe all that you are, I will never speak to you again, brother.'

The boy went scarlet at her words, his fair hair making his face seem all the more red. It was the colour of hurt rather than of anger, and Cressida regretted that she had to use such words to him. But it was a moment like those in their childhood, when she had sometimes had to be firm for their own sakes.

Francis did not speak again as they walked back to the house, but when at last they stood in the hallway, its warmth and comfort embracing them after the cold air outside, he put out his arms to Cressida.

She looked at him with some surprise. She could not embrace him with Richard in her arms. She looked round for Beatrice then, so that she could put him in her care.

'No need for the nurse, Cressida,' Francis smiled. 'I want to see my own nephew. Give him to me. Surely you know I would do nothing to harm him? You are too fearful for us all. You know we must shape our own destinies.'

Slowly, she handed the baby to her brother. She knew that he had given her the answer she wanted from him. The secret of Sir Robert's visit was safe, from Stephen at least.

That night she went to bed early, exhausted by the emotions the meeting with Robert had engendered. Stephen had been delayed long after Francis had left the Abbey, and she was thankful that she had the time in which to compose herself before his return.

When at last he came to their room she was half asleep. Stephen moved across to their bed in the darkness. A faint light penetrated the room from the direction of the river, which seemed never to sleep. Her eyes followed Stephen as he disrobed, his clothes as usual left in disarray where they fell. She smiled to herself, her whole being suffused with love as Stephen looked down at her from where he stood beside the bed.

She reached out a slim hand to him. In the half-light his lean brown body, the body of an ascetic, seemed to her like a figure in some magnificent painting, the shadows playing on his long limbs. Her hand reached out again. It was the first time, in all their passionate love-making, that she had dared to make the first approach. She touched his member, caressing it with a single long, smooth movement. As she did so, she looked into his eyes, and surprised there a glow of intense desire, mingled with pain.

'You know I cannot resist you, Cressida,' he said hoarsely. 'Mother of my son. My little wife.'

The words, which she had once thought she would never hear from him, fired her passion more surely than any caress. She felt the blood rush from her breast to her throat, and then beat wildly in her ears. Moments later, as his mouth found hers and then slipped to her breasts, her stomach and her thighs, she sank back into her own surrender, and cried out with love as he pierced her for the first time since the birth of their child, and found her the same.

As had happened once before, on the first night Stephen had come to her in River Lane, his ardent love-making drove all other thoughts from Cressida's mind in the hours that followed, even the image of the rider on the black horse disappearing into the trees close to where they now lay. And Cressida knew that the menace of Sir Robert's presence had this time been erased for ever, its place taken by the knowledge of Stephen's surrender to her love.

14

Cressida's relationship with Francis in the months that followed underwent an imperceptible change. The scene in the garden at Advent had never been mentioned again between them, and the fact that Cressida herself had put it from her mind made her think that the gap she felt widening between herself and her brother had some quite different cause.

Claire House was an ideal place for studying, and on the surface Francis spent the winter months happily enough. In the mornings he brought his books to the warmth of the great kitchen, and Beatrice scolded him and moved him from place to place, until, with the promise that his dinner would never be served if he did not get out of her way, he retreated for the afternoon hours to his own room and its view of the river.

His relations with Stephen seemed quite unchanged. It was as if there had been a tacit understanding between the two since the days Stephen had sheltered the boy at Oxford, and become his tutor. Their shared cause, and the secrecy it required, also gave them an unspoken unity. As Francis progressed in his studies in the new, vigorous English language that had even begun to be heard in certain cultured exchanges at Court, Stephen watched with silent approval. They all knew that the day would come when Francis would lead his fellows because he could write in Latin and French, but the treasure of their own language, to be written down and used in the making of their own laws as well as in worship, was something they hardly dared contemplate, as it became closer and closer to reality.

The rift with Cressida was more a clash of wills, and watching her brother at the rare moments when he played with her small son, she wondered if at the heart of it lay infant jealousy, the simplest of explanations. The child she had brought to freedom had been supplanted, or so it might seem to him, by her own child in her affections. But he was wrong. It was true now that Cressida, after Stephen, loved Richard more than anything in the world, but she would have been hard put to it to come to a decision had she been forced to choose between the baby and Francis.

In fact, she was wrong. Francis had come to manhood, and in her almost possessive treatment of her baby saw the threat that Cressida's strong character could be to his own independence.

It was a relief to them both when, as the days grew longer, Francis announced that he was going into the countryside to meet 'new friends'. He would be back at Claire House in time for Stephen and Cressida's wedding.

He made the announcement early one evening, when Stephen happened to be at home. They were in the ground floor living-room, a log fire blazing in the hearth. Stephen at once looked across to where Cressida sat in her favourite window seat. He signalled to her that she should make no objection. With a shrug of resignation she said to Francis:

'You know you must do as you wish, brother. Your freedom was hard won, and must be well used. That is all I ask you to remember.'

Francis gave an impatient nod of his fair head. He

knew only too well how much he owed his sister, but he was eager to prove to her that her aid was no longer needed. 'I do remember, Cressida,' he said in an even, controlled tone. 'Almost every day of my life I am reminded of it.'

A sharp, warning look from Stephen silenced him. Both men were aware of Cressida's role in her brother's growing restlessness, but Stephen would not tolerate open defiance of her, at least in his presence.

Cressida looked from one to the other, sensing that they shared some things she would never understand. But she had so much now to make her content that she did not choose to build the slight atmosphere of hostility that had arisen into anything more. She returned to her window, and her study of the twilight. The ships that passed so close to them, the river lights, and the often busy tow path at the foot of their garden, had become sources of endless fascination to her.

'When I learn to read,' she said airily, 'I shall have much more in my head than fears for the safety of my brother.'

And she was at a complete loss to understand why Francis and Stephen burst into laughter, as if at some further shared secret, and Stephen strode across to where she sat and put an arm about her shoulders.

'You do not know how close you are to becoming a scholar yourself, my dear,' he murmured into her ear.

The next morning, Cressida watched Francis ride away into the city, and guessed that he had other 'friends' to find before he made for the open country where, like the man Dominic she once knew so briefly, he no doubt held his meetings and sought out his rebels. As he looked back, he waved, and smiled. She returned his wave, and before she went back into the house looked up at the pale blue sky of early spring.

Somewhere in the trees behind the house a bird chirruped, and another sang in reply. They were the birds of the city, and she had first heard them in the yard behind the house in River Lane.

She awoke some mornings later to the same sweet, sharp sounds, but they mingled with a baby's hungry wailing from the direction of the nursery. Finding that Stephen had already left their bed, she sat up quickly, with a premonition that something was wrong.

Not pausing to put on a robe, she ran swiftly from the bedroom to the nursery, and stood in her shift watching Beatrice pick Richard up from his cradle.

'There's nothing wrong with him that a good feed won't cure.' Beatrice gave a rosy-faced smile. 'He's getting a big child, and wants his meat as well as his milk. It's high time his parents made themselves regular too, at the church.'

'That's enough, Beatrice,' Cressida said, but with only a tinge of mock anger. 'You know all that is in hand. I have chosen the month of May, and my brother will be at my side.'

'Master Stephen too, I hope,' Beatrice teased as she gave a resounding kiss to Richard's round cheek. 'It's his dark curls on this baby, and his grey eyes now the first blue has gone.'

Cressida could not resist, but walked to where Beatrice rocked Richard in her arms, and held out her own for him. She bent her head low over his as Beatrice handed him to her, and the sweet damp warmth of the baby and the small cries he gave as he recognized her served to reassure her.

It was late that morning that her nervous mood returned, with the arrival on the jetty of a royal barge she recognized as that of a messenger sent by the Queen. The man who paced solemnly to the door was unknown to her. She called to Beatrice that she would receive him, and the servants were to stay in their quarters meanwhile.

An hour later, she found herself on the royal barge bound for Westminster. It was Philippa who had sent word that she needed her friend. And the Queen, her namesake, had insisted on putting her own messenger at her disposal.

Cressida found Philippa alone in a small side room reserved for the more intimate gatherings of the ladies-in-waiting to the Queen. She stood at the window, staring out, and when Cressida was announced she turned and ran to her, revealing a tearstained face and great dark eyes deep with sorrow.

Their arms about each other as in the days when they had shared other sorrows, and other fears, the two young women walked to a high settle by the room's great fire-place, and as they sat down Philippa broke into more weeping.

'Philippa, you must tell me what ails you,' Cressida said softly. Her own heart beat painfully, as she tried to think what could have happened to put the usually merry Philippa in this state. For a fleeting second, she wondered if she herself, and Francis, were involved. Had something happened to Stephen, and only Philippa dared tell her? Or – had Francis at last gone his own wilful path and come to disaster?

'Is it Francis?' she asked. She knew by now that Philippa was deeply fond of her brother, and if he were in trouble, or worse, it could well occasion such grief. But Philippa shook her head, and tried to speak.

'It is my brother. I know he has always been hateful, but he cared for me in his way. And I gave him no peace.'

Cressida's heart raced. She hardly dared ask if what she suspected was true. From the way in which Philippa spoke of him, Robert could well be dead. And the knowledge brought with it a surge of relief, mingled with a growing fear that it had been Francis who had perpetrated their old enemy's end.

'Robert is dead,' she said quietly. It was a statement now, not a question. Philippa swallowed, and nodded, and blew her nose on the small kerchief which had been a gift from the Queen. It was an innovation which hardly served its purpose, but it was an improvement on past courtly ways.

'Murdered,' Philippa whispered, as if in awe of the knowledge. 'By a peasant farmer. He marked his son, for trying to escape again. It's against the law now, and I can't think what made him so angry or so foolish as to do such a thing. The men turned on him in the fields.'

Again she broke into a torrent of sobbing, and Cressida waited, a vivid picture in her mind's eye of the fields she had known as a child. She saw the squat, bent figures of the peasants working the poor earth, the taller figure of her father at the plough before he had gone to France. She remembered how she had sat under the oak tree at the corner of his thin strip of land as a child, and scattered the seed for him when she was old enough, the wind tugging at her hair and her short linen gown.

Then the squat figures turned, joined in an ugly blur, and felled some creature in their midst with harsh cries of satisfaction. At that moment, Cressida felt that she knew exactly how Robert had died, and why. It was the beginning of an anger that crept across the land, and would one day march. And yet it agonized her to think that the victim had been the blundering, passionate man who had so recently stood on the edge of her land and wanted her again.

Then she remembered Robert's last words to her. That there had been others who waited for him at home. His visit to her had been a strange farewell, and it was almost as if he had tried to tell her – though he failed – that he could do without her memory.

'Philippa,' she began, after a long silence in which they both hardly dared think of how terrible Robert's end must have been, 'how do you know all this? Has word come from home? Does Robert leave no one else to mourn him?'

Philippa half-shook, half-nodded her head, and swallowed, her sobs growing quieter.

'One of the men rode all night, and all next day. I had

to be told because of the lands. They are my responsibility now, Cressida. I will have to go home. After all this time. But – '

At the thought of parting from her friend after all they had shared Cressida put out a hand to touch her cheek. 'But you will come back. You must. Think how we all love you. The Queen. And – my brother.'

At the mention of Francis Philippa once more burst into tears, and Cressida knew then for sure that, as she had suspected, Sir Robert's own sister loved the boy who had fled from him years before.

'I don't know how to tell you, Cressida,' Philippa wept. 'There is someone as you said. In these last months, it seems, my brother has given status to a girl . . . I do not like to say . . . there have been so many. But it seems that this girl, Abigail, was of great beauty, but dared too to defy my brother in many things. And then – she bore him a child. A fair-haired girl, the messenger tells me. And my brother doted on this child – and called her – '

'What did he call her? Philippa, you must tell me.' Cressida stifled an impulse to shake her friend by the shoulders to wake her from her grief. She was both frightened and fascinated by what she might learn.

Aware of her impatience, Philippa looked up. The dark eyes stared frankly, yet questioning, into the blue. Cressida waited. And yet she knew.

'He called the child Cressida,' Philippa said softly. 'And she is to be brought up as his own. And I am to see that this is done . . . '

Cressida's first thought when she heard Philippa say the name was that if Stephen heard of this she would never be able to explain to him. She did not even understand it herself, except perhaps that something in Robert's face at their last meeting had spoken of more than lust. She had always sensed his admiration. But her loathing of what he had done to her had discounted the use of the word 'love' in her thoughts of him.

Now he had put his mark for ever on her life, so

cleverly and subtly that she would not have believed it was of his own doing. Perhaps his anger had bred such cunning in him? Perhaps he simply meant to mock her. For that is what it must be now, in her own village, she thought bitterly. A mockery. And she could not bear the thought that the place where her father and mother had brought her up should become a haven of scandal and slander. For there was no one else of that name in the district, that she knew. And no one with golden hair, to be labelled witch when things went badly.

With this realization, Cressida also understood what a life such a child would lead. Not only Cressida's good name was at stake, but the child's happiness.

'And what of her mother? Abigail?' Cressida asked Philippa at last.

Philippa shook her head. 'I cannot believe she loved my brother,' she said numbly. 'I understand none of it. But I do know that I must go home, and see what is to be done. And my lands – for they are mine now – must be cared for. Someone will have to see that all this tragedy does not leave its mark.'

'There is someone who would help you. Not far from there. Do you remember the Earl of Mansey's territory stretching into Ashby?'

Philippa grimaced. How could she forget Ralph of Mansey and his repeated attempts to wed her? To her knowledge he had still not found a bride, and with her brother's lands now firmly in her possession he would be sure to renew his grotesque courtship with zest.

'There is a man at Ashby called Peter, the clerk,' Cressida went on, choosing to ignore Philippa's wry expression. 'He has the power it will need to bring peace to your lands, if anyone has. I met him once. You know what happened to the travelling man, his friend. The man Dominic.'

She tried to destroy the picture in her mind's eye of Dominic as she had last seen him, and to replace it with the way he had been when he was alive, that last night at

Peter's house, and the children listened to his songs.

Now at last she believed she had found a way to do something that had lain dormant in her heart. She could carry on something of his work, but in a good way. It was he who had taught her that the true revolution would come from thoughtful, peaceful men. And his friend Peter lived close enough to Philippa's lands to carry their ideas to the peasants there. Swiftly and quietly, Cressida began to tell Philippa how Peter could be reached, and how he might help her.

In the stress of the moment, they had no sense of time. But as Cressida talked and her friend listened, they forgot something of their shared sorrow and pain. By the time Cressida rose to leave, both girls had the same sense of purpose shining from their eyes that they had shared on the night they fled from Ralph of Mansey to Grimthorne Abbey.

It was a perfect May morning when some weeks later Stephen and Cressida crossed the lawns at Claire House and took the river walk to London Bridge and the city. Although it would have been the natural consequence of Stephen's place at Court that they would marry at Westminster Abbey, and that the King himself would be represented at the ceremony, they had instead chosen a small city church, and a private service – to be conducted by a friar whom Stephen had known at Oxford.

The only witnesses to the marriage were Francis and Philippa, who had delayed her departure from Court in order to be present. The baby Richard was left at Claire House with Beatrice for the occasion. A dark-haired, rosy-cheeked child now with a strong will of his own, he had cried lustily in Beatrice's plump grasp when Cressida and Stephen left the house, but by the time Cressida turned on the river walk to wave goodbye he was laughing again. Relieved at this change in mood, Cressida walked to the church in quiet good spirits, her brother and Stephen on either side.

As there was still a crisp, spring-like brightness in the air Cressida wore a deep blue open-sided surcoat trimmed with grey fur over the gown she had chosen for her wedding. The gown itself was a pale blue silk, its tight sleeves banded with pearls, and the jewels were echoed in the mesh of the silver nets which bound Cressida's golden hair close to her face. From beneath her dress, there was a glimpse of grey leather shoes finely stitched with silver thread, and delicately pointed – in the latest fashion. As she walked, the sun glinted on the gold and silver helmet of her head, and Stephen was reminded of the figures of romantic legend stepping gracefully against Italian landscapes or walking in exquisitely formal gardens. As they walked, they did not touch, and in her happiness Cressida hardly dared look into Stephen's eyes.

Waiting for them in the shaded courtyard at the west door of the church, they found Philippa. She had come on horseback along the Strand, and a grey mare held by a young page stood at the church gate ready for her return. Gently, and without words, the two girls embraced. Their last meeting, and the plans they had made, had drawn them closer than ever.

Now that the moment for their marriage had come, both Stephen and Cressida approached it solemnly, and their companions were aware of their mood, and little was said. But as they came to the church entrance, Philippa whispered that she begged one favour – that the musician she had brought from the palace, and who now waited for them in the shadows of the porch, should be allowed to play for Cressida. Unable to refuse, Cressida nodded, and moments later she walked, with Stephen at her side, towards the altar, the trembling notes of a lute and the high chant of a young boy's voice echoing in the graceful curves of the painted ceiling above the transept.

At the altar, the friar waited for them, unsmiling. For a second it crossed Cressida's mind that such a man might not entirely approve of the ceremony he had been asked to conduct. Stephen's marriage was a loss to the friars, and to the Church itself. Not everyone knew that he continued his chosen work with as much dedication as a celibate man of holy orders might show – if not more. But if there was a glimmer of disapproval in the friar's eye, Cressida had no more time to dwell on its meaning as the sing-song rush of Latin that would wed her to the man she loved began.

Cressida had learned enough of the ceremony in advance, with Stephen's help, to understand its meanings. But the whole thing was now conducted at such speed that the words became a hazed, distant chant in her ears, and she had to concentrate on the fact that Stephen was close by her, his hand now firmly in hers, to keep herself from fainting. As the friar made the sign of the Cross before her eyes, she realized that the service was over, and Stephen's hand at her elbow helped her rise from her knees and turn to face the aisle again. Once more the young musician began to play, and Philippa, leaving her place, came to stand in front of Cressida and Stephen. Then, as they walked towards the west door, Francis took up his place behind them, and Philippa began to scatter fresh violets in the bridal couple's path. It was at that moment that Cressida's whole being sang at Stephen's touch, and at the knowledge that he loved her deeply enough to commit himself to her solemnly in this way.

Outside, the sunlight glinted on the bridle of Philippa's horse, and the birds sang in the few trees boasted by the churchyard. Again, Philippa and Cressida embraced silently, and as Francis moved forward to help Philippa remount for her return to Court it was he who spoke first:

'There will be feasting one day,' he told her, looking up into her eyes as she sat the grey mare. 'One day weddings will be a matter for rejoicing in the church itself – for the people to sing, and say "amen" – in a ceremony they understand.'

Philippa looked down at him keenly. He returned her gaze, shading his eyes against the bright light with a slender, boyish hand. 'It was still a thing of beauty, your sister's marriage service,' she said. 'And those who wish for such a wedding as you describe will have long to wait.'

'It would be worth it. Do you not think so, Philippa?' Francis replied.

She blushed slightly, and waving once more to where Cressida and Stephen still stood at the churchyard gate, she signed to her young page that she was ready to leave. 'This was a marriage that was meant to be, Francis. It matters hardly at all that it was not conducted in the way you would wish.'

'But you forget that my sister's flight, her bid for my own freedom, was what started all this. She believes in the new order of things as much as I – more. Tell me, Philippa, where do you stand? Why have you not returned to your great manor house and your serfs?' Francis held the bridle of her horse, his hand on the page's shoulder, so that she should not move off until he willed it.

Philippa leaned down and with an abrupt little gesture removed his grip. 'You do not know as much as I of these things, Francis, for all your studies. I leave tonight for my lands, and I am not sure that I shall ever return.'

Before Francis could stop her, she kicked at the mare's side with her heels, and her page regained control of the bridle as the horse began to trot smartly off in the direction of the Strand. As she went, Francis stood his ground, his eyes narrowed as he watched her. Then, as she turned to wave once more, he saw that she was weeping, and her parting words echoed for some time in his ears, long after the sound of her horse's hooves on the London stones had died away.

On the return to Claire House Francis dawdled thoughtfully, some way behind his sister and her husband. Soon they were lost to him, in the rattling carts and bustling shoppers that now filled the busy lanes approaching London Bridge. It was at Stephen's whim that they walked at all, and as it grew later in the morning the sun became warmer, the crowds less friendly, and Cressida wished that they could linger and gaze into shop windows, as it was months since she had been in the city at all and her old enjoyment of its teeming life, its spicy smells, the hint of luxury in the small boutiques, and the sweet freshness of the food purveyed on the open stalls around them tempted her.

But as they came to the bridge itself, Stephen – as if suddenly tired of the place, and of the occasion – quickened his pace, and drew ahead of her. By the time they were treading the wooden drawbridge she had almost to break into a run to stay at his side. As a great cart hurtled towards them, wheels flying and straw mixed with mud flying with them, she was glad it was not a time of year when the rains would have added to her discomfort. She lifted her gown, and stepped quickly out of its path.

Then, as she turned to rejoin Stephen, she found she had lost sight of him in the mill of shoppers and street vendors that made the drawbridge a market place as busy as that of any country town. She called, but her voice was lost as a stallholder shouted his wares in her ears. Hurriedly, she stepped into the centre of the path, so that she might make quicker progress.

Almost at once, a wide, tarpaulined carriage bore down on her, coming at speed. She was aware of a brown-garbed figure, a hooded head, and under the hood dark, gleaming eyes flecked with hazel in a brooding face. For a split second, the eyes bored into hers, and she returned the wild gaze of the man who drove down on her. Then, realizing it was too late for the cart to be diverted, she flung herself to one side, and at the same time found her brother's arm about her, and felt herself being dragged to safety.

While Francis cursed Stephen for neglecting her, and Cressida, curbing her tears, fought for self-control and tried to defend Stephen's neglect, there was one thought fighting for prominence. Making light of the incident, and brushing her surcoat free from dust as she walked on with her brother, Cressida told herself again and again that the man she had seen was not Brother Oliver, and that the encounter was not a bad omen on her wedding day, and that the night when she had faced him in the monastery and taunted him with her young body had not come home to roost. As they caught up with Stephen, she whispered to her brother fiercely that he was to make nothing of the scene. Nothing, she told him, was to be allowed to spoil her wedding day. But as she found herself walking once more at Stephen's side, and taking the path that led them along the south bank of the river to Claire House again, the sounds of the traffic and the market cries slowly receded into the distance, and she shivered in the bright sunlight.

It was not until they had walked by the river for some time, and the long low structure of Claire House glimmered ahead of them in the sunlight, that Cressida was able to wipe from her thoughts the memory of the day she had entered the city with Francis, Brother Oliver driving the lurching cart, and above them the grinning, crinkled masks of dead men.

'When we are home,' Francis said to Stephen as they walked, trying to satisfy his sister's request that he should not quarrel on such a day, 'will you spend the day with us? Do you have to go to Westminster?'

Stephen slackened his pace. 'It is to be home as soon as I may that I have made you walk so fast. There are things to do, and I would be with my wife and child at Claire House. I have told the bishops, the scribes, the King himself, that nothing will take me from home today.'

Deeply pleased by his words, Cressida fell into step beside Stephen, and gradually the happy mood in which the day had begun returned to her. By the time they crossed the lawns to the house, where Beatrice stood in the doorway, Richard in her arms, as if she had not moved from her place since they left, she was smiling. She broke into a run for the last yards, and took Richard into her arms, in time for Stephen to put a shielding arm around them both as he joined them. Then, signing to Francis to follow, he drew Cressida, still holding their child, across the wide flagstones of the spacious hallway, and into the room usually reserved for his private study.

Once inside, he led Cressida to a high-backed carved wooden seat in the window. From it she had a view of the high masts of a ship moored on the river, and a brilliant sky above it, the sea birds' cries as they wheeled round the ship reaching them in the dim seclusion of Stephen's very own room. With a sigh of contentment, she raised the child in her arms so that he could watch the scene. But she was almost instantly interrupted by a conspiratorial whisper in the doorway, and turned to find Francis and Stephen bent earnestly together over a small, bound book.

'You promised not to work today, Stephen,' she called. 'And before we are in the house, I find you at your books. My brother too!'

Stephen came across the room to her, his lean dark face gentle above the rich velvet of his tunic. His deep grey eyes had never, she thought, been so full of love for her. The smile at his lips was the rare, teasing smile she had grown to expect at their most solemn moments. Francis followed him, holding the book carefully in both hands.

'Give me my son. It is fitting that we spend some time together, today of all days.' Stephen smiled as he took Richard from her, and nursed him closely, gazing tenderly down at the dark curls. 'And your brother has something for you. A wedding gift.'

Cressida's eyes widened as she turned to Francis, and he held out to her the book he carried. Wordlessly, she took it from him, and stroked the smooth, rich vellum of its cover. Her eyes shining, she let the pages fall open, and tried to decipher the richly embellished lettering of the text. 'I – I cannot read, brother. A book for me? It is very beautiful, but you know well that I have not your skills.

What does it say? Tell me, what is written here?'

Francis came to her side, and as she still held the book open, at the first leaf, he told her: 'There is no secret to it, sister. And the book is the work of many who love you, and know your worth. It is in English – a primer of words in your own tongue. So that when you begin to read, as you must if you are to teach your own son, it will be in the language our mother loved. And now you know why we laughed so when you said you would learn!'

As she touched the page with wondering, questioning hands, Cressida's eyes filled with tears. 'Then tell me what it says, here where the blue flowers are painted and the small trees, each leaf as clear as if it grew in our garden.'

Stephen watched Cressida from where he stood by the window. Her delight was that of a young girl still, but everything about her figure spoke of her maturity. In four years she had made herself free, borne his child, and become his wife. The proud head, the high breasts, and the wide, sensuous mouth had not changed. But the blue eyes were solemn now, and the figure of the woman who walked towards him was voluptuous and more desirable than he would willingly confess.

'Tell me, Stephen. Have you seen my gift? Do you know what is written, here on this first page?'

'I know, little Cressida. For it is I who wrote the words, your brother who enscribed them, and many other unknown friends who made this book to our order. The words on this first page read "The Book of Cressida".'

With a cry of joy, Cressida ran to him. Then she called Francis to her, and all their recent differences forgotten, she kissed him, before the tears of happiness began again to cloud her eyes.

She turned from her companions then, leaving the child with Stephen, who held him proudly.

As she stood alone in the window she fought to conceal the strange mixture of emotions that held her in its grip. Joy that she and Stephen faced the future as man and wife. Delight in their child. Fears for her brother, and the knowledge that the path he had taken might lead to disaster. Pain at the thought that her friend Philippa must return home, to such tragedy. And yet her return would start a long chain of events that would bring changes only for the good, in the village where they both were born.

It seemed to her then that the wide grey-green water of the river that flowed so close to the house, the swift flow of its tide, were symbols of the journey into freedom she had made with the others with her in the room, and that she would forever forge her life in the same, headstrong, all-embracing way of the river itself, through the great city that was growing into being not far from where they stood.

BOOK II

Dark Tapestry

1

Shading her eyes against the brightness of a morning in early summer with a slim jewelled hand, Cressida stood at the open window of her bedroom and watched her young son Richard fasten his rowing boat at its moorings and run across the lawns from the river to Claire House.

The boy had her own straight golden hair. Her brother Francis shared the same colouring. But she never looked into Richard's deep grey eyes without recalling the ardent, impoverished young scholar her husband Stephen had once been. Their child had inherited his father's lean good looks and her own rebel spirit, and sometimes she feared for him. But for the time being, in such troubled times, they were safe.

She never tired of watching the Thames. It was a highway, much busier now than when she had first arrived in London over ten years ago. Swift running, vile smelling, and gleaming dark green and silver now in the sun, it seemed to her to be a symbol of the teeming life of London itself. On the far bank, where there had once been nothing but rough fields, the new turrets and spires of the Savoy Palace broke the skyline, like young sentinels set there by its builder, John of Gaunt, to guard the route to the seat of power at Westminster, where Stephen spent his days.

The voices of Beatrice and Henry in the hall below reminding her of the household duties that awaited her, Cressida leaned out and reluctantly closed the window. The scent of the honeysuckle that grew as high as the ledge lingered in the room as she hurriedly dressed and concealed her long hair beneath a tight fitting helmet of silver mesh. A brief glance in her only, ancient silvered mirror told her that she looked young still. She smoothed the white fur coverlet of the bed, a smile at the corner of her lips as she recollected the night she had just spent in Stephen's arms. After ten years of marriage she was still deeply in love with him.

As she descended the wide oaken stairs that led from the first landing to the living quarters on the ground floor the house struck her as unusually cold for the time of year, and she shivered. Perhaps it was her mood. There had been days lately when a wave of happiness had been followed, inexplicably, by a darker, almost fearful sensation. But the moods had passed.

She walked swiftly across the stone flagged hall to the kitchen door, resolving not to spoil the day. In the afternoon she would make Richard study, and snatch a moment for herself, to read the new poem in English by Geoffrey Chaucer she had managed to borrow from a friend who was a lady-in-waiting at the Palace. His writing never failed to entertain her, and her delight in her hard-earned skill in reading both the people's tongue and the Norman French still used in court circles had never waned. If only her mother, who prized such things and had foreseen their coming, had been able to hear her read aloud. . . .

In the kitchen she found Beatrice, arms akimbo, directing a disapproving scowl at the twitching corpse of a freshly caught fish which Richard had apparently deposited before her on the scrubbed table. He was now in the process of persuading her to cook it for her husband's breakfast, while Henry himself sat at a safe distance in the recess of the great hearth.

'This fish is not fit for human eating, and if you try to sell it at Chepeside you'll be carried to the stocks for your pains, boy,' Beatrice scolded. Richard turned his head as his mother came to his side.

'It came from clear water.' The grey eyes gave her the determined look she knew so well. 'And why should I hawk my catch round the market? I do not need to earn money in such ways! If Henry does not eat it I'll cook it myself on the spit now.'

He made to snatch the fish from the table, but Cressida was too quick for him. 'If you do that, Richard,' she spoke gently, but caught his wrist with her hand, 'you'll be in your room all day tomorrow, either as a punishment or from a sick stomach – and I can promise you there'll be no more fishing this summer.'

The stench of the fish reached her nostrils, as if to illustrate her words, and she drew back, trying to conceal her impulse to laugh.

The boy frowned, and she waited. She knew that he loved the river more than anything. He was already a skilled oarsman, and the small boat which had been a gift from her – in spite of his father's claim that she spoilt him – was by far his most treasured possession.

'Perhaps it does have a tainted look,' Richard admitted with a sigh. 'And next time I'll go further, to the clean waters above the city – and bring home enough for us all to eat!'

Beatrice and Henry broke into laughter. Richard always got his own way in the end, and they loved him for it. As the years went by and Beatrice bore no children of her own she had come to dote on Richard as if he were her son.

Cressida guided him firmly to the kitchen door. 'When you have washed your hands you may turn your attention to the Latin grammar you have to prepare for your father's approval.'

He shrugged as he stood in the doorway, looking back at her with a growing defiance in his flushed young face.

'Father will have no time for my Latin grammar, tonight or any night. It is weeks since he did so, and I am weary of working on my own. I think I shall go to Canterbury and study more serious matters soon. With my Uncle Francis – and there all my studies would be in the English tongue, and for a good cause.'

Cressida froze. Her throat tightened, and again she

fought with a sense of apprehension. Had she made a rebel of her brother only to lose her son to the same cause? Francis had been much the same age when they had fled together through the winter darkness. The French peasantry had already set the pace, marching on their apathetic leaders whose sting had been drawn by the English. It was their example that had driven Francis, before he was twenty, back into the countryside to train with the men of Kent. Although she feared for him, and missed him still, she had to admit that he had put his freedom to good use. But it was too soon for her son to have such notions.

'You will go to my solar and sit at your desk and study your Latin!' she said sharply. Then, more gently, 'Is that understood?'

Richard bowed his head, the determined line of his jaw turned from her. 'But I do wish father would come home early and read English with me, all the same. Even the King has his family around him.'

Not wishing to be sidetracked into a discussion on the private life of the royal family – which she knew in fact to be rather less idyllic than Richard imagined – she took refuge in her own love for her son, and held her arms out to him as she walked to where he stood.

'And so do I,' she said. 'As soon as Beatrice and I have planned the day – and we have much to do, for your father brings guests with him tonight – then I shall come to the solar, and we'll read together. Is it a fair bargain?'

She smoothed his hair and kissed him swiftly on his forehead as he nodded his agreement. Then, with a sigh, she turned back to Beatrice, suppressing the knowledge that much of what Richard had said about his father was true. But she could not tell him what it was that kept Stephen so long away from Claire House, and how important it was that he make such a show of devotion to duty at Westminster. It could mean death to those who knew the truth.

It was no wonder, she often thought, that the task of

rearing their son fell almost entirely on her shoulders. And still Stephen had the audacity to blame her for being too possessive. But if Richard was spoilt, it was not surprising. When she had wanted to conceive another child Stephen had argued that it was too soon, that their lives were too hazardous, that they should not risk bringing another child into their troubled world. Rather than end the happiness they still found in each other's arms she sought guidance from the herbalist who advised the ladies at Court in such matters. She knew now that there would be no second child of her marriage to Stephen unless she could be certain it was his wish as well as hers.

That afternoon, as she had promised, she sat with Richard and read with him. The new poem by Master Chaucer amused them both. But once or twice she looked up to find her son gazing into the distance, and knew instinctively that his thoughts were once more with the rebels in Kent. With a gradual sinking of her spirits she dragged Richard's attention back to his studies, and then gave up with a sigh and gave him permission to go to the river while the sun was still high.

The delighted cry with which he jumped to his feet and ran from the solar without a backward glance was her only reward. She welcomed the chance to be alone for a while with her thoughts before the onset of the demanding evening that lay before her as hostess to Stephen's friends.

As she dressed carefully, in a silver tunic over a pale blue gown, – the long wide sleeves edged with white fur showed she was of the highest social status a peasant girl could ever have dreamed of reaching – she frowned at the knowledge that she would not much longer be able to discipline her high spirited son.

Richard had been in bed for more than an hour when Stephen returned from Westminster. He was later than she expected, in spite of the fact that he brought guests with him, and she had some difficulty in persuading

Richard to go to his room at all without a glimpse of his father.

She checked the arrangements for the meal she and Beatrice had prepared, rearranged her hair under its smooth cap of silver mesh and pearls, and tried to read. But her ears strained for the sounds of the party's arrival, and at last as their private barge drew in to the jetty beyond the lawns and Stephen's tall, cloaked figure strode up the path to the house in the dusk, the subject of Richard was forgotten for a while.

As soon as she saw Stephen she knew that something was wrong. He embraced her briefly, as he always did on his return home, but his kiss was perfunctory and he seemed unduly concerned with making his guests comfortable and talking of the day at Westminster rapidly, as if wanting to give no chance to her to change the subject.

She had no choice as the supper wore on but to suppress her anxiety and concentrate on playing hostess. Occasionally her eyes rested on Stephen at the far end of the dining table. On either side of its gleaming surface laden with fruit and wine their guests gave their attention to the meal, apparently unaware of her preoccupation.

She sat very straight in her high-backed chair, her young face slightly flushed from the wine she had drunk. When one of the guests, an older man with deep set eyes in a hawk like face, unexpectedly turned to her and asked her opinion on the matter under discussion, she brought herself back to the present with a start, her slim hand tightening on the stem of her pewter goblet.

The man wore the black robes of a scholar, and seemed to be waiting for her answer with interest. Suddenly her blue eyes darkened with a threat of tears that seemed to come from nowhere.

'My lady.' The scholar half rose from his seat. 'Are you not well?'

She shook her head, the pearls in her headdress gleaming in the candlelight. 'I am perfectly well, sir.'

She became aware that Stephen had continued his

conversation with a second guest at the far end of the table as if nothing had happened. Was it an intentional refusal to notice that she was upset? He made no effort to come to her side, and she was thankful for it. This strange mood, half fear, half sadness, had plagued her all day. She would not allow it to mar the evening. With a smile at the scholar she blinked away her tears.

'You will forgive my foolishness?' she whispered confidingly. 'I have been in the sun too long today. A touch of giddiness – but it is already past. You were saying?'

The truth of the matter was that her son's references to her brother Francis in Canterbury earlier that day had served to renew old memories and fears. Suddenly she could not wait for word from him, and something told her that he was in danger. If she and Stephen had been alone she might have confided her mood in him earlier, on his return from Westminster. But his manner had hardly encouraged conversation on his arrival.

Telling herself not to be foolish, and that the summer, when roads were passable again, was certain to bring news from Kent, she forced a smile – and was rewarded when Stephen himself relaxed in his chair, and smiled quietly in her direction.

When their guests had said their farewells Stephen stood at Cressida's side in the garden, and together they looked up at a sky in which the stars seemed to keep watch over the city. The glow of the watermen's lanterns lit the dark waters as the scholar's barge pulled slowly away towards Westminster, and suddenly thankful to be alone with her husband Cressida raised her face to the cool breeze that now came from the river.

'I have been happy today,' she said. 'The summer has come. Richard was on the river soon after dawn. But we missed you.'

He looked down at the golden curve of her young shoulders, and his hand touched her elbow.

'For a moment earlier tonight I thought that happiness had been spoiled. I could have sworn that some word had reached you – '

She looked up at him, puzzled.

'Some word of the news I deemed better kept until now.'

Her heart missed a beat. She knew now that her strange fears of the day had some meaning. 'If it is bad news, you must tell me now, Stephen. I pray you, do not make me wait longer.'

He glanced back at the river as they turned towards the house. There was no sign of life in its waters. Cressida lifted her trailing skirts as they crossed the threshold of the house. Her heart beat loudly as they stood in the silent hall. The house seemed suddenly chill, and from the silence in the kitchen she guessed that Beatrice and Henry had already gone to their bed.

Out of habit, she followed Stephen into the solar where they spent their evenings together when they had no guests at Claire House. Out of habit she took the carved wooden chair on one side of the empty fireplace, facing Stephen's own chair. The scent of honeysuckle clung to the room, though the window was now closed against the night air.

Her eyes wide with fear she waited until Stephen seemed ready to talk.

'Word has come from Canterbury,' he began slowly, and she was on her feet at once, her hand to her lips to hold back a cry that might wake the house. At last she understood the strange apprehension that had stalked her all day.

'My brother,' she whispered. 'Has he come to some harm?' Then a wave of anger at Stephen's total lack of emotion swept over her. 'How could you sit through the evening knowing what you know? Why did you not tell me at once what has happened?'

He raised a warning hand. 'Our guests were important. You know that. And we had to be alone before I could tell you what has happened.'

She began to tremble, and went to him, kneeling at his

feet while he took her hand. 'Do you not trust me to be brave?' She spoke fiercely, staring into his face as though she would will him to tell her that Francis was safe.

He frowned. 'We are going to need more than courage. We must have cunning. And we must act as we did in the old days, when we were all fugitives – and silence was our master. When your brother comes here. . .'

'Then he *is* safe?' She clasped his hand in hers.

'When your brother comes to us we must hide him . . . for how long I do not know.'

'When does he come? I must prepare a room. Tell me, is he ill? Has he been harmed?'

She tried to jump to her feet, but Stephen drew her back gently to his side.

'He is a fugitive. And this time he is not a child we can hide for months in some upper room, or a babe to be concealed in the reeds nearby like some fourteenth century Moses. Perhaps the parallel is truer than we think – for your brother has become a leader, risking more than Moses himself. And he leads secret forces that cannot always be trusted. He has fled from Canterbury because those who followed the cause of rebellion with him have been indiscreet. Three of them at least have been murdered – by some hirelings of a local baron seeking the King's favour. They have no choice but to disband, for a time.'

'But how did you learn all this, Stephen? If such terrible things have happened to his fellows how can we be sure that Francis will reach Claire House alive?'

Stephen sighed heavily, and let go her hand as he got up from his chair. She watched him fearfully, her heart beating in heavy rhythm as he began to pace the room.

'Do you remember the boatman John Aske who saved your brother when he broke cover that Christmas to go to Chepeside . . .'

His voice trailed away, and Cressida knew that it was hard for him to speak of the incident, which she remembered as if it were yesterday.

'There were certain retainers, henchmen of your village overlord, who had pursued you both to London,' Stephen went on grimly. 'You have not forgotten?'

She shook her head mutely, and lowered her gaze. She knew that they skirted a subject which would never cease to make trouble between them, and try as she might she herself had not managed to forget it, except perhaps in Stephen's arms. For Stephen to mention Sir Robert, he must have some reason that would not be denied.

'John Aske worked for me long before he saved your brother,' Stephen said harshly. 'And still does.'

'And is it Master Aske who brought word from Kent?' Cressida asked eagerly, glad to be given the opportunity to steer the talk away from the memory of her ordeal.

'He has done more than that.'

She waited. Shc could remember the clear blue eyes of the waterman as if it were yesterday.

'John Aske waits in the darkness, on the far bank,' Stephen told her, and for the first time that night he gave her the loving, teasing look he had kept for her alone when they were childhood sweethearts. 'And your brother waits with him . . .'

2

'Until I know who it is who has betrayed us, and whether the killers have pursued us here to London,' Francis said, 'I need to hide.'

He sat facing Cressida and Stephen on the high wooden settle in the shelter of the kitchen hearth. They had come to talk in the warmest place in the house, the servants having long since made their way to their bedroom above.

In the glow of the dying embers of the fire Cressida saw that the year since her brother had last come to Claire

House had greatly changed him. It was a change that pleased her. His once unruly fair hair was cut severely straight where it met his collar. His blue eyes were surrounded by faint lines of fatigue. His golden beard was new to her. This strong, determined man who sat at her fireside was new to her too. Francis had changed his scholar's tunic for rough clothes woven in brown wool – the loose, hard-wearing garments of a peasant. For a fleeting moment she was acutely aware of the soft richness of her own blue gown.

'We will help you, of course,' she said. Her eyes went to Stephen's face, and found the reassurance she needed. 'But which of your rebel friends know you have come here to Claire House?'

'And what do they know of us?' Stephen added.

'Only the most trusted. And they know that I am with true friends. As for your place at Court,' Francis turned to Stephen, 'I would not put you at risk. I sent word by John Aske. He knows which of the boatmen at Westminster are to be trusted. My escape, and my safe arrival here surely prove it.'

Stephen nodded. 'The river has always been my most trusted messenger. And there is little John Aske does not know of my own clandestine activities. He is your link now doubtless with those who will seek out the traitors?'

Francis sighed. 'We lost three men. It was an ambush, after a meeting known only to those who attended – or so we thought. They were doubly outnumbered – by cut-throat mercenaries, paid to kill. The survivors say that the voices of the murderers were those of the men of the people, like ourselves. We were betrayed for gold, I'm sure of that. No baron would risk such orders to his own men these days.'

'You will learn that there are worse betrayals,' Stephen said harshly.

'But tell me,' Cressida interrupted, sensing Stephen's bitter mood. 'Are you prepared to face a long, perhaps stifling summer in hiding here, brother?'

Francis smiled at her. 'I learnt my lesson in River Lane. I promise to be the most patient of prisoners this time. I would not put you all at risk. Least of all my young nephew.' He jumped up from the settle and began to pace about the room. 'Surely he will keep my company?'

'If you can distract him from his endless excursions on the river I shall be in your debt,' Stephen said dryly. 'He has his own boat now. A present, of course, from a doting mother.'

'Stephen!' Cressida protested with a light little laugh that hid her true annoyance. Her eyes darkened. 'Francis will see for himself, soon enough, whether our son is spoilt. And if you are right, then his presence in this house can serve to remedy the matter. Richard needs the company of a man. Only this very morning I would have given all the gold in my purse for someone to keep him at his books.'

Before Stephen could reply, and before the sudden spark of anger in his eyes could lead to a scene, she stood, and held out her arms to her brother.

'Your presence can bring nothing but good, brother. You are welcome.'

As Francis clasped her in his arms, she remembered the night years ago when he had gazed into her eyes in the fearful dark of their road to freedom. Her own gaze now went beyond him, to where her husband stood, apparently impatient now for the day to end. The inexplicable tears that had waited all that evening filled her eyes again. She trembled as Francis released her, and to hide her emotion ran to the iron brackets that held the tallows and extinguished them one by one as Stephen led her brother into the dim light of the hall.

Later, when Francis had been escorted to the long, low-ceilinged room in the rafters above the main bedrooms where he might safely sleep on the rough pallet she had prepared, Cressida lay at Stephen's side and listened to the familiar sound of Claire House as it settled into its night-time stillness.

From the years they had shared a bed she knew that Stephen was wakeful, though he lay motionless beside her. They had been lovers, husband and wife, for so long that each knew when the other could not sleep, and Cressida sensed that Stephen's eyes were open, though their room was clothed in darkness.

At last she could bear the growing tension between them no longer, and reached a hand to touch his. Under the coverlet his long fingers curled round her wrist, then traced the palm delicately before he released her hand, and turned his back to her as if seeking sleep.

A small knife of pain touched her heart, and she bit her lip. It was rarely that Stephen turned from her in such fashion, and only the night before he had made love to her with such abandoment and pleasure as if it had been for the first time. She did not know what could have happened in the interim to send him into the black mood that had threatened earlier that evening and to which he now seemed to have succumbed.

Had they been able to spend more time alone since he had returned to Claire House for dinner, she might have been able to disperse his anger. His caustic remark about the gift she had made Richard of the boat had not passed unnoticed by her brother, she was sure of that. Had her brother's arrival secretly annoyed Stephen, in spite of his sympathy with the rebels? Had he turned the anger on her, rather than treat Francis badly after all that he had endured?

To her surprise Stephen spoke. 'We must take care that your brother's escape does not bring at his heels those who would destroy my own work,' he said.

For a moment it seemed that her fears had proved to be true, and with the knowledge came relief. Stephen's work had always been their first consideration and she could well accept his concern for its continuation.

She stared into the darkness. 'Francis himself seems well aware of the dangers,' she said quietly. 'After all, we ourselves take risks every day of our lives. We have even reared our son without thought for the danger with which we surround him – '

Stephen moved abruptly, turning towards her. 'Again, you speak of the boy. It is my cause that is in danger. I love our son, you know that. My position at Court is such that he need never suffer, or want for anything. This house is yours. If ever I myself have to leave London, it would still be your home. And Richard's.'

The thought that Stephen might once again leave London had not occurred to her. It was a prospect she could not bear. Controlling her voice as best she could, she asked him.: 'And are you to leave London? Is it that which has stood between us all night? Why did you not tell me?'

'There is nothing to tell,' he said. 'I wanted merely to remind you that my cause is not only the most important thing in our lives, but it has – by chance – brought you the trappings of wealth and security in times when our own people starve.'

'It is ten years, more, since the Black Death,' she argued. 'The land yields more fruitfully now. The wars are less demanding. The boys who survived the plague are men now – working the fields. Stephen, I did not come to bed with you to hear a sermon.'

They were silent again, their thoughts racing angrily, while each waited for the other to seek a truce. Aware that her last remark must have provoked him dangerously, Cressida spoke first.

'Is there some news from the countryside you cannot bring yourself to tell?' She raised herself on her elbow, and tried to see his face.

He nodded, and then, without warning, pulled her down beside him, and with a little sob of relief she lay again in his arms.

'I had promised myself to tell you nothing. But if things become more serious, you will hear from others. You are wrong when you say that the plague has left us in peace. Word reached us at Westminster today that it has struck again, and in the same place as the Black Death began.'

With a gasp of horror, Cressida clung to him.

'I fear for my mother,' Stephen echoed her thoughts. 'And yet I cannot risk the journey. I owe loyalty to you, and to our son. I cannot leave those with whom I have worked all these years when I know that I could not return without bringing death with me.'

Cressida kissed him swiftly, torn between the way in which her spirits soared again now that she knew the true source of his black mood, and the terror the news struck in her heart.

'Do they say that the plague travels fast?' she asked. 'Has it spread to the manor, to Ashby or Mansey?' Her thoughts went suddenly to Philippa, who now ran her dead brother's estate. If plague came to her door then she would see her people die, and the land die with them.

'If it were not for Richard, I would go myself,' she said fiercely.

Stephen smoothed her hair. 'Even if we had no child, I would not let you go. We must wait for news, and hope for my mother's safety.'

A long time ago, Cressida thought to herself, Stephen would have said 'pray' for his mother, and not for the first time she wondered what other changes had been wrought in the faith of this scholar-husband who might have been a priest had he not loved her.

At the knowledge that he did not intend to leave them and ride to his mother's village, she held him tightly to her. 'I am glad that we did not let the sun go down upon our quarrel, Stephen,' she said.

'When that happens,' he murmured as they were lulled into sleep, 'we are lost indeed.'

Before Stephen left for Westminster next day, they discussed quietly, out of earshot from Beatrice and Henry and their child, what steps they should take to protect the household against the plague should it return to London. They agreed that until Francis was able to come out of hiding there was enough cause for anxiety at Claire House without adding to it with threat of the black death. Though the approach of high summer would mean the epidemic might spread fast, it was still a long way from the city.

But as she watched Richard dress in the leather jerkin and leggings he wore for the river she thanked the providence that had brought her brother to the house the night before, giving her perhaps the only excuse her son would accept to keep him from the treacherous, evil-smelling water that might by now carry plague in its effluence into the heart of the town. Her lessons in such things from her mother had stayed with her, and she still mourned the way of her mother's death.

'Richard!' Her voice was sharp with concealed anguish at the memory of how she had dragged her mother on her death bed to wait in the sweet morning air for the passing burial cart. 'I have news for you that will make you want to stay at home today – and perhaps for many days to come.'

'Mother,' he groaned. 'I thought our quarrel on this score had been decided. I shall fish in clear water, and keep only the best of my catch for you all. I will return early, I promise, and perhaps father also will be early home tonight so that we can study together?'

She suppressed a smile at the incorrigible subtlety Richard could summon to argument when he wanted his own way.

'You will not have to wait for your father for a companion. Late last night we had a visitor. He is here in the house now, but still sleeping. He has travelled far.'

Richard frowned. 'Not one of the monks? They are dreary fellows, and make me read more Latin than English – I sometimes wonder if they can read in English at all.'

'No. But you should remember to respect the good friars. They are worthy men, and true to your father's cause.'

Richard dropped the fishing rod he had been inspecting with a bored look on his face. 'I prefer my Uncle Francis and his cause any day,' he said. 'For I can understand it, and he has talked of it to me in much plainer fashion than my father. It is action that I understand best.'

'Then you will not be disappointed when I tell you who has come to stay. You will not mind taking bread and ale to the attics, where your uncle sleeps this very moment?'

As she watched her son take the stairs from the hall to the first floor of the house in a series of leaps, the breakfast she had prepared for Francis balanced precariously in each hand, she was surprised to see how the likeness between Richard and her brother had increased. Though not as tall yet as his uncle, the boy had the same build, and in his dark leather clothes much the same aspect as Francis in his peasant garb. The head was the same, tousled shape as her brother's as a child. The quick movements, and sudden changes of mood were so similar that to watch Richard now was to remember her brother as a young boy.

Cressida shook her head, and made her way to the kitchen to start the day's routine. As she and Beatrice prepared to bake extra batches of bread to allow for Francis, she was silent. It had been easy enough to explain to Beatrice and Henry that they harboured a rebel who feared for his life, and that the runaway was the boy they had watched grow into manhood at Claire House. She knew they were to be trusted with her brother's life if needs be. But to add to their burden the news that plague had crept into the country again was not necessary as yet. If the time came, she and Stephen would prepare the household for siege, and fear would be kept at bay in the feverish activity she knew that would be sure to entail.

In the days that followed Cressida realized just how much Richard had needed a companion. The necessity of making a secret of Francis's presence at Claire House meant that many long hours had to be passed in the room under the rafters, and in the light of the tallows she supplied the two fair heads, so alike, were bent endlessly over the new English texts which Richard had recently neglected in preference for the river.

One afternoon when she had completed her day's tasks ahead of her usual routine, and an unusual breeze made the garden too chill, even for June, for her to sit under the trees with her embroidery, Cressida took her sewing upstairs with her. Climbing the last, winding approach to the room in the rafters she paused silently at the low door, intending to surprise the occupants.

The door was slightly ajar, and as she waited she could not help overhearing something of the conversation.

'I owe my life to a man of Kent who fought with my attackers till he himself was killed,' Francis was saying. 'The ambush was at night. We were taken by surprise. Two others died.'

'And did the attackers run when they found the rebels were a match for them?' Richard asked the question as if he already knew the story, and loved to hear the answers.

'It is not as exciting as it sounds, Richard, to be cut down in darkness and fight for your life when you cannot see the faces of the opponent.'

'When will you know who they were? Will they follow? Does John Aske know you are here?'

At the evidence of her son's familiarity with all the details of the rebels' situation, Cressida frowned. She had not realised how far he identified with the cause. She had taken his enthusiasm as part of his love for Francis, and perhaps also as a stop-gap for his need of his father's attention. But his voice rang now with fervour. Remembering his recent threat to follow his uncle into Kent, she wondered if she should have taken it for something more than a boyish whim.

She opened the door wider, to find Richard looking up into her brother's face with open admiration in his eyes. The room was stifling, in spite of the chill of the day outside. Both of its occupants were in linen shirts, and their golden hair gleamed dully in the light of the tallows. Their books lay forgotten on the floor between them. Then, as the draught from the stairway reached into the room, they turned and saw Cressida.

The tallow lights flickered and brightened, and in their glow Richard smiled at his mother. She was never to forget the expression in his eyes. It was a faraway look, and the smile could have been meant as a greeting to a stranger. At that moment Cressida knew that her son had taken his first step on the path away from his childhood. With a painful stillness of recognition in her heart she knew that it was a path she followed at her peril.

In an effort to speak normally, she said to Francis: 'This room is warmer than the June day outside. For once I envy you your snug prison.'

Francis got to his feet, and walked towards her, stooping a little under the sloping rafters he had to pass to reach her. 'Come, little sister,' he said teasingly, 'and we can play at conspirators. Tell me, is there word from John Aske the waterman today?'

Forcing a smile to please him, she shook her head. 'Do you believe he will come to us in person? Or pass word to Westminster and so to Stephen? If so, we may not hear at once. Stephen has to stay at Court for the next two nights at least. The King requires his presence.'

Francis gestured to the neglected books at his feet. 'Then we must use the time to study hard. And give news of your progress to your father on return that will please him,' he said to Richard.

The boy shrugged, his excitement of a moment ago fading from his face. Francis turned to Cressida again.

'I believe John Aske will come to me here at Claire House,' he said. 'For once we know who betrayed us, I must return to Canterbury. I plan to re-form our band of rebels, and move them to safer quarters. Perhaps even here to London. A city makes a good hiding place.'

'And you will seek revenge?' Cressida spoke with a sinking heart. 'Why else should you return? Your rebels could easily follow you to London if you sent word.'

'We must of course wipe out the traitors,' Francis answered. 'They must be taught that we are not fools. As yet we lack numbers, and arms. But we have one strength: we are in earnest.'

Knowing the truth of his words from the conversation she had overheard, Cressida said in a low voice: 'I would rather you did not go back to Canterbury as yet, brother. There are other things to keep you here, of which I cannot yet speak. But – ' she paused, seeking to change the subject rather than respond to the darkening in her brother's eyes – 'can we not speak of happier things? Will you not risk supper downstairs with us tonight, in the kitchen? Richard and I are alone.'

Later, when Richard had gone to bed and brother and sister sat by the great hearth, the candles unlit, Francis asked her what it was that troubled her.

At first she did not reply. She moved to the table, and brought the flagon of mead to where he sat, refilling his goblet with exaggerated care. He waited, his eyes not leaving her face.

When at length she took her place again by the fire, she said: 'Do you not sometimes think of the place of our birth, Francis? Of the village, of Stephen's village too?'

'And the Lady Philippa,' Francis rejoined, surprising her with a swift, warm smile. 'For she now runs the estate, does she not? It is good to know that our fair friend watches over our land.'

'It is her land, still, Francis. She is heir to the fields round our home. I hear that she is well-loved. A good landlord, and noted for her charity.'

Francis snorted, and drank deeply from his goblet. 'I have never wanted her charity. She is excellent company, and we were friends. But then – I was a child, and she had become a Court beauty, even before her brother's death.'

Cressida could not ignore the hatred in his voice. 'Philippa is not to blame for her brother's deeds, Francis. All that was so long ago. If I can forget it, surely you can wipe it from your memory?'

'I cannot forget that Sir Robert would have had no claim on your body and no claim on my labour, too,' Francis said coldly. 'To this day I believe he blackmailed you into those nights with him, when you feared he would recapture us both if you fled.'

Cressida was silent. She remembered only too well how fear for her young brother had made her play for time when Robert's men had seized her.

And how, in playing for time, she had lost her honour. Until that moment, she believed she had buried the memory deep. Now it welled up again, and her fair skin flushed so red as she recalled Robert's embraces that she was glad the kitchen was in darkness.

'Am I not right?' Francis persisted, his voice tinged with anger.

'If it were so, you can only be glad. You could not use your hard won liberty in a better cause than you now embrace.'

As she spoke, she wondered if the men who were closest to her, her husband and now her brother, would ever be reconciled to the way Robert had used her. It was as if her ordeal at his hands had not been punishment enough.

'That is true,' Francis replied more gently. 'And it is true that Philippa would make no more claim on us. But – I would dearly like to see her again, and to talk of old times, when we all first came to the city. Tell me, does she ever return to Court?'

Wondering at the obvious fondness that her brother, now so aggressively a man of the people, showed for the aristocratic Philippa after so many years, Cressida told him that their friend rarely came to London now. She spoke of the heavy responsibility Philippa had inherited in difficult times. She dared not break her word to Stephen and explain that no one would be leaving the forests while plague held them in its grip. Least of all would she tell him the real reason why Philippa had made the manor her home or of the child left in her care. If Stephen knew of the child's existence the old rift between them would open like a wound.

'No,' she told Francis. 'The Lady Philippa comes rarely to Court.' Then, at the unmistakable sound of footsteps approaching the house from the river, Francis held a finger to his lips, and they both strained to listen for some further sign or movement in the darkness.

Moments later, the sound came again; as if a heavy burden of some kind was being dragged on the rough path of the kitchen garden. Then silence, followed by movement. And at last, an urgent tapping on the kitchen door.

Still not speaking, Francis crossed to the door, and listened. Cressida caught a few, whispered words from whoever it was who stood on the far side of the door. Her heart beat so loudly that she did not know what else was said. Francis cautiously lifted the latch and opened the kitchen to the cold night air.

As he did so, she came slowly to her feet. Framed in the doorway, the light from the hearth just strong enough to make it possible for her to recognize his face, stood John Aske. At his feet lay the body of a man, stirring slightly. There was a crimson gash across the man's face. He groaned as the waterman rolled him into the doorway with a powerful lunge of his foot, cruelly aimed at the man's back.

'We have found your traitors,' John Aske said to Francis. 'The other one of the pair lies at the river's edge, already drowned. My companions will drop him to his grave in mid-stream. But when this fellow, who still has a little life in him, has talked – then perhaps he will deserve a more Christian burial?'

3

The sudden intrusion of violence into the customary serenity of the sheltered life at Claire House was followed by the death – and sudden, mysterious disappearance – of the wounded man John Aske had dragged to its doors. But not before Francis had gleaned the information for which he had waited while in hiding.

The ugly scenes which led to the man's confession – he had been sent from Canterbury to murder Francis, and before he died he named the Earl who had paid for his services – left Cressida in a mental turmoil which would, she knew, only be quietened by Stephen's return.

But it was more than she dared to risk her husband's safety and the role he played so well at Court by sending word of the night's events to him at Westminster. She would have to be patient, and while she longed for him, to take what comfort she could from the knowledge that now at least Francis would not have to return post-haste to Canterbury: for in the dawn hours after John Aske had returned to the river with his now lifeless burden, Francis had told Cressida that he had decided to bring his fellow conspirators to London.

'Before winter blocks the roads,' he told her, 'I aim to move the few, good men we have left. We have sorted the traitors. We know our enemies. With such enemies as this man has named we need friends to match them. Here in the city, where the revolution must one day burst into the open. That day has to come, Cressida. And to meet it I plan to make my headquarters on the road from which it will come – from Kent, and the south east. Nor shall I hide. I shall take heed of your husband's strategy. I shall pose as a pillar of society, a sober, freed man.' He smiled, as if at some secret. 'I shall need work. A fine house. And

– I think – a wife.'

Cressida looked at him in ill-disguised astonishment. She knew that for some time Francis had been old enough to marry, and in the years before he left Claire House the circle of ladies at Court who visited her there were free with their glances of admiration. But Francis had nothing of the courtier in his make-up, and she would not have wanted it otherwise. Now she wondered at the sudden decision to marry, and hesitated to ask where he thought he would find the income to maintain the establishment he had in mind.

That afternoon they walked across the lawns to the river, Francis inhaling the air deeply after his enforced confinement. The sun shone. They stood arm in arm as they watched Richard push his small boat out from the jetty and row into mid-stream.

'It would be good now,' Francis said quietly, 'to go home. To our true home. The days are long. I could take my nephew with me, to see the forests that bred him.'

'Never!'

Before she could prevent it, Cressida's angry refusal had leapt to her lips. She had kept the news of the plague's return to herself with some difficulty, and at the prospect of those she loved riding into its very jaws she could not conceal her horror.

Francis looked down at her coldly. His blue eyes were stunned, as if she had dealt him a blow across the face, and he fought with the impulse to retaliate.

'Have you outgrown our humble origins, then?' he asked, and at once seemed to regret the cruelty of his reply. The obvious distress of her manner told him she had not meant to insult him, or to reject all thought of their birth-place. Slowly, suspicion took the place of his rising anger. His eyes clouded.

'I can tell you have good reason. I am sorry. But am I not entitled to share your knowledge?'

The vehemence of the feelings she struggled to control brought tears to Cressida's eyes. Her usually wide mouth clamped in a narrow line, she shook her head.

'Have I stumbled on some terrible secret?' her brother persisted.

She nodded dumbly.

'And you are sworn to keep this – secret – from me?'

At his gentler tone, the tears spilled to her cheeks, and she brushed them away as she took his arm with her other hand and began to walk again along the river bank.

'When I see the sunlight on the water,' she said when she could speak at last, 'my son so safe and happy, you safe here with me again, I cannot believe that what we have heard from Westminster is true. It is a nightmare, reborn. I never thought to hear such things again.'

'But what can they have to say at Court of our small village, or our great forests? They are far away. Sir Robert is dead. Our land is well-husbanded by Philippa –' he spoke the name with a caress in his voice – 'and you and Stephen play your roles to perfection. Why should the child of such leaders of society not make a pilgrimage to his mother's birthplace? It is the most natural thing in the world.'

Seeing that he was not to be diverted by any lies, Cressida felt she could play for time no longer.

'You would not wish to take Richard with you, nor even go alone, if you knew the truth, Francis. For myself, I live in dread that Stephen will become reckless, and ride south in spite of it, and never return. My friend Philippa too – I live in dread of bad news of my dearest friend.'

At the mention of Philippa, Francis gripped her arm so hard that she winced. With a muttered cry, he turned to face her, and this time held both her arms to her side, in the same vice-like hold.

'You do not move from this place,' he said fiercely, 'until you tell me what ails your friend.' His face was white with emotion, and Cressida knew that her brother could be as good as his word.

'I did not say she was ailing,' she trembled. 'But – I wish I knew for certain that she is safe. You were too young to remember. But I saw the Death face to face. Our mother's death – '

'It is plague!' Francis's voice was a hoarse whisper, his eyes shot at once with tears of disbelief. 'When? And how fast does it travel? Will I be too late?'

'Too late?' Cressida realised with a cold dawning of fear what her brother planned to do.

'I must go to her,' he said, almost to himself. 'Tell Stephen that I shall of course go first to his mother's house. Then to the manor. If Philippa is safe, we return together. If not, you must believe that I'll not bring death to you here, to those I love too. I will ride only when it is safe.'

'But Francis, you yourself will be in danger as you approach the forests. I will not let you throw your life away in such fashion.'

He dropped his arms to his sides in a gesture of helplessness.

'Little sister, are you blind? There are more ways to throw one's life away than that. If Philippa is dead, I am already lost. If she lives, and is still unwed, then I intend to marry her.'

'But – ' Cressida began automatically to protest before the significance of his words had sunk in. When they did so, words failed her in the face of all the reasons against such a union, all the doubts that at once beset her.

She wanted to say that Philippa was high-born, even if they were old friends. She was older than Francis, stubborn in her ways. And surely too wealthy in her own right for a proud rebel serf to make her his wife.

Then she recalled how only moments before Francis had talked of a London house, a place in society. Surely her brother was too much of an idealist, too honest with himself, to wed a woman for her money and her land – in the manner of the aristocracy he claimed to despise?

'If you think her vast estates put her above me, you are wrong,' Francis seemed to read her thoughts. 'The land is as much ours, our birthright, as it is hers. My father worked in the fields. Philippa would be the first to admit it, and she has long known my beliefs in that direction. There is only one reason why I should plan to marry Philippa – if she still lives.' He suppressed a sigh, and had to pause to calm his voice before he went on.

'It is the best of reasons, Cressida, as you yourself should know. I shall ask Philippa to be my wife because in my long months of absence from you all I have learnt is that I love her.'

Before she could reply, Francis turned his heel, and walked quickly away from her, over the lawns towards the house. She heard him call to Henry that he wanted a horse saddled at once, and victuals for three days' ride. She knew that his journey should take him then to some hostelry where he could change horses, and buy more food. But these were the least of her worries.

As her brother's voice faded and the door to Claire House swung heavily into place, she was alone in the garden with the fear that she would never see him again.

Beyond the forests to the south west of London, almost a week later, another woman, dark haired, white-coifed, stood in another, walled garden.

In the plain tunic of a peasant woman, and the same drab brown linen underskirts of her companion, the Lady Philippa gathered herbs to make sweet-smelling fires to protect the children of her household.

Her dark hair drawn back severely from her brow by her coif, Philippa looked older than Cressida would have remembered, but the well-loved smile still lurked at the corners of the gentle mouth, and the brilliant eyes narrowed against the sun while her small, strong hands plucked deftly at leaves and flowers.

The lines of her figure were sturdier beneath her rough gown than Cressida's own, fashionable slimness. Her skin was bronzed by the sun, and shone in a manner that would have been quite unacceptable at Court.

The years spent mostly in the managing of her estate

had aged Philippa, but had added to her beauty, and her natural poise as a girl had become the innate dignity of a woman of position and wealth.

To an observer, her position might have been confirmed by the deference in the manner of her companion. Slightly older than Philippa, and of swarthier complexion and almost black eyes under winged brows, the woman wore the same white coif and plain gown, but held her skirts in folds to catch the flowers and leaves that Philippa gathered. As each flower was examined and approved, the woman bobbed her head. Philippa held a sprig of lavender to her nose, and smiled.

'We have ourselves to thank that we and our children are still free of the plague, Abigail,' Philippa said. 'If it begins to wane now – and they say in the village that it does – then I believe we shall survive.'

The woman whose name was Abigail gathered her skirts close to her to keep their collection of herbs safe as she walked to the wooden gate in the high garden wall, and opened it with a free hand for her mistress.

'But if our provisions are to last until I allow access to and from the village again,' Philippa continued, 'we must think of sharing the food more carefully as the days go by. The children come first of course. You must see that your child has her fill.'

The woman smiled again at the mention of the child, her rather lean, foreign face softened by some secret thought. Not for the first time, Philippa wondered where her brother had found this woman who had been the last love of his life. There was no one who seemed to know her in the village, where Robert claimed to have met her. She never spoke of family or friends, and since the birth of her child, Cressida, had shown no inclination to stray further than the grounds of the manor house which had become her home.

Yet there was something of the travelling people, the wanderers who came from far, even from across the seas, in her bearing. She walked with a loping, graceful panther tread, her narrow hips swinging, each step covering some distance with deceptive ease. Her hair was braided and greased in tight bands round her head beneath her coif. Philippa had never seen it free about the woman's shoulders, even in the privacy of their solar.

But whatever her story, Philippa had wanted to keep her vow to protect the woman and her child since her brother's death. It was part of her feeling for her that made her leave her in peace, asking no questions, never mentioning the relationship with Robert. All that mattered, after all, was that the child should thrive, and be safe, and enjoy some fair measure of her heritage.

Only once had Philippa seen any real show of emotion in Abigail's face; the day that Robert had been murdered in his fields by his own serfs, and his body dumped unceremoniously at the manor house gates, Abigail had placed their infant daughter, Cressida, in her small wooden cradle, and shut herself, with the child, in Robert's own sanctum. Refusing entry even to his personal servants, she had bathed his body, swathed him for burial, and keened in a low, strange voice as she worked. When at last Philippa had insisted on entering her brother's room, bringing his attendant with her, she had found Abigail sitting staring into space, the slow, endless tears of the night now dry on her brown cheeks.

Philippa had made her vow then. But there were some things she knew she was powerless to protect Abigail from. What would she think, she wondered, if ever she came face to face with the golden-haired woman whose name Sir Robert had chosen for their child? For if Robert had loved Cressida, then one thing more was certain: Abigail had also loved him deeply.

Now, as they left the garden and turned to the main house, the small figure of Abigail's daughter tumbled towards them across the rough grass, the red poppies as tall as herself contrasting gaily with her bright hair.

As she ran, the child called out to them: 'A rider! A strange rider! I flew my kite from the parapet, and saw him stop at the gates. But he rode on.'

Philippa looked sharply at the child's mother. With the plague not yet defeated, no visitor was welcome until they knew he or she was free of contagion.

'Did he ride from the village, or towards it?' she asked the child.

The child tossed her long golden hair over her shoulders, and frowned. 'Towards it. He did not wait long. He reigned in his horse – a grey horse – and seemed to watch for something. He did not wear my father's colours.'

At the innocent reference to her birth and the status of her father, the two women avoided each other's eyes, and Abigail caught the child's fingers in her own free hand and swung her in a small circle before they went on together through the field.

But Philippa lingered, and turned more than once to watch the rough road at the edge of the manor's grounds that led to the village.

On a deserted section of that road, beyond a great oak tree in the corner of a long field, and beyond the fork that led to the next village, Francis reined in his grey horse for the second time.

With mixed feelings, he dismounted and tethered the grey at a gap in a low hedge where a wooden gate had once stood. From the gate, the path had sloped slightly, towards the small, low built house in the corner of the plot of land. There was nothing there now but rough grass, and the door to the house swung half open, creaking at his touch.

The interior was in shadows, lit only by a slit of sunlight from the single window. Against the far wall, an oak chest still stood where he knew it had always stood. Half way across the room on the floor lay a small wooden model of a horse.

As he bent to retrieve the toy he had left there on the night he ran for his life, Francis heard as if it were yesterday his sister crying 'We take nothing.'

Thinking of all that Cressida now enjoyed from that 'nothing' – her freedom, her learning, her great house and her respected husband, Francis's eyes blurred. Suddenly he could not bear the memories of the house where they had grown up together, and ran from its single room. In two or three strides, he had reached the grey. And as he rode, not looking back, the ring of the horse's hooves echoed down the years and became the ring of his own pounding feet on the icy ridges of the track.

He followed the path by instinct now. It had not changed. The road forked to the manor, but he ignored the temptation to ride back to where he had watched for Philippa less than an hour before. If he learnt in the village that she was safe, he would go to her. But if the news was bad, he would ride to London, not even pausing to rest.

In the narrow street that passed Matilda's house there was no sign of life. The red crosses on each door told their own story. When he came to Matilda's home he dismounted, and led his horse to the door. At first he gave a low cry of gladness. There was no red cross, no 'Lord Have Mercy' scrawled above the lintel. The door itself swung open to reveal a cold deserted room. A faint smell of decayed food hung on the air. A brown hen scratched at a trickle of grain left half open on the table.

He knew then that they would never see Stephen's mother again. For whatever her fate had been, not even an urgent call to the sick in a village would have made her neglect her household in this fashion. The neat, swift movement of his mother's friend as she had busied herself in preparing a meal for them when he had warmed himself at her clean-swept hearth so long ago now returned vividly to his mind.

Wearily, he rode back down the deserted street. This was, he saw now, a village of the dead. He dare not open any of the scarred doors, in case he found that the scavengers had called on those who had not had Christian burial. As a child he had believed fervently, like all children, in hell fire. Not to be given proper burial would put a soul in risk of damnation.

Shuddering in spite of the warmth of the late summer afternoon, he looked about him once more. There would be no one here who could tell him whether Philippa lived. And now that was all he wanted to know, as he spurred his horse and rode out of the village towards her estate.

Long after she had re-entered the manor house, Philippa stayed at the window of her solar and watched the path from the road. The description of the rider had intrigued her. She had few men to set on watch, and she did not want to alarm the members of her household with unnecessary warnings that a stranger was in the district.

It was almost dusk when the grey horse and rider appeared. Before he rode into the grounds, one of her men ran quickly from the house, shouting orders. With two others, he stood in the rider's path. In the last rays of the sun, she saw the glint of a fair beard. The plain leather jacket the rider wore was the garment worn by a peasant. But his bridle gleamed silver as he rode closer to where she watched, her men at arms marching in some semblance of order at his side.

When she recognised him, she murmured his name. Her breasts rose and fell as her breathing suddenly quickened, and her heart pounded in her small, sturdy frame. Plague and all formality forgotten, she ran from her room, and down the wide stone stairs to the main hall.

As the rider reached the yard and dismounted, Philippa stood framed in the great doorway of her house.

Francis stood quite still when he saw her. 'Your men told me you are well. But I had to see for myself.'

'Francis,' she breathed. 'We are in danger still. You must come no closer. And yet I long for news.'

She looked down into his face, and held out her hand. Then, as she cried to him that he should leave if he valued his life, he ran up the last few steps to her side.

'If you live, I shall live for you, and with you,' Francis said as he took her into his arms. 'If you die, I die with you.'

4

The news that there was to be a banquet at the Palace in honour of the French architects who had now completed their work on the new nave at Westminster Abbey came just as Cressida had begun to believe that her brother was dead. Weeks had passed since he had left Claire House, and she was not to know that he spent them waiting with Philippa until they could be sure that the plague had once more spent itself out.

In other times the mention of a royal occasion at which she would take her place at Stephen's side would have brought a sparkle to Cressida's eyes. She would have busied herself at once with plans to buy new silks and velvet for a gown, and in deciding which of her jewels she should wear.

Knowing by now of Francis's headlong flight when Cressida had let fall the secret of the epidemic, Stephen eyed her coldly as she began to make excuses. 'I do not think I could do justice to such an occasion,' she said in a low voice, 'How can you expect me to make merry and play at greatness when those we love are in such peril?'

'You are my wife,' he answered. 'You will do this thing for me, if you still love me. If not, your presence will be sorely missed – not only by the King and my colleagues – but by me.'

'I cannot face the Court, knowing that Francis may be dead. Why is there no news, Stephen? He would not have left his return so late into the summer, when he planned to ride again to Kent and bring his men back to London before winter.'

'You must learn that a man makes his decisions as best he can,' Stephen said severely. 'You must let go. Francis is not your small brother now. If he lives, all well and good. If not – we may not hear the truth of death for many months.'

'How can you say such things? Do you feel nothing for those who might have plague? Not even your own mother?'

As soon as she spoke, she regretted her words. She knew in her heart that Stephen had been as loyal a son as was possible during his years at Oxford, and even now that his life in London laid such demands on his time he had made the long journey south as often as he could.

'I am sorry,' she said quickly. 'I should not have spoken in such fashion. But I – I fear for them so.'

Stephen took a step towards her, and gripped her hands in his. 'I have come far with you by my side,' he said, 'and I will not waste these years of dissemblance. The time may soon be here when my true work can come into its own. But we play this – this charade – until the very last.'

She was very aware of his closeness, and as always when he touched her something deep down in her responded immediately. Stephen, sensing her response, let her hands free, and with an arm about her shoulders led her to the window. Across the dark expanse of water, the torches flared along the terrace that separated the Savoy Palace from the river.

'The Duke of Lancaster, John of Gaunt himself, is now on our side,' he said, pointing to the gilded spires that caught the dying light of day on the far bank. 'The Prince is the first of many who will lead the way. He is for Wyclif's English Bible – though we may not expect him to go for our so-called heresy. But it is a start. They use English now in Parliament, and in our courts of Law. Are we going to waste all that?'

She shook her head, ashamed now of her lapse. She

knew they had come a long, dangerous road together, and in her heart could not imagine that she would not be at Stephen's side when his goal came in sight. From the first time he had talked to her of his work she had always thrilled to the idea of his success. But if only they could be sure of Philippa and Francis's safety!

'I will try,' she whispered, 'and perhaps it will pass the time. Tell me, when is the banquet to be held? Will Richard go with us?'

Stephen turned away from the window, frowning. 'He is old enough. But will he play the courtier? You'll have to teach him – and that will most certainly pass the time for you!'

Although the effort she made in the days that followed was for Stephen's sake, Cressida did in fact begin to enjoy herself, as she chose velvet for Richard's tunic, and embroidered shoes for them both, and silk for her own gown. Although her heart ached beneath the apparent fervour of her occupation, her step became lighter as the night of the banquet approached, and the lessons she gave to Richard in court etiquette made a welcome diversion from his endless questions as to his Uncle's whereabouts.

With the approach of winter she had almost begun to hope that the plague would have died out and her brother would come riding into the city one day as fast as he had left. If she heard the sound of hooves on the path that led to Claire House, she would stop in the middle of her task and strain her ears until she heard the riders pass. The cry of a seabird that had flown inland on a windy day would send her running to the window.

Late one afternoon only days before they were to go to Westminster, she was certain she heard a man's voice calling to her from the jetty, and that – as Stephen was not expected back so soon – her brother had reached Claire House at last, by the river. Dropping her sewing, she ran from her solar into the hall and flung open the main door.

All that greeted her as she stood under a sky of dark, scudding clouds was the sight of a galleon moving slowly past, down river, to some unknown, distant port. Her eyes brimming with tears of disappointment, she went back into her solar to find Richard waiting for her, his face white with anguish.

'If my uncle is lost to us – dead, maybe – surely I am of an age to be told, mother?'

Stifling her own answering cry of pain, she went to him and smoothed his hair, as much seeking comfort for herself in the familiar gesture as to comfort him.

'Your uncle is not dead, Richard. I cannot believe that he would die, when there is still so much for him to do with his life. He has gone into danger, it is true. But I am certain that he will come back to us!'

As she told Richard at last the reasons for Francis's absence, the relief gave new hope to her voice, and when she told Richard that she believed the long silence meant that the plague must have receded – or they would have received word to the contrary at Westminster – her words had the ring of truth.

'You must promise me to take care, Richard. And yet not to be afraid. I trust that the danger is past, and that London this time has been spared.'

'Mother,' Richard said evenly, 'I am not afraid of such things. I know my grandmother died of plague nursing and comforting the dying – did she not? It was a good death, however terrible. I believe that each man dies much as he deserves.'

Cressida looked at her son with new interest. She had judged him – on his own words – as a boy who would seek action rather than philosophy. It gave her deep pleasure to learn that behind his ceaseless liveliness there was such a gift for thought.

'Then you can also believe that Francis will come back to us,' she said fiercely, no doubt in her voice or her mind this time.

'Yes,' Richard said calmly. 'I know that my uncle must

come back. For his cause awaits him.'

Concealing the shock which his words had given her, Cressida sat down and took up her sewing again. She had realized when Francis was in hiding at Claire House that he had spent many hours teaching Richard about the strange, alien existence he had led in Kent as a leader of the new movement. She had seen the boyish admiration for Francis in Richard's face. But she had not been aware that he had developed this matter-of-fact attitude, as if Francis ran for his life and lay in hiding and took up his cause again all in the course of a day's work.

Hiding her concern, she bit into the thread with her small white teeth which, thankfully, she had retained even after the rigours of carrying a child. Then she threw her sewing down impatiently, and went once more to the window.

Outside, torches flared in the growing darkness as the barge bringing Stephen home was moored, but she peered anxiously into the dusk as Stephen's tall, cloaked figure, was followed by that of a second, younger man.

With a click of annoyance, she went to the door and called to Beatrice that they seemed to have a visitor for supper – just when she had hoped for an early night in preparation for a long day's work on her new gown. She had planned the simplest of meals for that evening, and – as a quick look in the small silver mirror she kept by the door revealed – she had loosened her long fair hair about her shoulders some time before in the belief that she would be spending the evening alone with her husband.

As he stepped into the hall, Stephen's face lit up at the sight of her hair, and he reached out to place a loose strand behind her shoulder, very gently, while he smiled down at her.

'I see you are ill-prepared for a visitor, Cressida,' he said solemnly, 'and tonight I bring you someone of the utmost importance.'

As he stepped aside for his companion to enter the house, Cressida was puzzled by the lack of annoyance he would normally have shown had he found her like this when he had brought someone from the Palace. But then, as a breath of night air sweetened with the first drops of a rain shower touched her face, she saw who it was who came towards her out of the darkness.

His heavy cloak spattered with dried mud, his fair beard glistening from the rain, Francis held out his arms to her as he came into the light. As Richard ran into the hall, shouting Francis's name, brother and sister stood clasped in each other's arms. They did not notice that Stephen's face was tense with concealed sorrow. They parted only to laugh at Richard's attempts to embrace them both.

Then, as they walked arm in arm towards her solar, Cressida stopped, and turned back to where Stephen stood.

'Stephen,' she asked, 'what news of your mother? Has Francis seen her?'

He shook his head, and Francis gripped her arm with a warning pressure.

'No, your brother did not see my mother. He told me at once, when he brought the Lady Philippa to the Queen – our whole village is waste-land. The pestilence has left it deserted. My mother's house is as if she had walked away from it to an unknown destination – and I cannot forgive myself that I was not with her.'

With an eloquent question in her eyes, Cressida let go her brother's arm, and ran to Stephen. There was so much she wanted to know, and the mention of Philippa's arrival at Court alone had sent her into a frenzy of curiosity and happiness. But with Francis safe at Claire House, her instinct now was to be alone with Stephen as he mourned his mother. As Francis led Richard with a finger on his lips out of the hall, she ran into Stephen's arms.

An hour later, in the quiet intimacy of their bedroom they sat without speaking. They had not moved since they reached the room, and had sat on the high bed like children, their arms about each other's waist, their thoughts far away in the childhood they had spent together, in the village of their birth. Now, with the death of Matilda, that childhood was over. Francis had described a village that had also died.

That night they slept quietly, clasped in each other's arms, and before she slept Cressida resolved silently to herself that one day she would make the journey back, perhaps with Stephen at her side, perhaps not, to the house where she had been born.

Next day Francis told her of his plans for marriage with Philippa, and confronted with his obvious elation she could not repeat the objections that had risen to her lips when he had first revealed his love for Sir Robert's sister. Even though Philippa was her closest woman friend she could still see that the marriage would be fraught with snares.

Permitting herself no more than some show of concern for the running of the estates now that Francis had succeeded in bringing their owner to London, she was told that they were in the good hands of Peter the Clerk of Ashby, and that in the few years she had passed at the manor since her inheritance Philippa had shown herself as capable as any man.

'When we have found the house I need,' he continued, 'we shall not wait. Philippa will move in immediately after the wedding, and as for the servants – I do not approve – we are to make do with the waiting woman and the child she has under her care.'

'The child?' Before she spoke, Cressida knew that this must be Robert's daughter. The knowledge that the child was now in London both surprised and frightened her.

'Little Cressida,' Francis said lightly, unaware of the dread the name struck in her heart when it was actually said aloud. 'A strange trick of chance, is it not, that her mother should have chosen the name? And the infant's head is as fair as yours – though Abigail herself is dark-eyed, black-haired.'

Cressida stared past him, wondering again how she could ever hope to keep Stephen from an encounter with the child who bore her name. The knowledge that Robert had chosen the name could do nothing but bring back into their lives the suspicion and hatred that had shadowed their relationship for years. If Francis and Philippa were to be married, then the members of their household could not be kept hid for ever from Stephen. The best she could do in the circumstances, she decided, was to go to Philippa as soon as possible, and ask her to see that Stephen's first glimpse of the child and her mother – if it came to it – was handled with tact. If her recollection of Philippa's nature was right, she would be met with understanding. But anything was better than waiting helplessly for trouble.

Leaving Francis to prepare for his journey, which he could postpone no longer if he was to bring his remaining conspirators to London before the snows, Cressida made the excuse that there were still some purchases to be made before the royal banquet, and as it was a fine wintry day she would walk to the city on her errands.

In a heavy cloak of mulberry wool with a hood edged with fine fur, she hurried away from Claire House in the direction of London Bridge. She knew that if she told Francis the truth, that her real destination was in the other direction and Westminster, he would have been tempted to go with her and see Philippa once more before he left.

Instead, she walked quickly along the river bank and as the crowds of pedestrians and merchants thickened she found herself jostled onto the bridge itself and carried along the bustling, noisy thoroughfare in the throng before she could pause.

As she reached the far side of the bridge and turned with the crowd in the mainstream of traffic that made for St Paul's, memories flooded back: the strange dance of suppliance with which the holy men of Flanders had prayed in the Cathedral yard, scourging each other's backs in a grotesque mimicry of putting the plague to flight. How she had fled from the sight in horror – and how they had failed to cleanse England of its pestilence even now. As she walked on it was as if she could once more hear their cries.

With a small start of recognition she came to a familiar corner, and a narrow street of tall houses sloping to a busy wharfside. River Lane – the street where she and her small brother had gone into hiding. And in River Lane, the house of the apothecary Master Valence – where, in the bedroom she had furnished so richly from the Queen's purse, she and Stephen had become lovers for the first time.

Now she knew that she had once more to defend that love. Based as it was on Stephen's adoration of her childhood innocence and his passionate, jealous need of her body once he had watched her grow to womanhood, it was worth defending. An hour later, as she turned at last into the Palace courtyard at Westminster and made for the rooms where the Queen's ladies in waiting spent their days, her step quickened – and with it her heartbeat.

To her relief she learned from a page that the Lady Philippa and her companions were in a room of their own, as preparations for a wedding were underway. As Cressida entered the room, Philippa looked up from her rapt inspection of a length of velvet. With a cry of joy, she dismissed the servants about her with a clap of her hands and ran to embrace her.

All the warmth and delight of their girlhood friendship was in the embrace, and her arms still about her, Philippa led Cressida to a window recess, endlessly chattering of Francis and the wedding plans. Then, as she turned to deposit her cloak on a chair, Cressida saw that one of the women had not left them. She sat by a window on the far side of the room, working on a tapestry. Her dark, braided hair shone in the harsh light of the winter day outside. At her feet a small girl played. The child's hair was caught back from her face in a white coif, but fell heavily about her shoulders – in golden strands.

At the sight of the woman and the child who played so close to her skirts, Cressida caught her breath.

The woman, as if sensing that she was watched, slowly turned. The child looked up at her mother, as if seeking reassurance. Did they know this richly dressed friend of Lady Philippa who took so much interest in their presence, she seemed to ask?

With an effort, Cressida smiled a greeting and crossed the room as if to inspect the tapestry. The woman waited, a proud gleam in her black eyes, and Cressida did not have to be told her identity. She knew also that the woman Abigail was perfectly aware of her own role in the story of Sir Robert's life. She had to admit that this strangely beautiful woman had been worthy of Robert.

'I do not know how Abigail keeps so calm while the world is turned upside down for us by your brother, Cressida,' Philippa said lightly, cleverly making it clear to Abigail that Cressida was her future sister-in-law and diverting all their thoughts from the past. But she watched the encounter from the window seat with more than a touch of wariness in her face.

Taking her tone from Philippa, Cressida bent to examine the sketch from which Abigail worked. The woman did not pause in her swift, almost fierce movements as her deft hands threaded the needle through the linen and pulled it back.

'The tapestry is my wedding gift to my lady,' she said in a low, vibrant voice.

Doubtfully, Cressida noted the strands of wool that lay at her side. They were without exception in rich, sombre colours. An odd choice for a wedding gift. And as she studied the picture itself she was unable to summon the usual formal words of polite admiration the occasion required.

The subject was even more outlandish than the colours, and she replaced the sketch hastily, strangely anxious to be rid of it. It was a scene that might once have pleased her – of a deserted path cutting through the tangled bracken heart of a forest. Far ahead on the path, as if about to quit the scene, a young boy was riding. Only the back of his head, a gleaming helmet of fair hair strangely vulnerable, was visible, as he rode into the waiting darkness.

'I see that you are familiar with the forests my brother and I roamed as children,' she said at last. The emotion in her voice betrayed the effect the tapestry had had on her.

The woman shrugged. 'They are full of danger, and one should keep to the open road. But – sometimes Providence decrees that we must brave the very heart of the forest. And there is no refusing its call.'

As she spoke, Cressida became aware that Abigail had considerable presence and that Robert had not exercised his *droit de seigneur* with some simple woman from the village. There would be no problem for Philippa in bringing her to Court as a waiting woman, even had she not wished to honour her duty to her dead brother's daughter. Abigail was clearly a woman who was not to be disregarded, and the way in which she addressed Cressida told of her proud nature.

In contrast to her mother's brooding expression the child at her feet now gave Cressida a dazzling smile – but still showed no inclination to leave her mother's side.

In answer to the smile, Cressida reached out to bring the child to her. 'We share the same name, you and I. Did you know that?'

The child hung back, though still smiling. Abigail answered for her, sharply.

'There was no need for her to know. It is a name, that is all. An ancient name.'

Realizing at once that she had trodden on forbidden territory, and that her self-imposed task of keeping the whole story from Stephen would in fact be much easier if Abigail herself did not wish to revive it, Cressida turned with some relief to Philippa. 'The Queen's namesake is also here,' she said with a little laugh, holding out her arms to her. 'How good it is to see you again, and how much there is to say.'

Strongly aware of the gaze of her own small namesake, Cressida took her place in the window recess with Philippa and for almost an hour they talked of the fate that had befallen their villages, of the good steward Philippa had in Peter of Ashby, of the wedding that had brought her once more to the city after so long an absence.

The time sped, and outside the winter's day began to darken. At last Cressida rose to take her leave.

'If I do not find a boatman to take me back to Claire House I shall find that Stephen has arrived before me, and I would have to explain a whole day passed in idleness!'

Philippa eyed her keenly. Since when did you have to explain yourself to your husband, she seemed to ask, but Cressida turned away, seeking her cloak, shivering a little at the thought of the return journey by water.

There seemed to be no opportunity to ask Philippa to protect her from the danger Abigail's presence could mean to her marriage. The woman herself had shown no sign of leaving them alone, and Philippa had not seemed to think it necessary. With a heavy heart, Cressida stood hesitatingly in the growing darkness, only to decide against some hurried, whispered exchange with Philippa which might only make things worse. Then, with a last farewell kiss Philippa led her to the door. As Cressida turned to go they were both surprised by the scurry of small slippered feet as the young child ran to her and raised her own face for a kiss.

This time Abigail watched in silence, and over the child's shoulder as she bent to embrace her Cressida looked into black eyes which smouldered with jealousy. Had Robert really loved her, and had he been so foolish as to tell this joyless woman of his love, she wondered? If so, there might be no limit to the resentment Abigail might nurse against her.

In the stone flagged cloister that led to the waterside,

she drew her cloak about her. The hood only half concealed her face, and she lowered her eyes as a young courtier, with a dark, sensitive face approached her. There was both curiosity and admiration in his glance.

She was in no mood for the polite exchanges of chivalry, and wanted only to get home. The encounter with Abigail had shrouded her in melancholy. Her fear of Stephen's reaction to the child Cressida's arrival at Westminster had been in some part subdued, but in its place was a less definable sense of impending disaster.

With a courteous inclination of her head, the very least required by the code of romantic chivalry, she passed the young courtier hurriedly. She was aware that he stopped and watched her as she made for the Palace quay. But her thoughts were elsewhere.

Later, as she huddled in the prow of the small boat which was all she had been able to hire to take her home, the clouds seemed to hang above the river with the menace from which she had just fled, and she vowed again that she would do all in her power to keep the past from once more threatening her marriage.

5

As they waited for the entrance of the King and Queen, the sweet gravity of the music played by the small orchestra in the gallery brought tears to Cressida's eyes. But they were tears she had learned not to shed. In a long, flowing gown of silver cloth, her high forehead gleaming beneath a wimple of pale blue embroidered with a circlet of silver flowers, she stood at Stephen's side. She knew that this moment was, in many ways, the most significant of their lives since they had been married.

For the first time for many days the fears that had returned from the past to haunt her receded. Her brother, betrothed to Philippa who had long been the Queen's favourite, could move freely at Court when he returned from Kent. Stephen, his difficult task as supervisor of the work on the new nave at the Abbey now complete, could spend more time on the work closest to his heart.

As she watched their son's grey velvet clad figure approach the throne, and his neat head bending swiftly over the Queen's extended hand, the small grunt of approval from where Stephen stood beside her sent a glow of happiness through her whole being.

It was at that moment that she became aware of being watched. As Richard walked quickly through the mêlée to rejoin them she turned her head to find herself looking into the dark eyes of the suave young courtier she had passed in the cloisters at Westminster.

The open admiration of that first meeting was, she saw now with some thankfulness rather more under control. But the boy – he could not have been more than seventeen – had an intensity about him that could not be hidden and which could not be attributed to the exaggerated romatic ardour assumed by most of the young men at court.

Once more acknowledging the boy's chivalrous bow with a slight inclination of her head, Cressida turned back to Richard and Stephen. She had noticed the strong lean lines of her admirer's body beneath his well-fitting bronze velvet tunic. His good looks pleased her as much as the alert, intelligent expression in his dark eyes. There was none of the usual young squire's extravagance in his dress, yet he seemed at ease amongst the richly apparelled nobility with whom he mingled.

Stephen moved away to take Richard to meet one of the Frenchmen who would soon be leaving the assembly, and Cressida found herself thinking again of the young man whose eyes were still, she was certain, upon her. But with a great show of application, she moved away from where she knew he stood, and began to search the crowd for Philippa. To her embarrassment, when Philippa did emerge from the crowd she was accompanied by none other than her young admirer, and as they walked towards her she had some difficulty in controlling the quickening of her heart. But there was no escape.

In a sweeping gown of burgundian silk beneath a tunic of matching velvet trimmed with gold, Philippa had never looked lovelier, and Cressida thought how slow she had been not to see from the very first that this vivid, smiling girl was the perfect match for her brother.

It was not surprising that Francis's name was the first word on Philippa's lips as she drew near, and the look in her eyes as she uttered it told how deeply she was in love.

'Francis,' she said, 'has told me that your son needs a tutor, Cressida. May I present an ideal candidate for the position? Gervaise – ' she indicated the courtier ' – is a scholar. More than that, he plays tennis, swims like a fish, and writes poetry.'

The touch on her hand as Gervaise bowed deeply over it was gentle, but firm, she thought, and she was glad she was wearing powder as a slight flush crept into her face when he looked once more into her eyes.

'Are your parents at Court, sir?' she asked. 'My husband would wish to meet with them if he decides that my son Richard is indeed to have a tutor.' She was disconcerted by the situation which Philippa had engineered, and it would be difficult to extricate herself other than by referring to Stephen's authority.

'My parents are dead, Madam,' Gervaise answered. 'In France, in the last campaigns.'

His voice was low, and attractive, and Cressida thought that she detected a slight accent of some kind.

'You have my sympathy, sir, for my own father died at the battle of Crecy, before France was safely ours again. But – my pride in the manner of his death has helped me bear the long years without him.'

Philippa made a little face at Cressida, her eyes speaking a warning.

'My own father died for your King's adversaries,' Gervaise said quietly. 'My family was French. But the

English Captain who killed him showed great mercy when it was learned that my mother had been murdered. We were poor. There was nothing left for me there. I was brought here to London.'

Cressida understood then the delicate, foreign intonation in his voice – and the intensity in his face. Her heart warmed towards his story. She knew that many officers had brought captives – of both sexes – back to England from the French wars. The fact that Gervaise was of humble origin, like herself, appealed to her. If he were to become Richard's tutor, she thought, she could expect no airs and graces. Perhaps the boy would, as Philippa clearly believed, make an ideal companion for her son.

'No matter which side a man dies for,' she answered, 'his children's grief is the same, is it not? But tell me, Master Gervaise, does your English Captain not expect you to serve his own household? Is my friend the Lady Philippa not under some misconception?'

Gervaise told her that he had only recently received permission from his benefactor to seek his own employment. As a serious poet, he wished to find work that would increase his knowledge of literature, and of the classics. The Captain himself was childless – hence his interest in the young boy he had brought with him from France. Now, it was agreed between them, he was prepared for him to seek his fortune.

'It is my dearest wish,' he concluded, 'to be independent. Not to be rich – but to be free, to study, and to write.'

Cressida frowned. It would not do to reveal how much his words pleased her, and how oddly they reflected her own thoughts when she had been this boy's age.

'I will inform my husband,' she said. 'It is true enough that our son needs a tutor. But his studies are far advanced, as his own father is – as you must know – an Oxford scholar of some distinction.'

'Yes, Madam,' Gervaise replied, 'your husband's reputation is of the highest. He is much respected at Court –

by us all.'

She could not be certain, but in the boy's voice there was a hint of more than respect. His last words were uttered in a low, almost conspiratorial tone, and looking at him more keenly, she said: 'Would it not displease you to leave Westminster? Claire House is some half hour by water from here. What of your adoptive friends and family?'

He shook his head, and for the first time she saw that he was capable of humour as well as intensity. 'Life at Court is not the best nursery for scholarship,' he said. 'They already have poets: it would be a hard task to set myself, to excel Geoffrey Chaucer. I would be foolish to turn down a post at Claire House – if it is offered.'

Cressida held out her hand, and again he bowed over it. 'Then we shall see what can be done,' she said, thinking to herself how vulnerable his young head seemed in its scholar's cap as he kissed her fingers briefly.

Then, as she walked away into the crowd of guests arm in arm with Philippa, she found herself wondering if she had made a mistake in giving Gervaise even the smallest encouragement. Philippa's excited account of her wedding plans, however – as soon as Francis had found them a house in a region suited to his purpose – soon put flight to any doubts. Before she could look round to find Stephen to tell him of the possible tutor for their son, a fanfare from the minstrel gallery proclaimed that it was time for the procession to form for the entry to the great dining hall.

As soon as the fanfare was heard, Stephen came promptly to her side with Richard in tow to escort her to her place at the high table with the French guests of honour. Richard joined a group of pages who were clustered further down the same table, ready to run errands if required. She had warned him that the banquet would last many hours, and that he should not eat and drink too much too soon. But she saw he was in experienced company, and decided to enjoy the occasion of Stephen's triumph without too much concern for their son.

As the King, a slight, bearded figure looking more aged than Cressida would have expected since she had last seen him, led his ailing Queen to her place, there was a second, thrilling cry of trumpets. Then the court broke into a babble of conversation. As the wine was passed and the music began again, Cressida raised her goblet to take her first sip of wine, her eyes caught Stephen's, and her heart lifted at the quiet happiness she saw in his face.

But the sudden return of good spirits which the evening had brought her was to be short-lived.

At a table some way from theirs, in the main body of the hall, Cressida saw that a group of clergy kept the servants as busy as any other table with their energetic attack on the food and wine. They were a mixed bunch – from dignitaries of the church in brilliant robes to simple monks and friars in sombre colours.

As the tables in that section of the hall were set from left to right from where she sat, half of the clerics were placed with their backs to her, and she found something amusing in the row of tonsured heads bent so diligently over the fare.

But her smile faded when she recognized a familiar figure amongst the clerics facing the high table. One of the monks was not carousing with the abandonment of the rest. He sat a little apart, his plate untouched. As he raised his goblet to his lips and drank, Cressida froze in her seat, unable to believe that the very last man she would have expected to find at Court, was here. Then, as he replaced his goblet, his cold, hazel eyes wandered briefly about the room, and rested on her – and she knew with a recoil of distate that Brother Oliver had indeed come to Westminster.

With an effort, she ignored his gaze, and asked Stephen if he would be able to stay home next day. 'The effects of the banquet are going to leave many posts at Westminster unmanned tomorrow, I think,' she said shakily. 'And it would be good to see you at Claire House. There is much to plan, with the wedding not far off.'

Stephen made some reply to the effect that he could not promise, but the idea was tempting enough for him to give it his consideration. His joking manner was lost on her as she only half listened to his reply, still acutely conscious of Brother Oliver's spectre-like appearance at the feast.

From the way he now studied her she was certain that he knew her. But in her rich gown and fashionable head-dress, her golden hair concealed, surely she must cut a very different figure from the weary, dishevelled young girl who had travelled in the monastery cart so long ago? If he watched her so closely, it was perhaps because he was unsure of her identity, puzzled by the likeness to the young girl who had once fired his senses. At the memory of the hostility and attraction there had once been between them, she found herself doubly angry at his reappearance, and determined to find out at once whether he was permanently at court or merely a guest for the occasion.

If she picked out the man as an object of interest, and spoke to Stephen about him, she knew it would only serve to draw attention to him unwisely. If Stephen did recognize the man from Grimthorne Abbey, known to be sympathetic to Wyclif, he would be likely to call Brother Oliver to their table, and she could not bear his proximity.

Her chance to make light of the matter came perhaps half an hour later, when the King clapped his hands. The charls stood back from the tables, lining the walls, and the pages ran hither and thither clearing a space directly before the royal table. From an arras behind them, a slow, rhythmic beating of a tambourine began, heralding a dance.

At that moment, Brother Oliver rose abruptly from his place. Shrugging off the appeal of his fellow clerics to stay, and with the panther-like walk Cressida remembered vividly, he made off swiftly from the hall.

Leaning towards Stephen, she whispered, 'Who is the holy man who will not stay for the dance?'

Stephen followed Oliver with his eyes. She was glad to see no start of recognition.

'The man is one of a series of new royal chaplains,' Stephen said dryly. 'It is hoped that his talk of hell fire will cool the blood of certain elements at court. But – did you not know him? I believe he is a product of Grimthorne. He has come a long way in more senses than one.'

With his answer, however, her heart sank. She watched the tall, dark-robed figure of the monk stride out of sight, and for the first time noticed the heavy sash of the scourge at his waist.

In the moments that followed Cressida struggled with a growing dizziness, and anxious to change the subject, whispered to Stephen that she believed she had consumed quite sufficient of the royal wine for that night. With an amused smile, he turned with the others at high table to watch the dancer who had just appeared.

When she saw the woman who curtsied to the King and then stood, head flung back, eyes glowing like black coals, Cressida forgot all her fears of Brother Oliver, and every sense she possessed became taut with awareness.

The woman's skirts began to sway, in the same, quickening rhythm. The men grew suddenly still. As Philippa caught Cressida's eye with a conspiratorial smile, the woman Abigail swirled into movement and a small, fair-haired girl who had crept unnoticed into the hall began to clap in time to her mother's wild dance.

It was not a dance that could be sustained for long. Abigail moved at such speed and with such sinuous grace that by the time the dance reached its climax she was a shimmering column of red silk turning faster and faster, like a child's top whipped into a blurr of colour.

Then, so suddenly that their audience sat dumb struck for a split second before it burst into applause, the child stopped clapping and her mother dropped, a bright circle of colour on the stones of the hall, before the King's feet. As she watched, Cressida saw the movement as an obeisance rather than a curtsey, and in strange contrast to the freedom of the dance itself. Reluctantly, she joined the applause. As she watched the girl and woman slip out of sight a cold hand gripped at her heart.

She knew that it could not be long before Stephen became acquainted with the identity of Abigail and perhaps her role in Sir Robert's past. Once this happened, it was certain that he would learn the name of her child.

That moment, and the reaction she had so dreaded, came even sooner than Cressida had feared.

With the end of the dance, the Queen pleaded fatigue, and was helped from the hall – a lumbering, exhausted figure – by her ladies in waiting. Within seconds, while the King's closer companions turned their heads away in feigned disinterest, a dark-haired, eagle-faced woman had darted to the King's side, and spoke to him so that everyone at the top table could plainly hear what she had to say.

Alice Perrers, the King's mistress, had taken the opportunity to gate-crash an occasion where until now she would have been unwanted. Her growing power over the King was, Cressida knew, a by-word at Court. But his love for Queen Philippa kept him within the bounds of decency, at least in public. Now, her finger tracing the line of the King's beard in a familiar gesture, she asked him if the woman Abigail danced better than his Alice.

As the King gave a weak laugh, and brushed her hand away, he asked: 'Where did we find such dancers? The woman is new to our Court. Was she hired from the travelling people for the occasion? Her dance came from the East, I swear.'

Alice shot a malicious glance in Philippa's direction. Knowing her to be the Queen's favourite and namesake, she could not let the chance to belittle her go by.

'The woman who danced is waiting-woman to the Lady Philippa. They say there is a closer tie, sire. Kinship, maybe. As for the child – '

'Ay,' the King looked about him, as if looking for the small girl who had appeared with her mother. 'The young fair girl pleased us greatly. Her mother does not resemble her. If it is her mother?'

Cressida held the stem of her goblet tightly, fearful of what came next. She and Stephen could hear every word of the conversation, as Alice Perrers fully intended they should.

'The vogue for fair women at Court – though our men have long been passing fair – ' she leaned on Edward's shoulder, an unpleasant smile on her face, as she pointed at Cressida – 'began with the arrival of a runaway in our midst. Do you not recall, sire, the day that Cressida, the wife of that oh so proud Stephen, came here to seek your Queen's help in her confusion? If confusion is the word. If poor Sir Robert were not dead he could tell us more.'

The King frowned. 'What has Sir Robert and the Lady Cressida to do with all this? The woman who danced is but a serving girl, a waiting woman.'

At the mention of Robert's name by the King himself, Cressida felt Stephen go tense at her side. Then with a suppressed oath he stood and pulled back his chair.

'We beg to take leave, sire,' he said to the King. 'This talk goes beyond the bounds of courtesy. I will not have such a night as this spoiled by mere gossip.'

The King shook his head gently, and placed a restraining hand on Alice's arm. She bridled, ready for the attack. But he was too late.

Cressida stood, knowing that their departure was now inevitable, and fearing that they could not avoid a scene. Her heart beat so loudly she was certain those around her must be able to hear it. To conceal her agitation she beckoned to Richard at the far end of the table, bringing him running to her side.

Stephen had not yet moved away. He stood very still, his dark head flung back, as Alice Perrers concluded:

'It is not mere gossip. The fair child and the fair lady

indeed bear the same name. The name Sir Robert gave to the child he kept well hid from us all. The name of Cressida!'

6

It was still some hours before dawn when they arrived at Claire House, and in the light of their boatman's flare they crossed the path from the river in silence. Richard, sensing there was trouble between his parents, knew better than to plead to be allowed to stay up any later – and ran obediently to his room at Cressida's request the moment they were indoors. She watched him go, wearily letting her cloak fall from her shoulders. When she turned to speak to Stephen it was in time to see the door of his study half-closed, and the yellow light of a candle flicker into life in the room.

Beatrice and Henry had not waited up for their return, and Cressida wandered to the kitchen, seeking some comfort in its warmth. She stood in the middle of the deserted room, in her silver gown, and inhaled the familiar aroma of new bread, charcoal, and herbs. Then she moved to the high settle by the hearth, and, as she sat gazing into the dying glow of the fire, she slowly removed her headdress, and shook her long hair free about her shoulders.

She knew that if she went to bed she would not sleep. She and Stephen had never allowed the slightest quarrel to remain in the air at the end of a day. Now this bitter, unspoken rift still gaped between them, and they were already close to the cold dawn.

The fact that Stephen's anger at Alice Perrers' words had taken the form of silence was the hardest thing to bear. She could have faced an open, angry outburst. She was ready with her answers, smarting as much as he from the remarks made at the King's table. If Robert's name stung Richard to fury, it still had the power to sting her into shame. But if their love was true, surely they would find the strength to overcome this setback? If Stephen wanted to know the truth of the child who bore her name, he had only to ask. But she was not prepared to run to him with abject apologies, and risk a cold reception.

When at last she found the courage to go to him – as she knew she must – it was with the intention of appealing to his sense of justice. She would ask him to exorcise the spectre of the past, for once and for all. She trembled as she crossed the hall. The house had grown cold in the small hours. At the study door she hesitated. With an aching heart she watched the dark head bent studiously over a manuscript, the thin hand speeding over the parchment as he worked. It was not in his nature, she knew, to feign occupation just to avoid her, and she stepped back, thinking to delay their encounter perhaps an hour longer, when daylight came.

But as she moved, Stephen looked up, and spoke. The candle light threw dark shadows under his eyes, and his voice came harshly.

'The child Cressida. Are you able to give me her parentage, her place of birth – and above all, her precise age?'

At the implication in his words, the blood began to pound in Cressida's head, and she knew that she had to control her own rising anger if they were to make their peace. Slowly, she approached his desk, and attempting to appear unmoved by his question, she said:

'You saw the child's mother. You heard the details of parentage. Do you need more?'

'I need to know the reason for her likeness to – to you. I must know the child's age. Was she born before, or after, your flight to London? When Robert pursued you, did he not in fact pursue the true mother of his fair child?'

It was out. The years of caring, the birth of their son,

the hopes for the future – all were nothing in the face of Stephen's deeply buried jealousy and hatred of the man who had dishonoured her.

She stared at him blankly, her face white beneath the powder. 'It seems that you know the answers to your own, vile questions Stephen,' she whispered.

'If I hear them from your own lips, I shall know the truth.'

'The truth. If you believe that I have been capable of years of lies and pretence, how can you be sure you shall ever hear the truth from me?'

He placed his quill pen slowly on the shining table before him, and moved the candle closer to her face. She was horrified as she looked into his eyes to see them totally bereft of life. His beloved face had become a grey mask of despair in the last hours.

Her breast rose and fell quickly beneath the long strands of her hair, as she waited.

'Well?' he said flatly.

She did not reply. She knew that if she spoke now she would fly at him, as she had once before. This time there would be no reconciliation, no passion arising from their anger with each other. He had gone too far. It was a stranger who now sat before her.

Suddenly, she recalled the tapestry the woman Abigail had been weaving for Philippa's wedding gift when they first met. Its sombre colours and mood had seemed to threaten her then. Now she knew that the threat was real. It was almost as if she were trapped between the smouldering jealousy of the woman, and Stephen's corroding suspicion. Between them they had conspired to destroy the one thing she valued above all else – her love for Stephen himself.

At last, she said: 'If you are my inquisitor, then I choose silence. If it is my beloved husband who speaks, then I beg him to see reason, and to wipe this madness out before it destroys us both.'

With a dry laugh, Stephen pushed back his chair, and

held the candle high. 'My humiliation at Court is not serious. I can ride it out. But my humiliation at your hands is something I will not tolerate. I have yet to hear my answer. The child has your name. Your golden beauty. The age is right. Have I or have I not been deceived all these years?'

Cressida stood slowly to her feet. Her voice and face were calm. 'There is one thing I myself have not known all this time,' she answered. 'In the child's name I learnt the truth. Though Robert took me violently, and would have branded my brother, he loved me. The message of love, sent to me over the years, is in the child's name. It may be hard for you to understand, Stephen, but knowing this I have been able at last to forgive his cruelty and violence. Robert is dead! Surely you also can forgive?'

He set the candle on the table, and began to pace about the room. Her eyes followed him as he turned and came to her again. 'How can I wipe out these memories, when your own brother is to marry Robert's sister – to live off his lands? Can it be that the profit to you both outweighs your disgust? You have done nothing to discourage the match – a coupling that should, in all justice, have seemed as unlikely as yours with Robert.'

'But Francis loves her! I have seen for myself, in both their faces. It is a love match, and started when they were no more than children. Do I have to explain such love to you?'

'And the woman who danced?' He sneered at the image Abigail seemed to have left on his mind. 'Did she also love Robert? She is a member of the Lady Philippa's household, it seems. Are we also to live with this token of true love under our very noses for the rest of our lives?'

Cressida watched him with growing alarm. She had known of his jealousy for a long time. Now, it seemed, there was nothing to restrain it. She wondered if exhaustion from over-work, had left him more vulnerable than usual to such destructive thoughts. And not for the first time, she asked if his mother's death, and the fact that he was not with her, had consumed him with guilt rather than sorrow. She moved towards Stephen, and her hand went out to touch him. The gesture was unplanned, instinctive, meant to comfort. But as he stepped back sharply to avoid her touch something in her went cold.

'Very well.' Her voice was flat. 'If we are to live, as you put it, for the rest of our lives, in circumstances that are not to offend your delicate sensibility, then we have a choice. But it is you who must choose. Either we never see my brother and his wife again – or you can remove yourself to some sanctuary where there is nothing to offend, and nothing to remind you of the past.'

For a moment she thought that he was going to come to her. His tall figure seemed to hestitate in the shadows, and his face softened. Then, abruptly, he gathered his papers together and resumed his place at his desk, avoiding her eyes.

'As it happens, there is a place for me at Oxford now. The translation of the Bible is no longer in such disrepute, and Wyclif plans a new, perfected form. Westminster can spare me at this juncture – tonight's festivities mark the end of an era. For us, it seems, they have been a farewell.'

'What of our son? And this house? Do they mean nothing to you?' She strove to keep her gathering fear from her voice.

'The house is yours for life, you know that. I lay no claim to it. As for Richard, you are right. The boy does not need a father now so much as a tutor. Someone who can give him more time, more companionship. He will benefit greatly from such a relationship.' Still he did not look up at her.

'Who will pay for these luxuries? Have you thought of that?'

'On completion of the Abbey nave I have received the King's purse,' he said heavily. 'It contains enough to keep a finer house than this in good order, for many years. You will find that you want for nothing.'

'Except for love?' she thought bleakly, not daring to

seem to ask for his love in words. The cold formality of his tone had left her without hope of a reconciliation. She walked to the door, and stood with her hand on the latch. As she looked back at him, he raised his head at last and looked into her eyes with the unseeing gaze of a stranger.

'Then I have my answer, Stephen,' she said aloud. 'In your own heart you believe the worst of me. We are better apart if this is so.'

'As you say, we are better apart.' He began to sort the manuscript on the desk, and this time she knew that it was a pretence.

'And you take up your duties at Oxford soon?'

The dawn light at last broke into the room, and the candle's glow seemed suddenly pale and lifeless.

'I ride today.'

Francis and Philippa were married at Christmas, some weeks after Stephen had left London. In the small East London chapel they had chosen for the ceremony the air was filled with the scent of the dried rose petals scattered at their feet. Cressida stood alone throughout the ceremony, and as they turned from the altar watched them until they had disappeared out of sight through the west door. Before she joined them, she sat in silent contemplation remembering her own wedding.

Outside, in the bitter cold of the snows that now gripped the town, their horses pawed at the hard ground. Richard and the young girl Cressida ran to stroke their noses. Abigail, who had carried Philippa's cloak during the service, now draped it about her shoulders. Then, with a remote smile, she walked to the heavy black horse that waited for her and, not looking in Cressida's direction, called the child to her.

Watching the dancing fair hair of the small girl as she ran to her mother, Cressida could not believe that a figure of such innocence should have indirectly wrecked her marriage and played havoc with her heart. She would not have stayed away from her own brother's wedding for the world. But the occasion had meant nothing but pain for her, knowing that by rights Stephen should have been at her side.

The ceremony had been in English, conducted by a friar sympathetic to Francis's rebel cause. There was nothing clandestine about it, as Francis was now accepted as Philippa's lawful husband and above suspicion. He had found a large, rambling house to rent some miles to the south east of Claire House, and had already set up a thriving business there as a scribe. The comings and goings of his customers, and of the artisans who were needed for the work, were the perfect cover for his other activities. Philippa herself knew nothing of her husband's true calling.

Watching them ride away, Cressida felt a pang of fear for them. They were so deeply in love that they had not paused to reckon with the forces that could bring them down. But then she and Stephen had not given thought for the future. They had simply been a team, with a single cause, welded by their love.

With a heavy sigh at the thought of their parting, she looked round for her own carriage. There had been no word from Stephen since he left for Oxford. The prospect of returning to Claire House for yet another night of loneliness held no attraction for her, and she dragged her feet through the snow as her carriage hove into view and Richard ran towards it.

Richard did not seem to miss his father unduly, and she knew she should be thankful that she had been able to engage Gervaise almost immediately after their meeting. The young French poet had proved the ideal companion for the boy, and on the occasions when she had sat with them during lessons at Claire House she had been impressed by his skill.

She had been thankful, too, that the code of chivalry which governed the young courtiers ruled that as a young married woman parted from her husband Cressida should be treated with the utmost politesse. The ardent glances which she had surprised in the tutor at their earlier encounters were now subdued. When he looked at her, it was with respect, and when he talked with her of Richard's progress his gaze was serious, and his manner formal. Philippa had been right – Gervaise was the ideal tutor. She had found pleasure in watching him become one of the family at Claire House – although her heart still ached for the presence of Stephen himself.

Now, as the driver of the carriage drew the horses in close, she heard Richard calling his tutor's name. For the first time that day a smile came easily to her lips as she saw Gervaise had driven to meet them.

As he helped her into the rough bench facing the driver, she was glad of the strong arm around her. Her shoes were slippery with snow, and the cold air had momentarily deprived her of her breath. She sank back on the few cushions provided, and waited for Richard to join her. Then, as the driver cracked his whip, Gervaise took his own place, facing her. The horses wheeled in the snow and made for Claire House.

As always, the journey was awkward and uncomfortable, and they jolted and lurched in their seats, glad of shelter from the snow but of little else. At each jolt, Richard fell against her, laughing. Gervaise smiled slowly in response. It was almost impossible to speak while the rough motion continued, and after a while Cressida took refuge in gazing through the small opening cut in the side of the carriage. As they came to the south bank of the river she saw that the water had frozen over, and children had taken to the ice with every toy they could find. The small, bright figures skated and slid in all directions, with handcarts and sledges, their feet tied in thick brown cloth which served as snow shoes and protection against the cold.

Cressida had always loved the winter landscape, and as she watched the children her face momentarily lost its tense sadness. Framed by the dark fur of her hood, she looked young and defenceless, and her blue eyes shone with a piercing clarity in the pallor of her face; she was so intent on watching the children at play that she was unaware of the admiration of her son's young tutor, and as the carriage slowed down and Claire House came into view Gervaise lowered his eyes.

In the bustle of their return, with Beatrice hovering with warm mulled wine, and Henry paying the driver, Richard slipped away before Cressida could plan how they would spend the rest of a day that now seemed to have no point to it.

She let her cloak fall on the bench in the hall, smoothed her hair. Since Stephen had gone and she had appeared less and less at Court, she had taken to wearing it in a simple, heavy coil at the base of her neck, and her previous love of jewelled wimples and gold and silver coifs had vanished. Today, even for her brother's wedding, her appearance had been almost severe; she had worn a tunic of dark blue velvet over a gown of the same shade. At the last moment she had even been tempted to wear her mother's treasured cloak. She knew that her brother would have appreciated the reason for her choice, but Richard had violently objected when he saw her take the sombre garment from the chest in her solar. She stood now, her velvet cloak shed, a slim dark figure waiting for word that she knew would not come.

These days she did not ask Beatrice if news had come from Oxford in her absence. She knew that her devoted maid would be the first to tell her if Stephen had made contact. Somehow, they had learned to run the house together as if his absence made no difference. It was understood between them that for the sake of his son things must go on as before.

Richard himself believed – correctly – that his father had gone to Oxford on important business. He was used to long absences when Stephen had worked at Westminster, and in winter had often not seen his father from one day to the next. Knowing this, Cressida made light of the matter in his presence, and now, with the snows deep over the whole of the south, she had the perfect explanation for Stephen's continuing absence.

With an audible sigh, she turned into the living room on the ground floor from which she could overlook the river. It had become her favourite, almost her only occupation, and there were not many hours of daylight now in which she could indulge it.

But as she opened the door, she was conscious of being watched, and looked up to find Gervaise on the wide stair.

Concealing her surprise, she said: 'Is Richard at his books? I thought this would be a day to celebrate, and he would be quick to make his excuses.'

Gervaise shook his head, and came down the stairs towards her. He told her that Richard had become so enthusiastic about his English that he thought the boy would soon be able to translate from both the classics and French poetry.

'He loves ideas,' Gervaise continued. 'It is a pleasure to teach him. And since I came here I have begun to write more myself.'

She looked out over the river, hardly listening. Her thoughts were with Stephen, who had stood here with her when they had first come to Claire House.

Bringing herself back to the moment with an effort, she said: 'Perhaps it is this house. It has inspired many things. Ideas, and ideals – and love.'

Gervaise was silent. She turned to see why he did not reply, and was surprised to see him blushing.

'Tell me Gervaise,' she tried to put him at his ease. 'Is my son to be a poet, or a soldier? Some months ago and I would have sworn it would be the latter.'

Gervaise came towards her eagerly, glad of a subject in which he could control the trend of the conversation. 'Perhaps he will be both – a true man of his time. Both poet and man of action.'

Cressida nodded. Then, as she turned back towards the window, she said: 'I trust there will be no call for him to go to war. Do you yourself ever think that you might have to fight for your adopted land?'

'Never. I could not fight my own people, if it came to war with the French. But – I believe if war comes it will be within this land. And between two factions of your people. If the common people once take it into their heads to throw off their yoke, then it will not be done by words. It will be a bloody business.'

'And yet I believe that the words come first, Gervaise. That my husband, for one, has already found expression for the common people. And my brother – tell me,' she looked at him again, 'do you know what it is that my brother really does? Do you believe this trade of scribe?'

'I – I have heard otherwise. But not from those at Court. He is safe. It is your son, Madam, who has told me. Richard lives for his uncle's cause. Did you know that?'

'I know it, and I fear it. But his father did not see the danger. Had my husband only spent more time with him, he could have diverted his interests, kept his affections. Now – if what you tell me is true – I know it may be too late.'

Gervaise went to her quickly as she put a hand to her forehead, and led her to the settle by the fire.

'I should not have talked of such things,' he said in a gentle voice. 'There are other times for such heavy matters. Today your brother's happiness should be your only concern. And, with such a woman as the Lady Philippa, he will be happy. I know it.'

As he spoke, Gervaise knelt by the fire, and looked into the flames.

'Tell me, Gervaise,' she said. 'What do you see in the heart of the fire?'

He smiled, not looking up. It was as if they played a children's game. 'I see – ' he began, slowly – 'a *belle dame, seule*. A beautiful woman, alone. She goes through hell fire. The flames are white. But, like the heart of a true saint, her heart does not burn. It is a heart that stays true.'

'That is a strange vision,' Cressida said. 'Do you believe in hell fire?'

He shook his head, vehemently. 'I know it is heresy, but if there *is* a hell, then it is of our own making.'

'And a heaven? Can we make that of our own will also?'

He looked up at her. For the first time since he had become Richard's tutor he allowed her to see the admiration in his face.

'I believe it is possible.'

7

The birth of a child to Francis and Philippa the following summer set the ladies in waiting at the Palace counting on their white fingers, but as she watched her brother take his baby daughter from Philippa's arms for her inspection, Cressida remembered how especially treasured a love-child could be.

Now respectably married in a large, ramshackle house at Blackheath, Philippa had left her lands, for the time being, to her steward Peter of Ashby. Happiness radiated from her dark eyes as she greeted Cressida, less than half a day after the child's birth. 'We are to call her Margaret, after our mother,' Francis told Cressida proudly, pausing to smile between mouthfuls from a large dish of wild strawberries and cream which he was consuming with relish. 'It is in memory of the past, of the village from which we all came. And Philippa wishes also to commemorate the way in which she and I met – she has sent for Brother Oliver, who drove us all to our hiding place in London that first spring. It is he who is to baptize our child.'

Cressida somehow managed to stifle the protest that sprang involuntarily to her lips before her brother noticed her reaction. After all, she thought, as she took Margaret into her arms, surely no harm could come of it.

If Brother Oliver was now a Court chaplain it was the most natural thing in the world for him to officiate at such an event. Philippa was loved by the Queen – no doubt a handsome gift would come to Margaret from the royal purse on the occasion of her christening. The presence of a royal household priest was to be expected. She could surely excuse herself from a ceremony that would be a mere formality to men of her brother's views.

'And when will this be?' she asked, taking the baby to her mother. Philippa stretched out her arms to receive the small, warm bundle with the sparkling eyes of a child who has done well and waits for the praise she knows is to come.

'Tomorrow,' Francis answered. He sat beside Philippa, gazing down at their baby with such absorption that Cressida had to turn away, unable to bear such happiness in others now she was alone.

It was at that moment that Abigail, bustling with importance and followed by her daughter, came into the bedroom, and with an air of authority, removed the baby from Philippa's arms.

Cressida looked on in some astonishment as she whisked the infant to a cradle in an alcove as if she were in sole charge. Then, with a cold glance in Cressida's direction, she left the room with the swaying tread that made her the strange, seductive creature she was. Cressida, realizing that this woman had carved a pride of place for herself in her brother's household, looked round uneasily for the tapestry she had been weaving when they first met. With a sense of relief she found it was absent.

'I must leave you to rest now, Philippa,' she said, as she got up to go. 'I see that I leave you in good hands.'

'Abigail is wise in such things,' Philippa smiled lazily. 'Her knowledge of children and child-bed came to her from her own people.'

'She is not, after all, from the village?'

'My brother found her there, it is true enough. But she is silent on the subject of their meeting. I believe that she had been left to fend for herself – perhaps by a troupe of mummers. You have seen her dance?'

Cressida nodded. She was not likely to forget that night at the Palace. Her voice was tight with annoyance. 'If she was left to fend for herself, then she showed great aptitude. She moves around this house like an equal. One cannot help but see it.'

Francis laughed, and put an arm about her shoulders. 'You forget how far we ourselves have come, sister. Would you begrudge a little equality to a fellow slave?'

She shrugged his arm away, but regretted the gesture before she had done so. 'You are right, of course. Yet – the woman makes me uneasy. She seems to wish me ill.'

Francis laughed again. 'Now that Philippa has told me so much more of the past, I understand quite well. Abigail loves her daughter, and has now come face to face with the woman Robert could not forget – surely she has a heavy burden to bear for life in her daughter's name!'

Cressida looked at him incredulously. She was certain that even her brother was under Abigail's spell. His defence of her was typically masculine and offhand – but defence it was. Catching Philippa's eye at that moment and seeing an anxious look on her face, Cressida decided not to argue further with Francis in her presence. It was of no use, and she could not wait and see how Abigail's role in their household developed with the passage of time.

'I know it is none of my business,' she said. 'I forget that my young brother is now the head of a household. A family man.' She hugged him suddenly to her, and turned back to the bed to kiss Philippa on the brow. 'Forgive a foolish elder sister. Stephen tried so often to teach me that I have this weakness – I will not let people go.'

At the mention of Stephen's name, her eyes blurred. She had thought that she had her memories of him under control, but the sight of others' happiness had lowered her defences. To conceal her tears she went swiftly to the cradle and touched the baby's small, curling hands.

Suddenly she wanted more than anything to be home again, at Claire House. With Richard and Gervaise.

'I must go home,' she said. 'Are the horses ready?'

Francis nodded, and led her to the door. As they went downstairs she was aware that two young men stood in the hall in deep discussion. She looked down into their serious faces from the landing before they moved quickly into a side room as if to avoid discovery.

She looked at Francis. 'Your scribes wear strange, country garb. Are they newly apprenticed from the fields?'

Francis laid a finger on her lips. 'My assistants come from all sides these days. They are apprenticed, it is true. But they will be wielding other weapons than the quill. If we could but find such weapons, or come by the gold with which to buy them.'

She gazed at him in horror. Although she had long been aware of his beliefs and his involvement in the revolutionary movement, this talk of violence – organized violence – was new.

'It is not your concern, Cressida. Forget what you have seen and heard. Perhaps I have gone too far. But a secret army of our kind will one day surge into the open whether I, or men like me, are there to lead them or not. It is better that someone has control . . . '

He ran lightly down the stairs ahead of her, as if the matter were closed. As she followed, trying to take in the full significance of what he had said, she was once again reminded of the likeness between her brother and her son. They could be brothers themselves, she thought, now that Richard had grown so tall this summer.

As he helped her take her place side-saddle on the small grey she had used to come the seven miles or so from the city, he gave a warning glance at the young groom who would escort her back to Claire House. It was as if he asked her again to forget what she had seen and heard.

Then, taking a folded parchment from his tunic, he

said in a clear voice that could easily be heard by the groom: 'Your way lies through Eastgate, and St Paul's is not far is it, sister?'

'That is so,' the groom called, mounting and bringing his horse close to where Francis stood.

'Then I have a small favour. Brother Oliver lives close by St Paul's, near St Andrew's Hill. I have prepared the directions for his journey here tomorrow, and the child's names. I would ride there myself, but – there is much to keep me here today.'

Cressida nodded to the groom, who bent to take the paper from Francis. She knew that there was no way in which she could refuse so harmless a request, but the thought of seeking Oliver out of his own house was anathema to her. It seemed that she was destined to cross paths with the monk, however much she planned otherwise. But, she thought, if the groom called at Oliver's door, she could wait at a distance until the business was done.

'I regret that I shall not be at the christening, Francis,' she said. 'Is it to be a simple ceremony? So little has been said.'

'A formality, merely. You are right. Philippa has no relatives at Court. I – set no great store by the ceremony. But, it is to please her and to bless the child. Brother Oliver comes early, before his duties at the Palace demand his presence. There will be no revels – you are excused. We will come to Claire House when you bid us!'

She leaned from the saddle to grasp the hand he offered. 'I will send for you very soon,' she said. 'Richard will not wait too long to meet his cousin.'

'Does the boy prosper? Does he make progress with his new tutor?' Francis asked casually, as he patted the horse's neck.

To her chagrin, Cressida felt herself blush at the mention of Gervaise.

'Yes, Richard makes good progress and is well. His tutor is hard-working. And clever. They give no cause for complaint, and with Stephen still at Oxford . . . '

She suppressed a sigh and Francis looked keenly up into her face. She was thankful that her horse pawed restlessly at the ground. If Francis continued with his questions he would be certain to ask if there had been word from Stephen, and when he was likely to come back. She did not trust herself to offer trumped-up excuses, and there had been no word since a New College scholar had ridden to London that spring with the news that her husband had arrived safely and was well.

'Tell my nephew that he is welcome here,' Francis said. 'There is much that he could do.'

She looked back at the old house flanked with numerous tumbledown outbuildings and wondered what secrets they hid.

'There is much here that I would not have him do, brother,' she said in a low voice which the groom would not be able to overhear.

Then, with a nod to the groom, she shook the reins and turned her horse, breaking into a fast trot along the dry, straight road that would take them to the city walls.

In the hour that followed, she tried to avert her eyes from the endless hovels that lined their route. But she still saw the thin bodies and dull eyes of the women who sat before them with their listless children at their feet, and was reminded that the poor of England were still starving and that her brother's cause was just.

As they drew nearer to London, the houses and streets became well-built and prosperous and with relief she followed her groom through the lively streets to the quiet enclosure of buildings where they would find Brother Oliver. She sensed at once that this was a cloister, reserved for the priesthood, and that even in the heart of London, Oliver had found a home suited to his ascetic nature. She knew, also, which of the small, trim houses was his – for in a narrow patch of well-dug soil before it grew a hedge of dog roses, spilling their summer colour into the dust of the road.

She waited at a distance and the groom made his way to the door, pausing to free his short cloak from a briar before he knocked. The scent of roses brought back memories all too vividly. The groom handed the note from Francis in through the door, which was immediately closed against him, and she shuddered, moving further away. Had Oliver seen her, she wondered? And would he know her again? It was to be a long time before she knew.

Since Stephen had left, Cressida had tried to salve her wounds in a frenzy of planning and spending. She had always wanted more outbuildings, and now that the gift of the house had been made for life and Stephen was not there to argue, she had sent for a master builder and carpenter and set the work in motion. As soon as one stable was finished, she had bought the small sturdy grey she now rode. Next it had been a logical step to hire a groom, and he now lived in the new loft. The grey served for Richard as well as herself, but with the arrival of summer she had wanted to buy a second horse. To her surprise, it was Gervaise who quietly advised her against it.

'Richard loves the river. He had his boat, and is as free to come and go by water as if he owned a whole team of horses. He had not used the grey to my knowledge since you said he may. Am I right?'

There was something so uncritical, so reasonable in his tone that she could not take exception. She had to acknowledge the truth of it, and told him, with a quick smile, that perhaps she would wait a while.

When he had gone to his room, she had sat alone wondering at the difference in the way he had advised her from the coldness of Stephen's objections to so many of the things she tried to do. More surprising, was the way in which she had taken his reaction. Not for the first time she found herself thinking of his sensitive young face and the way he had stared into the flames that night months before.

But, as always, the last face she saw before she slept was Stephen's, and her heart ached with growing despair. There was no denying that Stephen had now been absent, and silent, for more than half a year. Would he let a whole year go by? And if one year, then why not more?

In the dark emptiness of their bed she tossed and turned, unable to rid her senses of the memory of the love she and Stephen had once known. For a single, wild moment she told herself she would give up all attempt at sleep and rise at dawn – to ride for Oxford. Gervaise was perfectly capable of taking care of Richard; they would be fed by Beatrice. The summer days Richard spent on the river meant more to him than his mother's continued presence in the house.

But as she pictured her arrival at Stephen's college she knew that such a pilgrimage – for it would be a pilgrimage, of love – was out of the question.

She knew that Stephen's life at Oxford was that of a scholar and monk. The men who worked with John Wyclif were, for the most part, members of the clergy. She could already imagine the cold stares that would greet the arrival of a tearful wife in their midst, and her own voice chattering endlessly in explanation. She could not risk the rebuff that might be her only welcome.

Staring into the darkness, she wondered if Stephen might one day regret the anger and haste of his departure. He had never said he did not love her. Perhaps he too lay awake on his narrow college bed and his need for her would soon replace his anger. Perhaps.

But her brief optimism was followed by a deeper tide of despair. What would she do if Stephen never returned? She knew that he was still her whole life. The pretence of her preoccupation with Claire House and their son only preserved a mask of content on a face which grew daily more thin and pale.

Suddenly unable to bear the thought of Stephen so far away, she threw back the covers and ran naked to the blur of the window. There was no moon, but a few stars waited at a great distance, beckoning her to take wing –

to escape her loneliness in the vast spaces of the sky. Would Stephen follow, she wondered, if she ran to the edge of the world?

In her need to escape the stifling fear that haunted her bed, she opened the casement, and leaned out. The familiar scent of the honeysuckle reached her. Standing in the window like an exquisite statue, she touched her small breasts and lifted the long strands of golden hair, as Stephen had once done, to reveal her young shoulders and graceful neck. As she did so, she began to tremble and at last the tears ran down her face. She turned back into the room and flung herself on the bed, murmuring Stephen's name into her pillows so that no one else should hear.

In the garden below, the figure of a young man left the concealing shadows of the trees and quietly slipped into the house. Gervaise had been unable to sleep, and at the sound of the window opening above had turned to see Cressida's slim form in the light of the stars. Without meaning to hide, and wanting only to save her from fear or embarrassment, he had stepped quickly out of view. His blood pounded in his veins, and it took all the control he could muster not to look back at the house again.

Ruled as he was by his chivalric code of honour and romantic love, Gervaise had never let Cressida know that he desired her. The difference in their ages meant only that he respected her more than the young girls at Court who would willingly have continued their lessons in love had he stayed at Westminster. But he had wanted her from the moment of their first meeting. And the months in her company had turned the desire to love.

Now as he walked quickly towards the house he fought down the impulse to go to her room. He closed the heavy doors, as an owl called in the garden, and a bat darted and wheeled in the sky above the house. Their thin cries underlined his anguish. He would not go to Cressida until she asked it of him.

8

My dear husband . . .

Cressida began her letter to Stephen for the third time, and for the third time laid down her quill pen and sat staring into space. After a while, she got up from the small carved writing table and – her long pelisse of dark purple embroidered silk trailing as she walked – went to the silvered mirror that hung where it caught the light from the bedroom window.

Reflected in the highly polished metal surface she saw the waving branches and pale pink blur of blossoms from the old apple tree that now grew as high as the eaves. Then she stood close, and her own white face looked back at her.

Intent on completing the letter to Stephen before another day had passed, she had not dressed her hair, and it hung loosely to her waist. With an impatient gesture, she pushed it back from her shoulders. Her blue eyes stared lifelessly into the mirror. The set line of her mouth softened for a moment, as if remembering better things, and she turned away. It was five years since she and Stephen had parted. In those years she had fought a long battle with loneliness and despair, and almost won. The war had left its mark in her fair skin, which now showed delicate lines at the corner of the eyes. When she was alone the proud look and determined walk sometimes left her . . . as they did now.

On the eve of yet another anniversary of her wedding day she had heard that a friend of Gervaise was to ride to Oxford. He was to arrange his studies for the following Michaelmas Term, and would return after spending only a few days at the University. Her heart had leapt at the news, bringing as it did the possibility that if she wrote to

Stephen and he knew the messenger was to return so soon to London he might find it in his own heart to reply.

But now that it came to putting into words all that she wanted to say her spirits sank. For the first time since their separation she wanted guidance from Stephen, and was afraid of his rejection if she asked it of him. Until now she had lacked for nothing but his presence at her side – he had seen to that. Claire House was still one of the finest homes in London, and her friends at Court were still assured of good company and hospitality there. Richard was in the capable hands of Gervaise. The King's patronage meant that they would never go hungry. But no friends in high places could bring Stephen back to her, and now that their son approached his sixteenth birthday the question of his future could no longer be left to chance.

The presence of Gervaise at Claire House in recent years had been a source of increasing comfort to Cressida. He had grown from admiring, boyish courtier to a thoughtful, handsome man who was never far from her side. Yet he always sensed when she needed to be alone, and at those times, if his lessons with Richard were finished for the day, he would retire to his own room along the corridor to write. His prowess as a poet was acknowledged at Court, where he spent his free days. Sometimes she wondered if he had some secret love that took him so often to the Palace. But she had heard no talk of it, and he showed no sign of wanting to leave Claire House.

She knew however, that she could not expect Gervaise to remain indefinitely in her household, as tutor to a pupil who had now almost reached manhood. And although he had taken the responsibility in his stride, and made a success of Richard's studies, she could not ask of him to make decisions that would affect the boy's whole life.

She wanted those decisions to be made jointly, by herself and by Stephen. If necessary, she wanted Stephen to bring to bear the discipline she had once found too severe. For she was aware, with a growing sense of helplessness, that whenever he could escape the house Richard found his way to Blackheath, and his uncle's household. The passion for the river had been exchanged for a love of riding. Richard had his own black stallion in the stables behind the house, and the groom had orders that it should always be saddled.

Her greatest fear was that one day he would ride out of their lives and choose not to return. If he did so, he would not be the first young revolutionary to go into hiding against the day of the planned rebellion.

But what if Stephen had lost all interest in their son? He had sent birthday gifts each year, no more. Perhaps his devotion to Wyclif's cause meant that there was now no room in his heart for more human concerns. He had always been an ascetic – at the first real excuse he had left her for his old life. Over the years there had been no word of regret from him; in answer to the few, impassioned letters she had written in the early months of their separation there had been nothing but silence.

She sat at the table again and picked up her pen with new determination. This time she did not intend to beg for love or plead for his return. She had learnt that it was useless. But Stephen owed it to her and to their son to respond to the appeal she knew she must now make. If he did not, then for once and for all she would accept that he was lost to them and that she must seek guidance elsewhere.

Angrily, she thought how often she had had the chance to turn to one or other of her admirers at Westminster or in the City. Her beauty was no longer that of a young girl, she knew that. But she had long been an object of envy of the other women at the palace, with her slender body and her instinctive gift for dress. She had, more than once, set a new fashion, and turned the heads of the men who surrounded the ageing King. The more timid courtiers admired her from a distance, respecting her status as Stephen's wife. But her new role as a wife to a man who never came to Court, left her open to advances from the bolder of the young bachelors. Her constant love for Stephen had been her only protection in a court where moral behaviour was not as it had once been.

The most persistent of her admirers was the merchant Andrew Blake. He had recently lost his young, childless wife, and in his visits to her since the bereavement had made no effort to conceal the fact that he was ready to fall at her feet. A handsome, rather fleshy man with sad, brown eyes and a vast private fortune, she knew he could give her anything she desired. But she made certain that Beatrice or Henry were always with her when he arrived. She did not have to put into words to them that she needed to be chaperoned. They both knew where her heart still belonged.

My dear husband . . .

She mouthed the words silently, and began to write.

'A friend of our son's tutor will carry this letter for me, and I trust that you will find it within your power to send word by him, for he is to return to London within days and I have much need of your answer. Doubtless he will give you news of Westminster should you ask it. The Queen is exceedingly ill, and we do not expect her to see the end of another year. Philippa, my sister-in-law, grieves already for her. But my brother Francis has other trials, and it is of them that I must speak with you, in person. By my long silence, and by the fashion in which I now break that silence, you must know that my need is great. And when you learn that our son is involved, I trust that you will in turn find it in your heart to make speed, and come to us.'

As she signed her name, a sound in the corridor outside made her look up. She walked quickly to the door and opened it to find Gervaise about to walk away. He turned back, and bowed slightly as she stood framed in the doorway, her hair in a golden cloud against the light from the room beyond.

Gervaise was dressed in a white linen tunic with full sleeves that made his shoulders look even broader than they were above his slim waist. On his arm he carried a short cloak. With a start of surprise, she noticed that he wore a dagger at his belt, in a leather sheath. His eyes were serious as he apologised for disturbing her, but she shook her head quickly to reassure him.

'I did not hear your knock. I would have called for you soon. The – the letter for Oxford is ready.'

Gervaise waited while she went back to the writing table and folded the letter, pausing to seal it with the small, round emblem she used for all her communications. The smell of the wax caught at her throat as she extinguished the taper, and her voice was low and strained as she handed the letter to Gervaise.

'You go armed to Westminster, Gervaise? I do not remember ever seeing you carry a weapon before.'

'It is nothing. A rumour, but one I do not choose to ignore. There is a new brand of rogue merchant at large in the city this summer, they say. Rough fellows from the Netherlands, and their loyalties are not yet clear. It is said they are the King's men, and it has been made worth their while to settle here. If I go by the river from this house it is better that I go armed.'

Her eyes widened. 'From this house? Why should you go armed from here? What are these men to us?'

Gervaise hesitated. 'As I say, it is nothing, a mere precaution. Yet you must know, my lady, that your brother's name is linked with those who work for a new order. These newcomers could well be dangerous to his kind. It has not escaped you, that your own son has also taken the cause to his heart?'

A glance along the corridor told her that they were alone, but not wanting to spread alarm further than need be, she opened the door of her bedroom wider, as if to usher Gervaise inside. He followed her to the window, where she turned to him, her hands clasping and unclasping nervously.

With an effort, he kept his eyes away from the pulse that beat in her white throat.

'How long have you known such things, Gervaise? And how deeply involved has Richard become? I believe you know more than I, even if I am his mother. He has grown away from me of late, and it is only natural. That is why I have written to Oxford. I have asked his father to come here, to Claire House, to decide on our son's future.'

She was so nervous of explaining why she had at last written to Stephen that she did not notice how Gervaise's expression changed at her announcement. Something akin to anger flashed sharply in his eyes, and his lips tightened.

'I have known of your brother's two lives for many months. But his lady Philippa is the best guardian of his secrets a man could wish for. She is constantly at Westminster, playing the butterfly. No one would guess at the great issues at stake in their house.'

'Then how did you learn of them, Gervaise? How many others share this secret?'

He looked down at the letter he was to send on to her husband. 'As yet, only those who are already for it. But – it is from your own son that I learn most. My lady, in writing to Oxford now you are perhaps only just in time. Richard is almost a man – and you cannot keep him captive here much longer.'

'Captive!' Her voice was harsh with fear now. 'Do you believe, as his father does, that I have tried to keep too firm a hold on him?'

He stepped towards her, and laid a gentle hand on the silk sleeve of her robe. Not for the first time, she was aware of the hidden strength in his unhurried movements. She looked up into his eyes, expecting the reassurance he always gave her.

His eyes held hers, and his voice was gentle. 'You have done well by your son, my lady. Although you have been alone you have given him the strength that comes from a father, as well as your love. You have nothing to fear on that score. If he is captive – though I used the word foolishly – it is from his own choice, until now.'

'And now you think he is about to make his escape?' she whispered.

He nodded. 'This life is too good, too comfortable for a young rebel. However much he loves you, he cannot explain it away forever to his fellows. Sooner or later, he will have to return to the land, or learn to lead others less able than himself.'

'But it is such a waste! Gervaise, his father and I left our village no better than slaves. My own brother was a child, and would have ended his days in bondage had I not fled with him. Now is all that I have achieved to be rejected by my own son?'

As she turned to gaze out of the window at the river, Gervaise fought the need to go to her side.

'You must not think of it like that. You must see it as the natural outcome to your own bid for freedom. Your son is part of a great movement that is gathering strength. It may take years to come into the open, but when it does, it will be a tide that no man will hold back, and you would not want Richard to stand aside then.'

She listened, knowing the truth of what he said. Wearily, she led the way to the door. 'Then, if his father comes, you deem his journey wasted before it has even begun? Just now you told me otherwise.'

His voice trembled a little, and this time he did not meet her eyes. 'If I say it is time for your husband to return,' he said, 'it is not because I believe he will influence Richard to change his beliefs, or put a halt to his inevitable departure. It is because I know your son, and I know that he is thinking of leaving soon. And therefore – therefore I would not wish to see you left alone, my lady.'

'Gervaise, you have been a true friend to us. We rarely talk together, yet I would welcome it. You know my son, but – you do not know my husband well. I must tell you that the answer to this letter may be yet more silence.'

'Then why send it? Why ask for rejection, when you deserve something so different?' The vehemence of his reply so surprised her that her hand flew to her throat. In the shadow of the corridor they faced each other in a sudden, frozen silence. He seemed to regret his words as soon as they were uttered; she reeled from his unexpected display of emotion.

Before she could stop him, he walked quickly away from her to the head of the stairs, and ran down into the hall without looking back. Shaken, she turned back into her bedroom, but as she heard the front door close heavily into place she found herself running to the window, wanting to see Gervaise once more before he left for the Palace.

In the garden, Gervaise had been joined by Richard. With new insight into his feelings she watched sadly as Gervaise put an arm about her son's shoulders. He spoke to him earnestly for a while before signalling to the boatman that he was ready to depart. To her relief, neither her son nor his tutor looked back at the house. If they had seen her watching them she would have found it almost impossible to wave or smile. Her heart was heavy as she watched the boat pull out into midstream. Gervaise, sitting in the prow, did not look back.

But as Richard turned back towards the house he looked up in time to see Cressida standing there, and broke into a run, calling to her to join him in the garden. Raising a hand to greet him, she closed the window, and hurried to her garde-robe to choose a gown.

The letter to Stephen was on its way at last, she told herself, and she might just as well spend the days of waiting for an answer in some semblance of happiness, if only for Richard's sake.

But as she let her silk robe fall to her feet she looked over her shoulder to where the spring sunshine latticed the floor, and she would have given everything she possessed at that moment to see Stephen standing there, admiring her as he once had done – in the place where, only moments before, Gervaise had stood, with eyes that shone with anger. For it was only anger, she told herself, as she pulled her hair tightly back from her high forehead and glanced quickly into her mirror.

Gervaise was a loyal man who simply wanted to protect her. It was only natural. His confession that he believed Stephen should be at her side was that of a chivalrous member of her household, no more.

As she crossed the hall to join Richard, she remembered that her first encounter with Gervaise had been when she had fled from the open hatred of Abigail. With a bitter smile she reflected how things had changed since that first strange meeting. If Abigail had not come to Court Stephen might never have found the excuse he needed to leave her. For she was certain that his jealousy and anger were fleeting, spurious emotions with none of the lasting depth of his dedication to his work.

She held out her hands to Richard, and he led her to a seat under the trees overlooking the river bank. She tried to forget the child Cressida and the terrible effect her existence had had on Stephen. But could she honestly expect such feelings to have survived the years? For the first time in many months she had a growing conviction that if Stephen answered her letter, and came to her, it would be without bitterness. If she could forgive him for his suspicions then surely by now he would forgive her for her pride?

She closed her eyes, lifting her face to the warmth of the midday sun. 'I have written to your father today, Richard,' she said softly. 'Gervaise has a friend at Court who rides to Oxford, and word will come soon.'

Richard moved impatiently, and she opened her eyes to catch a bitter look, quickly suppressed.

'It is not my birthday yet, mother. We shall hear soon enough. A gift, if no word with it, is at least a sign that my father is still alive.'

'Richard!' She reproved him gently. 'You must hear me

out. You talk of your birthday. Do you realize that you are sixteen this year, and must decide on the course your life is to take?'

The lean jawline he presented to her as he turned abruptly away was so like his father's that when she spoke again her voice was sharp.

'I would like you to talk with your father before you make any decision. He is wise. It is him we have to thank for all that we have.'

'It is my father we have to thank for your place alone in London. For the place Gervaise has with us. For wealth that means nothing.'

'I have not seen you refuse to ride your horse, which the King's purse paid for,' she cajoled, fearing that she might not be able to avoid a serious scene if she took his remarks at their face value. But his words had made her heart beat painfully faster. She had never wanted her son to be aware of her loneliness. She had wanted him to benefit from the position and wealth that were her only comforts. But it seemed she had lost on both scores, and his next words struck home, more deadly than before.

'I will ride as and when I wish, mother. And the horse will carry me one day to those who fill the King's purse with their taxes and their labours. If I use it in their cause, then I use it well.'

He stood, and she thought for a heart-rending moment that he intended to leave her without a look. But he took her hand, and pulled her to her feet with a sudden smile of such extraordinary sweetness and love that it was as if she were transported to the days when he was much younger, a small boy demanding her attention with a tugging hand.

In those days, she had been closer to the beliefs he held. She herself had known what it was to be a rebel at heart, and to grasp at whatever came her way on the road from poverty. It was not so long since she had seen starvation on the faces of the poor – some who lived only a few miles from where they now sat. She knew in her heart that her son was right, but she could not bring herself to lose him willingly to his cause.

Silently, she let him take her arm and walk her to the river side. Together they looked out across the wide water. The tide was high, and the small boats sped on its depths to and fro about the business of a thriving city. She hoped that Richard would stay at her side like this until his father came to them.

For if Stephen did not come, she knew that Richard would sooner or later prove as good as his word, and that argument now was useless. She would do better to enjoy this time with him, and trust that Gervaise's friend would travel fast and bring good news.

But just as she began to relax, and to enjoy watching the small craft, a voice called from the house. She turned to find Henry, his kindly face red with exertion, running heavily across the lawns towards them. As he drew near, he looked anxiously from one to the other, as if deciding whom he should speak to first.

'Henry, what is it?' she said at last. 'Is Beatrice unwell? Quickly, let us go in to her.'

He shook his head, gasping for breath. 'Beatrice is in the kitchen as usual. No harm has come to her.'

The emphasis he gave to the last word was not lost on them. 'Who is it, Henry? Is anyone hurt?'

As they walked back to the house, Henry told them that a rider had come from Blackheath. He had called first at the stables, so that in the gardens they had not been aware of his arrival. Now he waited – with word from the Lady Philippa.

The man, dressed in the loose peasant garments worn by most of Francis's workers, was in the hall. Cressida was aware of very blue eyes, and rough hands turning and turning a riding hat as the man tried to speak.

In a hoarse, low voice he told Cressida at last that her brother wished her to ride back with him to Blackheath. The Lady Philippa sent word. The child Cressida had died of fever – a lightning summer fever. The mother had disappeared. And, that morning, Margaret had collapsed with the same symptoms.

As she sped to her room Richard went straight to the stables to make sure that their horses were ready. She heard the man call after her: 'I ride now to St Andrew's Hill. The Lady Philippa did not wish it, but the priest should be with her.'

She hardly gave a thought to the fact that the priest the man went for would, in all probability, be Brother Oliver. For her hatred of the monk was as nothing compared to the immediate, unreasoning lift of the heart she had experienced when she learnt that the child who symbolized the hated past had been removed – however tragically – by the hand of Providence just as she had asked her husband to return.

9

Philippa sat at her child's bedside and stared blankly into the hollow darkness. The small hand lay damp and still in her own, and the breathing from the slight figure on the bed came in shallow rasps. It was the sound of a small animal fighting for its life, and when Cressida came silently into the room her friend did not even look up to greet her. The mother was as much at war with the fever as the child it had brought down.

Margaret had always been a lively, vivacious child. But this sudden, vicious sickness had struck her down without warning. On the journey to Blackheath Cressida had heard from her brother's messenger how first a young apprentice printer, then the fair child who bore the lady Cressida's name, had succumbed to the fever – and all in a matter of hours.

Knowing that her brother had not much use for the services of an apothecary, and that their rambling old house was too far from the court for Philippa to send for more distinguished medical help in time to be of any use, Cressida had brought with her the various potions and herbs she had learnt to use when her mother was alive, and later when she herself had assisted Master Valence.

As she hurriedly unpacked them, she thanked Providence for her knowledge, and giving her instructions quickly and quietly to the young girl who had led her to the room, she removed her cloak and began to roll back the sleeves of her gown.

In a daze, Philippa watched her work to bring down the fever. Neither of them spoke unnecessarily. At Cressida's instructions, Philippa wiped the perspiration from her daughter's body and forehead, wrung cloths tightly in cold water, and sent for an infusion from the kitchens.

As she held the child's wrist, searching for some sign that the humours were restoring themselves slowly into balance, Cressida looked for a moment into Philippa's eyes.

It was not the time to mention the child who had died earlier that day, and yet Cressida wanted to ask what had happened to Abigail, and why she had fled from Philippa, who had always cared for her.

'Margaret has outlasted the child who died,' Philippa seemed to know the questions that teemed in Cressida's mind without being told. 'By some five hours now. Is there hope, Cressida? Will she live?'

Margaret's breathing was, in fact, easier, but at that moment her thin frame arched on the bed and she cried out in pain. At once, Philippa went to put her arms about her, but Cressida put out a restraining hand.

'The crisis has come. Only she can do what must be done now. We can only wait.'

With a moan, Philippa turned away, and Cressida looked up to find her brother standing at the foot of the bed. Philippa ran to him, and Cressida returned to her task. The smell of sickness rose from the bed in a foetid wave, and she gagged. But as she recovered, her tongue still coated with bile, Margaret opened her eyes.

An hour later, while Francis insisted on taking his turn by the sick bed, and the child in it slept peacefully, Philippa and Cressida sat together in the living room. It was late, and the apprentices had at last gone to their dormitory, thankful that no one else in their ranks showed any sign of the fever. Now that it was too late to return to Claire House, Cressida had reluctantly agreed to allow Richard to join them.

She knew that Henry and Beatrice had been prepared for her not to return that night. As arrangements were made for beds for herself and her son she found herself thinking of Gervaise. Had he given her letter to their messenger by now? And had he stayed at the Palace, or returned to find her gone? In her mind's eye she saw him standing alone in the shadows outside her room, as she had found him earlier that day. And again she shuddered at the sight of the dagger in his belt.

'Is it not strange,' Philippa broke into her thoughts, 'that Brother Oliver did not come? And sent word that he would pray for Margaret rather than prepare the last rites. His ways are such that I shall never understand him. Do you know, Cressida, that he said he would not come to bury a child he had so recently named for God?'

Cressida did not reveal that she had been distinctly glad not to have Brother Oliver looking over her shoulder while she worked. She had renounced his world of belief in heaven, hell and eternal damnation many years before, and Margaret had need of more than prayer. Yet it was unbelievable that a priest who had known the family so long should refuse the call to what might well have been a death bed; she brushed aside the thought that perhaps Oliver knew that she had gone on to Blackheath ahead of him.

'He is a dedicated man,' she said. 'That much I understand. As it is, he was right to stay at home and pray. The outcome is more than a saint could have hoped for, is it not?'

Philippa clasped the hand she held out to her, and for the first time that day she smiled. Then, just as suddenly, tears sprang to her eyes. 'How can I feel gladness like this, when less than one day ago I saw Abigail's own child die? Is it wicked of me, Cressida? Does death always make those left behind so wickedly glad that they have survived?'

'There is no wickedness in your joy for Margaret's recovery,' Cressida told her. 'But tell me, how could the child's mother leave her poor body to be buried by strangers? Even if you are Robert's sister, you had your own torment here today. Surely Abigail could have seen her daughter to her last rest?'

At first Philippa shook her head dumbly, the tears still waiting to be shed. 'These last years have been a torment, Cressida, as much as these last hours. Abigail missed the forests, and the countryside. She was a wild creature, and stayed with us only for the sake of her child. Once that link was snapped, she disappeared from our lives – as swiftly and strangely as she came.'

Cressida was silent. She had seen how wildly Abigail danced, and how close mother and daughter had been. They had never been far from each other, every time she had seen them – like two strangers in an enemy camp. She could well believe that her daughter gone Abigail would see no reason to stay.

And now that Philippa had to bury her brother's child, would this last vestige of the past be buried too? With the child who bore her name gone for ever there was no reminder that Robert had loved Cressida.

With an effort, she changed the subject. 'You must rest now, Philippa. Abigail is lost, and you must think of your own child.'

'I must order broth for her now. And then, perhaps honey?'

'And later, wine. A little.'

'You have done well by us, Cressida. How can we

thank you?'

'A measure of mulled wine perhaps?' Cressida smiled. 'Then I too must sleep. It has been a long day – longer even than the day we spent with Ralph of Mansey, the Earl you refused so often.'

At that recollection they both broke into laughter. And Francis, when he came to tell them that Margaret was still asleep, found them both giggling like young girls.

Next morning, in the courtyard, Francis waited with their escort, and as Cressida approached he fumbled awkwardly with a scroll of fabric which he seemed to be attempting to conceal.

She eyed it curiously, and he said: 'I have a gift for you, sister. You saved our daughter's life, and words of thanks are not enough. I know how much you like a new tapestry, and this one is of great, strange beauty. But I will not pretend – it was designed and worked by Abigail, and I think it best that it now goes to another house.'

Cressida stared at him disbelievingly. She knew he must mean well, and that the tapestry, when she had seen it in its early stages, was indeed very beautiful. But surely its sinister aspect could not have escaped him? Could it be that he secretly wanted to rid his house of it and that this was the only way he could persuade his wife to let it go?

'Are you certain that Philippa would wish Abigail's work to be given away, after all that has happened here?' She hoped that her face and voice did not betray her own distaste at the thought of the tapestry in her own possession. One thing was certain – it would never grace the walls of Claire House, even if she had to accept it from her brother.

'She agrees with me, that it should be yours. Perhaps it holds too many memories for her. But it is a valued gift – and she hopes you too will find it so.'

Cressida took the scroll from him, her eyes lowered. She could hardly refuse the gesture, but neither could she pretend to be overjoyed. Francis knew her too well for that.

'Of course. I shall treasure the keepsake as a token of Margaret's recovery,' she said carefully. 'And you will send word of her progress?'

She mounted her horse with Francis's assistance, and looked down at him. He answered:

'Richard will bring you news, when he comes to Claire House again.'

She looked round, not at first taking in what he said. 'Where is Richard? And the stallion – is it not saddled?'

'He has begged to stay here at Blackheath for a while,' Francis said. 'Did he not tell you?'

The significance of what he said began to dawn on her, and a sudden wave of anger with her brother and her son made her cheeks flush heavily.

'He did not ask me,' she corrected. 'And if he had, my answer would most likely have been "no", as he is all too aware.'

'Perhaps that is why he did not ask, Cressida,' Francis smiled up at her.

'It is not a matter for joking, brother. Richard knows full well that we wait for Stephen to ride from Oxford. He may not wish to see his father, but he will not avoid it by staying here with you. Stephen will come for him soon enough if he is not waiting for him at Claire House.'

'Are you so sure? And even so, can he not spend a day or two here – he will serve to make us more cheerful, after all that has happened.'

'Should he not make his mother happy too?' she asked sharply, then, her voice lowered, she said: 'You know he has other reasons for staying here, Francis. And you do nothing to dissuade him.'

'You should be glad that your son is a rebel at heart,' he said. 'And I do not dissuade him because with a boy of his age that would have the opposite effect – he would only join some rogue band of the same views and fall into disrepute. It is better this way.'

Cressida remembered that Gervaise had talked only the day before of rogues. 'There are disreputable fellows in all walks of life, and I believe we could all be in danger,' she said, shaking her head. 'I must see Richard, at least. If he is to stay, there must be a fixed day for his return.'

'Very well,' Francis turned away with a slight shrug of annoyance, and beckoned to a boy apprentice in brown tunic and stockings who stood in a doorway across the courtyard. The boy listened, then ran into the house. Cressida called her escort to her side, and handed him the tapestry, before she shook the reins and trotted her horse towards the house.

When Richard appeared in the doorway, shading his eyes against the morning sun, she was shocked to see that he was dressed in the brown garments worn by her brother's workers.

'Where are your clothes, Richard?' she said coldly, without greeting.

'They are safely stowed, mother. I am better like this, when I stay here.'

'And why was I not asked? You know that I expect word from your father. If he comes to London and finds you are not at the house he will be angered – and rightly. His time is precious.'

She knew that her choice of words had been indiscreet when she saw the sneer on her son's young face.

'My father's time is so precious that it takes five years of his life before he comes to you – if he comes to you, mother! At such a time as he does come he will find I am no longer a child. Will it be too much to expect that he waits a day or two for my presence when we have waited so long?'

The truth of all that he said, and the controlled anger in his voice, pierced Cressida's whole being, and she could not find it in her heart to continue the argument without betraying her own despair. She could boast that she had rarely let her son see how deeply she felt his father's absence. It would be a waste of the long years of self-discipline if she were to weaken now. Yet the very loyalty to her in Richard's protest was enough to move her to tears.

'Very well,' she muttered, beginning to turn her horse in the direction of the gates. 'But I want your word, Richard – you are to come home within five days, and by daylight.'

With a sudden smile, he at once ran towards her, and took her bridle. Breaking into a run he trotted her horse to the gate. Then, all the anger gone from his face, he looked up at her, and his deep grey eyes had never reminded her more forcibly of Stephen.

'Thank you, mother,' he said. 'You have my word. Ride safely, and give my love to Beatrice.'

'And what of your tutor? Is not Gervaise also worthy of your love?'

He stepped back, and gave the horse a smart tap on its rump. 'Oh my tutor has been my best friend these many years. I thought you knew that. Tell him I do not waste my time – and he is not to waste his!'

'I shall tell him that I am ashamed to return without his pupil,' she said, smiling in spite of herself. For as she rode through the gate she found to her surprise that she was glad to be on her way to Claire House, and with a message for Gervaise on her lips – but on the heels of the thought came the knowledge that she would spend the days to come in an agony of suspense, waiting for an answer from Stephen and the sound of his footsteps on the hall stone flags.

Was their son right in judging his father so? She had never wanted to explain the cause of the rift between them. But now that, in one long day, the evidence of Robert's love had been so cruelly wiped out, her body throbbed with a hope that she knew was unreasoning, but which would not be denied.

The ride to the city and on to the South bank seemed endless, as her thoughts circled round her dilemma. At last, as the house came into view, she asked her companion if he wished to return directly to Blackheath, and when he thanked her and handed her the scroll in which the tapestry was packed, she did not wait to watch him turn and leave her, but broke into a canter and made straight for the stables, calling for her groom.

Moments later, she ran into the kitchen from the stable yard and sank gratefully onto the bench by the table where Beatrice was preparing a meal.

It was not until she had removed her cloak that she remembered the tapestry and reached for it where she had let it fall at her feet. With a sigh, she retrieved it, and chattering to Beatrice of Margaret's good recovery, began to unroll it from its cover.

Frowning, she studied the dark scene as the picture came gradually into view. As the figure of the rider appeared, she became aware that she was being watched, and looked up to find that Gervaise had just come into the kitchen from the hall.

They held each other's gaze for an endless moment, while Beatrice continued her work her head bent with studied concentration over the great table.

'I am so glad to be home,' Cressida was the first to break the silence.

'And all is well?' His question seemed to veil a dozen other, more important questions. His dark eyes did not leave her face, and in them she saw that he too was glad that she was back at Claire House.

Suddenly everything seemed of secondary importance to this moment of homecoming.

She re-folded the tapestry slowly, and moved to her favourite place on the high settle by the hearth. As she gazed into the bright fire her face glowed with some fierce, secret resolution. Life seemed at that moment to be a treasure she had almost discarded, without thought for what it held.

She looked back to where Gervaise stood in the doorway, still waiting for her answer.

'All is well,' she said softly.

10

The death of the young girl who bore her name, and the flight of Abigail, were to Cressida a turning point. It was as if the heavy weight of the past had been lifted from her heart, and the way was clear for Stephen to return to her. All that had destroyed their happiness had now been itself destroyed, and however tragic the death of Robert's daughter had been, Cressida swore to herself that out of it would come the rebuilding of her marriage.

Watching her as she gazed into the fire late that night, Gervaise thought that she had never looked more beautiful. It was a loveliness that shone through exhaustion, for she had nursed the child Margaret for long, vigilant hours. But the blue eyes vivid in her white face, and the delicate lines of fatigue at the corners of her young, determined mouth, made Gervaise's heart ache more than ever with the love he had concealed for her.

It was true that they did not yet know whether Stephen had received his wife's message but Gervaise was aware that suddenly all the omens indicated that they might soon expect the return of Cressida's husband.

Later, in the privacy of her bedroom, Cressida unrolled the tapestry which Francis had given her, and with a slight frown studied the detail of its intricate, undeniably skilful work. Now, with the threat of Abigail herself removed, she was able to see in it dark, outlandish beauty. The sinister threat that had seemed to hang over the figure of the young horseman who rode through the mysterious woodland seemed now in abeyance.

But she knew that if Stephen returned to Claire House she could never consider using the tapestry on its walls, and with a sigh at the memory of Little Cressida's death, she placed it firmly in the bottom of her garde-robe, pulled a long silk gown from the cupboard, and began slowly to undress.

That night she did not sleep, but lay in a state of suppressed excitement, tinged with a happiness that had long been a stranger to her. Even the fact that her son had stayed on at Blackheath could not diminish the quickening of her spirits, and when the dawn came at last she rose quickly, and ran to the bedroom window as if she could not wait to begin the new day.

She was just in time, as she opened the window, to glimpse the figure of a man standing with his back to the house. He was staring out across the early morning mist that still cloaked the river. At the slight sound of the window opening, the man glanced behind him, and then walked quickly away along the tow path in the direction of London Bridge. She knew at once from the man's short cape and his familiar walk that the man was Gervaise. She wondered as she watched him go why he was up and about so early, and why he had left so abruptly without a greeting when he must have heard her at the window.

She was not to know that Gervaise walked blindly, without purpose; that he had not slept, and that he dared not greet her with the marks of his long tormented struggle of the night still evident on his sensitive face. He had never forgotten the beauty of Cressida's naked body from the night five years ago when he had seen her at her window – but now he loved her for so much more. The thought that she who had suffered so much was now to return to her rightful husband made him angry. He could no longer trust himself to remain at Claire House. He silently cursed Stephen, the man who had brought Cressida so much pain yet who would soon be offered her lips with unchanged love.

As he strode along the river bank, he decided that he would ask Cressida that night for permission to remain at Court for a few days – at least for as long as her son stayed with his uncle. The boy could come to harm there, he knew. But perhaps with Margaret's recovery he would find a youthful companion who would dispel the more serious concerns of politics and rebellion. There was also the bitter thought that when Richard did at last come back home he would probably find his father – and his future – waiting for him.

If that happened, Gervaise's days at Claire House would be numbered, and, wanting nothing for Cressida but her happiness, he would go with good grace. To leave her could not bring more agony than to stay and watch her at her husband's side. Or so he told himself. But at the thought of such a parting, his grey eyes darkened. He turned on to London Bridge where, mingling with the noisy morning crowds, and though jostled from side to side as he walked, he heard nothing but Cressida's name again and again echoing in his mind.

That night he returned to a house that had been swept and polished and scented with herbs. At the sound of voices in the great ground floor solar he paused, all his senses honed into a steely awareness. One of the voices had the low timbre of a man's; the other was Cressida's. Believing that Stephen had indeed come home Gervaise hesitated, a hand on the balustrade, reluctant to face them together.

But if Stephen were home, then it was his duty to find out if Richard had come back to see his father. Squaring his shoulders, he crossed the hall and knocked at the solar door.

With a mixture of annoyance and relief, Gervaise saw that Cressida's companion for the evening was not her husband, but the merchant Andrew Blake. On the shining oaken table which flanked one wall stood a flask of wine, and Cressida and her visitor were drinking from goblets placed in front of them.

Cressida looked up as Gervaise entered, and as he stood in the doorway he caught an expression of almost reckless excitement in her eyes. In her hands lay a sample of crimson velvet, a colour that did not suit her pallor. A thin intensity about her made her even more desirable than usual, and though the merchant watched her covertly Gervaise was completely aware of his interest.

His eyes still on Cressida's face, Gervaise asked: 'My lady, is there news from Oxford yet? Or word from Blackheath?'

With a sidelone glance at Andrew Blake, Cressida answered Gervaise in a bright voice: 'Yes, my husband will ride to London the day after tomorrow. And there is just time for me to make a new tunic, if I sew it myself, to herald his return.'

As she gestured to the length of red velvet draped across her knees, Gervaise thought how apt her choice of words was. The colour was a colour for heraldic banners, for flags. It had a hectic quality that was matched now in Cressida's eyes. Yet he could not help but be glad of her happiness, however brittle and fleeting this moment might be.

'Will Richard be here for his father's arrival?' Gervaise avoided the need to comment on Cressida's choice of gown by turning to a more important subject.

She sighed, her head a little on one side. 'If only my son had returned with me there would be no need to beg this of you Gervaise, but you have come to the heart of the matter – of course Richard must be here, and I would be grateful if you would go to Blackheath for me tomorrow, and bring him home. Perhaps he will listen to you. In any case my brother Francis will know that Stephen must find his son here to greet him . . . after . . . so long an absence.'

Gervaise sensed that Cressida had not wished to draw her visitor's attention to the question of Stephen's separate existence at Oxford, and to cover her momentary confusion he quickly told her that he would give orders for a horse to be ready at first light. As he spoke he stayed in the doorway, as yet uninvited to join Blake and Cressida. Torn between taking a seat at Cressida's side without her consent and leaving her to the admiring attentions of the merchant, he paused just long enough for Cressida herself to settle the matter.

'Then we must not keep you,' she smiled. 'In the morning I too will rise early. I have gifts for my niece Margaret. She must be fully recovered from the fever now.'

Nodding his assent, Gervaise bowed to her, and with a briefer bow to her companion drew back into the quiet hall and closed the door. He wondered uneasily whether Beatrice and Henry knew that their mistress was closeted so late with the merchant, but after a glance in the direction of the silent kitchens thought better of it. After giving the groom his orders, he took the stairs two and three at a time and sought his own room.

Flinging himself on the narrow bed, he gripped his hands behind his head, and stared into the darkness. Then turning, he felt for tallow and flint, and in a few moments the small room was lit by a pale yellow flame.

In its light, he went to his armoire, and one by one, took out the few clothes he possessed. On the bed beside them, he piled the manuscripts of his poems. After he had brought Richard back home next day, he would leave for Westminster. With the knowledge that Stephen was really on his way to London at last, Gervaise knew that he could not stay with Cressida another day without declaring his love. That declaration would violate his chivalric code, and maybe even earn her hatred. It was this last risk that he could not take.

With a single gesture, he swept clothes, manuscripts, and books to the floor, and flung himself on the bed, knowing he would not sleep before it was time to ride to Blackheath. As he gazed sightlessly at the low ceiling he also listened keenly for the sounds of Andrew Blake's departure from the house. There had been an element of familiarity in the merchant's demeanour when he found them together, and as he watched them Gervaise had found himself wanting both to protect Cressida from Andrew Blake, and from herself.

Angry at the memory of the length of scarlet velvet, he began to compose in his head a poem to Cressida's beauty, comparing it to that of the speedwell – the small wayside flower, blue as her eyes, and as wild and ready to be plucked as he imagined that she had once been.

Next morning the poem already half forgotten, he found her in the kitchens, a demure aproned figure, her golden hair coifed stiffly in white linen as she prepared his breakfast of new bread and fresh meat herself. Half ashamed of his thoughts of the night before, he watched her from beneath lowered eyelids. She went about her tasks, until, sensing his eyes upon her, she turned from where she bent over the rekindled fire in the kitchen hearth.

'I am glad you are able to bring Richard to me,' she said quietly. He noticed with some relief that the heightened mood of recent hours had left her.

'It is my duty, and my privilege,' he said. Still he could not bring himself to look directly into her blue eyes.

'I have never felt that you worked with Richard out of duty, Gervaise.'

'And you have been right in that, my lady. But these last hours, before your son's future is decided by the one who has the right to do so, are not so easy. It is a sense of duty that takes me through them. And I shall do as you ask no less willingly, you must believe that.'

She walked to the table, and hastily he took a long draught from his tankard of ale, so that she should not read the look in his eyes.

'And where will you go?' she asked.

'To Westminster at first.' He was ready with his answer, and glad of it. 'I wish to study more here in London, and I have much to learn from the poets at Court.'

'And then?' There was a softness in her voice, but she obviously did not intend to let him off easily. This time he had no choice but to look up at her. The code of politesse demanded it.

'And then, my lady, perhaps I shall seek my own land again. My own people.'

Her eyes widened. 'You would go back to France, after your own foster father has loved you so well? Have we displeased you here in England?'

He shook his head, wishing she would find some distraction in the kitchen, or that Beatrice would come in and bustle them out of her way.

'Nothing has displeased me here,' he said evenly. 'But France has been through a turmoil that still awaits you here in England. Now that my work with Richard draws to an end I must confess that I have for some time been drawn to the new France.'

'You are as much of the people as I, Gervaise,' she said, smiling. 'I believe you would side with the rebels. Am I right?'

He held her gaze. 'They are part of a tide that will not be stemmed. When that tide rises in London, as it must, I would not want to see you at its mercy. Your menfolk are on the right side, my lady.'

'And yet?' She detected a hesitation in his voice.

'And yet it would be better perhaps,' he explained, 'if the peasants, when they come into the open, are able to tell who is their enemy, and who not. If I may say so freely, my lady, it will be dangerous to continue in such – such style and comfort as is enjoyed at Claire House if ever – whenever – the time comes.'

Cressida sat down with a swift, graceful movement on the bench on the far side of the table. Cupping her chin in her hands, she narrowed her eyes. It was a long time since she had had the opportunity to talk of the cause still so close to her heart. It had become blurred in her mind, now that she saw her brother's involvement as a danger to her son, and her husband's work as one cause of their long separation.

'There is no fear of that, Gervaise. We do not flaunt our beliefs in this house, for the success of the cause depends on our duplicity. I have never told you of such things. It has been bettter so. But of course you know of my brother Francis's activities – and the danger to my son. And I thank you for your concern.'

He was silent. This was the moment when he might tell her that he cared nothing for Francis, and only a margin more for Richard. It was Cressida herself, her safety and her future, that concerned him especially now that the time was coming when he would have no choice but to leave her.

'But why should you leave Claire House?' She seemed to have read his thoughts, and she lowered her small hands, opening them expressively towards him as if welcoming him to her. 'I do not know how I could have been so foolish, but now I see that if you wish to stay at Westminster for some time then why not continue to live here, and go each day by river to your studies and your poets?'

He smiled at her eagerness, and pushed his plate away, the food half-finished.

'It is better that when something is ended, it is known to be ended,' he told her. 'My lady, your offer is the kindest I have received since I was brought to England after my father's death. But –'

She waited. He shook his head helplessly. 'But?' she asked.

'I have made up my mind.' He stood, and looked round for his cape. As he retrieved it from the bench by the hearth, he knew that her eyes followed him.

He turned to her, fixing the clasp on his cape while he searched for words. 'These have been good years, my lady. And now I pray that your husband returns to you for ever. When your son has gone out into the world you will not want a stranger in the house. You will see . . .'

She stood very close to him now, and he controlled the trembling in his voice with some difficulty. Slowly, it began to dawn on Cressida that the young tutor's emotion was due to much more than their talk of rebellion and parting, of his homeland.

The gentle warmth that flowed through her as she realized that she was loved by this handsome, gifted man, brought a soft glow to her face beneath the white coif. The absurdity of his love for a woman of her age was not lost on her, and yet that love made her feel once more like a young girl. Her heart beat a little faster, but out of concern for him she did not allow any sign of her emotion to show in her voice.

'You speak with great understanding,' she almost whispered. 'And as a true friend. Perhaps you are right. But, if ever you change your mind – you will come back to me?'

She held out her hand. Gervaise bowed, and brushed it with a kiss. He dared not answer her this time, for he knew that if he did so he would confess to a love that was both treacherous and dangerous. Treacherous to Stephen and Cressida's married vows, and dangerous to his own sanity.

Taking refuge in the need for an early departure, he walked quickly to the door. 'Is there any word you would wish me to convey to your brother? Or to the Lady Philippa?'

She followed him, the moment of dangerous emotions past. But her heart was still beating quickly, and she knew that colour touched her cheeks with a becoming hand.

'Only that I wish them well, and that my brother should take care. I shall indeed by happy to see my son safely home again. By nightfall, perhaps?'

'The days are long. I hope to bring him to you before sunset,' he told her. He did not add that by returning as fast as good manners would permit from Blackheath, he also hoped to spend at least one more night under the same roof as her before Stephen's return. It was an innocent need on his part, to enjoy a sense of responsibility for her and her son, before that role was relinquished to Stephen for good.

She listened for a moment or two as the sound of his horse clattered in the stable yard and then gradually died away on the road. Then she hurried back to the kitchen, where Beatrice was waiting for her orders.

The message brought back from Oxford had been brief and to the point: there was a lull in work at the University as high summer approached, and Stephen was able to come to London within the seven' night. Which meant that they had two more days in which to prepare the feast with which she planned to welcome him home. As Beatrice set to, measuring ingredients and kneading dough on the great scrubbed kitchen table, Cressida opened the heavy cupboard in which her preserves were stored, blissfully unaware of the way in which her servant grumbled under her breath that a man who could stay away so long from such devotion deserved no welcome at all.

Once or twice a day Cressida paused in the middle of her tasks, savouring the joy of knowing that Stephen was at last on his way. She tried not to dwell on the fact that he had drily explained things were quiet at Oxford. She was certain that he would not have come to London at all had he been reluctant to do so.

As she took a moment's respite in her solar, the day's work almost finished, she listened for the sound of the returning horses, and smiled secretly to herself at the love she had seen in Gervaise's face that morning. Her pleasure in his devotion was innocent enough, she told herself. It was flattering to be admired by a younger gifted man. And it would give her confidence to face her own husband after this long separation.

Then, inevitably, her thoughts led to the love she and Stephen had known in the sanctuary of their bed. The anger and jealousy that had brought that love to so abrupt an end now had no cause. But could she be sure that her husband had not stifled his body's need for her? She knew that his iron will could prove her enemy if she tried, as she longed, to reawaken his desire.

Anxiously, she went to the mirror, seeking the signs of age that five years must surely have brought. Turning her head from side to side in the silver gleam of the mirror's surface, she was reassured. After a moment she crossed the room to her armoire, and brought out the red tunic she had made with Andrew Blake's velvet. The merchant had insisted that she take it as a gift, to celebrate her husband's return. It was true she had always been an excellent customer, and the gift was acceptable – though the colour was a little wrong for her. She had seen that the red velvet had not pleased Gervaise. She had made the tunic against his, and her own, better judgement.

Holding it against her body as she gazed into the mirror she knew she would not wear it. The vivid colour suddenly dissolved into a smear of blood-red, and she remembered Dominic, the minstrel who had given her the mirror and the terrible sight of his broken body that she had been forced to witness.

Dominic's murder had been her first lesson in what the power-hungry landlords thought of those who would bring them down. Dominic had brought the new thinking to the villages where he sang the old songs. For that he had given his life.

Her eyes blinded by hot tears, she threw the red velvet into her wardrobe, unconsciously concealing Abigail's tapestry as she did so.

She ran down to the hallway, and saw that evening sunlight was slanting across the flagstones. From the stableyard came voices, and the sound of hooves. With her hand to her breast she raced to the kitchen, calling Beatrice to prepare supper for Richard and Gervaise.

But as she opened the door into the stableyard she paused. She had expected Richard to come running with all the news of Blackheath and her brother on his lips. But the stables had gone suddenly quiet, and as she approached, the groom turned his face away from her, pretending to fasten the door of the horse-box. Inside it was Richard's black stallion.

'Richard?' she called softly, thinking he had returned in high spirits and was hiding from her as he used to as a child. She turned about, as if playing blind man's buff, waiting for him to jump out from the shadows that stole across the courtyard.

It was then that she saw a man standing very still in the far corner of the yard. She knew at once that it was Gervaise, and her heart lurched as she realized that he was alone.

She ran a few paces towards him, and then stopped. As she did so, he came slowly into the sunlight.

They stood face to face, looking blankly into each other's eyes. 'You are alone?' Cressida's voice was almost a sigh, her words a statement rather than a question.

Gervaise turned away, his eyes searching the grey waters of the river.

'Where is my son?' The question was a whip, bringing him back, meant to hurt. Cressida saw the blank stare change to grief.

He took her arm, and held her hand very tightly. They walked a yard or so towards the house, and their steps faltered as Cressida looked up at him, silently asking for an answer, a denial, to a question she could not frame.

Gervaise stood and faced her again, his hands on her shoulders. He shook his head. 'We were followed. Perhaps it was Richard's likeness to your brother. You know how strong it has become of late. The fair hair. He wore – '

'Those clothes! I knew they were an omen. When I saw him in them, I felt as though he was lost to us . . . '

'Richard fought like a lion. Your brother rode after us, when warning reached Blackheath. But he was too late. The . . . assassins . . . turned on him, when they saw their mistake. Then the boy went into the fray like a wild thing, Cressida. And to some purpose. Francis, your brother, is safe. The murderers escaped once they saw they were losing ground.'

'And Richard?' As she said her son's name there was a high-pitched scream of protest already in her throat. The light turned blood red and her head swam, then Gervaise caught her ice-cold body as she fell.

She was unconscious, and her face was buried against him, but as he rocked her in his arms he told her that her son was dead.

11

'I believe that each man dies much as he deserves.' Her son's words, spoken in such innocence and yet now proved with the cruellest conviction, burned into Cressida's brain as she lay alone in the darkness of her bedroom and mourned for him.

Ever since Gervaise had told her the truth she had not left the bed to which he had carried her. She lay fully clothed, her long hair tangled about her and wet with her endless tears. Sometimes she twisted in agony, her body bent almost double in her effort to seek some comfort and escape. Then she would double her fists, and hold them to her gaping mouth, biting into her knuckles to stifle her crying.

She knew that someone waited and watched in the corridor outside. When there was silence, she believed it was Gervaise, and that he kept vigil alone. Every now and then there would be a small bout of whispering, and she knew that Henry and Beatrice took their turn. Then she dared call out, and Beatrice would come to her, carrying a bowl of soup or a beaker of mulled wine. But she would only wet her lips before once more she broke into a paroxysm of angry tears.

She told Beatrice that she would not see Gervaise. It was not that she blamed him. But she could not bear to see the love in his eyes, which he had made no attempt to conceal since her son's death. She did not trust herself in the face of such love. Again and again she asked Beatrice why Stephen had not come. It was her husband, the dead boy's father, she wanted at her side.

She did not know that with the shock of Richard's death all sense of time and place had deserted her. It was only a few hours since Gervaise had returned from Blackheath, yet it seemed like weeks. The room was in darkness, the linen curtains drawn against the summer, at her request. She believed, with an angry bitter certainty, that Stephen had once more failed her, and would not come.

She found her mind wandering to the winter's day now sixteen years ago, when she had given birth to Richard in this same room. Her agony had been almost as violent as the pain she was enduring now. She had endured that alone, too. Even then Stephen had not been with her, and she railed as much against his absence then as she screamed protest at his imagined lateness now.

Once she thought she heard voices in the garden and, as the first night since Richard's death closed in on her, she ran to the window and drew back the curtains. She watched the flicker of torches from the river on the ceiling, and in her feverish state imagined they were the flames of a hell fire she had always denied existed. Contradicting all she had learnt from Stephen, she found herself crying inwardly against the flames that might consume her child if he were not forgiven his sins. Everyone she knew believed such things. Perhaps they were true! Her son, struck down without warning, had not seen a priest or been to confession in all the short years of his life.

If Stephen were with her she knew he would help her fight such thoughts, but alone in the darkness she was at the mercy of the whole heritage of her generation in the face of death. She had known death before, and had watched her mother go to her end bravely. But the loss of her son had completely disarmed her. As the tears at last began gradually to dry she lay limply, her exhaustion making her prey to the wildest thoughts.

She was dozing fitfully for the first time when she heard

voices on the stairway. Henry and Beatrice seemed to be answering questions, and the voice that questioned them was that of a man, but he was speaking so quietly that she could not be sure of his identity.

Moments later the bedroom door swung open and Beatrice came in with a tallow lamp. The wavering light threw shadows on the old servant's ravaged face, and Cressida saw that she was not the only one who had wept all day.

She held out her arms to Beatrice with a cry, but as she saw who followed her into the room the cry froze in her throat. She leapt from the bed and pushed her brother bodily from the room.

Francis held her at arm's length as she screamed at him to leave. Her extraordinary strength shocked him, and he grappled with her with some difficulty, taken by surprise.

At last Beatrice and Henry took her arms, and led her sobbing back into her room, while Francis stood helplessly in the doorway waiting for her to calm down.

'I came to tell you that Richard died bravely, in my defence,' he said when her sobs had subsided enough for him to be heard.

'I know it already, from those who loved him,' she snapped back. 'You did not have to come. I order you to leave my house. You have led my son to his death.'

She coldly surveyed his fair hair, assessing with hatred the likeness that had caused Richard to be killed in his uncle's place.

She almost spat her next words. 'And tell me, did my son sport the brave rebel garments when he died? Did that make the picture complete for you and your fanatics?'

Beatrice looked fearfully from one to the other, and shook her head at Francis, her eyes begging him to leave his sister to her grief.

'There was a time when you yourself would have been proud of him, sister. Have you not asked yourself at whose knee I learnt the doctrines that brought us to this moment? You were the first rebel in our midst. Can you deny it?'

'I do not deny anything, least of all my pride in my dead son!' She had drawn herself into a kneeling position on the bed, and her hair shone in a thick cloud of gold about her. Clutching her head frantically, she shrieked: 'I will not have you in my house. Nor your wife, nor your child. From now on it will be as if we have never known each other – '

Francis stared in horror at his sister. In spite of her wild gestures and crazed words he came towards her. 'But Philippa is your oldest, dearest friend. And our child has done no harm. Cressida, it is now that you need us most. Let me bring Philippa to you – '

'No!' The vehemence of her refusal made him take a step back. He saw that she was in earnest. 'Your wife and her estates began it all. It was her brother who made us flee slavery, who destroyed my marriage. If she had not made you love her you would never have come to London – and Richard would still be alive.'

As she said Richard's name, her voice broke, and in another fit of sobbing she flung herself violently into Beatrice's arms.

Beatrice signed to Francis that he should leave them. Her brother's footsteps sounded on the stair and the front door closed behind him. Cressida sank back into her pillows and gripped Beatrice's hand as if she were drowning.

'Is it because their own child still lives? Is that why you cannot bring yourself to see them?'

The harsh words, with their ring of truth, struck into the icy calm that had taken grip of Cressida's feelings, and she surveyed the speaker coldly.

'My brother caused my son's death,' she told Brother Oliver. 'It is quite simple. He knew that those who murdered his fellows in Canterbury might follow. His household is a hotbed of rebellion, and word must have reached his enemies of his whereabouts. The rest follows . . .'

The monk eyed her silently. The Lady Philippa had sent him. She had heard that Cressida had once again begun to rave and that Stephen though expected, had still not returned to London. Oliver had arrived in time to see the last moments of Cressida's rage before she relapsed into an even more terrifying apathy. He did not want to revive either her grief, or her anger. Now she spoke to him like a mechanical doll, her face staring and unseeing, her limbs – when they moved at all – jerking artificially as if controlled by a puppet master.

The monk had not forgotten the young girl who had taunted him with her beauty, accusing him of unchristian lust. It was hard to believe that young girl had become the thin, staring creature who now spoke so harshly of her brother.

Knowing the bonds that had held brother and sister close in those days he was shocked by the hatred he saw in Cressida's eyes. He knew from long experience that it was not an emotion that would disappear in the dark comfort of the confessional. Only time, perhaps not even that, would cure the sorrow akin to madness that held Cressida in its grip. And the Lady Philippa had fondly imagined that a man of God could cure it!

As he kept vigil at Cressida's side he went back in his mind over all he had known of the two families. The Lady Philippa had led them a dance at Grimthorne, with her winning ways and her gifts of jewels to mother church. Once they had reached London, however, she had disappeared into the protective arms of the Court.

As a court chaplain, Oliver had witnessed the sad changes in the Queen who had befriended Philippa.

Her approaching death kept him almost constantly at Westminster now. There always had to be one or two chaplains at hand to comfort her, and in the worst event, to administer the last rites due to the King's wife.

At the thought of Edward's own decline into the

wandering, drooling plaything of Alice Perrers, Oliver called silently on God to punish them both. He was secretly glad to have been called elsewhere. He felt unconsciously for the scourge at his waist and remembered that, on an impulse, he had given it into the safe keeping of his young clerk. The impassive woman who sat straight-backed before him would, perhaps, have benefitted from the shock and revelation of the whip, he thought. He watched her through the narrow hazel slits of his eyes, waiting for some sign that it would be propitious to speak again.

He had forgotten the golden glory of her hair, which still hung about her shoulders. But the beauty of her body, encased now in plain grey linen, had often returned to him in the nights when he had taken his full vows and there was no going back. He had never joined the other monks in their worldly excursions, in search of a little relief from the exigencies of their order. He knew too well the dominion that such tastes could hold over a man, and he had dealt with his own temptations ruthlessly from the start.

Once he had glimpsed Cressida on a spring day, when he had been driving into London for the monastery supplies. He had known her at once, though she wore a silver bridal coif over her hair and a rich blue gown. It was the eyes, the tilt of the head, that had told him at once who she was, and he had whipped the cumbersome horses into a fast trot at the sight of her. He had not known that Stephen had married her that day. But he was not surprised that such a sinful union had been cursed by the death of their son. The boy Richard was, he gathered from the family, all that was left of the marriage. He bowed his head to conceal the question in his eyes as he wondered, half fearfully, if Stephen would come to London after all, now that the boy was dead.

The bald circle and dark ring of his tonsured head gleamed in the light of the tallow. Cressida gazed at the monk unseeingly. If her defences had not been so weak she would never have allowed him into her home. But in the last hours all such considerations seemed unimportant. If Oliver was a figure from the past, then, with her brother, with Philippa, with Stephen and their dead son – he was no more to her than a cold cypher. Now that her raging had left her she felt as if she would never be capable of feeling again. Listlessly, she raised a hand to Oliver, indicating that he should speak if he wished.

The exhaustion and indifference that was eloquent in the gesture made Oliver hesitate. It was no use wasting his sermons on her. If he hoped to convert her to remorse rather than grief then he would have to bide his time.

'I bring naught for your comfort, Lady Cressida. The Lord Jesu himself was not a man of soft speech.' He stood, and bowed slightly. 'Think on what I have said. Your family, your friends, would bring you solace – if you could find it in your heart to forgive.'

She levered herself from the chair with the slow, ponderous movements of a dreamer and led him to the door. Suddenly the square set of her young shoulders seemed to crumble, and he put out a hand to save her as she stumbled. But she reached the doorway, and opening it, leaned on the frame, her eyes averted as he passed her and stood helplessly in the deserted hall.

She called for the servants. Beatrice appeared within seconds, as if she had been waiting.

Beatrice opened the main door and called to her husband that the good Father was ready to return to Court. Henry's voice sounded strangely distant to Cressida as he in turn called to the waiting boat on the jetty. She turned her head slowly in its direction, as if remembering some other voice from the water. As she did so, Oliver saw in the clear light of day that her eyes were lack-lustre, and red-rimmed. In a sudden surge of compassion, his mistrust of her beauty vanished. He restrained an impulse to place a hand gently on her sleeve. The moment passed as swiftly as it had come. Cressida watched the brown robed figure stride quickly across the lawns towards the river with dull eyes, unaware Oliver had wanted to fight for her salvation and her soul but had once more lost his own battle against her loveliness.

With a sigh, she wandered back into the solar and allowed Beatrice to settle her in her chair with a cup of her remedy for all ills – a measure of her home-brewed wine laced with honey and herbs.

She sipped from the cup as Beatrice held it, unaware that it contained other ingredients guaranteed to bring sleep to her exhausted mind and body. The draught was doubly strong. Within moments she had closed her eyes and her head lay back against a small cushion. Then, as the shadows lengthened on the white walls, Beatrice snuffed out the tallow lights and quietly let herself out of the room.

It was there that Stephen found Cressida at dawn next day. She opened her eyes slowly, aware of the singing of the birds in the garden and of a presence in the room.

When she saw who it was she tried to sit up, and the giddiness left by the potion made her grip each side of her chair. She stood slowly, breathing deeply, and her eyes, revived by her long sleep to their vivid blueness blazed in her white face.

'So you have come to us at last. Or rather to me.'

At first Stephen did not speak. He stood in the growing light, his long riding cloak still fastened. She saw that it was spattered with dry mud and realized that he had ridden far without stopping for rest. But now that they faced each other he could not bring himself to take the last step and embrace her. She was unaware that her cold eyes and wild hair would have struck terror into any man – and that even to Stephen, who had loved her so deeply, they were like warning beacons on a dangerous shore.

'For you know that I am alone? That our son is not here to greet you?' She persisted cruelly.

Stephen's grey eyes bored into hers. She believed they shone with anger, not with grief. She could not help taunting him. It was the first solace she had found since Richard's death, and she was incapable of anything else. In her heart she blamed Stephen for what had happened, and though, even after five years' separation, she still ached with love for him, she did not intend to spare him.

He nodded curtly. When he spoke at last his voice was low, and icily controlled.

'Richard's tutor, the Frenchman, waited for me at Westminster. Of course the attack was not known of there. It would not be prudent to call attention to your brother's activities so openly. Gervaise asked me what should be said. Before I came to Claire House I announced that our son had died victim to the fever that claimed others at Blackheath. It seemed best.'

'Your words hold more truth than you know. It *is* a fever that grips my brother and his men. But if you had not left London you could have kept our son safe. He was drawn to my brother in his father's absence. Whatever parted you from me, did Richard have to suffer so?'

'I came in answer to your letter. What more could you ask of me? You were right – the time had come to settle our son's future . . . '

The irony of his statement suddenly struck him; Richard's young life was now bereft of a future of any kind, and his voice trailed away. When he spoke again it was in a harsh tone, fighting with rising tears. The grey eyes softened, and he asked Cressida again: 'What more could you ask of me?'

At that moment her heart ached for him and she longed to throw herself into his arms and grieve with him for their lost child. But something still held her back. Oliver had spoken to her of the need to forgive. Perhaps she could, in time, learn to forgive her brother. But she knew that she would never be able to forgive Stephen's accusations, nor all the years they had been parted because of his mistrust.

Now, as she sought for some further excuse to vent her anger at Richard's death, she opened the old wound.

'I would have asked you,' she hissed at him, 'to come to me years ago, and beg my forgiveness. For the evil you thought of me. For the jealousy, the suspicion, that destroyed our love.'

She knew at once that she should not have revived the subject. The familiar expression of suppressed anger made a mask of Stephen's thin face. For the first time since he had come into the room, she looked straight at him and saw how pale he looked. The deep lines at each corner of his sensitive mouth spoke of suffering as well as of the five years that had passed.

'If our love is destroyed, as you claim, and our son is dead,' Stephen said coldly, 'then can you give me one reason why I should stay here in this house?'

Her heart pounded in dread that she might have gone too far, and that Stephen would turn and leave her before she could retrieve something from the meeting she had longed for for so long. Instinctively she put out a hand to stop him.

With a quick, angry movement he twisted at the fastening of his cloak and dropped it on the nearest chair. She watched him in silence, wondering at the sudden resignation with which he sank into his familiar chair, opposite her own.

He shook his head from side to side, and motioned to her own chair.

Slowly, she obeyed.

'It will always be thus between us,' Stephen said wearily. 'And now there is nothing to keep me here. Even our son's burial is out of our hands.'

Cressida leaned towards him, and the tears began to spill down her face. 'Nothing has been said. I – I have been ill. Gervaise, the servants – did they arrange things for me? I waited for you, but I did not know the time passed.'

He looked at her. In his heart he felt compassion for this still young, still exquisite woman who was his wife. But he also had not forgotten the reasons for their long, fierce war. Yet Cressida had waited for him, as if it had been a minor quarrel that kept them apart.

'There is no need to trouble your heart. Gervaise told me what he dared not tell you. But I believe I knew our son well enough to know that he has gone to a quiet grave. One he would have chosen. I – ' he faltered, seeking words that would not cause her more pain.

'You need say no more, Stephen. Our son's body was not found? But his tutor knows where it lies?'

Stephen nodded, unable to speak. He covered his eyes with his hands. Cressida rose and walked slowly to the window. It seemed to her that at all most important moments of her life she had been drawn to the great wide stretch of water that flowed by the house.

She rested her forehead on the cool window panes, and closed her eyes.

'So Richard has ended in the river he loved?'

Stephen reached her side as she turned away from the window, and held her gently by the shoulders as she began to weep again. He looked down at her golden head and his eyes blurred.

All the speeches she had planned, the venom she had nursed, were forgotten as he drew her firmly into his arms.

'Whatever the future holds for us,' he said, 'Tonight I shall stay with you. We will not let the sun go down upon our wrath this time.'

12

When Gervaise had told Stephen the news of Richard's death he had seen in the great scholar's face the torment of his grief and bewilderment. From the way in which Stephen turned abruptly from him without a word of thanks or farewell and raced to the palace quayside to order a barge, he knew that Stephen had to be with Cressida, and that they should be left to themselves.

He had got to Westminster planning to intercept Stephen with the news. A young follower of Wyclif, who had travelled with Stephen, informed Gervaise they had been delayed because of talks which might bring Wyclif himself to London. John of Gaunt, their sponsor awaited a report of the meeting at the Savoy Palace; but Stephen left word with Gervaise that he would have to postpone his encounter with the Prince.

Realizing that if Stephen found such a meeting of secondary importance there must still be some residue of feeling left in him for Cressida, Gervaise spent the next two days miserably at the Court, squandering his time, and grieving for his dead pupil. If he went back to Claire House he knew that he risked finding Cressida and her husband reunited in their sorrow – and he was not sure that he could bear to be with Cressida again if that were so.

He knew now that he loved Cressida so deeply that he only wanted her happiness. If she was destined to find that again with her rightful husband, then he would accept it. He was glad that he had not courted her, nor dared to make her his mistress in the long years of her husband's absence. If he had done so he doubted that he would have been able to renounce her so easily.

As a poet he knew enough of the human heart to guess that the boy's death would bring, at least, a temporary reconciliation for Cressida and Stephen, but he could not bring himself to think of Cressida in any other arms but his own. The secret love he had nursed for so long had become a part of him. He lived with it, with her image in his heart, every moment of the day.

He also knew enough to see that Cressida was not perfect. In his years as Richard's tutor the young Frenchman had studied the boy's mother and found her as complex, and as subject to moods and changes of heart as any other woman. He knew her above all to be ruled by her pride, by her fierce independence, and that she would not sacrifice that independence even to a man she loved – as she loved her husband.

In his role as messenger, Gervaise had learnt for certain that she still loved her husband. He had been aware of the agony of uncertainty in which she waited for her answer, and of the strange elation when she returned from Blackheath on the night after her namesake had died. He knew that he might never know the truth of the child's story. But it was plain that the little girl's death and the disappearance of her mother had, in some strange way, removed a weight from Cressida's soul.

At the thought of how wrong her prophecy, that all would be well, had been, his heart contracted. So on the night Stephen returned to Claire House Gervaise stayed away, pacing the corridors of the Palace, aware with every step he took of Cressida's grief – and of the solace she might seek in her husband's arms.

About midnight, as he began to think he should find a corner and at least try to sleep, Gervaise found himself outside the solar where the Queen's ladies in waiting usually passed the time. There was no sign of life. The Queen was at Windsor, and not expected to live the summer out.

With a pang, he remembered how he had first seen Cressida – when he still lived at Court – and how she had hurried past him in this very corridor, eyes averted from his gaze of open admiration. He blushed at the recollection of his boyish audacity. From the first glimpse had come a depth of emotion he had not guessed could exist.

With a sigh, he gave a last look about him and walked quickly away in the direction of the main hall. There was still the sound of singing in the distance, and if he could not sleep then at least he could join the musicians and compose a sad rhyme or two to touch their hearts. Now, perhaps for the first time, he knew that his poetry would have the ring of truth.

*

At Claire House the downstairs rooms were bathed in darkness and silence. The servants had retired early once Stephen had eaten what scant refreshment he had been able to take.

On the landing outside the room they had shared during the first years of their marriage, Cressida paused. She and Stephen looked silently into each other's eyes. It was a fleeting look, but it said everything each of them needed to know. The anger had gone, and they were exhausted by their shared sorrow. By wordless consent, Cressida opened the bedroom door, knowing that Stephen would follow.

As the door closed behind them, she turned to see how he welcomed this room where their son had been born. The candles were lit, and Beatrice had smoothed the bed and put the room in order. The heavy furniture shone in the soft light.

Something in his bearing as he stood on the edge of the shadows told her that he too had memories. Her heart beating painfully, she crossed the room to him and went like a small bird into his arms. At first he held her stiffly, and she tensed in her fear of rejection. Then his lips brushed her hair in a protective, almost brotherly gesture.

They were both too stricken by Richard's death for their embrace to change to the more urgent clasp of desire. She also knew that Stephen needed to sleep – even more than she did herself. If sleep would come.

Breaking from him gently, she went to the wardrobe to find a fresh gown in which to spend the night. Stephen walked slowly to her bed and began to unbutton his jacket.

His head turned sharply when a moment later she came upon the tapestry Abigail had worked, half hidden beneath folds of red velvet. Her gasp of anger called Stephen's attention to the discovery.

As she pulled it from its hiding place, wishing that she had destroyed it in the kitchen fire, it unrolled. Once more – now with Stephen gazing over her shoulder – she found herself contemplating the bleak, threatening scene. The young rider, vulnerable and solitary on the path through the dark wood, now had true meaning. She was certain that the woman Abigail had with every inch of the embroidery, stitched a lasting reminder of hatred and jealousy – a hatred of Cressida that had borne fruit in Richard's death.

'What is this work?' Stephen's voice was harsh with judgement made in advance. 'A sad purchase that fits these sorrowing walls.'

She did not reply. She had long been used to his carping at her spending, but if he knew the true origin of the tapestry it could spark off more than she could cope with emotionally. She thrust it back into the depths of the wardrobe.

'I have never liked it,' she remarked as she closed the cupboard door, the robe she had chosen over her arm. 'And it was a gift, not a purchase.'

With a strange laugh, Stephen began to pace restlessly about the room. 'To think that I should pick at old quarrels when we have such shared grief – at least for tonight.'

He sank into the room's only deep chair, still muttering to himself. She paused in her tracks, on her way to her garde-robe, where she had intended to undress in privacy. So her instinct had been right. Stephen had indeed come to London – perhaps solely for his meeting with the Prince – only to find that all reason for staying with her had gone. Perhaps he still loved her in his own, remote way, enough to share this night of sorrow. But he had not changed his cold manner toward her.

With a supreme effort of will she made no reply. She still loved him, and he still had power to hurt her. He was the father of her son, and she determined to snatch what solace she could from his presence. The fact that he even broached old subjects of their married quarrels at such a time was, in a way, a sign that he was still close to her. There had been indifference in his voice, it was true. But at least it was a voice she recognized. In happier days she had been able to change his indifference to something else once they were alone at night.

In her garde-robe mirror she scrutinized herself with a critical eye. Her tangled hair, swollen face and staring eyes made her ugly, she knew that. Her body felt stale and heavy. She seemed to have been wearing the grey robe for days.

Hurriedly, she pulled off the robe and poured cold water from the pitcher into a bowl. Again and again she splashed the water into her face, gasping at first as her skin and eyes tingled, and then throwing her head back in enjoyment, licking the drops from her lips. Refreshed at last, she dried her hair roughly and ran her hands through it, putting it into some semblance of order. Then she drew the night robe she had chosen at random over her head and returned to the mirror. The face that stared back at her was still marked by grief, but calmer now. Her hair sprang back in a wide halo from her high forehead.

Extinguishing the candle, she moved quietly into the bedroom. There she found Stephen, his tunic and breeches discarded carelessly as ever, stretched on the bed. As she drew near to him, her heart beating with slow painful thuds, she saw that he slept.

To be so close to him after all the years alone, watching him without his knowledge, was both deeply painful to her and at the same time a strange pleasure. She saw again how his long dark lashes curved above the high cheek-bones, and noticed that there were grey hairs in the thick curls and neat beard. She reached out, longing to trace the sensitive lines of his mouth as she used to when they were lovers. But she drew back quickly, remembering that her touch always awakened him, and brought him back into her arms.

Tonight Stephen needed to sleep, and she dared not disturb him – for fear that if he did wake he would not turn to her. She was willing to accept this night as a token of their shared love for their child, but as for the future –

she prayed that grief and anger would pass, but knew she would have to wait patiently for what would come in their wake.

From the foot of the bed, she took a coverlet which always lay folded ready in case the nights turned chill. Then, moving carefully, she lay down at Stephen's side and drew the coverlet over them both.

In the flickering light of the candles she stared at the ceiling. Was this to be her way of life from now on? She still felt young, and knew that other men desired her. But she had kept her marriage vows, always believing that one day Stephen would come to her again. There had been no way of knowing that it would be such a desolate homecoming, with no child to run to greet him, and no laughter in the house.

At the thought of children, her body contracted. The knife of her grief turned in her stomach, and her throat went suddenly dry. She fought the need to sit up, to run to the window for air. If she disturbed Stephen now he would find her in tears. She turned her head on the pillow as a single candle flared and died, and stifled the thought that if Stephen had returned as her husband in the truest sense she could that very night have conceived another child.

Somehow, briefly, she slept. When she woke she was immediately aware that her whole world had changed.

As grey and relentless as the dawn itself, the words came to her lips: 'Richard is dead.'

She sprang out of bed, throwing back the coverlet. Then she remembered how the night before she had drawn its warmth over herself and Stephen, and stared unbelievingly at the bare space where he had lain.

Still in her robe she ran barefoot into the corridor, and down the wide stairs. The kitchen door stood half open, and she could hear the servants' subdued voices and smell the newly baked bread. She paused, wondering if Stephen were with them, breakfasting early. But a narrow chink of light under the study door told her that he had taken refuge there – with his only true solace, his work.

Everything in her cried out against the hurt he had dealt her by leaving her side so readily. She ran across the hall and pushed wide the study door. She stood there, a wild figure with tears welling in her staring eyes, while Stephen looked up slowly from the papers he was reading.

When she spoke, her voice was a whip. 'So you can work? You can come back to this house, to such sorrow, and yet start a day like any other? Tell me, could you not sleep in our bed? Was your guilt too much for your conscience this once, Stephen?'

'My guilt?' His tone was cold, but he saw that she was still distraught with grief. He got up from his desk and walked towards her. As he tried to close the door and lead Cressida into the room she gripped his wrist with a hand that felt like ice, in spite of the humid warmth of the summer morning.

'Are you afraid that our servants, who doubtless loved your son more than you yourself, Stephen, will hear what I have to say? Let them – it is time they knew what I have endured. The years of isolation. Even when you lived in this house I was alone. And when at last you come to your son, you find him dead!'

She threw herself at him in a storm of angry tears, and her hands flew for his cheeks. He was too quick for her, and as he held her at arm's length he looked down into her ravaged, staring face and was reminded of a moment many years before when she had flown at him in her fury. When he had been unable to accept the horror of her rape by Sir Robert.

'Perhaps you are right, Cressida,' he said softly. 'There is some justice, and I deserve to be judged for many things. But not by the death of Richard. I came to you when you asked. Is that not enough?'

'It was too late! And for all I know you only came to see the Prince.'

Stephen knew better than to take up the challenge in her voice. He held her hands more gently as he answered.

'There was much to do at Oxford. I had to prepare a full report for Gaunt – and he'll not wait much longer for it. That is the only reason why I rose early today. Did you think otherwise?'

The words that should have served to quieten her were as red rag to a bull. With a twist of her body she freed herself, and stood back from him, disgust etched in every line of her face.

'Then you have come to the right place after all! If it is Lancaster you want to see, and not your wife? The Duke's Palace can be seen from our own windows – or had you forgotten? A ferry will take you to him within the half hour – or sooner. You could have gone to him last night had you only dared explain to me that you came to London for Wyclif and not for my sake!'

'I can explain nothing to you, Cressida, while you are like this. You try me to the limit with your unreasoning anger. Even if you are brought down with grief for our son you could surely spare me some small understanding?'

'I understand all too well – husband!' The word was a dagger, intended to draw blood. 'You are my husband still, I take it? You have not taken your full vows and denied our marriage yet?'

Stephen shook his head. 'My work is not the cause of all this, I know. There was a time when you were proud of my achievement, my partner in all the years of deception. Did I destroy all that when I doubted your purity? Is everything I – we – worked for, to be blamed for the one mistake I made?'

He spoke quietly, but without pause. When he had finished Cressida was silent. Her breath came in heavy pants of exhaustion. She raised an arm only to push the hair back wearily from her face. She knew that Stephen was right. She had still not forgiven him for thinking she might have had a child by the man who raped her. That when she still lived in their childhood village she had been Sir Robert's whore.

'You need hate the past no longer, Stephen,' she said at last. Her voice was bitter. 'The child you thought was mine, and bore my name, is also dead. From a summer fever. Is that not strange, that I lose both the children you believe are mine in the space of a sevennight?'

'I am sorry for the child's death. But you are mistaken if you think I have ever believed she was yours. It was the voice of jealousy that said so – and of love for you.'

'What do you know of love?' Cressida faced him scornfully. 'You were right when you guessed that Robert loved me. The child's name proved it. The hatred the child's mother bore me was caused by it. And now I have reaped her curses.'

Stephen stepped towards her, and gripped her cruelly with both his hands on her half bare shoulders. 'You know too much to believe such things. You are an educated woman, not a peasant. The curses of such a woman have no power.'

'Then why has she left my brother's household, now that her task is done? Why did she not stay, to mourn her child and help my friend to nurse my niece Margaret?'

'So she has left Blackheath . . . '

Cressida nodded. 'We do not know where she has gone. And I do not care.'

'Then you have truly changed, Cressida. For the girl I knew and loved would have followed, and brought her back. These are no times for a woman to travel alone. The roads are packed with ruffians intent on theft and murder. If she falls in with the wrong band her end will be unthinkable.'

Cressida remembered the dance Abigail had performed at the Palace and the effect it had on the men at High Table. Could even Stephen have fallen under the woman's spell?

'You care more for her fate then than for mine,' she

said sullenly, and even as the words were out she regretted them. But to her astonishment, Stephen laughed. It was a rueful, sad little sound – but nonetheless the first laughter at Claire House for many days.

She looked up at him, questioning his mood. But her heart sank as she saw his head turn back to the papers on his desk, and she knew that the moment of communication had passed. How ironical that the mention of the woman who had caused them so much harm had so nearly brought them closer together.

The stubborn line she knew only too well had set in Stephen's lean features. She sighed.

'You meet with John of Gaunt today, then?'

'I have no choice. As I planned when I first joined the King's entourage, I have learned who will befriend our cause, and the time is approaching when they can come into the open for me. The years of playing the King's loyal servant have made me a respectable figure. Even the English language must be respectable, if I choose to write it!'

'And you say that Wyclif may come to London?' She dared not seem to plead, and wanted rather to know if Stephen would accompany the great scholar and churchman.

'To preach. It is an historic decision for us all.'

'And when will you return to Oxford?' She could not conceal a wistful note in the question.

He dropped his hands to his sides. 'Our son is laid to rest where he would perhaps have best liked to be. There is nothing I can do. My answer to his murderer is to work on, to show that no amount of killing can stem the tide of the rebellion. It is true I am not a man of action like your brother – '

At the mention of Francis Cressida turned away. 'Do not speak to me of my brother ever again. I have forbidden him to enter this house, and I shall never see him again. It is he who led our son to his death.'

Stephen followed her to where she stood by the bare

hearth. She did not look up, but studied the cold ashes of a fire that must have last been lit when Richard and Gervaise studied together in the spring. She wondered idly why Beatrice had not cleared the grate. At the memory of Richard's fair hair bent over his books her eyes filled with tears.

'But if your brother is barred from this house who is there to care for you? You cannot live entirely alone.'

'So it is true? You intend to live on at the university? There is no question of your return to Claire House? Tell me, Stephen, when you think of home – do you think of this place where we have lived so deep and suffered so much? Or of some dry scholar's room lined with your dusty papers and your dry thoughts?'

He shrugged despairingly. He could see that her grief had put her beyond his reach, at least for the time being.

'There are others who will care for me,' she rapped out when she saw that he had no answer for her. 'I have friends in the City. Beatrice and Henry will never leave me. Have no fear, Stephen, your wife is well loved!'

In the garden the sunlight grew suddenly strong and clear, and Cressida turned distractedly as a thrush broke into song. She did not want to think of Gervaise again. With Richard gone the poet might never return. Why should she expect it of him? Yet the bird song made her think of him, and his serious, devoted young face glimmered at the corners of her mind as she went to the window.

'I know you have to go now, Stephen,' she said. 'But I have one last favour to ask of you.'

She saw that he had not moved, and sensed that he had been watching her silently for the last few moments.

'If you are to ride to Oxford soon, as you say, then I do not think I could bear to say goodbye. Nor to see you in this house again before you go. As you say, our son is buried deep. At least you have work in which to drown your grief.'

She did not know whether she expected her words to

bring Stephen protesting to her side, or send him angrily from the room. But his reaction, when she thought about it in the long days that followed, was as typical of her husband as anything she had known him do.

'If you send us all away, then I pity you, Cressida,' he said. 'But in my case there is no choice. I am not master of my destiny, you have always known that. Whereas you, little Cressida, have always been mistress of your own. I wish you joy of it.'

Then, gathering his papers into a single sheaf and rolling them neatly into a scroll, he looked about for his scholar's cloak, and when he had found it left her.

13

If Cressida had known that two more long years would drag by before John of Gaunt would in reality find the courage to come into the open for the Lollards' cause she might not have allowed Stephen to close the study door on their lives and leave for Oxford.

She was never to know the exact nature and outcome of Stephen's meeting that day at the Savoy. Just a boat-ride away from where she sat and brooded on her loss, and the apparent end of her marriage, Stephen was fighting for the language of the people as she herself would once have fought.

At almost forty, Stephen had the mature presence and experience to impress the Prince. But the Prince, almost ten years Stephen's junior, had still some way to go. His gift for diplomacy conspired with his hunger of power and made him hang back, waiting almost a decade before Stephen's hearing that day would bring any real results.

It was ironical, Cressida thought, that just as her husband seemed so close to victory she could not say that her heart went with him. In the hours since her son's death all thoughts of rebellion and politics had become anathema to her. She had turned into a creature capable only of grief, and of anger. Believing that Stephen rejected her love she had finally – or so it seemed to her in her confusion and despair – allowed the fire of her anger to consume what was left of her love.

All that day she roamed aimlessly about the house where they had all once been so happy. As each room became unbearable with its store of memories she left it, and moved to the next. Several times Beatrice tried to persuade her to eat, bringing her delicacies piled on a small silver tray. But she could not bring herself to touch them.

When Beatrice heard her climb the stairs to her bedroom, she followed her with a posset which would bring her sleep. But Cressida refused even that, and Beatrice left her with a despairing glance. As the door closed, Cressida sank to her knees in front of the cupboard in the bedroom and began to ransack its depths.

Late that night, when the house was silent, Cressida went down to the deserted kitchen, a scroll of fabric gripped tightly to her breast. For a while she sat crouched before the dying embers of the fire. Then, her face a blank, she thrust the tapestry into the ashes and waited. One by one small flames spurted into life, and a thick acrid smoke swirled into her face from the burning linen and silks. Choking on its bitterness, she watched until every vestige of the tapestry had turned to ash. Only then did she go to her bed.

In the sleepless night that followed she tried to decide what she should do. At first she thought of giving up everything – her place at Court, Claire House itself. There was nothing to keep her in London. She suspected that even Beatrice and Henry would gladly leave with her, bereft as they were by Richard's death.

But where should she go with her servants? There was only one place that seemed to beckon – her own village. Beatrice had been born there, too, and had met her husband at the village fair. But she knew from the latest news that the place was a waste land, laid low by two plagues and the loss of many farm workers. What land was well cared for was under the domain of Philippa, her sister-in-law – and, indirectly, her brother Francis. She had known Peter of Ashby, Philippa's steward, once, but it was unthinkable that she should seek a home in a region where she would be dependent on the good will of people she never intended to see again.

She turned angrily in her bed, trying to sleep before the dawn light chased away all hope of any rest. As she closed her eyes she found herself half dreaming of the day they had come to London together almost twenty years ago. Cressida had lost everyone she loved to the cause that had brought her to the city.

Her last waking thought was, strangely, of Gervaise. With a pang of remorse she wondered why he had stayed away since his pupil's death. Tomorrow, she would bathe and dress early – and seek him out at Westminster. If he was to leave her employment, she thought sadly, there were things to be settled . . .

But her resolution to do something about his situation was forgotten next day when she woke blinking her eyes in brilliant sunshine to find Beatrice standing at the foot of the bed. In her arms was a long shapeless wrap of palest silk, which seemed to be concealing some other garment. Wearily, Cressida shook her head. She did not want to give her attention to matters of dress at such a time. But she was suddenly hungry and thirsty, and asked Beatrice to bring meat and drink to her room.

'So you're feeling a mite better, my sweet?' Beatrice asked, her kindly face breaking into a smile for the first time since Richard's death.

'I must not become a burden to you, Beatrice,' Cressida answered. 'If I am to make plans for us all I need my strength.'

'Plans?' Beatrice narrowed her eyes doubtfully. 'What plans would they be then, my lady?'

'When I have eaten and quenched my thirst I shall come to the kitchen and talk – with Henry too if he is about.'

Beatrice came round the foot of the bed and placed her parcel with great ceremony across the coverlet.

'When you have quenched your thirst you will wash your face and put on this gown and come down to the great gentleman who has brought it for you. He'll not leave Claire House till he sees you in it, I'll be bound.'

'I ordered no gown.' Cressida looked at the parcel, wondering if she had indeed forgotten some recent creation made for her in the city. Her hands touched the silk with little interest, and Beatrice pushed them away, in order to unwrap the contents herself.

'It's a sad robe, but none the less a beauty. And you're right in saying you didn't order it, for it's a gift. From him who waits below.'

She drew out a long black silk underdress and a short black velvet tunic with a low cut neckline. The long, graceful sleeves were edged with pearls, and Cressida gasped in surprise. Involuntarily, she pushed her mass of golden hair back from her shoulders and knelt on the bed, taking the gown from Beatrice with a little cry of admiration. Then from the silken wrapping Beatrice produced a small meshed helmet made entirely of pearls sewn on a base of black silk strands, so closely that they shone like a mass of silver in the sunlight.

'Who has sent this sad robe for me?' Cressida breathed.

'A very good customer you've been to him in your day, so there's no charity in it,' Beatrice said. 'It's Master Andrew Blake the merchant and he waits below.'

'I cannot see him,' Cressida said firmly. She sat back against her pillows and stared at the dress. 'You must tell him that it is the noblest, kindest gift – but I cannot see him.'

'If it's your red eyes you're hiding, there's no need.' Beatrice dived for the last time into the package, and brought out a long veil of sheerest black that seemed to

Cressida to be made of gossamer. 'No man will expect you to appear unveiled at this time.'

For a moment Cressida's brow wrinkled in puzzlement. Not only was the gift, however sad, a timely and welcome affair – but with the fact of the way in which her son had died being suppressed so carefully she wondered how a man of Andrew Blake's walk of life had heard of her loss.

'Is – is Richard's death then common knowledge?' she asked, the tears springing to her eyes as she spoke her son's name.

'It will be afor long if it is not now,' Beatrice said, bustling in the direction of the garde-robe, as if intending to have Cressida washed and dressed in a trice. 'And if you have to face the world, or your friends at Court, bless your good friend who has provided you with the means to go forth, and let him be the first to approve . . . '

Knowing her servant's mind was made up, Cressida placed the robes carefully at the foot of the bed, and slid her feet to the floor. A sudden wave of dizziness came over her as she stood, but as she turned Beatrice's sturdy arms came round her and led her to the garde-robe. Then, as Beatrice ran to and fro with pitchers of warm water spiced with lavender and rosemary, and the small room clouded with perfumed steam, Cressida ate and drank, and after soothing her face and body into some semblance of well-being, slowly donned the new, sombre clothes that waited for her.

Too disinterested to look at herself in the mirror, Cressida finally allowed her maid to bind her long hair and tuck it into the pearl headdress. As she stood forlornly in the centre of her bedroom, as if waiting for someone or something that would bring her to life, Cressida felt the soft, black veiling fall about her shoulders, and found herself gazing out on to a dim, grey world whose occupants could now not read the anguish in her eyes.

With this at least to thank him for, she followed

Beatrice slowly down the stairs and into the solar, where Andrew Blake stood, his back to the door, staring out at the river scene.

As he swung round to greet her, the merchant's full mouth opened in a gasp of admiration, but, sensing the gravity of the moment, he said nothing, sweeping a deep bow and waiting for Cressida to speak first.

'Master Blake, you have been generous, and I thank you.' Cressida's voice trembled, but she walked steadily towards her benefactor, her shoulders very straight and her head held proudly, almost imperiously in its crown of pearls and silk. The veil lifted slightly as she moved, and Andrew Blake's eyes went to the golden line of young flesh above the low cut of the black velvet tunic.

In the grief that still beset her Cressida was unaware of his glance. She held out a slender hand, which he brushed with his lips.

'You will take wine? It is the least I can offer you. You have come so early on a warm day. And with such gifts.'

The merchant moved to the chair Cressida indicated for him, and sat when she had taken her own place at the chair that faced his.

'It is nothing. I simply happened to have in store this length of velvet, and it had to be for you, Lady Cressida. There will not be much more of it in London I fear, if the rumour of the renewed wars in France is true.' He sighed. 'My very best silks will soon disppear from my shelves.'

At the mention of war in France Cressida's thoughts went at once to Gervaise. Would this be the lever that was needed to make him return to his own people? She hoped not. She could not see him in battle. And she knew from her own father's death at Crecy that war often claimed those who most deserved to live.

She frowned. 'War in France? Are we to be content ever in this land of ours?'

Her companion shrugged. 'England is a land of soldiers now. The new ships are fast, and carry great numbers. When a country becomes so strong, it has to spread its wings.'

'It is a pity that such wealth has not been spent on those who most need it,' Cressida said. There was a pause, in which Andrew Blake eyed her carefully she thought, as if surprised that she could broach the matter of politics at such a time. In fact she had surprised herself, but in the last hour she had begun, however slowly, to come out of her numb sorrow, and something of her dead son's spirit was in her words.

Entering the room with the tray of wine, Beatrice gave her an approving motherly glance, as if to say 'life must go on.' And in the aloof, muted world beneath her veil Cressida suppressed a deep sigh, her small chin tilting proudly.

'How did you learn of my son's death, Master Blake?' she asked in a low voice as the merchant sipped the wine Beatrice poured for him.

'The sad news reached me through a merchant. A Flemish merchant who lives on Chepeside. I did not pursue the source of his information, I fear. I was too shocked on your behalf, my lady. I could only think what I could best do for you in your sorrow.'

She bowed her head in acknowledgement. But her mind was racing. If the merchant was one of the roguish Netherlanders whom she had heard rented houses openly in the turbulent city of London, making what pickings they could, then could it be that one of their number had been a paid assassin? Paid, that is, to kill her brother and not her son. It was the kind of deed she believed was well within their scope. If they had allegiance to anyone, it was certainly not to the rebel cause.

'You could not have done more. The gown is exquisite. I thank you again.'

The merchant must have noticed Cressida's hands clenched on the wooden arms of her chair, for he finished his wine quickly, and said that he must not outstay his welcome.

Unable to stand on ceremony in her present mood,

Cressida stood and walked with him to the main doors. As Henry ran across the hall from the kitchen to open them, she could not miss a rather disgruntled, suspicious look he despatched in their visitor's direction. But Andrew Blake, it seemed, had eyes for no one but herself.

He bowed over her hand, and she was aware for the first time of a heavy perfume. She suppressed a wave of distaste. The man was more of a dandy than she had realised. Perhaps it was as well. If his admiration was a pose, then it was safe. She could not have dealt with anything more ardent while Stephen's recent presence still haunted her.

As he walked with Henry through the gardens and round to the stable block where the groom waited for him Cressida watched. She did not allow her gaze to stray to the river beyond. She could not trust herself to look at the wide water that held her son's body in its depths. She could not bear the sound of the boatmen calling to each other across its grey reaches. It was Richard's world, and until her shock and her grief were at bay she could not bring herself to enter it again.

The doors closed against her visitor, and a warm summer breeze reached her from the garden, laden with the scent of newly cut grass. Finding herself alone in the hall, she lifted her veil and threw it back over the pearl headdress. Her high forehead gleamed from her recent bathing, and her eyes were sapphires in her white face. Unaware of the new beauty that sorrow had brought to her body, Cressida stood for a few moments in the silent hall. In the kitchen, Beatrice moved quietly about her duties. Suddenly there was no movement, and the unmistakable sound of weeping reached Cressida's ears.

Her veil flying, she ran across the flagged stones and pushed open the kitchen door.

From the great scrubbed table Beatrice looked up into Cressida's eyes. Before her was a dish of silver-scaled fish, fresh from the river. Her worn, reddened hands gripped the edge of the table as her whole body shook with grief.

As she wept out her heart for the small boy who would never bring fish to her kitchen again, Cressida ran to her and took her silently in her arms, her heart surging in the knowledge that she did not mourn her son alone.

Richard had been dead for ten days when a brown-tunicked rider rode to Claire House with a letter from her brother.

While the man waited she opened the parchment with visible distaste. There was no likelihood of her wanting to send a written reply, but she could not bring herself to refuse entirely to communicate with Francis.

Sister . . . Philippa and I know and understand your feelings. We are patient, by nature. By need, we wish to talk with you. Send word to us when we may see you. If that is not soon, then remember you have friends and come to them however late. Francis.

Her wide mouth in a tight line of anger, Cressida did not re-read the missive. She turned to the messenger and told him curtly:

'I thank you for your journey. On your return, pray tell my brother that I will not come to him. He knows my reasons.'

Eyes downcast, the man backed his way out of the house. As she heard the sound of his horse's hooves growing fainter in the distance Cressida knew a brief moment of regret. But she had not been impulsive. Her cold response was born of deep-rooted anger. Even had she wanted to see her brother again she would not have trusted herself yet to make anything of an encounter but yet more quarrels, yet more despair.

Yet she could, she told herself, have found the good grace to enquire after Margaret's health. Could Brother Oliver's judgement of the situation be verging on the truth, she wondered? Was she now doomed to hate anyone whose child still lived, and especially the brother who should have died in Richard's place?

For the first time in days, she went to her favourite window seat from which she could see the river. A barge passed dressed with garlands for some summer festival. The sound of music drifted across the water to her, and she brushed hot tears from her face as she listened. Even when the music had long since disappeared into the distance, she remained at the window.

Then, calling to Beatrice to help her, she ran from the room and to the stairs. 'Thank providence for Master Blake and his gift,' she said to herself as she reached her bedroom door. 'I can hold my head high at Court beneath my veil. I must go to Westminster. To find Gervaise.'

14

'I feared that I would be too late. That you would have sailed for France.'

They were sitting in the rose arbour beneath the window of the Queen's solar, where Cressida herself had often watched the royal children at play. Gervaise looked into her eyes, and quickly looked away, watching a giant bee drone in circles towards a rose of such deep crimson that it was almost black.

As he had watched her come towards him over the Palace lawns from the quayside, her black veil rippling about her shoulders, he had experienced a sharp anguish, as if he had fallen in love with her only at that moment.

'I would not have gone without sending word to you. But it is true, I have in these days begun to feel that I should make a new life with my own people.'

'And perhaps live to fight those who have brought you up, loved you, as their own? I do not see that you – a man of peace – could ever take arms against those you love.'

'You know me well, my lady. I am not certain that I could kill any man. But if France is defeated – as I believe she will be this time, perhaps for ever – then I would not want to stay here, in this land where corruption and ambition have taken the crown.'

The bitterness in his voice made her realise that Gervaise also felt her son's death deeply. 'But things will change, and soon. Would you not want to witness the better things – for which – ' she faltered, unable to say Richard's name in front of this young man who had been his constant companion.

'For which your son died?'

She thanked him with her eyes, and without thinking held her hand out to him. He took it, holding it tightly in both his hands, all the agony of the last few days eloquent in his grasp.

Since Stephen's arrival Gervaise had spent all his time at Westminster, not daring to return to Claire House in case he should disturb a reconciliation, some chance of happiness for Cressida out of her sorrow. But his spirits had risen sharply when he had heard that Stephen had once more left for Oxford – after less than two days in London.

He had been forced to recognise that it was not Richard's death that had convinced him there was no longer a place for him at Cressida's side – but the fact that her husband had returned at her request, and that it was this she most needed and desired.

The difference in their ages was nothing. Cressida was at the height of her beauty, in spite of her recent suffering. He had often received more than encouragement from older women at Court, and had found them more pleasing and interesting than the girls who blushed and laughed at the approach of a young gallant. And he knew that she would always rival the loveliest women.

The desire he had known for her as a mere boy had now turned into an all-embracing love. With Richard's death he had thought that love must be denied for good. His only hope of sanity had been escape, and even the wars in France seemed better than living close to the woman he loved with no hope of fulfilment.

'It is in my son's name that I am asking you to stay,'

Cressida spoke at last, her voice vibrant with questions.

His grip of her hand tightened. 'I still cannot believe your son is dead. Nor will I ever accept it.'

'Then why not stay here, where his memory will always live. What harm is there in that?'

They both knew that when she spoke of harm she was not talking of Richard or his death. The waves of growing passion that flowed between them as they touched made her lips quiver as she waited for her answer.

'The scholar Stephen. Your husband. Would he see the harm in it?' Gervaise searched her face for some sign that she still loved Stephen and would react to his name.

She answered quickly. 'My husband belongs in Oxford. He has no right now to see ill or not in what I do. It is better that I leave him in peace, to pursue his work. If Wyclif does come to London, then I am assured my husband will come as his colleague . . . and not because he cannot bear to stay away from me.'

Her breathless manner when she spoke of Stephen gave Gervaise his answer. He was certain she still loved him, but that the pride which underlay so much of her behaviour in the past was in play. If Stephen had indeed shown his preference for the scholar's life, and left Cressida alone so soon after her bereavement, then she would never betray how deeply he had hurt her by doing so.

'Are we to watch over our shoulders for months, maybe years for Wyclif and his party to come to London? Could we two live in such uneasy fashion?'

'There would be more to our lives than that,' Cressida spoke earnestly, and with her other hand touched his shoulder, her eyes shining for the first time since she had received the news of Richard's death. 'There is so much we could do. I would take up my studies again. You could be my tutor!'

He smiled gravely, and raised her hand to his mouth, brushing the palm with his lips. 'And you my teacher in many things.'

In the quiet garden they sat, unobserved, for some time. Cressida rested her head on Gervaise's shoulder, suddenly at peace with herself. They both knew that the consummation of their desire for each other would wait on their grief. But in the unspoken declaration of their feelings they had opened up new paths and the process of laying Richard's memory to rest had, imperceptibly, begun.

As they walked back into the main cloisters round the palace they moved at a slight distance from each other, but Cressida did not care who saw that her hand rested lovingly on Gervaise's arm. She had thrown her veil back from her face, and members of the Court who knew that she had lost her son paused and bowed as she passed, their eyes filled with admiration. Andrew Blake had done his work well.

As they reached the quayside and the boatman called for the barge which would carry Cressida home, she became aware of other eyes, which watched her more critically. Taking her seat in the centre of the boat, Cressida raised a hand in farewell to Gervaise and smiled. He would tell his friends at Court of his plans to live at Claire House before he returned to her.

But her smile froze on her face as over his shoulder she looked into Brother Oliver's cat-like eyes. The venomous judgement in his gaze reminded her forcibly of another day when she had been almost run down in the crowded streets by this zealous man of God. Her wedding day. Would he always be there, she wondered, to cloud any moment of happiness for her? What did he want of her?

When he had come to her in her wild grief he had spoken of remorse. He had told her that she resented those whose children were still alive, when her own son was dead. How did a man like Oliver know of such things? If he were right, she thought fiercely, the remedy was in her hands, not his. She could remedy her loss. She was still young enough to bear another child. And if she did so it would bind Gervaise to her for good.

*

The delight and fulfilment of the two years that followed were not to include the conception of a child, but they compensated for the vacuum left in Cressida's life in every other way. On his return to Claire House Gervaise established himself as her tutor and mentor. They began lessons in French literature, and in the composition of poetry. Beatrice and Henry, glad to have the house once more filled with activity, watched over them with a benevolent, parental eye. They did not judge Cressida for her new-found love. In the early months there was, in any case, a formal relationship between tutor and mistress – there was nothing to condemn. By the time Gervaise and Cressida began to share a bed Stephen's continued absence and silence had turned Beatrice against him; and where Beatrice walked, Henry followed.

It was in the heart of the first winter after Richard's murder that Gervaise became Cressida's lover. With the approach of the Christmas festivities they were both acutely aware of the fact that they had no family to visit, no callers to rejoice with them. Beatrice took to standing gloomily in the kitchen saying that Christmas was nothing without children to cook for, and for her sake Cressida suggested to Gervaise that they go into the fields to find holly and mistletoe and decorate the house.

The path behind Claire House took them southwards, and a light fall of snow underfoot made walking a hazard. Cressida wore her mother's ancient grey-green cloak, and followed Gervaise, planting her small leather booted feet in his footprints. At one moment she almost slipped, and Gervaise turned and was struck by the change in her. There was colour and sparkle in her cheeks, and as he caught her hand to steady her, her lips curved in a smile – the first he had seen on her face for many months.

'I thought you were a country wench,' he teased, 'and that walking in the snow held no fears for you.'

'I have run far in the snow in my time,' she replied, remembering the icy ridges of the rough track that led from her home to Stephen's village. 'If the river were frozen hard I would teach you to skate like a bird.'

They walked on side by side for a while, his arm about her waist, and she felt the warmth of this embrace through the heavy fabric of her cloak. In the distance a group of children laughed and scrambled for holly in the hedgerow. Gervaise glanced down at Cressida to see if the sight of the children troubled her. Since the summer she had seemed to avoid the London streets with their packs of tumbling urchins, and the stiffly dressed children at Court held no attraction for her on their recent visits there together.

But Cressida watched the children with an untroubled expression on her face, and pulled the hood of the cloak back, letting her long hair fall free as they reached the holly trees. With her arms filled with the spiky green branches and bright red berries, Gervaise thought she herself looked as delighted as a child. As they trudged back to the house together he had an almost uncontrollable desire to stop and take her in his arms.

That night they sat in the ground floor solar and wove the holly into wreaths. Beatrice and Henry bustled in and out with advice and cries of admiration at their work. When they had finished, Cressida asked for warm mead and honey to be brought to them. Beatrice returned with the drinks, and then hurried away saying that she had to be abed early as there was work to be done in her kitchen as soon as it was light.

As they sipped their warming drinks, they grew silent. Although Richard was still present in both their hearts they did not mention him. The day had, in some new, precious way been theirs, and they wanted to end it as serenely as it had begun.

As she drained her goblet, Cressida sensed Gervaise's eyes upon her, and placing the goblet almost too carefully on the table she rose and went to the window. Drawing back the curtain that kept out the chill of the night, she pressed her face against the glass pane and watched the first heavy white flakes of snow fall and settle in the garden.

Beyond the lawns the river shone in the light of the watermen's torches and she saw that its surface was now a solid sheet of ice.

'The children will be out on the river tomorrow,' she told Gervaise. 'I shall find them there at first light, for sure, when I look from my window.'

She turned, to find him at her shoulder, and with gentle hands he turned her fully towards him and pulled her close.

Her heart began to pound beneath her ribs, and she wondered if he could hear it. But as he bent to kiss her and she looked into his deep grey eyes she was aware only that she felt suffused with sweetness and that Gervaise was the source of that sweetness.

'I do not believe you will be at your window so early,' he said in a voice low with desire. She could not answer him at first, except with a swift, light kiss on his bare throat.

He responded with a deeper, rougher kiss and she parted her lips to his tongue. For some minutes they stood locked in each other's arms, oblivious of the snowbound world outside. Their whole world was in the warm, silent room, and their blood pulsed through their veins as if they were one, until Gervaise pulled away from her and led her to the hearth.

He forced her gently down on the thick furs which edged the fireplace and she did nothing to prevent him. Her head swam from the intoxication of being loved. She was aware of the flicker of candlelight on the ceiling, then Gervaise's form blotted out the light. He began to whisper his love for her as his young body bore down on hers. His hands sought her breasts, and with a recognition of her own body's desires she arched against him.

Her movement excited him, and he moved quickly, pulling her robe away from her. At the sight of her he paused, and said: 'I knew that you were as lovely as this.

In my heart I knew that I loved and desired a young girl who goes disguised as the Lady Cressida. You are perfection.'

To be loved again after so long a time was something Cressida had only allowed herself to imagine at the height of her loneliness. She had in some ways feared the reality, wondering whether all her pain had made her cold and she would disappoint a lover – especially a younger man. The only man she had ever really desired was Stephen, and on the nights she had longed for him she would have found it in her heart to forget all wrongs if he had come to her bed. But he had been far away on those nights, and as silent as ever.

Now, to her delirious joy, she found that as Gervaise touched her she was moist and eager with love. She was proud of her smooth skin she had cared for all the years she had lived alone, and thrilled to Gervaise's caresses. But more than all the physical rapture of being loved was the depth of love she felt flowing from Gervaise into her as he gently made her his own.

The sorrows they had shared, the patience with which they had waited for this moment making it perfect for them both, gave to their love-making a meaning and passion that she would not have believed possible. Her body ached for Gervaise even when he possessed her, and she returned his kisses and embraces with complete abandon. When his first rush of passion was over he lay in her arms in the firelight and told her of the years he had loved her without hope. As they went upstairs and stood at the door to Cressida's bedroom it was tacitly understood between them that he would not share the bed she had shared with her husband, and he kissed her long and tenderly in the shadows, whispering to her to come to him again before it was light.

It was almost dawn when Cressida stood naked in her room, shivering with a mixture of the chill night air and excitement. Leaving the garments she had worn that day carelessly on her smooth bed, she chose a fresh gown and slipped into it quickly, blew out the candles and made for the room where Gervaise still slept.

As the new day came, they lay close on his narrow bed and talked of the future. Cressida paused between words and to kiss Gervaise, on the brow, the mouth, and the warm skin of his body.

'Will you not find a young girl to love now that you have possessed me?' she teased, and in the way he turned to her, his desire aroused again, she received her answer.

This time her own passion matched his and outmatched it. Her cries of love delighted Gervaise, and he reached a peak of loving again and again until it was she who had to cry mercy and insisted that they should dress and go down to the kitchens. She was hungry for the first time in months, and as Gervaise watched her consuming her breakfast under Beatrice's approving administration, she did not care that he found it amusing.

Later, they sat with their books in the solar, and as each of them turned a page or made note of some word they paused, and gazed into each other's eyes, alive with discovery of each other.

Before dark, Gervaise insisted that they seek the fresh air. 'Lest I forget altogether the outside world and die of a surfeit of love,' he said.

She acquiesced, running to the chest in the hall for her great cloak, and calling to Beatrice that they would be home before nightfall.

They walked along the river bank, heedless of the mud and wet snow that had been churned up by the day's travellers, until they came within sight of the bridge. The flares in the street were brilliant in the twilight, and the bustling crowds of shoppers and merchants that were still about in the busiest season of all beckoned to them.

Huddled close together, they wandered from stall to stall, sampling sweetmeats, laughing at the odd antics of mechanical toys, sad only for a brief moment that they had no one for whom they could buy such gifts.

At the low doorway to a mercer's well known for his

choice silks and ribbons, Cressida paused. She was tempted to go in, but knew that her appearance might cause some comment. No one would know her for the great lady she had become in recent years. But she nursed another fear – that if she began to buy such things in the presence of her young lover he would be made aware of his lesser income.

Making a mental note to see what could be done to find a patron for Gervaise as a poet, for this was the accepted, practical way for him to be able to pursue his craft, she pulled at his arm, leading him on into the crowds. But it was as if he had read her thoughts, and his enthusiasm suddenly seemed to evaporate.

'It is dark already. We have no torch, and the bye-laws forbid the river path to those who carry no light.'

'Very well,' Cressida said. She did not want to spoil their excursion with a difference of opinion. She would return to the mercer's alone, another day. 'But we have to go quickly, if you are right, my dearest.'

It was as they turned and hurried south over the bridge again that a beggar woman began to trot at Gervaise's heels, mumbling her prayer for a small coin or a morsel of bread. It was not Cressida's plain, peasant's garment that attracted her, but perhaps a glimpse of the velvet tunic and silken hose that Gervaise wore beneath his long winter cloak. His face softened, and he brushed the woman's hand once or twice gently from his sleeve, walking on at Cressida's side as he did so. They had little or no money left after their unexpected excursion, and neither of them believed in the superstition that to turn away a beggar brought bad luck.

Then something familiar in the woman's voice made Cressida pause, and she signed to Gervaise that they should search their purses for whatever they could find. They stopped in the light of a flare to do so, and Cressida turned to tell the woman to wait.

To her horror she found herself looking into the dark, accusing eyes of Abigail. But it was not the fear of a curse or a scene in the street that made her draw back. It was the tell-tale swelling of polluted flesh on the woman's face, and the livid pallor of the twisted hand that still plucked at Gervaise's sleeve.

Cressida looked about her in amazement, wondering how the woman had gone unnoticed and unmolested in a crowd that would certainly have hounded her from the scene had they searched the evil face under its ragged hood. Abigail was a leper!

'Dear God in heaven,' Cressida gasped. 'How have you come to this? Does my brother know? What will become of you?'

Gervaise, not knowing who the woman was, tried at once to drag Cressida from the spot once he had seen the leper's marks. He was too kindly to call for the Watch and have the sick dog of a creature run out of the city to starve in the winter fields, and only wanted to get Cressida as far away as was physically possible. But Cressida stayed her ground.

'Where do you lodge? How can we reach you? If I come to you with the means to take you to some hospice with the good nuns, will you go with me?'

The woman pulled her hood closer round her head, with a clumsy, fearful movement. Cressida had to lean close to catch her words.

'There is a ruined boat beneath the old jetty at the foot of River Lane. Do you know it?'

'Of course. I lived there at the apothecary's once, many years ago.'

'You may find me there. You may not. I wait for the travelling men who would have taken me with them to the spring fair at Exeter. But it is too late.'

'Then will you do as I say?' In her need to save the mutilated body of the woman who had once been so seductively alive, Cressida had forgotten all the evil of which she had once suspected her.

Abigail nodded, several times, and then seemed to

huddle deeper into her rags before she limped away into the crowds.

As they stumbled their way back to Claire House in the dark, Gervaise angrily demanded why Cressida had put herself at such risk. The thought that she should catch such a disease herself sent a knife of fear through his heart – and the woman's presence in the city was a flagrant breach of its laws.

But when Cressida explained who Abigail was, and what she had once been to Philippa and Francis, Gervaise changed his tone. 'Then we have no choice,' he told her. 'Whatever your feelings for your brother, you must seek his help in finding proper shelter for this poor creature.'

They had reached the jetty that served Claire House, and there was more light from the river. Cressida looked back at the outline of the bridge where they had found Abigail, and could not believe the horror of her condition and the way in which she limped away into the crowds, perhaps spreading her disease with each step that she took.

'When we go in,' Gervaise spoke severely, as if to a child, 'you will send for hot water – all Beatrice can manage – and you will bathe. If anything harmed you, I think I would die.'

The concern in his voice, and the authority with which he told her what she must do, made her feel strangely protected. As for informing her brother of Abigail's condition, she knew that he was right. She had no choice. It was information they could not trust to another soul, if Abigail was to survive long enough for them to take her to shelter.

'Will you come with me to Blackheath?' she asked Gervaise.

'When you have bathed, the horses will be ready. We must lose no time.'

15

Their party reached River Lane just as dawn broke, avoiding the last night-watch and riding in from Ludgate. They had crossed the river in darkness, Francis leading the way over the bridge at the reins of the small covered wagon he kept for the use of men on the run. Gervaise and Cressida followed on horseback.

As he paused to turn into the lane, Francis glanced at his sister and in the sad smile with which she returned his look he knew that she too was thinking of their first days in London.

There had been no time to talk of reconciliation, or of blame when Cressida and Gervaise arrived at the Blackheath house with news of Abigail. Such things had seemed of no import, and as they made their way down the narrow street where Master Valence still lived, brother and sister knew every cobbled stone over which their horses moved – and with each ring of the hooves the memory of their early struggle was hammered home.

With Gervaise's love surrounding her in a cocoon of tenderness and well-being, Cressida had found it easier to face Philippa and Francis in spite of her vows of enmity. She even found it possible to ride past the house where she and Stephen had first become lovers, and was surprised that the anger and resentment that had smouldered in her heart for so long against him seemed suddenly to have diminished.

She had embraced Philippa tenderly, before the rush of words about Abigail's horrifying condition poured out. Her embrace had been returned, then Philippa had led them quickly into her solar before Margaret, who leaned over the balustrade on the floor above, could hear too much.

Looking up at the child's face, Cressida had been struck by the increasing resemblance to her own mother. There was the same gravity and pale beauty in the fine-boned face, the same energy and vitality lurking in the bright eyes and firm chin.

Gervaise had paused when she waved to the child, asking her identity, and, looking down into the poet's handsome face, Margaret had blushed and fled.

Philippa decided to stay at the house as she would not leave her daughter alone at night, and Francis, knowing of a lepers' hospice south of Blackheath in the roughland between the city and the fields of Kent, had organized everything from then on.

As they drew close to the quayside they could see in the half light a huddle of derelict boats and huts. They paused, wondering how to identify Abigail's hiding place, but a water-carrier trudging past with early morning deliveries slung across his shoulders shot them a suspicious glance which made them move quickly on as if certain of their destination. If Abigail were discovered by anyone but themselves she would be hounded from the district, to die in the open. It was silently understood amongst them that the woman who had loved Philippa's brother did not deserve to die in such fashion.

Some yards along the quay their search came to an end. The sound of the horses had no doubt warned her of their approach. A hunched figure of a woman with her hood drawn low over her face broke into view and ran away from them across the mud flats bared by the low tide.

At a signal from Francis, Gervaise spurred his horse into a floundering chase. No one dared call the woman's name, or pursue her on foot and perhaps be forced to touch her. Gervaise had made it abundantly clear to Cressida after their encounter with Abigail earlier that he would not put either of them at such risk.

He stopped her flight at length by overtaking her and, turning his horse, stopping dead in her path. She fell back in the mud, and looking fearfully up into his face with her dark eyes knew him at once as Cressida's companion of the day before.

Waiting on the quayside, Cressida and Francis could not hear what passed between Gervaise and the woman but he seemed to persuade her successfully to return with him, and she followed meekly enough as he rode back to them.

His young face bemused with horror at what he could see of Abigail's condition, Francis gestured silently to her that she should climb into the rear of the wagon, and she scrambled in, looking round anxiously at the signs of the river and its people slowly coming to life for the day.

Gervaise reined in his horse at Cressida's side, where she watched at a slight distance. 'The matter is out of our hands now,' he said in a low voice. 'Your brother knows what must be done. It is for the best.'

Gervaise followed her home in silence. He too had been shocked by what they had seen. Cressida felt as if an era was dead and that she should face life anew. With the loss of her child she and the woman Abigail had become equals; with the terrible affliction that had seized on her Abigail had ceased to threaten her. At the door to the house, Cressida took a deep, cleansing breath and stepped firmly over the threshold, knowing that she had come home.

With the revival of her lifelong friendship with Philippa, Cressida went more frequently to the Palace in the two years that followed. Even though the Queen she loved so fervently had died, Philippa still had many friends in royal circles. She did not have to explain to Cressida that she cultivated these friends so that suspicion would be diverted from Francis's activities. No one would suspect a woman with Philippa's vast agricultural estates of a liaison with an active dissident. But a scholar and scribe, with a houseful of apprentices, made a more romantic match for a liberal aristocratic woman, and it was accepted that she had married for love.

That the offspring of the love-match was therefore a beauty was inevitable, and Philippa frequently confided in Cressida that she dreaded the day her daughter Margaret would be of age to be presented at Westminster and the heady business of courtships would begin. She was certain there would be no shortage of applicants for Margaret's hand.

Listening to her at such times, Cressida wondered if Philippa was aware that her small world could soon be void of such niceties, and that the work her husband did in grouping rebels for action against oppression at their home meant that the revolt would come right to their door.

But Philippa moved in a gentle haze of happiness, still the laughing girl who had defied her own brother so effectively, and showed no fear of what her husband might bring down upon their heads.

It was Cressida who had grown into the true courtier: avid for the rich pageantry and fine conversations of court, and soothed by the open admiration she received wherever she went. Her liaison with Gervaise now served to give her the extreme confidence that she had lacked as Stephen's wife. In the shadow of the great scholar, and always longing for his approval, she had played a secondary role. Now her place as consort of a handsome, younger man put her in the limelight, as an object of envy to the women and one of secret, amused congratulations by the men.

It was to one of her admirers at Westminster, Thomas Belcampe, that she went to request a patronage for Gervaise. Belcampe was the scion of one of England's noblest families, unmarried, and as rich as Croesus. As one of the King's financial advisors he had rooms at the Palace – and a reputation as a womanizer who had long eluded marriage as a snare. Cressida knew from gossip that those rooms were put to other purposes than conferences on the well-being of the royal purse.

With no intention of becoming yet another lamb led to

the slaughter of Thomas Belcampe's bed, Cressida nonetheless knew that if she looked her most beautiful for the occasion she stood more chance of success.

For some days before her decision to approach Belcampe, she and Gervaise had begun to quarrel, lightly, but more than once, about money. She was still wealthy enough in her own right to have supported him, but with no pupil to justify his role as tutor at Claire House he had adamantly refused to draw a stipend from the month of Richard's death. However often she explained that the house was hers for life, and that they lived by the King's generosity, Gervaise would not listen.

'I have not worked for the King. I need my independence. I work as a poet, and now that I have found happiness with you I need more than ever to succeed.'

'But you are a success. Honour is sure to come to you. It will not be long before the King himself gives you recognition, I'm sure of it.'

Gervaise stared moodily into the fireplace of the study where they sat. In her bid for a new life she had deliberately removed all trace of Stephen's presence there and opened it up as a small but pleasant library for them both.

'Not if the wars with France continue. They do not encourage the French at Court at this time.'

'Do you regret not going back to your homeland?' Her voice was sharper than she intended, revealing the fear she believed she had mastered of losing him. Though they had been ardent lovers almost every night over the past months there was still no sign that she had conceived. And secretly she still hoped to bind him to her with a child of their own.

The tone of her voice was not lost on him. 'Of course not, my love. I was persuaded by arguments no man could have denied. And there are you own studies to plan. I am needed here, I know that. Yet I must have my own means.'

Early one morning a few days later, Cressida had left him engrossed in his work and gone to the city to order from a new batch of fabrics that Andrew Blake had sent word to say, had arrived from Italy. Her errand was genuine; with her growing social life she was constantly in need of new gowns. But it also afforded an excuse to leave the house without Gervaise, who had soon shown that he did not enjoy the prolonged sessions at the merchant's house, and from there she planned to go on to the palace.

Andrew Blake received her with a long, critical look at the tunic and gown she had selected for her interview with Thomas Belcampe.

'Blue has always been your colour, and yet something about you has changed. It is a subtle change, and calls, I think, for a more vibrant colour.'

He snapped his fingers and an apprentice staggered towards him with a bale of silk in a brilliant, emerald green. Cressida looked at it, her eyes shining.

'I had not thought of such a colour. It is pleasing – and the silk is perfect in grain and softness.'

'You will not regret the choice,' Andrew Blake promised her. 'And it would give me infinite pleasure to design the gown as a gift.'

'Oh no,' Cressida said hurriedly. The mourning gown and headdress he had brought her had been the gift of a lifetime, and she did not want to be further beholden to this persistent, wealthy man. 'Your generosity after my son's death was too much, sir. And your thought in choosing this new colour for me is gift enough.'

He sighed, perhaps at the reminder of her grief, perhaps with regret at her refusal. 'Did they ever find the killers?'

She shook her head, her eyes lowered. It was strange how this merchant seemed so watchful in the matter of Richard's death. She knew enough, and understood more these days, of the current political scene, to suspect that, depending as he did on the wealthy city community for the greater part of his business, Andrew Blake would not be above trading information with them as well as cloth.

To her relief, they were interrupted by the arrival of a young apprentice from a mercer in Chepeside. Blake turned to him impatiently.

'And what is Master Whittington's desire?'

Cressida was glad to observe that the boy, his fair country complexion darkening only slightly, did not cower at the imperious manner of the great man.

'The scarlet velvet for Master Fitzwayn, and a sample of green silk for his daughter Alice would be much welcomed,' he said.

The boy's composure intrigued her, and she longed to question him on the origin of the slight burr of dialect in his speech. Then, as the merchant gave orders for the fabrics to be parcelled up, the visitor surprised them both by approaching Cressida and, with a slight bow, begging permission to address her.

As she looked into his steady eyes, she thought to herself that, though he could not be more than eighteen, this was more than a mere apprentice in the making.

'If Master Fitzwayn can give us of his time,' she acquiesced with a smile. 'But first tell me your name.'

'Richard, my lady.' Her heart contracted with a return of grief, which she stifled for the boy's sake. He doffed his small, feathered hat. 'Richard Whittington, at your service.' She waited for what he had to say.

'My lady Cressida is known to all at Chepeside,' he said solemnly, 'and well loved. But tell me, is it true that she was once a poor peasant girl and her brother a slave?'

Andrew Blake gasped in indignation and tried to shoo the boy from the room, but Cressida raised a restraining hand. 'The boy shall have his answer.' She smiled at the apprentice. 'If he can give me a good reason for daring to ask his question in the first place.' She was intrigued at the courage the boy must have needed to approach her on such a matter, and was certain there was more to it than idle curiosity.

Without hesitation, Dick Whittington gave her his answer. 'Why, because I myself plan to rise in the world, and

I believe I have it in to be the richest man in London. Maybe even the city's Mayor.'

Cressida threw back her head and laughed delightedly, while the boy himself smiled.

'Then I can tell you that my story is true, and I'm sure that yours will come to pass. Master Blake, I believe we may well have in our midst a future Lord Mayor of London. What say you?'

Unable to risk offending her by sending the boy packing, which was clearly what he wished to do, Andrew Blake contented himself with a surly nod, and 'I daresay, I daresay. All things are possible in this shifting world of ours.'

Cressida's smile still hovered at the corner of her lips when, an hour later, she was ushered into Thomas Belcampe's rooms at Westminster and the great man bowed over her hand. It was true that all things were possible, for here she was, a poor peasant girl, brought into the presence of one of the most powerful men in England. In her secret delight at the irony of the situation, she was unaware that she had taken the first false step in her relations with Gervaise.

'Never! From a man who is a known lecher, and without my knowledge – never would I have allowed you to seek such patronage!'

Gervaise's face was white with anger, and he paced about the library like a caged lion. He had hardly heard her out before he turned on Cressida, accusing her of duplicity and deception.

'In what way have I deceived you?' She protested warily, frightened by this first show of real anger from Gervaise. 'I came here directly, to tell you what I thought to be good news. I have nothing to hide.'

'If I could be sure of that . . . '

Her heart sank as she recognized in his words and in the anguish on his face the same doubts and jealousy that had once consumed her husband. 'Do not give voice to such foolishness,' she cut in. She could not endure the same sort of wrangling that jealousy had caused between her and Stephen year after year. 'I sought patronage for you so that you may continue your work and keep your pride. It is what you asked. I do not see what I have done wrong.'

'How can I keep my pride when a woman intercedes for me with men like Belcampe. Have I to teach you logic as well as Latin?'

'You need teach me nothing if it is such a burden to one so proud – '

'Pride is your speciality Cressida, not mine. I once admired and loved you for it. But it is a dangerous attribute. Do not let it come between us.'

She looked at him in amazement as he slumped in a chair, refusing to turn in her direction. She was seeing yet another aspect of her poet-lover, who could be as moody as a November day. She had thought that his recent dark moments had been caused by his money problems, and had tried to solve them – only to fail dismally.

'I have done nothing to drive a rift between us, Gervaise,' she said in as controlled a tone as she could command. This, she thought, is where my age must make me the more prudent of the pair of us. 'And when you have come to see that I meant no harm, that I may even have achieved some good, then a look – a touch – will tell me. Until then, I fear I must leave you to your sullen ways.'

'You address me as if I were a child,' he muttered, and with a stab recognition she knew that he spoke the truth. She had used the voice she had once used when her son was intent on getting his way. It was an unfortunate slip, and Gervaise, sensitive in the extreme, had caught her out. But his sensitivity also saved them, for as he spoke he seemed to know at once how cruelly the words could have hurt her, now that she had no child to correct. She moved quickly to the door, on the verge of tears which she did not want him to see. Before she could open it he was at her side.

Close in his arms, she almost swooned with the joy of knowing that the dangerous moment had passed. He held her in a fierce embrace, whispering to her that they should not waste their days together in such fashion.

'Then I am forgiven?' she looked up at him.

'And I?'

This kiss that followed was the most passionate they had yet known, and Cressida's mouth received his with a mingling of delight and desire that was almost pain. She felt him harden against her, and drew back a little, gasping.

'Beatrice is preparing our dinner. She will be bound to come to the library any moment to find us . . . '

'Then she will find the students have played truant, and will have to keep their supper warm,' he smiled, opening the door and grasping her round her waist.

Together they mounted the stairs to his room, and fell on his narrow bed, embracing each other hungrily after the desolate moments of their first serious rift. As Gervaise thrust aside her skirts and parted her legs Cressida received him with a moan of desire born of familiar knowledge of the course their love-making would take. Her young lover's ability to make love to her endlessly had made her, though she did not know it, a victim of her passion for him, and even as she was quarrelling with him minutes before, she had felt her body stir with love and need for him.

It was quite dark in the room when Gervaise at last lifted himself gently from her, and they lay close together, their hands touching. Cressida was too fulfilled to speak, and rested her head on Gervaise's shoulder, fighting with sleep. She knew they must make at least some semblance of spending the evening downstairs and eating Beatrice's repast. She was about to say so when she became aware of a certain stillness in Gervaise that was not part of the aftermath of love.

'Tomorrow,' he said, 'I must go to Westminster and make certain that Master Belcampe has no plans for me. And I shall, I think, spend a few days there. My fellow poets may have news of some work for me, with which I can pay my way.'

Her heart sank, and she fought the impulse to answer him quickly, begging him not to take things into his own hands. But her better judgement triumphed. She would keep Gervaise at any price, and had to think quickly.

'Then, my love,' she whispered, 'it would give me great joy if on your return you bring your fellows with you, and they spend some days here with us.'

In the way he kissed her before he came to her again in a sudden whirlwind revival of their passion, she knew that she had won him back to her.

16

The quarrel over Thomas Belcampe was a turning point in their lives. The incident had served to bring Cressida to her senses, and she knew that if she was to keep the love of her poet she must allow him the freedom – and selfishness – of a young man. In return, she watched her home become a centre of culture, filled with his poet friends and their animated talk.

It was nothing for Cressida to come down to the library in the morning and find a red-eyed poet who had been at work there till dawn, or a group of writers who had ferried across to Claire House from the Savoy for the entire purpose of staying up all night and talking.

But it was rarely that such a night would keep Gervaise from her bed, and far from finding their new regime meant that she was left to her own devices, she found herself more ardently loved than before.

The good talk, the stimulus of young company and the sense that Claire House had at last come into its own, brought a new purpose and vitality to Cressida herself. She studied hard, and mastered the new, vigorous tongue her visitors favoured. She listened to their work, criticized with a shrewd ear, true understanding – and no false generosity. Her extravagance, which she was still unable to curb, was justified by the need to have generous supplies always at hand for their numerous visitors. She blossomed under the writers' admiration – and she had no trouble in justifying a new gown every time a formal party was planned.

Her reward was to see Gervaise smile conspiratorally at her across a room filled with laughing, talking young men. His pride in her and her love for him protected her in such lively company, and she moved amongst her lover's guests as an equal, without fearing that she would be molested as they grew rowdy or boisterous. At such times, Gervaise would always manage to be at her side, and when the mood of the gathering quietened down, the revellers would make their way to their own homes or to the beds they used at Claire House like so many weary children. Later, in the darkness of their own room, Gervaise would take Cressida into his arms and thank her, with his face buried in her hair, and his body alive with desire.

The expense of their way of life was not lost on Cressida, who as Stephen's consort had known what it entailed to keep open house for the highest in the land. The house was still run by the good grace of the King's purse, for she was still Stephen's wife and the throne's debt to him was there for all to see in his work at Westminster. And she would not have been surprised if Thomas Belcampe had also some influence to ensure she did not suffer from Stephen's continued absence.

But her spending on herself and on the embellishment of the house began to get out of hand in the second year, and one night she found herself only half listening when the guests' talk turned to Wyclif, for she was worrying about a batch of unpaid accounts she had found in her desk that morning.

'They've slipped him into London to preach and taken

the anti-Lollards by surprise,' one young writer told Gervaise.

'It is too soon,' another enjoined. 'He'll not last. He'll have the need of the devil's own luck if he's to avoid being dumped in the river before the week is out.'

The choice of phrase, with all its terrible associations, at last brought Cressida back to the present. On realizing who it was under discussion her heart beat faster. If Wyclif had come to London surely he would not have travelled alone? Which of his supporters would he have chosen to accompany him on such a dangerous mission? She dared not ask openly if Stephen was among them.

'Does John Wyclif travel with his Oxford colleagues?' she asked the first speaker, assuming a casual interest.

There was an embarrassed silence. 'Or is he alone?'

Still no one answered her. Everyone in the room knew the identity of Cressida's husband. Their admiration of him in no way prevented them from accepting the relationship between his neglected wife and their friend Gervaise.

Eventually Gervaise himself broke the news to her, as the others resumed their conversation in subdued tones.

'I found out this morning that Wyclif was in London, and of course I enquired of your husband. He has stayed at Oxford. There is nothing to fear. It seems this is to be a very short visit. Wyclif sees it as a test of opinion. At least it will give hope to those who think as he does.'

'You do not have to give me false comfort, Gervaise,' Cressida told him. She spoke quietly, under cover of the buzz of laughter that now filled the room as one of their guests began to sing an improvised comic song. 'It was always possible that the great days for the Lollards, for all those who work with Stephen, would not come for many years. I have been prepared for his long absence. And –' she looked about her, a small smile of bravado on her lips, but not in her eyes, 'it would hardly be convenient for us all if my husband were to walk in at this moment, do you not agree?'

Gervaise knew her so well that he interpreted the smile as the attempt by a perfect hostess to put her guests at ease. It would not do for his friends to see their liaison as a light of heart affair easily threatened by the sudden homecoming of an irate husband. He loved her too deeply for that. That their guests continued the evening as if the subject of Stephen had not disturbed anything reflected their respect for Cressida, and for that love.

The awkward moment past, and he looked at her with eyes dark with desire. She was wearing the vivid green silk from Andrew Blake's shop, and her small high breasts were like those of a young girl in the fashionably tight velvet bodice. The rest of the gown flowed gracefully about her body.

He had never found her more desirable, and the impulse to grasp her hand and slip away with her to the privacy of his room was almost uncontrollable. But he curbed it, and simply raised a goblet of wine to her lips, the intimacy of the gesture expressing much of what he felt.

He could have persuaded her to leave their guests. They had done so before, hugging and laughing their way to the upper floor and consummating their love urgently as soon as they reached his bed. But tonight there was something in Cressida's face that he had not expected. Beneath the brave smile he read unerringly what he always tried to forget – that she still loved her husband.

It was a different love from theirs, he knew that. It was the only reason that he was secretly glad Cressida had not conceived. He knew that she wanted a child. But much as he adored her he was pursued by a sense of impermanency in their relationship, and was always on his guard against the day when their happiness would steal away as softly and inevitably as it had come.

For the time being, Stephen's continued absence was a fortunate respite. He made up his mind to help Cressida forget her disappointment.

It was not until Wyclif's fortunes changed once more

that Stephen was to come to London again.

It was a February that gripped the city with biting cold. With the death of the Black Prince all hopes that the brilliant young warrior would succeed his father and oust Alice Perrers from Court were dashed to the ground. The ageing King, grief-stricken, was more of a pawn than ever in the hands of his courtiers. His grandson, who would succeed him as Richard II, was prey to the older Princes who waited their chance to seize more power. John of Gaunt, Richard's uncle, was at once the most dangerous and most likely of these. As the anti-Lollards' protestations against the activities and heresies of John Wyclif grew more vociferous, he eased himself diplomatically out of the arena and allowed them to bring Wyclif to an indictment at the spiritual court of St Paul's.

All London knew that the trial was a symbol of the struggle for power, by the lords both spiritual and temporal. It suited no one who wielded authority in the grim year of 1377 to see the common man gain ground. If the church services and the Bible were there for all to understand, it could only lead to trouble. The mystique maintained by church and State depended on fear and ignorance. Wyclif's crime – and Stephen's – was that he had worked to dispel both.

The news of Wyclif's trial renewed in Cressida all the dedication she had felt for her husband's cause. It nearly drove her to distraction not knowing if he would stand trial with Wyclif, or whether he would lose his privileges as a scholar now that all the Lollards were to lose their licence. There was no way of telling, and she dared not give away her beliefs by asking outright at Westminster. She still had her brother Francis and his family to think of, and in such a crisis it would be far too easy to bring officialdom down on them, with disastrous results.

Since their reconciliation, Cressida had seen more of Philippa but Francis was now completely immersed in the organization and the arming of his rebels.

More than once in their chance encounters at the

Palace Philippa would whisper fearfully to Cressida that Francis walked a tightrope of danger; and on the occasions she brought Margaret to Claire House her gaiety was forced and she seemed increasingly on edge.

'I would not have Margaret know of her father's true work. She is still too young. There is so much else I want for her. A year from now she should be presented at Court. It will be something I know Francis would forbid. But if she is to inherit my – our lands – then she needs to learn the ways of the world. We have no son to follow us.'

'Surely Francis will protect you both when the time comes. I do not see my brother at the head of a rabble. And he loves the land, the village where we were all born.'

Philippa nodded. 'Francis disapproves of the marauding bands of trouble-makers. They pass up from Kent on their way to the city and he gives them short shrift. When he comes into the open it will be for the true revolution. Perhaps not in the old King's time. But have you thought, Cressida – what will become of you? You live so close to the Savoy. It is not known that you are anything more than the wealthy, privileged wife of an important man. Stephen was seen to be the King's man for so many years.'

Cressida looked at her sharply. It had never occurred to her that the rebels might not know her for one of their own. 'But he has played a double game,' she protested. 'We lost our own child in the rebel cause.'

'People have short memories, Cressida. All they see now is a woman who dresses in silks and velvets and has the golden young men of the Court at her feet. They did not know you when I first met you, a peasant girl who spat in the faces of nobility.'

'Then,' Cressida said slowly, 'when the time comes I shall have to remind them. Perhaps my husband's position will not be so impressive by then. If I know him, and if Wyclif falls, then Stephen will not be the man to go underground yet again.'

She was to remember her own words some weeks later, when she sat with Philippa in a corner of the dim interior of St Paul's church and waited, shivering in spite of her fur-trimmed surcoat, for the arrival of the Bishop of London, William Courtenay, and the Chancellor's men. As the red-robed dignitaries took their places, hard-lipped and hard-eyed, the small dark figure of John Wyclif came into view at the West door.

He walked slowly, eyes straight ahead, towards his judges. The crowds who had come to watch him parted to let him go by. With a surge of recognition and delight Cressida saw that amongst the small group of loyal supporters who walked with him was Stephen. His dark head held proudly, his face devoid of expression, he seemed oblivious of the whisperings of the crowd eager for blood. She was certain he would not see her in her obscure corner, and she did not want him to know of her presence. If he saw her, he might think she had come to crow. He had no means of telling that his cause was still her own, and that to watch him as he took his place at Wyclif's side revived all her pride in him.

The fact that he had not come to see her did not surprise her. There had been no word from him for five years or more. Perhaps he wished to protect her and their home by doing nothing to remind the authorities of his connection now that Wyclif was disgraced. He had done more than devotion to their cause demanded, by displaying his loyalty in open court. It was unlikely that anything more than an example was to be made of Wyclif – anything more drastic would be risky, even for the fanatic William Courtenay. But whether Stephen ended up in prison, or in disgrace, or she never saw him again, Cressida felt closer to Stephen in those grim moments at St Paul's than she had ever been. When it came the punishment was cruel enough – to be denied the pulpit and the speech of the common man. For the preacher Wyclif it was tantamount to the end of his life's work. The men who stood with him blanched, and stood immobilized, unable to take in the verdict.

The courtiers round Cressida were silent, more from

prudence than shock. But as Wyclif's procession began to leave through the West door, Cressida could not suppress a cry of protest. In the silence of the great church it echoed eerily, seeming to come from all sides and from everyone present. 'Never . . . '

At the head of the procession, Stephen turned sharply at the sound, seeking out his anonymous sympathizer. Cressida knew she had given herself away to those around her – but was unsure of their reaction. She drew her fur-trimmed hood closer round her face, but Stephen's eyes found her. He knew at once that it was Cressida who had dared voice her protest. Across the stone flags of the church and across the years they faced each other, their anger with each other forgotten.

Stephen's grey eyes were as clear and penetrating as they had been when they had first met. His face was blank, but she knew it concealed the same zealot who had chosen his work before his family. Yet there was a flicker of something else in his eyes – of recognition, of course, but also, perhaps, of thanks.

She was not to know that to walk away from Cressida, knowing that she had betrayed herself with her own lips was the hardest task Stephen had ever set himself. If he acknowledged her he would call attention to her and her sympathies – and after the indictment the position of such sympathizers at Court would be hazardous for some time to come. If he greeted her as her husband, it would be to revive old wounds at a time when he had no hope of making his position clear. He would have to ride to Oxford at once, to make sure of the supporters there. It was none too certain that the University would continue its support, and the scholars might find themselves without a home or a place to continue their work. For continue they would, in spite of the blow to Wyclif himself.

But the moment he saw Cressida in the crowd his heart pounded beneath his robes. Had he been able to approach her, he would not have trusted his ability to speak. Her beauty had changed in quality over the years, and was now that of a mature woman. She was groomed perfectly, if anything her garments were richer, and more elaborate than most of the other women in the church. Yet under the skilled painting her face still retained a trace of the young girl who had been his childhood playmate, and the only woman he had ever loved.

He moved out into the grey light of the winter's day as if in a dream. A crowd of Londoners, muffled against the cold, waited for the verdict in the courtyard. As Wyclif's supporters came into view they turned away, huddling together in mock conference. Inwardly, Stephen echoed Cressida's angry cry. So much work destroyed in a single day.

In the cheering, brightly dressed crowds that lined the streets of the city less than four months later it would have been impossible to recognize that these were the same people. The crowning of the young King brought new hope to the capital. Gaunt, now Duke of Lancaster and the King's protector, encouraged the Londoners' belief that the city would not fall prey to the edicts that were making bondsmen of their fellows in the provinces. It had even been said that the boy king would sympathize with the rebel landworkers' cause – but that had yet to be proved.

In the meantime, Richard left the Tower. He had lived there for seven days in a symbolic claim to his authority over the whole land. As his brilliant coronation procession began to wind its way through the city, the July sunshine seemed to reflect the new spirit his reign had brought to its people.

The old King had died less than a month before, and Alice Perrers had snatched what rings she could drag from the royal hand and mysteriously disappeared. A sense of relief had swept through the Court.

In Chepeside the stalls did a thriving trade. Refreshments were loaded on to trays, and trays perched on white-capped heads, as the victuallers' boys ran to and fro between the displays of food and drink and the high wooden stands which lined the streets. Row upon row of wealthy citizens, tradesmen on holiday, and children dressed in royal white and silver, sat waiting for the procession to pass.

Cressida and Gervaise had seats on one of the stands with a party of Philippa's friends from Court. Francis, of course, did not feel he could give a show of loyal support to the crown, and so Philippa attended with her daughter Margaret. Above them a royal banner emblazoned with the symbol of the white hart lifted in a refreshing breeze. Philippa fanned herself frequently, complaining of the heat, and Gervaise sent a boy with a pitcher to a nearby fountain which ran with wine for the occasion. Glancing sideways at her friend, Cressida could not help but notice that she seemed to have put on weight. Her brow creased in curiosity. Surely Philippa was not pregnant again, after all these years. She turned, to Margaret, and caught the young girl blushing and laughing with Gervaise. With a hand on her shoulder, he was pointing out the antics of a tumbling clown, who was turning somersaults with a monkey on his shoulder. Then Margaret's child-like laugh was drowned by a shrill cry of trumpets, heralding King Richard's approach. They all craned their necks as the small figure, dressed all in white rode past them on a prancing horse bridled in gold and silver.

In her excitement, Margaret gripped Gervaise's sleeve. Cressida saw that Gervaise was too delighted with the spectacle to notice the girl's gesture. But when the King had passed and she still held on to his arm he looked down at her, a teasing grin making his face look suddenly very young. Apprehension tugged at her heart, but she told herself not to be so foolish.

Gervaise had loved her more passionately than ever in recent months. It was as if he knew her unspoken fears about Stephen and strove to blot all thoughts of her husband from her mind. Sometimes, in search of oblivion, she took the initiative herself, curling into his body in his narrow bed in the hours before dawn, and waking him with her touch. Then her hands became urgent, and he would make love to her very quickly and violently, as if to appease some new longing. Remembering the way he had fallen asleep in her arms early that same morning after such love-making, she told herself, again, not to be foolish. But as Margaret followed her mother down the steep wooden steps she noticed that the girl's once childish walk had changed in recent weeks to the demure and formal bearing of a lady of high birth.

It was with mixed feelings that later that day she listened to Philippa's request that Margaret's debut at Court might be arranged to take place from Claire House.

They had returned there in a group from Chepeside, and Beatrice had greeted them with a *fête champêtre* of countless delicacies on a table on the lawns.

Margaret was sitting at a little distance from them under the trees, her gaze fixed rapturously on the busy river scene before them and white-flagged towers of the Savoy across the water. Gervaise had begged to be allowed to do some work in commemoration of the royal day, and had gone to his room.

'I know you are fond of my daughter,' Philippa said. 'And I need this favour from you, Cressida.'

Although Francis had elected not to accompany Philippa to the coronation procession for obvious, political reasons, as a landowner and a member of the nobility, Philippa had had no choice – just as she had no choice, either, but to present her daughter at Court within the coming year.

Cressida watched, her eyes narrowed against the sunshine, as Margaret plucked a small flower from the grass and held it to her straight little nose. 'She is so like my mother, her namesake. How could I not be fond of her?'

'Then would you do this for me? You must know such a thing would be impossible from the house at Blackheath. Such things are quite beyond Francis, who lives only for his work. And it is so far out of town.'

Cressida sighed. The house had been full of Gervaise's friends for so long now that if she began to think about how complicated it would be to organize her niece's debut she might never agree.

'And would you stay here with us for the presentation?'

'If you will have me, dearest friend,' Philippa put out a hand to touch Cressida's sleeve. There was something so sad in the gesture that Cressida found herself remembering when she had been dependent on this supplicant for her very life. And if Philippa were, as she suspected, pregnant again then she needed her help more than ever.

'Then it is settled. You may tell my brother that his daughter will be in good hands. But Philippa – will this lead to a life at Court for Margaret? Is that what you wish for her?'

Philippa shook her head. 'There is nothing at the manor for her. She will inherit, it is true. But I do not see her as a great landownder. She seems made more for the city, don't you think?'

In the weeks before Margaret's presentation, Cressida found her mother's assessment to be true. Music and dancing were the girl's first loves. In the dance she became a graceful butterfly, her movements at one with the melody, and she soon had complete mastery of the often complicated steps of the fashionable Westminster dances.

Philippa watched the lessons with motherly approval, while Cressida kept an eagle eye on the pupil's progress – wanting their money's worth from the expensive dancing teacher they had hired.

In the middle of one lesson, Gervaise came into the ground-floor solar which had been cleared for the lessons, and stood watching, an expression of amusement on his face, until the sequence had come to an end.

Margaret was flushed at her success with a particularly

difficult new step. 'Do you laugh at me, sir?' She ran to the door and, seizing Gervaise by his hands, challenged him. 'I daresay the laughter will be mine if you try this step with me. Come!'

To Philippa's amusement, and Cressida's displeasure, Gervaise was drawn into the dance, making very little show of reluctance. As she watched them together, Cressida was conscious of how close they seemed in age, with Margaret emerging so gracefully from her girlhood, and Gervaise still so young and alive.

With a glance at Philippa to see if her thoughts were shared, Cressida came to her feet the moment the music stopped, and broke into a little show of polite applause. Gervaise was too breathless and too amused by his companion to take note of the slight irony of Cressida's action. He formally led Margaret to her mother, her hand resting lightly on his, and then bowed himself out of the room pleading the need to work. Margaret stamped her foot playfully in remonstrance.

'You shall have many partners if you attend the King's celebrations in the white gown your aunt has chosen for you,' Philippa said.

'But none of them will be of my choice, Mother,' the girl said, gazing so innocently at the door that Cressida's heart sank, and she shivered although the solar was quite warm.

17

With the success of her Court debut and the birth of her baby brother, Simon, the following spring, Margaret became a constant visitor to Claire House. Increasingly convinced that her niece was drawn to Gervaise, Cressida was helpless in the face of her apprehension. She knew herself what jealousy could do, through Stephen's destruction of their married life. She did not intend to fall into the same trap and challenge Gervaise about the budding friendship, which, on his side, she was certain was innocent enough. There had been no sign that his love for her had diminished since Margaret had come into their lives, and his love-making still had the power to delight her.

Careful not to make any move that would betray her secret annoyance, she still treated Margaret as a well-loved niece, and made light of the occasions when the girl succeeded in dragging Gervaise away from her.

'He is my tutor for today,' Margaret would laugh, her young face alight with pleasure when Gervaise at last agreed to read with her, or walk with her in the garden.

At these times Cressida noted the girl's vivacity, and the firm set of the young chin above the long slender throat. Beneath the laughing exterior there was character and determination. If Margaret resembled her grandmother in any other ways, then it would not be easy to divert her from any path she chose to follow.

For the time being Cressida knew that her safest strategy – if strategy was needed at all – was to tolerate her niece's behaviour as if it sprang from youthful high spirits, and to wait for Margaret to be swept off her feet by some wealthy suitor. Now that Philippa and Francis had a son there was no need for their daughter to be involved in the future management of her mother's country estates. Her choice of a consort was no problem. Cressida hoped that she would soon be wooed and won by some young nobleman who would remove her to his own territory and out of harm's way. The girl was certainly sufficiently beautiful to attract the most eligible of the young gallants at Court. For this reason alone Cressida did not discourage her staying at Claire House – close to where the majority of such suitors were to be found.

There was only one area in which she would risk no rivalry. When Margaret begged to sleep at Claire House, pleading that her young brother devoured all the space and attention at Blackheath, Cressida insisted that she go to her bed early, like a child. She did not want her present in the evenings . . . when she was still the flame round which Gervaise's friends gathered.

Because Margaret's youth lessened her confidence Cressida increased her efforts to keep the interest of Gervaise's friends. She would not let a week go by in which she did not devise some new entertainment; she drove Beatrice, who had now begun to slow down with the approach of age, to distraction with her demands for new recipes for supper; she searched restlessly for rich furnishings and new gowns for herself; and she began to go deeply and steadily into debt with the city merchants.

It was on a hurried return from Chepeside and after a long consultation with Andrew Blake on the desirability of the latest fashion – long, scalloped sleeves lined with scarlet silk – that she noticed a visitor's horse tethered in the stable yard, and entered the hall to find Gervaise standing angrily waiting for her, a sheaf of papers in his hand.

'We have a guest, I think?' Cressida asked innocently. She had guessed from looking at the top paper that whoever had come to see her had come in connection with one of the many unpaid bills she had recently allowed to accumulate.

'By your tone, Cressida, I fear you do not know that our visitor is unwelcome. Nothing I could say could persuade the fellow to leave before he had spoken with you. He has been waiting in the solar for almost two hours.'

Depositing her cloak on the hall chest, Cressida held out her hands for the accounts but Gervaise turned away from her, frowning. 'I feel honour bound to study these further,' he said, walking towards the study door. He turned again, his hand on the latch: 'I have the marks to pay the fellow who waits for you. I will bring them to you.'

Cressida felt herself blanch with anger and surprise. Never once, since their first quarrel over patronage had he intruded on her household dealings. He had supplied his share of their keep, and more. He had always left the matter of payment to her, as the acknowledged mistress of the house.

'If you had the money, why did you not pay the man what he is owed and let him go?' she said coldly. Something in his manner made her defiant, and she was uneasily conscious that she had been through such scenes before, with Stephen.

'Because on reflection I wanted you to see yourself the sort of man you betray when you do not pay for your grand ways, Cressida. Your own kind. A craftsman whose children eat only if he is rewarded fairly for his labours.'

'You do not have to remind me of my origins,' she flared. 'I have not observed that you dislike your "grand" surroundings.'

'I like to see you happy, that is all,' he said flatly. 'But not at the price the man who waits for you must pay.'

'I shall decide for myself what to do about our caller.' She walked quickly to the door as she spoke, frightened of the turn their discussion had taken and anxious to bring it to an end.

'It is already decided. As I have told you, I shall bring the money to you. Tonight we will close the doors against our friends, and go through these accounts together.'

Unable to believe the unaccustomed severity in his voice, Cressida avoided his eyes as she opened the solar door and straightened her shoulders. Whatever quarrel between her and her lover, she would greet this tradesman with the dignity that befitted her station.

But as she stood in the darkening room her resolve weakened. There was something familiar about the bent, ragged figure that waited for her, and as the old man came towards her, she gave a start of recognition. It was Peter Linley, the carpenter who had carved the bed for her first home in River Lane, and which still stood in her bedroom at Claire House.

The craftsman had been a young man then, and she remembered that he had been courting a girl who lived close by in Ludgate. Had the years treated him so harshly, when she herself enjoyed such well-being? She could not believe that the active, bright-eyed man she had commissioned to make her furniture had changed so much.

'Peter Linley – ' her voice warm with the memories of those early days, she led the old man to her own chair by the hearth. 'I trust you have been cared for in my absence?'

The carpenter nodded in the direction of a tray of wine and meat which had been hardly touched. She saw that Beatrice had done her duty, even if the old man had been unable to eat what he had been offered.

'I have dealt with your apprentice and your assistance for many months,' she said. 'And now my – I have been told that you have come for the settlement of your account. You will be paid, of course. The purse is being prepared for you.'

Now that she knew the identity of the creditor and saw the low condition into which he had sunk she could not quarrel with Gervaise to pay the carpenter what he was owed. She spoke quickly, not looking the old man in the eyes. 'And what news is there of your wife? Did you marry the girl from Ludgate?'

'Aye.' The old man spoke at last, his voice husky with some long-endured illness. She noticed how his chest caved in above the ribs beneath his worn surcoat. 'Married, and buried. And three of our four children in the same grave.'

'Master Linley, I do not know what to say. Did you know that I too have suffered loss?'

He looked about him, a sardonic glint in his tired eyes. 'Loss of your son. The news reached us, a long time after. But all else is well with you, my lady? And my work to your pleasure?'

'Of course, of course.' She looked at the door, beginning to wish Gervaise would make haste with the promised money. She found herself suddenly embarrassed, tongue-tied, with this old man who had once been virtually a friend. Gervaise was right, she thought bitterly. She had come a long way if she could afford to forget people like this. But he had no right to judge her, or to correct her as he had done.

To her relief, Gervaise appeared, the purse in one hand. Seeing that the purpose of his visit had been answered, Peter Linley rose and walked towards Gervaise, touching his forelock. The abject humility in his bearing, and the inference that Gervaise was master in the house, brought a flush of anger to Cressida's cheeks. She bit her lip, only wanting the old man to be gone.

She heard the front door close and Gervaise returned to the solar to find her still in her chair by the hearth, staring blankly before her.

'You were right, Gervaise,' she said softly. 'I am glad that the old man waited. You can be very wise.'

Gervaise knelt by her side, and took the hand that lay lifelessly in her lap. 'I would not be wise at your expense, my dearest. But I was angry. My place in this house is not easy – though you have done your best to make it so. But this time I had to speak out. I cannot see you go in such a direction without making some attempt to stop you.'

'It is not for you to correct me. Nor to judge. You cannot know the joy I have had in making a home for you, a place fit for our guests. If I owe money - it is perhaps because I do not think. And many of the merchants with whom I deal rarely submit their bills.'

Gervaise gave a short laugh, and got to his feet. 'That is their way, their cunning. You will find that one day the reckoning will come, and they will not hesitate to ruin you if they so decide. Such men blow with the prevailing wind. If things change for you, my love, you will find them at your door like a pack of hounds.'

'Why should things change? We have this house. The

young King has not altered his father's allowance to me as Stephen's wife.'

'And will you always want that?' Gervaise gazed at her frankly, his eyes dark with questions.

'What do you mean?'

'It is a long time since you have seen Stephen. His fate is uncertain. The Lollards are not so welcome at Oxford. Much has happened since the indictment at St Paul's. If your husband is to lose everything, then would it not be better to learn to do without – before disaster? As my mistress, you could let all this go – all that came to you as Stephen's wife.'

She looked at him in amazement. He had never talked to her like this, and she had never dreamed that such thoughts were in his mind.

'But we are so happy here. You and your friends – this is as much your home as mine.'

He shook his head. 'It is no home for any of us if it is paid for by Peter Linley and men like him. Each time you use the labours of a poor man and do not pay him you are no better than Alice Perrers – a thief.'

Cressida flushed angrily. 'That is a cruel comparison, Gervaise. You have never talked to me like this before.'

'Many things are changing,' he told her. 'I with them. Finding so many, unpaid bills in the study – where they were left openly, for all to see – while that old man trembled for his money has forced me to talk like this.'

She waited, sensing there was worse to come. 'If you no longer love your husband, Cressida, then this house cannot mean so much to you. When Richard died I thought that the moment had come for you to leave here. Yet you stayed. Have you ever asked yourself why?'

She shrugged. 'It is my home. And when you had come to me here I clung to you, as well as to the past. Have you not been happy?'

'My happiness depends on yours, Cressida. But I have held back, perhaps seemed distant from you lately, because I seem to have lost the power to talk with you.

We should have no secrets.'

She wondered if he referred in any way to his friendship with her niece. It was little comfort to hear him say he wanted her happiness when she knew he was being tempted in another direction – even if he did not know it himself. 'Then I cannot hide the truth from you. I do not think I could ever leave Claire House,' she replied at last. 'And as Stephen's wife I do not have to do so.'

He sighed, and rose to his feet. 'You are as stubborn as you are beautiful. But I have my answer. Tonight, we must decide how to deal with this matter of debts.'

She shook her head. 'That is something I cannot let you do. It is my affair. It reflects on me alone.'

'But there will come a time when you may not be able to keep such things at bay, Cressida, I warn you. Do you want to be seen as a wealthy aristocrat, treading on the poor, when the rebellion comes? They would make short shrift of Claire House if ever they decided to attack. As attack they will, one day, and no one will stop them. Peter Linley may be too ill, too old, but there are those who come on after him, and will clamber over his dead body to avenge him.'

'You do not have to tell me, of all people,' she replied stiffly.

'Your brother is a brave man, but I would rather not see his family caught up in his activities,' Gervaise remarked. She caught her breath, annoyed at his concern for Margaret.

'My son died on his behalf,' she said, bitterly stung by jealousy. 'Surely you have not forgotten?'

The way in which he caught her in his arms was all the answer she needed. She had begun to despair of their discussion, which showed every sign of lapsing into an ugly quarrel. But, as always, the thought of Richard brought him close again. Gervaise buried his face in her hair and she fought back her tears. This time she would not cry. She had listened to what he had said, and knew that much of it was true. She wanted to think.

Gervaise led her to his room and began to undress her in the shadows, and for a while she could not think of anything but his young, urgent hands. It was not until some time later when he lay exhausted at her side that she remembered their unresolved discussion. Did Gervaise really want to leave Claire House, she wondered? And why could not she find it in her heart to make the final break with Stephen? Their son was dead. The last she had seen of her husband was a proud face across the nave of St Paul's. For all she knew, she might never see him again. But, if she faced the truth, was she not really waiting for him here, as the years rolled by in silence?

Then as she slipped into sleep she remembered again that last view of Stephen, and heard her own voice echoing through the vault of the cathedral. There had not been only silence between them after all. Perhaps it was that single word – 'Never' – which still linked their lives together.

It was some weeks later that she was reminded of a remark which Gervaise had made during their quarrel. He had mentioned that the Lollards were no longer welcome at Oxford. But there had been no word from Stephen – or from those who would have known such things at Westminster – that he had moved away.

A heavy fall of snow in February of the new year had kept Margaret at her parents' home for some days, and Gervaise had spent long hours in the library, hard at work on a new poem celebrating the start of the decade which the year, 1380, had begun.

On an impulse, Cressida took her cloak from the hall chest and, wrapped in its warmth, hired a barge to Westminster. She needed company, and, for the first time for many months, found herself missing the gossip of the ladies in waiting there. Though much had changed at Court since the crowning of Richard, he had a young Queen, and Cressida knew she would be sure of a welcome from the bright young daughters of the nobility who attended her.

On her arrival, Cressida saw that the Palace was in the grip of the snow. Its red brick gables were touched with white, and the walls of the gardens were capped with thick, sparkling ledges of ice.

As she hurried towards it, she saw in the distance a trio of dark-robed monks moving like crows up the garden path. She at once recognized the older man who walked between two younger friars.

She paused uncertainly as the three men approached. Since Richard's death there had been little communication between her and Brother Oliver. She shuddered at the sight of the scourge at his waist. Before she could move away, he surprised her by raising a hand in greeting, and seemed to quicken his pace, as if he wished to speak with her.

Her cloak drawn tightly about her, she waited, shivering in the cold. She hoped that whatever it was the monk had to say to her it would not take too long. A royal chaplain he must be given at least the courtesey of a hearing.

'You wanted to speak with me, Brother Oliver?' Her voice was clear on the sharp air, and her blue eyes shone coldly above her pink cheeks.

He bowed, and gestured to his companions. 'It is rather my guests who would speak with you, Lady Cressida. They are newly arrived from Oxford, and have information for your ears.'

He spoke quietly, almost conspiratorially. She remembered that Grimthorne Abbey had been a rebel haven. In spite of his influential post at Court it was not likely that a zealot of Oliver's calibre would have turned his back on the old ideals. There was still a fanatical gleam in his eyes. The younger of the two monks said, 'We arrived before the snows; thanks be to God, my lady, before we left we debated the risk of our journey at this time of year. But we had little choice.' He looked about him, making sure there was no one else nearby. 'The city of Oxford has given us to understand that we are not wanted there. So much has changed. The last haven for those who think as we do – your husband also – is no longer safe. When our brother – ' he motioned to Oliver – 'told us who you were, we felt it was a sign. You should know that soon the followers of John Wyclif will be leaving the University. At least until our patrons can once more come into the open.'

Cressida listened in a daze. If what the young monk said was true, then Stephen would be forced to leave the sanctuary in which he had hidden from the world – from her and their love – and if he followed these young disciples to London, as he might well do, then where would he choose to live? Her heart beat painfully.

So Gervaise had been right. Oxford was no longer safe for Stephen. No wonder he had pressed her to choose between her house and a new way of life. What would he feel, she wondered, when he discovered that their existence in London might have to stand up to the scrutiny of Stephen himself – or of those who had been close to him during the years in Oxford. If Stephen were to come and claim his rightful place would he suffer her presence there, knowing it had been the scene of her long love affair with Gervaise? She was silent, aware of Oliver's penetrating gaze. How he must be enjoying this test to which I am to be put, she thought. With an effort, she composed herself.

'It is well to be prepared for such things,' she said gravely. 'I thank you. Tell me, did you not see the scholar Stephen before you left? Is he well?'

'He lives more or less as a recluse since the indictment,' the other monk told her. 'They say he works harder than ever before. Though none of us can preach in public he is determined that our work on the Bible should never stop. One day we believe it will come into its own. Though there are many dangerous years ahead for us all.'

Thanking them again for the news and their concern, Cressida hesitated before continuing her visit to the ladies in waiting. Suddenly her heart had gone out of it. She needed some reassurance. But if Oliver saw her retrace her steps he would be certain to think that the information had sent her running to Claire House. And everyone at the Court knew that she lived with Gervaise.

Slowly, she made her way through the cloisters to the solar. She would rest, and maybe ask for a warm reviving drink before she left. Then, she would go to Blackheath before dark. She was so deeply moved by the thought of Stephen's return she did not want to be alone. If there was anyone who would understand, and who would listen without judgement, it was Philippa.

There was not time to return to Claire House and then set out for Blackheath before dark. Gervaise might be anxious for her, but when she left he had been completely engrossed in his poetry. By the time he missed her his friends would have joined him. Anyway he would assume she had stayed on at Court in such weather. She had done so before, and by morning she would have sorted out her feelings and would be able to return home.

As she had hoped, it was still not quite dark when she rode into the courtyard of Francis's house. She had insisted on riding alone in spite of the entreaties of the groom at Westminster. She knew the way well, and there were few people about. But as she rode she had regretted her decision. There were more ragged brown figures in the London streets than she had anticipated. Huddled in groups and the corners, they turned and stared as she passed. One fellow dressed almost in rags held out a hand in a mockery of begging alms, and clicked his tongue in an echo of her horse's hooves as she passed. She was glad that she wore nothing more glamorous than her mother's old cloak. If she had, they might have stopped her in her tracks and demanded the alms they so clearly needed.

By the time she dismounted she was shaking as much with fear as with the cold, and the voices of Francis's apprentices as they ran to take her horse were welcome music to her ears.

In the hallway, she pushed the hood back from her hair, and blew on her fingers to bring them back to life. Margaret ran downstairs to be the first to greet her, and asked eagerly after Gervaise before she saw that Cressida was in some distress. Then she called her mother, and led Cressida through to the main solar, where a high-banked fire spat red and orange in the gloom. To her surprise, Cressida saw that the room, usually reserved for the family, held several groups of the young rebels who posed as her brother's apprentices. They looked up in greeting, but when Philippa appeared they returned immediately to their conversation.

Touched by Margaret's concern, Cressida kissed her. Then, turning to Philippa, she reached out her arms for the small boy who clung to his mother's skirts.

Simon gazed up at her with wide dark eyes. He had the ruddy skin of Philippa's Norman ancestors, and some of the robustness of his dead uncle. Since he had begun to walk and talk, his likeness to his mother's family had increased, and to see him now, when her emotions were already heightened, brought Cressida suddenly and painfully face to face with the past.

She held Simon close, nestling her face in his warm neck until he complained that her skin was cold. He ran to the fireside and watching him, she delighted in his sturdy frame, and remembered how her own son had been at the same age.

Philippa led her to the settle by the fire, an arm about her.

'Is something wrong, Cressida? What brings you so far on such a day? You will stay, of course, and not attempt to return tonight.'

'It is news from Oxford,' she began, and Philippa grasped her hands tightly. She launched into the story she had heard from the young monks.

Philippa listened, frowning. From time to time she nodded, as if she knew all too well how things were.

Then, as Cressida seemed drained of words, she told her:

'It is all part of a pattern, my friend. You must see that.' She looked round at her husband's followers, who had fallen silent while Cressida talked. 'Very soon, perhaps within this year – certainly next – the conflict will be out in the open. The men who rule this land cannot have it their own way forever. They will move with the times, or die.' She shook her head, and her daughter eyed her anxiously.

'Surely my father has not worked for so long to bring death to the land? What will become of us, mother? And Simon – will he be safe?'

Philippa placed a hand on her lips, as if to beg her silence. 'Simon will be safe. And you, Margaret. We must trust your father. If things turn out well, this secret life we have led for so long will bring its rewards. Now – it is too late for Simon to be up. Margaret, will you take your brother to bed?'

As Margaret disappeared with the small boy in her arms Cressida held Philippa's hand tightly in hers. All they had been through together seemed to give her strength.

'Will it be war, and so soon?' she whispered. In her heart she was praying that Stephen would have decided to leave Oxford and return to London before any blood was shed.

'Francis thinks it will be soon. We are prepared. But still the rebels prefer to win their demands by treaty. The talk can only last another summer. But I do not think the men of Kent will be held back much longer. It is then that your brother must come into the open as a leader – or there will be chaos.'

Suddenly the two women clung together. Remembering the clusters of angry, hungry men she had seen on her way to Blackheath, Cressida knew that what she had heard was the truth. Within a year she might see the fruits of refusing to stay in her dying village and watch her brother grow to manhood as a slave.

18

It was high summer, Ascensiontide of the same year, when word came at last from Stephen. Cressida had refused to go with Gervaise to the Richmond fair, and spent the day in the garden. Her excursions into the city had been fewer since she had started to curb her spending, and what she had seen there had not encouraged her to return. London steamed under the threat of rebellion, and yet a strange quiet seemed to hold the people in its grip. The wealthy citizens went about their business with a great show of knives and daggers at their belts. The rumours of plague and poll tax flew from one narrow street to the next. Yet nothing happened.

News of Stephen was slow in coming. When she had first known what was happening at Oxford she had expected her husband to ride into the stable yard at any moment. Gervaise, knowing the reason for her anxiety, refused to make any decision about their future until he was certain that either Stephen was to return or that they would never see him again. He would not leave Cressida alone with her torment, although he had been forced to accept that she would never put him first, or leave her house with him as he begged.

They were still lovers, but their relationship had assumed a tolerance that belonged more to friends than to two people who had shared such passion and pain. Cressida found herself setting much less store by Margaret's flirting, and to be fair to Gervaise she had to admit he did nothing to encourage her advances.

On the day of the Ascension fair Margaret had joined a small party of Philippa's friends to go to Richmond by river. Gervaise had agreed to go with them when Cressida had declared her preference for remaining behind.

Now she sat listlessly on an oaken bench beneath the apple tree. There was no breeze from the water, and she watched through half-closed eyes the passage of the few small craft that still plied the river in the heat of the day.

One of the boats drew into the Claire House jetty and the oarsman fastened his mooring before clambering heavily ashore. Cressida suddenly became alert. There was something familiar in the elderly, leatherclad figure that walked towards her. Before he had covered all the ground between them she knew it was John Aske.

It was thirty years since she had received word through him that Stephen would join her in London. Now it seemed they had come full circle. As he crossed the lawns in the sunshine, his grey head bared to greet her, she knew with every sense in her body that once more he brought news of her husband.

John Aske's shrewd eyes measured Cressida's reaction as she read the letter he had delivered. How well the years had treated the fair girl he had known in River Lane. Her figure was that of a much younger woman, and the bloom on her cheek told him that she had loved, and known much love. He saw that grief had touched her life, but the lines it had added to her face only gave her face more character and depth.

Oblivious of his scrutiny, Cressida read and re-read the letter from Stephen. The neat handwriting leapt up at her from the page, and it was as if she were reading some lesson he had penned for her brother when he first taught him to read. He had clearly taken great pains to write carefully to her, and each word had been chosen with restraint. But between the lines the message was plain; Stephen had chosen to go to ground in Oxford, and to wait for things to improve for Wyclif. If things got worse in London – which was likely – they would find no refuge there. He was writing not only to tell Cressida of his continued whereabouts, but to warn her that with the complete loss of support for their cause in high places Stephen's own source of income from the Crown had recently been cut off. From now on he could not keep Claire House for her, although as the King's gift it would always be theirs.

Torn between fear for his safety in an unfriendly city and dread of what her own future would be without means, Cressida suddenly swayed forward, and but for John Aske's support would have fallen.

'It is the heat, nothing more,' she said. 'My maid will bring refreshment, if you can stay?' Her question was a plea for him not to leave her immediately. Nodding his reassurance he insisted on finding the kitchens himself and helped Beatrice bring a salver of cool white wine into the garden.

The sight of Cressida's white face told Beatrice at once that something was wrong, and the old maidservant fussed and clucked over her as if she were a child.

Back in the kitchen, she told her husband that she would not rest that night until she knew what ailed their mistress. 'Things go badly enough for us all as it is. She has had news, and it is not good news.'

Henry shook his head. Beatrice had always shared all the troubles as well as the joys that came to the house. She was ageing and slowing down, and for himself he did not feel able to take on any more cares than he had already. Cressida had gone her own blithe way since her son's death and her husband's flight. For flight it was, he often reminded Beatrice – from a headstrong, passionate woman who would turn a man's thoughts from his life work.

Beatrice did not have long to wonder about her mistress. As soon as John Aske had taken his departure, Cressida sent for her and her husband. The sunlight had left the garden at the front of the house, and she waited for them in the coolness of the ground-floor solar.

'I have heard from my husband today,' Cressida said, going straight to the point. 'And the news is bad. We shall not see him for some time, perhaps a long time still. That is, for me, much more serious than the rest of the information I received today. But for you, my dearest friends, the news is such that I hardly dare tell you. The truth is, we are no longer to receive the support of the royal purse. If I stay at Claire House – as I mean to do – then there will be no way of providing you with a home, and no means to pay your wages. I have to tell you that you are free to go – to find other work, perhaps. Perhaps to go back to our own village. Only you can decide . . . '

There was a heavy silence, broken only by Beatrice's gasp of disbelief and Henry's growling disapproval. At last Henry voiced his opinion.

'Dost think my girl that when your husband has chosen to desert you and the King's purse has dried up that we two would walk away? Who would want us, worn out and slow as we have become? Easier to scratch a living here, than to try elsewhere at our time of life! And as for leaving the city altogether and going home – ' Beatrice interrupted him, 'Everyone knows our village was laid waste. Twice by the plague. Only Sir Robert's estates remain, and the few labourers Lady Philippa managed to keep loyal to her. We'd eat less than here, money or no, and besides,' Beatrice sat firmly on the bench at the table, as if to make it clear it was her own decision and no one would shake her, 'I'd never live to finish the journey. So here I stay – and Henry with me.'

Smiling gratefully at what she had guessed might be the outcome, Cressida sat at Beatrice's side and took her hand. 'Then I have no choice, Beatrice. You have made up my mind for me. If you and Henry are to stay at Claire House, I myself cannot possibly leave!'

Beatrice looked at her sideways, mollified but still having something to say. She glanced up at Henry, as if asking him to finish some incomplete business for her.

Henry coughed. 'There remains the question of the other resident,' he began pompously. Cressida had to bite her lip to prevent the laugh that suddenly rose in her throat. She knew what was coming, and could not let Henry land himself in further trouble.

'No one in this house need fear,' she answered quickly. 'If it is to remain home for me, then it remains so for all whom I love, and who – love me. Is that understood?' She looked at each of them in turn, and they both nodded hastily, as if regretting that they had nurtured any doubts. But she suspected that Henry had no doubts at all about wanting Gervaise out of the house if there was going to be no money coming in. He did not know that Gervaise's pride might save them all, and that her lover would prefer her to be dependent on him in order to feel more secure.

'There is no need to fear,' she repeated. 'Now – there will be guests for supper, goodness knows how many, when the Lady Philippa's party returns from Richmond fair. Shall we see what is left in our pantry for this last great banquet before we have to set to and earn our keep like the good peasants we are?'

She laughed again, out loud this time, and crossed the hall to the kitchen, Beatrice and Henry in tow.

As the red of the dying sun stained the waters of the Thames and the flares were lit one by one on the terraces of the Palace of the Savoy, Cressida sat motionless in her favourite windowseat in the solar. There was nothing to wait for now except the return of friends on a summer day. No child to come running across the lawns. No Stephen. At last she would have to give up listening for his footsteps and his voice. This time had made it clear. Even if he ever returned to Claire House he might not expect to find her there. How could he expect her to run such a place without the royal patronage?

But even as she entertained such thoughts the shrewd half of her character was working out how she could keep Claire House for herself, for Gervaise if he stayed with her . . . perhaps even for Stephen. For the present, all that mattered was survival. Something long dormant in her, some native country girl's resilience, was reawakened in her as she sat in the darkness.

That night, as she had anticipated, there was company for supper. Flushed with the long summer's day in the open air, Philippa and her daughter sat at the far end of the dining table. A group of their friends were placed on each side, and Gervaise sat at Cressida's right hand. The meal Beatrice had provided was sumptuous – perhaps as a last, careless gesture in the face of poverty. Cressida said nothing of what had happened. She was content to see Claire House as it should be perhaps for the last time, – filled with laughter and good living. Even Margaret's flashing eyes, which always seemed to seek out Gervaise from the far end of the table, could not annoy her tonight. But as the meal drew to an end she made it clear to Philippa that she expected the whole party to return to Blackheath – her niece included.

'You cannot leave small Simon to his father's care more than a day, I'll not have it,' she made a joke of it, knowing that Philippa would take the hint without offence. 'My groom shall escort you. The torches are trimmed, and the night is fine enough for a ride, is it not?'

Gervaise looked at her quizzically, wondering how she dared make it so clear that she wished to be alone with him, and rid of her guests. But she held her ground. Within an hour the party had cantered out of hearing on the river path, and the lights disappeared one by one as they took the turn that would lead them across the Thames.

Then, Cressida made Gervaise sit with her and told him all that had happened that day. When she had finished, she could not bear to wait for him to speak, but crossed the window and flung it wide, bringing the heavy scent of honeysuckle and the night air into them. She need not have dreaded his reaction. It was just as she had known and hoped for.

Gervaise came to her and turned her to him. 'It is time we earned our happiness in this good world we have made together,' he said. His hands smoothed her hair on each side of her face, and he bent to kiss her eyelids. When she opened her eyes, his expression was serious.

'There is much worse to come than what you have told

me, Cressida. I could not leave you here unless I knew your husband claimed you again. By then, perhaps to be in London will be the least desirable state for any man. Those who are still alive will flee. But until such a day, you must know that for a long time now this has been my home . . . I know no other . . . because it is yours.'

There were myriad questions she wanted to ask. How could he bear to speak of Stephen as if he might one day come back for her? What of the young girl Margaret, whom every day she could see was becoming more of a fit match for Gervaise? And how were they to survive?

But he stopped her questions before she could begin. He put his arm about her shoulders, and leading her to each of the lights that flickered wanly in the warm night air, extinguished them one by one without letting her go. The last candle he took in his free hand, and held it high as they crossed the hall to the stairs.

At the door to her room, he paused, and held the candle so that he could see into her eyes. 'You will come to me tonight.' It was half question half statement. Weary as she was, she wanted to be in his arms when she slept. But he had given her the choice. She nodded, and he kissed her tenderly. 'We must sleep,' he said, not teasing. 'For tomorrow we return to your true calling. Have you not thought what could be done with all the grassland behind this house?'

For the remainder of the summer, and the long hard winter that followed, Cressida worked as she had not done since she was a child. She had been happy trudging beside her father's plough, her long hair caught back in a white coif and the wind teasing at her skirts. Though the threat of rebellion now seemed very real and there was no further word from Stephen she was, in a strange fashion, happier than she had been since her son's death.

With Henry's knowledge, her own peasant instinct, and Beatrice's willing hands, they tilled and sowed and harvested the few acres of land to the south of Claire

House. Every inch of grass was sacrificed except one corner where a single cow grazed. Their only horse they had retained kept her company. Even the lawns between the house and the river were not sacrosanct. Beatrice made it her special task to plant young fruit bushes to the very edge of the garden, and took infinite delight in screaming at the predatory birds and children who swooped on her first young crops.

Once Gervaise had pointed the way for them, Cressida was glad that he chose to continue to make his living by his craft. She had not wanted him to give up poetry for her sake, but knew that if he had wished to do so she could not have stopped him. Instead, he began to diversify – writing pamphlets and songs for the rebels and taking goods in payment, bartering his poems at Court for the young seedlings and cuttings Cressida coveted from the royal gardens, and writing endless sentimental love songs for gallants at the palace who were free with their gold in return. As she watched him develop all these sides to his once serious talent, Cressida waited for some sign of resentment to set in. But it never came. Gervaise seemed to find it all vastly amusing, and each day brought its reward – in gold or in kind – to her feet as if it were all some adventure, or even a jest.

When Margaret came to the house, the new regime demanded that she join in the work, and Cressida watched with some amusement as the tall young woman tugged at the small plough, and waded up and down between the ridges of their solitary field as if to the manner born. On one morning early in the following spring, when the work had become even more demanding than Cressida had imagined it could be, she woke late to find Gervaise's place beside her was empty. Yawning, she went to the window of his room, which overlooked the back of the house.

On the far side of the field, Margaret, who had stayed the night with them, stood barefoot, her skirts caught up to her knees. Her long legs gleamed in the sunlight. In her arms she held a rough sack of seeds which Cressida had planned to scatter that day herself. She was laughing. As Cressida watched, the figure of Gervaise, his back to the house, came into view. He was dressed in a light grey tunic, and his shirt sleeves were rolled back to reveal his brown arms. He was hatless, and Cressida realized that he was not up early in order to go to Westminster. As he drew closer to Margaret, she plunged a hand into the sack she was holding and with a gesture of extreme grace scattered the seeds into the air about her. She was still laughing when Gervaise reached her, and lifted her face for a kiss that she seemed to expect.

Gervaise bent towards the girl and Cressida drew back quickly into the shadows of the room. Hot tears stung her eyes, and she breathed in great sobs of protest and surprise. She had been so sure of Gervaise. How could she have been so foolish? She had reckoned without Margaret's growing beauty – and without the effect his newly gained independence had on Gervaise himself.

Dreading that for some reason he might come back to his room and find her in tears, she ran down the corridor to her own bedroom. Looking in the mirror she found herself face to face with a wild-eyed sallow creature. For the first time in months she studied her reflection. Since she began to work in the field she had not found time for such things. She now saw what havoc her new life had wrought with her appearance.

In a young girl it might have produced a becoming depth of colour and glowing eyes. For Cressida it had made her golden hair coarse and harsh. There were deep lines about her eyes and mouth. Her once smooth skin was stretched, and sallow.

She raised a hand to smooth her hair, and noticed how rough her touch had become. Tears came again, suddenly, and she choked them back. Weeping would only make her face look worse, if that were possible. With a low cry of anger, she ran to her garde-robe and searched for the pitcher of scented water which Beatrice usually left for her each morning. It was not there. She remembered that Beatrice and Henry had risen even earlier that day, to sell some of their produce at market.

Splashing cold water on her face until she gasped, she found her wooden comb and began to tug cruelly at her tangled hair. Then, with a silk kerchief she had not used since she was at the Palace, she took each strand of hair and began slowly, luxuriously, to restore its burnished softness.

She worked for an hour or more, and then went back to her mirror. The face that looked back at her was more composed. The neat head shone with a golden light. But she turned quickly away. The reflection was that of a woman who had reached her prime, and suffered deeply. The eyes that gazed out at her had an unmistakable expression of sorrow. The brave face she had kept for them all in the last months had not changed the truth, and what she had seen that morning had sealed her agony.

For a while she sat on her bed, very still, her hands hidden in the folds of her gown. She had not realized how red and sore they had become. But there were worse things to brave out now. She knew that if she challenged Gervaise she risked losing him at a time when she needed him more than ever before. Not only in her bed, but as a partner in her fight for her very existence. She also risked throwing them together, when Gervaise might only have been briefly tempted, and meant no more than the kiss. The girl had looked so lovely that Cressida's heart ached at the memory.

If Gervaise really loved Margaret, on the other hand, she knew that one day he would find the courage to tell her so. But he had shown no sign in recent weeks of ceasing to love her. She could not believe she had lost him. But if she had, she would not let him go until she was sure the liaison was right for him. The thought brought a wry smile to her face. Would she never learn? Even her lover could not escape her possessive need to shape his destiny. It was Stephen who had first objected to this trait in her nature. How right he had been!

The thought of Stephen made her smile. If he walked into Claire House today of all days, how welcome he would be. Suddenly her heart ached for him, and she experienced an almost frenzied need to know where he was and how he fared. The long months since John Aske had brought the last news had been so crowded with work that she had thought the wound had healed. But it still smarted, and now, with the shock of knowing that Margaret had stolen at least a kiss from Gervaise, the wound opened again.

Perhaps because she knew she had gone too far, perhaps because she was shy of her growing love for the poet, Margaret did not appear at Claire House again for some weeks. When she did so, it was late afternoon, and she found Cressida alone in the kitchen preparing a meal. Startled by her sudden arrival and her unkempt, almost frightened appearance, Cressida asked her sharply what she was doing there unannounced. At once she regretted her tone.

Her niece burst into tears and knelt beside her. 'Please don't send me away, Cressida. It would be more than I could bear. Mother says I will be safer here, and she will follow. With Simon.'

'But what has happened?' Cressida looked at her aghast. Margaret began to tremble uncontrollably. Lifting her to her feet, Cressida wiped her eyes with her own apron, and made her sit down at the table while she poured a beaker of fresh milk. Then she sat at the far side of the table and watched her as she tried to drink.

'The people have gathered at the city walls,' she said at last. 'My father's men are armed, ready to join them. To lead them! The house is filled with strangers. My father wanted us all to come away, but mother refused. He could not bring herself to leave him straight away. She says there is so much to do, so many to feed. But really I know it is because she will not leave him.'

She faltered, and then as if the thought of her parents'

love had made her think of Gervaise, she asked where he could be found. Her innocence disarmed Cressida completely, and she found herself gripped by fear. 'At Westminster,' she answered, concern ill-concealed in her voice. 'But he will soon be home. He did not intend to stay, and when news of the gathering reaches the Palace he will want to be with – with us.'

It was already dark when Gervaise did finally appear, and when he saw the women's frightened faces he surprised them both by bursting out laughing.

'There is more to rejoice about than to fear if all goes well,' he tried to reassure them. 'It is true, the people march on London. But Wat Tyler is a man to be respected. It is certain that after a skirmish or two the young King himself will hear his cause. Only good can come of it.'

But that evening, as they all sat in the solar, Gervaise rose more than once and went to the window, seeming to gaze out at the still June night, but carefully watching them both when he thought they were not looking.

Margaret broke one of the many long silences, nervously clearing her throat and looking at Gervaise defiantly, as if telling him that she would have her own way.

'If my mother does not come soon with Simon, then I shall go back. I should be with them. I can help with my small brother . . . ' her voice trailed away tearfully, and Cressida tried to catch Gervaise's eye and signal that they must not allow this whatever happened.

'They will come,' he said quietly. 'You must have patience. If it is humanly possible, they will come to us here.'

Cressida's blood ran cold at the phrase he had perhaps accidentally, perhaps not, let slip into his answer. Was he trying to warn them? To prepare them for the worst?

She turned anxiously to the window, which Gervaise had left open. It was then that the voices began. Across the river they heard the shouts of guards, warning their fellows. In reply came the angry voice of a crowd growing to a fierce cry. All three ran to the window, but Gervaise pulled them back as a white turret suddenly pierced the dark sky across the water, lit from inside by curling flames.

'They are out of control,' Gervaise said. His voice was like ice. 'They have fired the Duke's palace, and nothing will stop them now. It is the worst thing they could have done.'

They looked at each other dumbly. They were all aware that this was exactly the kind of wild folly that Francis had planned to avoid. An unspoken fear hung like smoke in the room about them – if Francis and his trained men were not at the head of the rabble to take the city with a firm hand, then where were they? And why had Philippa not come to them before it was too late to get through?

As if to keep their thoughts from imagining the worst, Gervaise abruptly closed the window and swept the curtains back into place. The noises of fighting, and of women screaming, faintly reached them. Cressida wondered what she would do if Claire House itself was attacked, and was grateful that she had heeded Gervaise's advice to lead a simpler life. No longer the Court beauty or the hostess of poets and writers, perhaps she had become less of a target for the rebels. Claire House was these days as poor as any slave's hovel – and just as hard work.

By mutual consent they did not try to sleep. Moments after the first fires had lit the sky Beatrice and Henry joined them in the solar, and they sat listening for any sound of approaching danger.

At last the Savoy seemed to grow quiet. The rabble's shouting receded, and Gervaise went to the window again. They all watched as he drew back the curtains. Across the river a great cloud of smoke and a run of small flickering fires marked where the Palace had been. With a cry, Cressida ran to Gervaise. But he would not let her linger on the desolation that marked the end of a whole era. She remembered how she had watched the Palace grow, and wept for its loss, her head in Gervaise's arms. Margaret looked on, tears running down her cheeks.

Again, the girl broke the silence first. 'The Duke's Palace may be destroyed,' she said flatly, her eyes fixed hopelessly on Gervaise, as if she spoke only to him. 'But I fear also for my parents' house. Why else did my mother send me here? Did she know that my father's enemies would be too quick for him and his men? I must know what has happened, Gervaise. Please help me!'

At the tone of command in Margaret's voice, Cressida raised her head. She felt Gervaise stiffen at the same moment, and was aware that the time had come when he was forced to make a choice in public. It was clear that Margaret would not be denied, and in her grief and fear she assumed a wild beauty that no man could have resisted.

Slowly, Gervaise released Cressida from the shelter of his arms. She stood back from him, her eyes never leaving his face. He looked down at her with great tenderness, and his hands went to her shoulders, gripping her firmly as if he would convey much more to her than he could say.

Margaret waited, her head flung back as she listened for signs of action from the river. Cressida thought how she had changed in the last few hours. There was no mistaking the fact that she not only needed Gervaise, but expected him to help her. Her eyes willed him to do so.

The impish, lively child had turned into the woman who openly challenged her for Gervaise's love. How ironic, that she had once fought for Margaret's life, and won. Had she not been at Blackheath that night, would Margaret also have died of the fever that gripped the household? It was the first and only time she was to feel hatred for her niece. Gervaise gave Margaret a glass of wine and told her that she must stay calm. He would not allow her to leave the house while it was still dark. Cressida felt the hatred ebb from her. She knew now that the kiss she had seen that morning in the garden had been inevitable. Margaret loved Gervaise. In his touch as he let Cressida go there had been conflict mingled with remaining tenderness. But, he had let her go.

With a growing sense of helplessness she prepared to wait for the dawn. As Gervaise took the chair next to where Margaret sat, she closed her eyes, feigning sleep.

It would be some hours before they could learn the extent of the disaster that had struck the city, and whether the rising had succeeded. She wondered where her brother was now, and pictured the scenes at Blackheath. Had all the years of preparation for rebellion come to fruition in one night? Had her brother's long years as a rebel leader ended in the skirmish and fires across the river?

She tried in vain to rest, her thoughts returning again and again to her son, who had died before these one-night rebels had had the means or the will to strike. She was surprised to find that she nursed no bitterness. Just as her anger had drained away, leaving a numb void in its place, the thought of Richard's death now brought only a quiet sadness . . . even a sudden gladness that he was not out in the darkness now, killing and waiting to be killed.

Her last thoughts before she drifted into uneasy sleep were of Stephen. She was glad that she had stayed on at Claire House. If he came to London he would know where to find her. If he wanted to.

19

As the first light crept through the chinks of the closed curtains they stretched their limbs and shivered, exhausted by their sleepless night. In a small, close-huddled group they moved into the garden and stood gazing across to where the Savoy Palace had stood.

The air was very still and warm, heralding another hot summer day. The thin spires of white smoke that rose into the sky from the ruins were like a mockery of the graceful spires that had once been.

There was no one about. The river was deserted, and an uncanny silence lay over the whole city. It was a lull that struck even colder fear into Cressida's heart than the strident sounds of the rabble during the night.

As they turned to go into the house, Henry insisted that he should go for news. He argued that whatever had happened, there would surely be someone who would tell a harmless old man the latest developments. And his wife agreed. Beatrice pointed out that Henry was less likely to attract curiosity or violence than a younger man, or one of the women. None of them knew what had really happened, or which way the rebels or their opponents would turn next. Young master Gervaise would be more protection to the women if danger threatened Claire House.

Margaret objected most vehemently. She pleaded with Gervaise to take her home to Blackheath, and became almost hysterical when he refused. He did not tell her that he feared what they might find there, but that she should stay where her parents knew her to be, and where they could reach her as soon as they were able to do so. He did not voice his dread that Francis and Philippa might not be alive.

Watching him soothe Margaret, Cressida knew that she could not begrudge him a future with someone who could give him a real marriage, and children.

She was relieved when Henry had returned before noon, and she heard him talking in an urgent voice to Beatrice in the kitchen. When she saw his face she knew they had to be prepared for the worst. As they gathered round him he shook his head from side to side, too moved to speak, until Margaret almost sprang at him, seizing him by the shoulders as if she would force the truth from him.

He told them that the rising had started in Essex some days ago. The rebels there had refused to accept imprisonment as punishment of non-payment of yet more new taxes. They had made for Kent, and the whole ill-disciplined mob had marched on London armed with every shape and size of rough weapon they could find.

At Blackheath, knowing that Francis and his trained men were there, their leaders had set up camp. But a band of merchants from the city, expertly prepared, had been too quick for them. Whilst the most violent of the rioters had marched on the Savoy those who remained behind – Francis's men with them – had been routed.

His voice trailed into silence. He turned helplessly to Cressida, as if seeking her support.

'Well?' Margaret remonstrated. 'There is something else. You have not told us all.'

Gripping the table's edges, his voice shaking, the old man began again. This time he told them that the Lady Cressida's brother Francis was dead. And that his wife, the Lady Philippa, had died with him.

Margaret cried out that it was not true, that he had been mistaken, and that he was a foolish old man who could not hear what was said to him. Cressida covered her face with her hands.

She was aware of Gervaise going to Margaret and holding her tightly. But the whole room seemed to be at a great distance, and she felt nothing but cold despair. It was the end of a long road. Even her son had died for nothing, now that the man he had tried to save was also dead. The brother to whom she had preached rebellion when he was only a child had paid the same price as Richard. And still nothing had come of their sacrifice.

Stunned through her reverie she heard Margaret crying for her mother and father. She came slowly back to reality.

'What of the child? Was Simon killed too?'

They looked at Henry for an answer, but he shook his head and shrugged helplessly. 'Those who told me did not know about a child. I came here as fast as I could when I knew the rest.'

Margaret suddenly came to life, and tearing herself from Gervaise's arms she rushed blindly into the hall. Before she could reach the door Gervaise had caught up with her, but she struggled with him, crying out that she must go home or she would go mad.

'I will go to Blackheath,' he told her gravely. 'I beg you not to leave this house. By nightfall I shall return. If your little brother has survived I give you my word he will be with me.'

The remainder of the day passed like a bad dream. Cressida eventually persuaded Margaret to drink one of Beatrice's sleeping draughts, and she dozed on Cressida's bed.

Outside the stifling heat of a day in mid-June hung over the city. Her ears straining at every sound, Cressida waited with the whole of London for the outcome to the night's events.

At last, unable to bear the confines of the house, she went to keep watch in the grounds. She paced the lawns by the river, and the field to the south. In her belt she had concealed a kitchen knife, diamond sharp, and her fingers were never far from its hilt.

As she patrolled she had time to think. She was surprised at how calm she felt in the cooling air, and found that without knowing it she had been drained of all grief.

At the edge of the field she looked back at the house. In the last months it had become a mere shelter from which to till the ground. It served the same function as the single storied, one roomed hut in which she had been born. For all the scenes of splendour and success that the house had seen, it was now, quite simply, her home. Whatever had happened in London, and whatever the outcome of the rising, she knew she would never leave it until Stephen had come back.

For the first time in many weeks she imagined how she would feel if Stephen did walk back into her life. With a fierce lift of her heart, she knew she would open her arms to him and that all her anger had finally died.

The sound of Gervaise's stallion broke in on her thoughts. She gathered her skirts and sped in the direction of the stables. Gervaise had his back to her, fastening the stable door. As he turned she saw that in the folds of his cloak he held a bundle – the rounded, sleeping form of baby Simon.

Handing the child to Cressida Gervaise went to tell Margaret her brother was safe. Cressida took the child into the kitchen and sat herself down with him in the high settle by the fire. A sudden chill had crept into the house as the heat of the day died and Beatrice had made the room into a warm haven. Without voicing their feelings, everyone wanted to stay in a close group, as if companionship dulled their fear.

Looking down at Simon as he lay curled and contented in her lap, Cressida realized how much she would have loved another child. It was too late now. Perhaps she would have kept Gervaise's love had she conceived. She would never have survived the years since Richard's murder without his love. Nor could she have got through the last two days without his support.

She fell into a light sleep, and woke to find Gervaise looking at her. His grey eyes were tender, and blushing she straightened her skirt and held Simon close.

'Could it be that out of so much pain you will find peace, Cressida?' he asked. On an impulse he knelt at her side, and took Simon's hand in his. The boy yawned and resettled in her arms like a plump cat.

She smiled, then asked anxiously if Margaret was awake. He told her that she had been, but that the news of Simon had sent her back into a deep, healing sleep. 'You are both so brave,' he told her. 'It is good to see you smile.'

'I have no right. My brother is dead. My dearest friend, Philippa, died for a cause only because she loved him. Their children are alone.'

As soon as she had said the words she knew that by chance, or perhaps by intent, she had given him the opportunity to tell her of his love for Margaret. Gervaise took her hand, and raised it to his lips.

'The time has come for me to return to France, my dearest Cressida. If Margaret will come with me would you want to stop her? She is not alone now, but she will need much to re-build her life and forget these terrible times.'

Cressida drew her hand away, pretending she had to push a hair back from Simon's eyes. 'And her brother? Is Simon part of this new life you plan for her?' There was a plea in her voice that Gervaise was quick to understand. He knew at once that Cressida wanted Simon.

'There is much to discuss, of course. It is too soon to put the cold facts before Margaret, but I know I must. The death of your brother and his wife means that the estate comes to Simon. Even if he came to France with us he would have no choice but to return one day and take his heritage.'

From then on it was understood that Gervaise would do nothing to prevent Cressida from keeping the child with her in England. In the days to come she was glad to have something to live for.

The young King kept his word and came from the Tower

to meet Wat Tyler and his men. The rebels' grievances were listed. A vow was made to the great crowd of labourers and peasants that surged towards the royal party. Then, at an imagined threat to the King a merchant scuffled with Wat Tyler, and struck him down. At the feet of the King himself rebel blood was shed, and England moved with one sword-blow into the darkest days it was to know for a century. The rebels were discredited, the King no longer trusted by his people. The legend of Wat Tyler's martyrdom fed the flames of rebellion for years to come.

The failure of the rebel cause coincided with a renewed campaign against Wyclif and his reforms, and William Courtenay, as Bishop of London, prepared to have all Lollard doctrines condemned. It was a delicate matter with so many of the men in power, including John of Gaunt. Men of Cressida's husband's brilliance and determination had not deserted their work. It was to take the Bishop almost a year after the incidents of that summer, before Oxford at last closed its gates to Wyclif's disciples. By then Cressida had lived with baby Simon but without Gervaise, for a whole winter and a brief spring.

One afternoon in May, Cressida was in the garden with Beatrice, tending the rows of spring flowers that she had decided to grow for sale in Chepeside, when Simon called out that a rider wanted to see her.

Puzzled, she turned to see a heavy figure in crimson tunic and short black cloak watching her with an expression of amused surprise.

Wiping her hands on her long apron, she shaded her eyes as she walked to greet Andrew Blake. It was many months since she had bought a new gown, and she could think of no reason why he should call on her. She had made certain that his account was paid as soon as she had begun to benefit from her new way of life.

Blake bowed without dismounting, and turning his horse, indicated that he wished to speak to her out of earshot from Beatrice. She followed reluctantly, put out to be called from her work. She suspected that with his questions about her brother and her past, Blake had had some connection with the rogues who had destroyed his headquarters at Blackheath. But she had no proof, and wanted such things to go forgotten now, for Simon's sake. Before she heard the merchant out, she turned anxiously to make sure the boy was safe.

'You need not fear me, my lady Cressida,' Blake said softly. 'I have come to you with the best of intentions, and with only your welfare at heart. Now that the city is in less of a turmoil I had expected you to send for some new gowns for the summer. I heard quite by chance that you no longer allow the Court the privilege of your presence. I came to see if there was any reason for this. And if I could help.'

Cressida eyed him indifferently. She could not be sure whether he knew that Gervaise and Margaret were married and in France. She did not want him to know that she lived without protection, with only her ageing servants to guard her and the child.

Ther merchant's horse pawed the ground. She shook her hair back from her shoulders, playing for time. She did not intend to ask him into the house.

'If you had come to me for silks,' Blake said in a low voice, 'I would once more have advised you a change in your dress. A change for the good, of course. I find you even more beautiful, Lady Cressida. Perhaps your new beauty now demands simpler treatment. I no longer see you in black, either. There is a great tranquillity in your bearing.'

She inclined her head at the compliment, but avoided his eyes. She knew rather than saw that the wide lips were moist with excitement, and that the merchant had known she was alone from the start. He would not dare offer such lengthy speeches if she were still with her lover or her husband. With a pang she remembered when she had Gervaise's protection, and when she and Stephen had eyes only for each other. She had spent the long winter working so hard that she had forgotten such things. Now she could see that she might have to face the hazards of life without a man.

'Then you will know, sir,' she replied at last, 'that all is well with me. And with my household.' She glanced back to where Beatrice stood glaring rudely in their direction. Perhaps her old maidservant was as good a protector as any man!

'Ah,' he nodded as if satisfied. But he still did not move. She shifted impatiently where she stood. Surely he could see that she was not going to invite him into the house?

'I beg you to forgive my lack of hospitality, Master Blake, but – as you can see – I am in the very middle of something that will wait for no man. My flowers are demanding task-masters.'

He curled his lip. For a moment she thought he was about to spur his horse and ride off. He had only called on her seeking business after all – or some pleasure she was certainly not going to allow him. Surely she did not still have to show gratitude for the black gown?

Tears of vexation smarted her eyes, and she had to fight the impulse to ask him plainly to leave. But he at last dug his heels into the horse's side, and turned.

'Then I trust that your task will be done before your husband comes home tonight. When I saw him at Ludgate, but an hour ago, I'd have sworn he was bound this way. But perhaps he had business at St Paul's – if he is allowed over its threshold!'

With his last words he snapped the reins and doffed his hat in an exaggerated gesture of farewell. Cressida saw that his face was scarlet with anger, and at last she understood. If Andrew Blake had really seen Stephen in London then he would want to know how things stood between them. His interest in her all these years had been more personal than that of a vendor of silks, after all.

With a shudder, she watched him go, thankful that she had given no sign of surprise at the mention of Stephen's name. But as soon as her visitor was out of sight she began to shake uncontrollably. She called to Beatrice to take Simon into the house.

If the merchants who consorted with Blake were amongst those who had murdered her brother then it would be the most natural thing in the world for them to turn their attention to Stephen. The allusion to St Paul's was not lost on her. The Bishop had more than once threatened to make public the disgrace of the Lollards and post their listed sins on the cathedral doors.

Back in the coolness of the house, she tugged off her coif and ran to her room to bathe her face. When she came down, Beatrice and Henry were plying Simon with sweetmeats in the kitchen. The sound of his laughter reached her on the stairs, reminding her to keep calm, if only for his sake.

In her solar she paced to and fro, returning again and again to the window as if expecting Stephen to arrive by barge as he had done in the old days. But there was no sign of him. As evening approached she told herself that Andrew Blake had only come to torment her after all, and to make sure for reasons of his own that she lived alone.

It was late when she heard scratching at the front door that turned her spine into a column of ice. At first she was certain that the merchant had returned and meant to harm her. Then she thought that Stephen had come under cover of darkness as a fugitive. Taking a candle from the table, she ran into the hall and listened. The whole house was in silence. Henry and Beatrice had retired long ago, exhausted as they were these days by their new duties.

When the scratching came again she whispered that she would open the door. But first she demanded the identity of the caller.

'A friend. I have news of your husband.'

Cressida's heart sank. She was certain now that it was a trap. But if Stephen was in need of her she could not risk turning the caller away.

'I will not open the door until I know your name, and have some proof of your friendship.' She tried to keep her voice from shaking, and knew that she only just succeeded.

'My name is Oliver. I was a friar at Grimthorne Abbey. I – I carried a young boy and a young girl once into London, many years ago.'

Cressida held her breath. 'Tell me,' she asked, her lips close to the dark oak of the doorway now, 'if you are indeed Brother Oliver you can tell me what else was in that wagon that crossed into London so long ago.'

There was a brief silence. She waited, fighting down a scream.

'I grew roses. There were roses with you and the children, and when I lifted you down from the wagon your small hands were scratched and bleeding from the thorns.'

Cressida opened the door, and the thin, ageing figure of Brother Oliver stepped swiftly inside. She saw that his robes were torn and mud-stained, and he was out of breath, as if he had run all the way.

She led him into the solar and made him sit by the fire. She had lit it earlier, knowing that she would not sleep that night. But she had thought it would be Stephen who would join her there, not this wild figure who had come out of the past. She noted with some relief that his scourge was no longer at his waist.

'I shall not be with you long,' the monk said. 'I ride for Grimthorne as soon as I can find – or steal – a horse.'

'But why? Do you flee the young King? Who are your enemies?'

'They are on all sides. In my somewhat privileged place at Court I had prior warning. This time all those who have sympathized with Wyclif and his work are in real danger. Bishop Courtenay will make a clean sweep of us all. My rivals at Westminster have chosen to remember that I came to them from Grimthorne – a haven of the new thought, as you yourself know. I have no choice but to return there, to warn them – and to seek what will perhaps be my last sanctuary.'

Cressida listened in growing fear. She dared not ask the monk if Stephen had returned to London, for it was clear that if he had he was now a fugitive. And she was not yet certain that Oliver was sincere. The best thing she could do was to get him out of Claire House as soon as possible. Then she would take her life into her hands and go into the city to search for Stephen herself.

'You have come to the right place, Brother Oliver, and I am glad,' she said. 'There is a fine stallion in my stables. He will not fail you. When you are ready, I will take you to him.'

There was a bright moon in the summer sky when they left the house and made for the stable yard, and Cressida was thankful that they did not have to carry torches. She did not want to alert her servants or to wake Simon, and she did not know who watched the house these days.

While Brother Oliver prepared the stallion and swung into the saddle, she stood in the darkness keeping watch. At last the monk was ready, and she put a finger to her lips as she led him to the path that would take him to the road. Brother Oliver took her hand, and she asked him to wish all at the Abbey well, though she feared there would not be many there who remembered their strange visitors that winter so long ago. As she watched him canter away into the distance she wondered if he would ever reach them and if the monks at Grimthorne would ever be safe again.

Back in the safety of the house, she replaced the latch with a sigh of relief. She was suddenly exhausted with fear and uncertainty. If Brother Oliver had to flee from London, where would Stephen make his hiding place? Her spirits sank as she climbed the stairs to her room. Before she undressed she stood in the window. The scent of honeysuckle spun up to her through the darkness. It was the only thing in the past years, she thought, that had not changed.

For the first time in weeks, she slept deeply. It was as if she could bear no more, and the visitors of the day had taken what strength and patience she had left. She awoke refreshed, to hear Simon knocking impatiently at her door. She called to him to enter and he ran to her, immediately snuggling down beside her under the ancient blue coverlet.

They lay close, dozing lazily again and watching the sunlight creep across the bedroom floor. Cressida wondered when she should take the child to the lands that were his. How strange that she should have in her care the owner of the estates where she had once been a serf and his father a slave!

She set the problem aside, as one too difficult for her to solve alone. She could not envisage making such a journey without more help than her ageing servants could give, devoted though they were.

She held the child tightly. 'One day, Simon,' she said, 'you and I will go on a long journey. To the place where I was born, and where you will have a castle of your own, and fields to grow more than flowers, and wild blackberries each September.'

She sighed and closed her eyes. Soon, she told herself, she really must shake off her apathy and see that the cow was milked and that the dough had been set to rise for the day's bread. Beatrice had been increasingly tired since the events of the last few days. She believed her servants would more than welcome the chance to leave the city behind them for good.

A sound outside made her open her eyes, suddenly on guard. It was not a step she knew, and if Beatrice and Henry were up they would make more deliberate noise.

As she sat up, the door opened slowly. A cloaked man came into the room. It was Stephen.

She saw at once that he was exhausted, and that his dark hair was streaked with white. His cloak was heavy with dust, and his grey eyes shone with the look of a man who had not slept for many days.

Her heart beat so fast as he came towards her that she could hardly breathe. She edged her arm away from

Simon so that she should not wake him, and held out her hand to Stephen. The joy and disbelief in her face gave her the look of a young girl again, and without speaking, he swept her long hair back from her shoulder, and stroked her brown hand that betrayed all the long hours she had worked in the field.

'I was told you had been seen at Ludgate,' she said at last, 'but I dared not hope that it was true. But when the days went by, I feared that you would not come . . . I had almost lost hope.'

He held her hand tightly. All the anger and pride that had kept them apart had disappeared.

'I stayed at River Lane, our old refuge. I had to be certain that I was not followed before I came. I would not bring you more sorrow. Our old friends at Ludgate told me all that has happened here.'

'If you have come home, Stephen, I can endure anything. But are you really safe? Who would follow you?'

'Safe enough,' he said heavily. 'But Oxford will have me no longer. I stayed as long as I could, as long as it was necessary.'

'And now?'

'Wyclif is a sick man, maybe with not long to live. But what his enemies do not yet know is that we finished our work. A year from now, maybe sooner, there will be copies in English of the Bible in many places – for all men to read.'

His eyes had the fierce and dedicated look she had known and loved when he was young. 'So all these years have been worth it, Stephen,' she said.

He nodded. 'The rebel cause and Wyclif's teaching are only briefly defeated – I'm sure of that. You and I may not live to see it, but these set-backs will bring them even more strongly into battle before the century is out.'

She gazed at him in wonder, her heart going out to him. How could he speak with such hope and faith when he was obviously at bay?

'Why should we not see the century out, Stephen?' she

smiled. 'We have much to do, and our young nephew here – ' she looked down at the sleeping boy – 'is too mischievous a child to be left to his own devices for long.'

Stephen studied the child's dark head and for a moment she held her breath. Would the boy's likeness to Robert mean anything to Stephen? Would the old scores return to keep them apart?

But Stephen reached out and held Simon's clenched fist. 'I heard the promise you made to him. This city is no place for the boy, nor will be for many years. You are right to plan to take him home. But – ' He looked at her keenly, the old teasing look creeping into his grey eyes. She waited.

'You have forgotten that his village was your birthplace and mine. I would not let you make such a journey alone.'

'Could you live there, Stephen? After all that has happened. They say it has been laid waste, by plague.'

'There would be much to do. But the countryside will lick its wounds from plague and rebellion. There will be better times.'

Cressida lay back on her pillow, and closed her eyes. She thought of her mother's house, and the small herb garden she had loved as a child. She saw the great manor house which was Simon's inheritance. Stephen was right. There was much to do.

'I shall wear my mother's cloak for the journey,' she said. 'But this time I shall not walk. Nor shall I flee in winter, and in the dark.'